too much of a good thing

allie giancarlo

ISBN-13: 978-1-7342377-0-2

Front Cover Art by Elizabeth Ames @elizabethamesart
Editor: Elizabeth Gordon

To my number one fans, for believing in me always.

Charlie Kate Murphy was completely and utterly terrified.

At five years old—almost six, she reminded herself—she was entering the public-school system for the first time. She had watched her older sister Kelly and brother David pass through these hallowed halls before her. But right now, clutching her mother's hand as if she were being dropped off at a battlefield instead of bubbly and bright Room 201, she wasn't so sure she was all that excited about going to kindergarten.

She had spent the better part of last night tossing and turning, her nightmares riddled with scenes of bullies and evil chocolate milk cartons and showing up to school in her underwear. As her mother edged them forward towards the threshold of the classroom, she stayed rooted in her spot. Her mother smiled, turned slowly on her toes, and knelt down in front of Charlie Kate. When they were eye level, Mom's fingers brushed her rosy cheeks.

"Don't worry, sweetheart," Linda Murphy began, her smile more forced than anything. After all, this was the last baby she would send through the doors of Countryside Elementary. She had a right to be at least a little melancholy. Charlie Kate stared determinedly down at her shoes, avoiding her mother's gaze at all costs. If Mommy cried, she would cry, too.

"You'll make friends in no time. There are plenty of little boys and girls in there who are just as nervous as you are. Why don't you go in there and make a new friend?"

It was this moment that Charlie Kate feared the most. Not learning how to read, or braving the lunch line, or fumbling through adding and subtracting. No, she was already pretty good at all of that. She had, after all, watched her parents put two children through the learning ringer already. If anything, she was ahead of the other newbies. It was making friends that worried her the most.

Being the youngest of three, her childhood up until this point had been largely spent with her family, playing together in the yard, going on vacations, and watching the Red Sox. Naturally, David and Kelly were her best friends. Although she often played with the neighborhood kids, the comfort of her close-knit family coupled with her siblings' overprotectiveness had shielded her into a little bubble of safety that was about to be popped. She had never had to make friends before. They were handed to her, just like the hand-me-down clothes that were once Kelly's. But now, even with David and Kelly somewhere down the hall, she was about to be truly on her own for the first time.

"Charlie Kate." Her mother's soft voice shook her from the cat and mouse chase happening inside her head. Tentatively, she met her mother's gaze, which mirrored her own tear-brimmed eyes. "Everything is going to be okay. I just know it. Kindergarten is where you go to meet your very best friends."

"Promise?" Her voice, so small and trembling, almost broke Linda Murphy. But she knew that she had to be strong, if not for herself, for her daughter.

"Pinky promise."

A smile finally tugged at the little girl's lips, as she jutted her small finger out to meet her mother's. As she linked them, Linda pulled her daughter's forehead in for a kiss.

"Have so much fun, sweetie. I love you."

"Love you too, Mommy."

As she watched her daughter take a deep breath, Charlie Kate's tiny fists clutching the straps of her purple Jansport backpack and her honey-colored pigtails bouncing as she took the first steps into her future, Linda let out a breath. A few stray tears bounded off her smile on their way down.

"I can *do* this," Charlie Kate muttered to herself.

She quickly found a cubby brandished with an ABC sticker that said "Charlotte Murphy," tucked her things carefully away as all of the other children were doing, and pattered tentatively to a circular table filled with coloring sheets and buckets of Crayola crayons. A boy with a blonde bowl cut occupied one of the four chairs gathered around the table, scribbling sloppily and outside the lines. He reminded her of

David. *Safety*. Not removing her eyes from the boy, she slid a coloring sheet to her spot, grabbed a purple crayon, and sat down.

"Hi, what's your name?" she asked, beginning to add color to the dress of the little schoolgirl printed on the paper.

"I'm Charlie," the boy responded, not bothering to remove his concentration from his picture. His brows were furrowed, and his bottom lip was pulled between his teeth as he continued scribbling.

"That's my name, too!" Ecstatic, Charlie Kate's eyes lit up for the first time since arriving in the strange new place.

But then, for the first time since she sat down, the boy stopped coloring.

"Well that's *stupid*. Charlie's a *boy's* name."

Her eyes fell to her picture, a distinct purple now wavering outside the lines.

"It's just my nickname," she began, breathy and nervous as sweat began to bead on her brow. "My real name is Charlotte, but my daddy calls me Charlie Kate—"

"But you're a *girl*. Your dad must be stupid if he gave you a boy name."

She wanted to leave, wanted to pick up and find another table with a different child who wasn't so rude. But she was frozen to the spot. Cheeks reddening by the second, she put her head down, concentrating now on salvaging the picture that she had begun. While she finished filling in the dress, and the tension slowly began to waver, she took deep breaths. A new student seated herself at the table then. She was wearing a purple dress, and her chocolate pigtails resembled Charlie Kate's. There was hope yet.

"Hi," the little girl began, waving a pudgy hand in the air.

"Don't talk to her, she has a *boy* name," Charlie interrupted, pointing his red crayon at Charlie Kate, his eyes passing threateningly between her and the new little girl.

Charlie Kate's lip was quivering now, but true to her brother's words that morning before he bounded down the hall to second grade, she wouldn't cry.

"Kindergarten's easy peasy, Charlie Kate. It'll be okay. Just

4

remember, nothing in kindergarten is worth crying about, okay?
You're smarter and tougher than all of those other kids. Be brave."

As two other boys joined the table, gathering around the culprit of her taunts, she clenched her teeth, balled her hands into fists, and stomped off to another part of the still unfamiliar classroom.

At recess, she found herself alone on the playground, underneath the jungle gym with her knees pulled up under her chin. Despite David's advice earlier, as soon as she stepped foot outside, she let tears trickle down her cheeks. With her eyes focused on the ground to count the wood chips, a pair of light-up Power Ranger shoes blinked into her line of vision.

The shouts and laughter of the other children disappeared around her as she realized that the shoes were there for her. Her eyes followed the shoes upwards, running over a pair of jean shorts and a Red Sox t-shirt, before finally landing on the round face of a little boy whom she recognized from her classroom.

She wiped her eyes with the backs of her fists, noticing the way his head cocked and his eyebrows furrowed. She prepared herself for more taunting and teasing.

"Why are you sittin' all by yourself?"

As she wiped the last stray tear from her cheek, the boy settled himself next to her, pulling his knees up to mimic her position in the wood chips. Before she could answer, he spoke again.

"I think Charlie Kate is a nice name," he began. "I'm James."

She found his eyes tentatively. After the cruelty of the morning, she didn't want to be belittled twice before lunch.

Shrugging, she offered him a simple, "Thanks." Then, after a beat, feigning indifference, she said, "My real name is Charlotte. Charlie Kate's just a stupid nickname."

She fumbled with her fingers, her gaze fixed on her knees as she looked away from James. But as she picked at the purple nail polish that her mother had freshly applied the night before, his sweet voice suddenly perked at her ears again.

"I like Charlie Kate better." The smile that he passed was a lopsided, goofy grin, creeping up the left side of his face. The warmth and sincerity lifted a weight that had been building on her shoulders since she had walked through the classroom doors that morning. She smiled back small at first, but her lips nearly reached her pigtails by the time James stood and outstretched his fingers towards her, saying, "Come on, you can play with me."

She stood with him, their hands clasped together as they wound their way out from under the jungle gym. He broke into a run as soon as they were free.

"My dad just taught me how to pump by myself on the swings. I can teach you if you want!" he called over his shoulder.

Mounting a pair of swings, and watching as the little boy with unruly chestnut hair demonstrated how to gather your momentum and pump your legs, Charlotte Katherine Murphy found herself laughing for the first time that day. And it certainly wouldn't be her last.

Later that day, after her teacher had introduced the different centers to the class, Charlotte took up shop at a table that mirrored the one she found herself at earlier: it was covered in blank sheets of paper and had markers galore. She was hesitant at first, noticing the snickering eyes of the kids who had teased her earlier. It wasn't until she felt James by her side that she felt confident enough to take a seat.

Her markers glided carefully across the page, reds and blues and browns and greens coming together as neatly as she could to form the body of the boy who was scribbling wildly to her right. Using her free hand to cover her gaze, she snuck glances at him, realizing quickly that he was so focused on his own drawing that he wouldn't notice that she was drawing him.

In the end, her wobbly marker lines showed his mop of brown hair next to her bright yellow curly pigtails. She wasn't so great at the trademarked Boston *B* that her brother practiced so diligently, so she settled for a red shirt with a blue baseball. After, she gave herself a purple dress and matching shoes, linking their peach hands in the middle. The top of the page read *Charlie Kate and Jams Bst Frns* in kindergartener style blocky handwriting, fit with backwards "e's" to boot.

She carried the picture gingerly to her mailbox, sliding it carefully inside and triple checking that the picture stayed put before returning to the table.

"DONE!"

As she took her seat next to James and slid a fresh piece of paper in front of her spot, James dropped his green marker dramatically to the table, beaming at his picture.

"What did you draw?" she asked, pausing her own marker above her paper to peer at his, that was nothing but a mess of green with random black lines and backward numbers.

"It's the Green Monster. *Duh*. Hey, what'd you make? I didn't get to see yours."

Her cheeks blushed.

"Oh, I messed up. I threw it away. I'm starting over."

"That's cool. I'm gonna draw Fenway Park next!"

She giggled as he picked up the green marker again, indistinguishable blobs filling his page that was beginning to look, unsurprisingly, just like his previous picture. She settled her sights on drawing a butterfly, focusing on the symmetry as James colored to her right, and made occasional comments like *Look at this, Charlie Kate, I put Troy O'Leary in the grass!* and *Your butterfly is pretty! Maybe you could give it a Red Sox jersey.*

When it was time for pick-up, she made sure that her picture from earlier made its way safely into her take-home folder before she joined the car rider line. She smiled as James took her hand on their way out the door.

When they met their moms in front of the building, he dropped her hand to take his mother's, turning to wave and offer her the half smile that she was growing so accustomed to.

"Bye, Charlie Kate! See you tomorrow!"

When she got home, she made a beeline for the basement playroom, setting up shop at the craft table with a fresh piece of lined paper and a bucket of markers. The first day of kindergarten had a fictional tale brewing in her head all day, starring main characters James and Charlie Kate, with a bully to boot. Told in mostly pictures, Charlie Kate and James defeated the bully with the help of the Red Sox, and remained best friends *forever and ever*.

After stacking the papers neatly and in order, she adorned the edges with staples, sealing the picture from school at the top like a cover. Her grin was wide and growing as she flipped through her book, one of many that littered the Murphy household, each of them with *By Charlie Kate Murphy* written proudly at the bottom, just like David had taught her to do. This story, she decided, was her best yet.

It was then that her brother came bounding down the stairs, whipping his backpack at the couch and heading straight for the PlayStation. As the machine booted up, he joined his sister at the table, ruffling her hair as he bent down to her level.

"So, how was your first day of kindergarten, squirt?" had barely passed by his lips before his eyes caught the thick packet of papers she had been working on. "Hey, what's that?"

Before she could answer, he snatched the book from her grip and began mocking her pictures out loud. All of her hard work was suddenly reduced to belittlement by her big brother, who could really be a jerk sometimes.

"Oh man, Charlie Kate," he chuckled, "do you *love* James?"

"No! David, give that back!"

She reached for her book, but he held it above his head, dangling it just out of reach no matter how high she jumped.

"Charlie Kate and *Jaaaaames* sitting in a tree, K-I-S-S-I-N-G."

She was crying now, her face as red as a tomato as her small fingers curled into fists at her sides. Once the noise caught Mom's attention away from making dinner, David was scolded and her book was returned, and she fled to her room, clutching the now wrinkled paper to her chest. Though she diligently tried to flatten out the wrinkles, creases still remained. It was then that she made the promise to keep her stories inside of her head. No one else needed to read them after all.

"Lemon Sauce Productions. Ginny Edley's line. Charlotte Murphy speaking. How may I direct your call?"

"You can direct my call to the receiver, because you're already twenty minutes late, and I'm pretty sure your boss can hear my stomach growling from four stories up."

Charlotte Murphy's lips, pursed in annoyance not seconds prior, unfurled into a full grin. She shifted her desk phone between her shoulder and her ear as she finished filing the paperwork that was clutched between her fingers and reached for the brown paper bag that was tucked under her desk.

"I'll be down in five minutes, Rango. Don't get your panties in a bunch."

She chuckled, imagining the tall, lanky man on the other end of the receiver reaching behind him to unfurl a wedgie. It was not so much imagined as it was pulled from her memories of that same man as a child, wrestling in the backyard with her brother, as David hoisted him into the air by his boxer shorts.

"It's not my panties that are bunched, it's my stomach! Now, hurry up. I'm starving!"

"Okay, okay! I'm coming, I'm coming!"

Grabbing her purse from the bottom drawer of her desk, she headed to the office elevator.

James grinned, that same sideways grin he'd had since boyhood, as he ended the phone call. The picture on his cell background caught his eye as he closed out of the phone app. He smiled at the image of a blonde woman cradled against his own chest, before a familiar scent of vanilla and lavender lifted him out of his thoughts.

He spotted her honey curls, already frizzing slightly in the Los Angeles heat, as she turned out the door and away from him. She was frazzled, head jerking this way and that, searching for him. Rather than flagging her down right away, he took a moment to relish in her airiness, loving the way that her brows knit together as she searched aimlessly for him. Once she began moving down the sidewalk in the opposite direction, he chuckled, pocketed his cell phone, and skipped to grab her elbow before she actually crossed the street without him.

When they reached the park, they found a comfortable spot in the grass. Hands reached into brown paper bags to pull out two almost identical sandwiches, each cut diagonally to form two triangles apiece. His fingers buzzed with the memory like they always did.

"I have peanut butter and jelly. What do you have?"

"Peanut butter and fluff," Charlotte replied with a wide grin.

"Aww, man!" James's sandwich plunged into his lap, his jealousy brewing a giggle in Charlotte's throat. *"Your momma's so cool! My lunch is so boring."*

Plucking one of her sandwich halves from its plastic baggie, she thrust it towards him.

"Here, wanna trade? Then, we could both have both."

His floppy head perked up from where it had been hanging, more so in forged contempt than anything else. With eyes bugged, he passed half of his own sandwich to her.

As they munched on matching sandwiches, the roofs of their mouths sticking together, James broke their contented silence.

"Hey Charlie Kate, why were you crying yesterday?"

"'Cause." She shrugged, her gaze dragging from her sandwich to her lap.

"'Cause why?" he pressed. When she didn't answer, he offered her a sideways glance, his eyes screaming I'll get it out of you one way or another. *Twenty-four hours of friendship, and he already wasn't letting her get away with anything.*

She let a beat pass, taking a deep breath as she gathered her words.

"My mommy told me that I would make lots of best friends in kindergarten. But then that mean boy made fun of me and I didn't have any friends."

James cocked his head, his eyebrows crinkling as he watched the pigtailed little girl drop her head and roll her shoulders forward in defeat.

"Charlie Kate, those other kids are stupid,*" he began, the words trotting off his tongue as if they were facts and not opinions.*

Her head perked up. She wasn't allowed to say "stupid," so hearing the only friend that she had use the word so freely made it seem real.

"First of all, that boy Charlie Cox was the naughtiest kid at summer camp. Nobody actually listens to him." He waggled his eyebrows, watching his friend giggle in response. "Second of all, I don't care if you have a boy name or a girl name."

She was smiling now. Genuinely smiling.

"You're nice, and you're pretty, and if those other kids don't wanna play with you, forget about them. That's what you've got me for."

She sat up straighter, her smile reaching her pigtails.

"I'm glad we're friends, James."

"Best friends."

"*God*, I needed this."

The park was buzzing with life: mothers pushed babies in buggies, joggers got in a quick afternoon workout, college students passed a frisbee around in a circle. Charlotte let out a huge sigh as she stretched out her legs, leaning back on her elbows as James passed half his sandwich to her like it was muscle memory.

"Boss already has you workin' like a dog, huh?" he chuckled. She could only nod, peanut butter and fluff rendering her temporarily speechless.

"Kindergarten graduation was *yesterday* James. *Yesterday.* And yet, here I am, already back in the thick of it. It doesn't *end*."

She flopped backwards onto the grass in dramatic fashion as James wiped a smear of peanut butter from the corner of his lip with his thumb.

"So, the burning question of the afternoon then, Murph: *why* did you take the job again? You spend *every summer* complaining. So, quit!"

She rolled her eyes, trying and failing to suppress a smile. "I'm sorry that my glamorous day job of teaching kindergarten doesn't allow me the luxuries of affording Los Angeles rent without having to work a second job over the summer."

"So, move back in with me," he replied with a shrug, his tone casual but serious as he popped a Frito into his mouth. "Just remember, I expect my underwear folded and my coffee ready to go by six on the dot."

Charlotte sat up and rocked sideways, bumping their shoulders as she snorted.

"I complain because I can," she sighed finally. "And besides, Ginny isn't *that* bad."

"Not that bad? Need I remind you about the—not one, but *three*—separate occasions in which she tried to jump me in the dorm showers? And that was just the *first* week of college."

She laughed at his misfortune, enjoying the cool breeze and quiet summer ambience for a still moment.

"Seriously, though, Charlie Kate. You've gotta do what makes you happy. I mean, why keep putting yourself through all of this misery when you could be, I don't know, doing something better with your summers? Didn't you drag me out here so we could spend all of our free time at the beach?"

She reached across the space between them to slap him in the chest, quirking an eyebrow as she retorted, "*I* dragged *you* out here? You're full of shit."

His expression said, *I'll win this argument if you keep pushing.*

"I guess...yes, spending a ton of time in the sun was definitely a perk of moving out here but...I don't know, James. We're, like, *real* adults at this point. We had our fun. But we have to live in the real world and make big kid decisions now. At least *one* of us has to be responsible."

"Now where's the fun in *that*?" he chuckled, pushing his gangly body up off the grass. "Being a kid is what I do best!"

Eyeing the vast park before him, he picked up a stray frisbee and tossed it to the throng of college students that awaited its return. As he nodded his head back at her, Charlotte picked herself up off the ground, the roll of her eyes contradicting the way her lips were pulling into a grin.

As they strode down the sidewalk, taking their time before returning to their respective offices, a thought gnawing in James's head provoked him to return to their lunchtime conversation.

"Hey, so, seriously though. What gives? You're working like a dog, and you're clearly unhappy about it. Why not just get a different summer job? Or...I don't know, move or something?"

"Are we really doing this again?" Her annoyance was partly playful but mostly true; she really didn't want to dig up her skeletons, not when the sun was shining and the weekend was looming close.

"We, in fact, are," he said bluntly. His feigned seriousness was an art that had been perfected from the time he was six years old.

But as he stared down at her, a full foot between the tops of their heads, she knew she wasn't getting out of this one.

Her eyes found the bright blue sky as her head rolled back, an *Ugh* echoing in her throat. James laughed quietly when her footfalls became heavier, as if she were stomping like a petulant child. But the way that she carried her body, the manner in which her shoulders fell and her head lolled back into place and her chest heaved in a defeated sigh, told him that getting to the underlying cause of her frustration was going to take longer than one of their lunch break heart-to-hearts.

"I just...God, James, I look at you and all that you've accomplished, and then, I look at me, and..."

She trailed off as they approached a *DO NOT CROSS* light, her green eyes finding their resting spot at the less-than-white laces of her shoes, settled next to the shiny brown of her best friend's Hugo Boss Oxfords.

In her silence, James took in the dejectedness of his best friend. As words failed, he brought his hand around her shoulder to give her a tight squeeze to his side as the orange hand transformed into the bright white of a walking figure.

"You know, Charlie Kate, just because I'm smiling on the outside doesn't mean it's all sunshine and rainbows on the inside," he began as they strode across faded white lines. "For all you know, my job could be eating me alive, my condo could be harboring a rat infestation, and I could have Vanessa bound and gagged in the back of my closet."

"Don't even pretend that you don't absolutely love your life," she challenged.

He rolled his head back, arms thrust upward, as he continued his argument.

"But that's just *it* Charlie Kate: you're basing your successes off of mine. People just...they don't progress at the same pace." He pondered for a beat, begging the clouds to give him answers in the remaining block and a half of their journey. "Don't you remember when we were in the fourth grade and you got put in the blue reading group and I had to stay behind in the red reading group?"

It was a long shot, but at least she was giggling now.

"Well yes, but I don't think my reading level being superior to yours when we were ten is the best comparison to *you* growing up and *me* sitting behind a shitty desk and going home to my cats for the rest of my life."

"Oh, stop it. You don't even like cats. You have nothing to worry about." She sidled into him, barely moving him as her petite body bounced off his hip.

"You'll be fine Charlie Kate, I promise," he tried to reassure her, pulling her against his side forcefully. "Just give it some time. You're in a rut. You just have to find your groove again. Think of it like a hitter's slump. David Ortiz always got himself out of it, and when he did, he had everyone on their feet. It might take some time, but just be patient. It'll all work out in the end."

He pulled her into a tight embrace, mumbling the last of his sentence into the curls atop her head.

He turned his upper half to extend one more goodbye wave before making his way three blocks east to Apex Solutions, where his desk overlooked a beautiful courtyard, and he could shoot hoops on his downtime. As his feet beat the warm pavement, he mulled over their conversation.

James Ramsey really didn't have many complaints about his life. He had a stable job in sales marketing that afforded him a nice condo in Los Angeles. A condo that he shared with the woman whom he'd spent the past two years of his life with.

But as he rode the elevator up to the seventeenth floor, his heart ached a little for his best friend of over two decades. She wasn't happy. And in the Charlotte Murphy corner of his mind—the one that was larger than he sometimes cared to admit to—that made him unhappy, too.

"So, did you bone him yet?"

Ginny Edley was nothing if not subtle.

She was Charlotte's stark opposite in every way, but somehow in the first week of college, they had clicked. All those years later, Charlotte spent her summers as an assistant to her college best friend while she was on summer vacation from teaching kindergarten. Something about a teacher's salary and the cost of living in California just didn't quite mesh.

Ginny's bluntness was a matching pair to her inability to censor herself. She was perched on Charlotte's desk the second she returned from lunch with James, Ginny's fingers curled around a half-eaten apple.

"I'm not having this conversation again, Ginny. You know we're just friends."

The conversation was not uncommon, and Charlotte brushed it off as she would a fly that had followed her into the office. She sorted through the fresh list of scripts that had been dropped off on her lunch break. Being Ginny's assistant at Lemon Sauce called for a lot of answering phones, going on coffee runs, and copying scripts when they came in. She wasn't a writer's assistant by any means, but with her friend's credentials often landing her as the head writer on many a script, Charlotte was gratefully accepted as an extra set of hands during the summer.

"Uh huh, because I'm *that* friendly with any of *my* male friends without getting a little action on the side."

Ginny had moved onto a yogurt now, swirling the spoon in her mouth as she spoke.

"You don't *have* any male friends that you aren't having sex with on the side."

"That's exactly my point. You either fuck 'em, or you don't socialize with 'em outside the break room."

Tossing the empty container into Charlotte's garbage can, she grabbed the top script off of the pile in Charlotte's hand and began flipping through it.

"If you don't go for it soon, I'm going to have to step in and take things into my own hands. I don't know how much longer I can go on calling you the two of you my friends when I have had to watch you socialize with him for too many years without getting any."

Charlotte's cheeks turned a deep shade of crimson almost immediately, and she promptly buried her nose into the new topsheet.

"Oh my god, Charlotte Murphy! You *did* get some! *Spill!* When? Where? How—"

"*Ginny!*"

Ginny hopped off Charlotte's desk and followed her to the copier.

"It's nothing you haven't heard before," Charlotte began quietly, willing the burn in her cheeks to subside.

"That's the problem. I swear, when you two tried to *get it out of your systems,* you did something wrong."

Blush creeped into Charlotte's cheeks again as she watched papers stack, hole punch, staple, and pile at the end tray of the copy machine, willing her own memories to the back-burner.

"Is he still dating that frigid little thing?" Ginny continued, off in her own conversation, as was often the case. "You'd think by now he'd have found someone who didn't have her G-string stuck so high up her ass that it has her face turning purple."

Charlotte nearly choked on a laugh, her eyes bulging at the petite blonde with the upturned nose who offered her a simple shrug in return.

Eyes fleeting, she was distracted by images of a different petite blonde.

Vanessa Harding, draped around the man with whom she had just shared lunch, speeding through her mind in fleeting forms, before she was brought back to earth by her friend's incessant nit picking.

"I mean come on Charlotte. He's got her so high up on this pedestal, but that's only because that's where the leash lands her. If she pulls that thing any tighter he's going to choke, and then," with a motion that resembled popping the head off of a dandelion, she continued, "bye-bye Jamesy; hello lonely little Charlotte, without a best friend and potential fuck buddy for the rest of her life."

Ginny's posture exuded smug satisfaction; her arms crossed triumphantly across her chest. As Charlotte brushed her off, heading back to her desk with a fresh stack of papers, her thoughts twisted with details of James's latest relationship.

"She's not *that* horrid," she tossed over her shoulder, knowing that Ginny would be on her tail. "She's always been nice to me. I know if I had a boyfriend who was as close to another girl as James and I are, I'd at least be a little bit skeptical."

The glide of a highlighter filled the silence as Charlotte mulled over the scenario that Ginny had wound. Vanessa wasn't necessarily her favorite person in the world. But James loved her, and that was what mattered. Right? Sure, Vanessa's hours at the hospital gave her limited time to see James, and she essentially dictated his free time with her hectic schedule, but wasn't that what relationships were built on? Spending time together? Compromise?

It didn't matter that his past two years spent with Vanessa had significantly hindered the time that *Charlotte* and James spent together. There were always sacrifices with relationships, and Charlotte just so happened to be *his*. And yet, she had never thought about it that way: that any part of James's stress stemmed from Vanessa's—what— jealousy?

"Maybe that's why she has him so tightly wound." Charlotte cocked her head sideways, thumbing through her prints to assure that she had them labeled correctly before shoving them into mailboxes. "You think it's my fault?"

"Is it your fault that she's so insecure? Nope. I'm pretty sure her terrible nose job and lopsided tits do that on their own."

Despite her vulgarity, Ginny always had a knack for making her laugh.

"Maybe she's just afraid of losing him to you, so she feels like she has to up her game. That would explain why they're constantly having sex."

"So I'm their motivation for sex. Thank you. That makes me feel *so* much better."

"Think of it as a positive thing. At least one of them is thinking about you." Ginny winked, reaching past a wide-eyed Charlotte to snatch her own topsheet from her desk as they passed by. "Why don't you just confront him? Tell him how you really feel?"

"Right, because waltzing up to my best friend and telling him that I don't like his girlfriend of two years and that he should dump her is clearly the best option."

It wasn't that she didn't *like* Vanessa. As a person Vanessa was kind, compassionate, definitely a hard worker. But for James, she was all wrong. Charlotte couldn't be the only one who noticed.

"I was talking about politely telling him that you'd like to get in his pants. Not all that mushy sentimental bullshit. You know I wouldn't touch that with a ten-foot pole." As Ginny flipped through more paperwork, she continued laying the groundwork for her reticent friend. "Try actually using that extra key he gave you to do some good. 'Why excuse me Mr. Ramsey, but I rather fancy that large package you've got sitting in your lap. Would you mind if I took a quick peek?'"

Charlotte backhanded Ginny across the arm before eyeing the to-do list that awaited her. She rolled her eyes slightly as her butt hit the chair.

First day of summer vacation, my ass.

It was after eight PM when she finally shuffled her feet through the doorway of her one-bedroom apartment, her shoes and purse forming an amorphous pile on the scratched laminate. After changing into oversized sweats and exchanging contacts for glasses, she claimed the dip in her couch with a plate of microwaved pizza and a glass of wine. The sounds of Jerry Remy's Red Sox broadcast filled her apartment as she finally let herself breathe.

A text from James during the third inning, ***Jesus Christ, can Mookie Betts do no wrong, or can Mookie Betts do no wrong?*** gave her a breathy giggle, but it pulled her right back to their conversation from earlier in the day.

Her eyes wandered around the living room that she had moved into just a little under two years prior. It wasn't big by any means, but it suited her lifestyle of not needing much anyway. Her couch was a decent enough distance away from the kitchen table that she could convince herself it was "open concept" and not just "a small step above a studio." And besides, she could watch TV while she ate breakfast. Definitely a bonus, right?

When her eyes met the clock on the cable box, the *8:52* seeming to taunt her, she felt her chest tighten.

But she rolled her eyes, the constant reminder that *the majority of corporate America worked through the summer* scolding her from somewhere in the back of her mind that complained about *not getting the summer off even though she was a teacher*. She groaned, tossing her head against the back of the couch as she struggled to pity her own situation. Maybe James was right. Maybe it *was* time to find a job at a school somewhere else, or a new place of residence.

Maybe moving back to Massachusetts wasn't the worst idea in the world.

But the thought of picking up and starting over at square one without her best friend by her side spiked terror up her spine. Instead, she poured herself another glass of wine to numb those thoughts and enjoyed the fact that the Red Sox were off to a pretty great start this season, pushing her worries about what to do with her life to the wayside for one more night.

June 1996

As they crossed the path of Brookline Avenue over to Yawkey Way, Charlotte's heart thumped faster in her chest. The brick walls of Fenway Park peaked over the horizon, the same walls she had seen so many times on TV. But as they walked underneath the banner that read *Welcome to Fenway Park*, her hand clammy in the clutches of James's, it was so much more.

Charlotte was born into the Red Sox lifestyle, but she didn't mind in the slightest. There was something familiar and exciting about sitting with her family five nights a week starting in April, though it often ended in heartache and lots of tossed pillows by Daddy and David in the middle of September. Still, watching players like Mo Vaughn and Jose Canseco take the field had her body buzzing with excitement. These guys were part of her family.

And it made her all the more grateful that the Ramsey family was as big into baseball as the Murphys were.

It was the summer after kindergarten graduation, and as both a Father's Day gift to Jerry and Will, as well as a "get these kids out of the hair of a pregnant Julie Ramsey," Charlotte and James found themselves attending their first Red Sox game together.

"Oh my god! Charlie Kate! *Look at that!*" was the phrase she would hear most commonly throughout the day, as he pointed out *The seats!* and *The banners!* and *Oh my GOD it's the Green Monster!* Though one of his hands remained stickily grasping hers, the other pointed wildly and frantically.

They were attending a Sunday afternoon game, and without a cloud in the sky, the afternoon was looking to be a perfect one. No one could have prepared them for the first feeling of walking through the tunnel behind home plate, but as they squeezed each other's hands a little tighter and turned to grin, Charlotte felt the butterflies roam from her stomach to her throat, her entire body tingling as her legs carried her up the walkway.

Her face was splitting in an ear to ear grin as her eyes shot around the field that, until now, was only present in her life on channel 13. It smelled like dirt and popcorn and Fenway Franks, the aroma wrapping around her like a tight hug as the sounds of bats cracking and balls popping into mitts had her ears buzzing with anticipation.

These men that she watched with her father from their superstitious spots in the living room looked so much bigger in person, and it slightly shocked her to realize that Troy O'Leary was a *real life person* and not just the t-shirt that she wore to school at least once a week.

James, beside her, was cutting off her circulation with his grip, but she didn't care. The way his eyes were bugging wide and the way that his body was literally jumping up and down beside her as he yelled things like *Dad, it's Tim Wakefield! Oh my god oh my god oh my god!* mirrored the excitement that was bubbling within her.

Their seats were in the grandstand behind the Sox dugout, and although she spent plenty of time on Daddy's lap in order to see, most of her time was spent standing next to James, clutching the seats in front of them as Mo Vaughn went 4 for 4 and Jose Canseco and Reggie Jefferson each hit a home run. The Sox bested the Rangers 10 to 9.

They fell asleep on the car ride home, with noses and cheeks red from a day in the sun, James's lips open and slightly drooling on Charlotte's shoulder, their eyes heavy under two new ball caps.

It had been the perfect day.

And it was that outing that lead to talk about the lake house, and planning vacations together as a family duo. It was thrilling to Charlotte when, on their next trip to Disneyland as a family, James and his brother and new baby sister accompanied them at the airport. Now, David had someone else to talk to in James's older brother, Kyle, and Kelly was all a flutter with holding baby Abby and making her giggle and wave her chubby hands in the air.

Charlotte and James remained in their own little corner of the terminal, sharing a Mickey Mouse coloring book on laps where the feet attached didn't touch the ground, but swung freely in the open air of Boston Logan Airport. Charlotte's pigtails bounced wildly as she expressed her glee about heading back to California, telling James of all the wonderful things that Disneyland had to offer.

"Do you wanna know the best part?" she whispered through a gap-toothed smile where her front two teeth were missing. "There's snow here at home, but when we get to Disneyland, it's like summer all the time!"

"Summer all the time? That's crazy, Charlie Kate. You can't have summer all the time. What would you even do during Christmas?"

"You'll see," she chided, her eyes simultaneously saying *Get over yourself* and *Trust me on this one.*

They boarded the plane with hands clasped together as they walked down the center aisle. As they approached the row next to the wing, Charlotte slid into the window seat first, quirking an eyebrow at James's dumbfounded, gaping expression.

"What?"

"Uh, how come *you* get the window seat?"

"I always sit by the window," she shrugged, buckling her seatbelt.

"Well *that's* not fair."

James crossed his arms, his lips now furling into the beginnings of a pout. Charlotte, with her lips parted and her eyes wide, glanced from side to side, intent on staying in her spot. She saw the light bulb go on in James's eyes before he dug around in his pocket, his tongue stuck out past his lips until he pulled out a dull quarter.

"Flip for it?"

She smiled smugly, told him, "You're going down," as he chose heads and she chose tails, and giggled when he ultimately flumped his bony body into the middle seat.

When they returned from their week away, it was James, ultimately, who shared with their first grade class how they had missed a week of school to go to *This awesome place called California where they have summer all the time and it never snows!* while Charlotte used her share time to tell the class about meeting Mickey Mouse and going on the Matterhorn.

Though it wasn't the only place that the Ramseys and Murphys vacationed together, California was a fan favorite. When the Murphys took a solo trip in third grade to San Diego, James cried jealousy the whole day before they left. What was supposed to be one more sleepover before a week apart turned into James being pouty and Charlotte rolling her eyes until his mom picked him up in the morning. Charlotte brought him back a button, but it wasn't the same as the stories she shared of palm trees and beautiful weather and her wish to *live in the summer forever.*

But the families continued to grow close, especially when Will and Jerry became the coaches to James and David's little league baseball team, the one that eventually turned into a team that would travel around the country for different tournaments throughout the summers. The women swapped recipes and child rearing tips, the men helped one another with projects, and the kids looked out for one another. Kelly often babysat the Ramseys when Kyle had orchestra performances or Julie had to take Abby to a doctor's appointment. Charlotte's sleepovers at the Ramsey household were sometimes out of necessity rather than for fun, but she never saw a difference.

Their whole life was only thought of as *together.* Those rare moments that Charlotte looked back on that didn't contain James in some way were often filled with missing him or wishing he was there.

June 2018

"Cheers to the summer!" James exclaimed.

As per Friday night tradition, Charlotte found herself clinking beer bottles with James across his living room couch. After surviving kindergarten graduation on Tuesday, and her first week and a half inside of her summer office, she was greeted by a surprise party of one waiting for her at the condo that James shared with Vanessa.

When she let herself in that evening, she found a six pack of beer, a pizza, and a bouquet of balloons anchored to his kitchen table. A shoddily drawn sign that said *You Survived!* hung from the light fixture overhead. She smiled. Art had never been his forte, but it was the gesture that had her heart doing flips. She truly had struck gold all those years ago.

"Yeah. Another year down, only forever to go." Taking a swig from her beer, she rolled her eyes with a grin tugging at her lips.

"Oh, come on, Negative Nellie. Stop being such a downer. It's *summer*time. You have three months of freedom between you and the new tater tots, so start enjoying it. And besides, the Sox are still on, so we actually get to watch a game that doesn't end after lunch."

"Alright, alright."

She sighed in defeat, threw herself into her spot on his couch, and settled in right away. It wasn't the same couch that they'd had in college, or even the one from the apartment they shared when they first moved to California. It was a couch purchased with his "big boy money," one that Vanessa had said would "make his place look more grown up" than the faux leather recliners they had taken from his parents' basement. While the living room did certainly resemble a Better Homes & Gardens catalogue, Charlotte couldn't help but adjust herself every twenty minutes or so. It wasn't comfortable at all.

James turned to Charlotte, his mouth stuffed with cheese and pepperoni as he asked, "So, Miss Murphy, what kind of takeaways do we have this year?"

He had one hand pressed to the side of his head as if to hold an earpiece in place, while the other was thrust in front of her face, mimicking a microphone. They'd done this before, making fun of local newscasters, and she took right to the charade.

"Well, Bob, I'd have to say, number one: pack extra clothes. It isn't only the *kids* who get peed on," she replied, her tone sly with a fake accent.

"*What* insight. Care to continue?"

"I'll take you back to the first incident, Bob. It was a bright September day, a slight chill in the air, when little Tommy Knowles first sat on my lap…"

The banter continued, transitioning in and out easily from watching the game to chatting about nothing and everything while beer slowly began to disappear and make their words toss and tumble.

In her few years of teaching experience, this year truly took the cake as the most awful. Charlotte had spent many a night in tears on the phone with her mom, instituted "Wine Wednesdays" with her kindergarten team, and had more than plenty of venting sessions on James's couch.

He heard it all that year, from challenging behaviors, to kids in her class speaking four different languages that were not English, to not meeting test score expectations ("They're five, James. *Five*! They shouldn't be taking *standardized tests*!"), all culminating with the bomb threat that had the whole town on edge for two weeks straight.

On that particular night, she didn't need to say a word. After seeing the broadcast on the local news in his office lobby, the phone was glued to his ear for the entire drive to the front door of her school building. He arrived before the final bell rang, took her wordlessly home, and held her close as she cried. His own heart finally broke when she'd muttered with tears dried, "Is it sad that I kind of expected this to happen to me one day?"

As the post-game interviews wrapped on a 6 to 2 Sox victory, Charlotte took the opportunity to pick up their mess of garbage, stumbling in her tipsy haze as she deposited an empty six pack and more into James's recycling bin.

"So, any big plans for the summer?" James asked as Charlotte flopped back onto the couch.

"You ask me that question like you don't already have my schedule on your calendar," she said with a snort.

"You're not wrong." He pointed the tip of his new beer at her before taking a healthy swig. "So what, aside from going home for Emma's birthday, you're going to do absolutely nothing exciting?"

"Yep." She gave him a large smile, satisfied with her choices as she closed her eyes contentedly.

"Wow, Charlie Kate. Just...*wow*. I mean, the school year from hell is finally over and you expect me to believe you're going to do absolutely nothing to celebrate?"

"I did celebrate. I *am* celebrating. I just emptied your fridge of beer and ate half a pizza. Is that not celebration?"

"No. We used to do this every Tuesday back in college."

She snorted again, a flash of dorms and underage drinking bringing her back in time for just a moment.

"You're not wrong," she mimicked him, reaching across the table to pop open another bottle, beer fizzing down the side to meet her thumb. "Technically speaking, I *am* doing something exciting. I'm spending the three months off that I earned inside of a stuffy office making copies and running petty errands for my old college roommate. Very exciting. Super great summer plans."

He curled his lips and cocked his eyebrow at her satirical nods and faux serious edge.

"Oh *please*. You hate that job."

"I do not. I *tolerate* that job. That job keeps my air conditioning running during the summer. And besides," she continued, swigging back her Sam Adams, "I love my *actual* job. So there. I win."

He chuckled as she sloshed back her beer bottle hard enough to send liquid dribbling down her chin, her fingers fumbling to catch it before it dripped into her lap.

In the stillness that passed between commercial breaks and polishing off more alcohol, James found his gaze wandering over Charlotte's profile, noticing the way that her eyes were fighting to stay open, the way her shoulders were shrugged forward. He could do his best to blame it on the exhausting week, on the alcohol, on the late hour, but he knew better. His next words, not so carefully chosen, he blamed on the alcohol.

"Then how come you look so sad?"

Charlotte's eyes found him slowly, following the lines of the couch to the edge of his basketball shorts, up his arms and neck and sharp chin until the gold flecks in his green eyes were insistently upon her. Her own state of inebriation brought tears to her eyes that she quickly shucked away, her face scrunching in anger at herself for letting her emotions bubble up and almost foam over the top.

"It's just hard, you know?" The words, edged with tears, seemed to tumble. He could do no more than just let her go. "I mean, I bust my ass for the better part of a year, and then the kids are just...*gone*. Like, I spend all this time watching them grow and become better little human beings, and they get these little personalities, and then they're in 5th grade and barely remember who I am anymore. And then, for my reward, I get to work a second job to make ends meet. Am I doing something wrong here? I don't know, James, I just...I feel so...lonely?"

Her eyes were searching, wide and pleading, bringing him back to the first day he met her, five years old with her knees tucked beneath her on the playground, just looking for a friend. He had promised to be that friend.

Wordlessly, his arms were tight around her, curls tumbling against his cheek and in the crook of his neck.

Oftentimes when they were young, they would be knee to knee in conversation, the clock hands hitting two or three in the morning before their mothers came and turned out the lights of a sleepover, or exhaustion pulled their eyelids closed. But then, there were those times when silence was what conquered.

Tonight, with her body pulled into his lap, her small hands wrapped around his waist, he settled his cheek atop her head and remained in the necessary.

It wasn't uncommon to wake up on a couch with her wrapped up in his arms, against his chest, especially after a night of drinking. He left the tie blanket slung over the back of the couch for just that purpose, despite Vanessa's insistence that *it didn't match*. There were times when she would fall asleep before him, passed out to the sounds of a movie or Netflix marathon at two in the morning, her body curled up in its own corner of the couch. Those times, he would adjust her head accordingly so that she wouldn't wake with aches, tuck the blanket around her feet and under her chin, and retreat to his own bed.

But tonight, after hearing her anxieties to the tune of tears, real tears, he couldn't leave her. Not tonight.

Not when her breathing slowed against his own heart that was still racing with a need to make her feel better, just like he always had, still knowing that he had no power to fix what was breaking her on the inside. Not despite the fact that he was wide awake with the feel of her body weight against him. Not now, not when she was so fragile and so scared.

In the hours that he lay awake, he held onto her tighter, wishing her pain and her fears would go away just as they had when they were younger, and a hug from her best friend was all it took.

Here, with her in his arms, her shampoo tickling his nose, he was pulled back in time.

To last weekend, when he was on *her* couch, and her laughter accompanied thrown popcorn, a bad movie, and a wide smile.

To the apartment on 5th, the one that they had shared, the one where he would make her breakfast, where he would laugh and roll his eyes at the way that she folded his underwear even though he secretly loved it.

To the way that they made a valiant effort to date others in college when everyone on campus knew that it was *James and Charlotte against the world.*

To high school prom, and middle school awkwardness, and climbing the trees in his backyard to hide from their siblings and remain in their own world, a sacred bubble with just the two of them.

To meeting her all those years ago, never truly realizing the impact that two pigtails and a pair of purple shoes would have on his life all those years later.

So now, with her face years older, yet still so young and peaceful in sleep, he held her more tightly, rubbed his cheek against the top of her head, and willed sleep to stay away as he cemented this feeling, so distant in time and yet familiar all the same.

When he awoke hours later, they had shifted, but only slightly. He was laying on his back, a crick in his neck from the uncomfortable arm of the couch that he had rested against for seven hours. But Charlotte was still curled on his chest, her fists folded underneath her chin, the furrow in her brow finally gone.

At least she wouldn't wake with aches and pains.

He had always been abrupt to wake, unable to fall asleep once his eyes peeled open. It made Christmas mornings in the Ramsey household an early affair. But this morning, as the grey of dawn began to peek through the curtains they'd forgotten to draw, he cherished the moments he had, re-familiarizing himself with the way that breath whispered from her nose in her sleep, the way her eyelashes fluttered, the slight part in her lips as she breathed so softly.

It was so different than the way that he woke to Vanessa still asleep like the dead most days. If she wasn't in an exhaustive hangover, then she was cranky and irritable, non-communicative until she had her coffee, but still unpleasant until she had truly readied herself for the day.

Mornings with Vanessa were something he did his best to avoid. But when he thought of his mornings, past and present, with Charlotte, he smiled, thinking about how adorable it was, the way that she grumbled in a playful way, and turned her annoyed waking into fun.

It wasn't until his legs began to grow restless that he finally peeled himself from the couch, a piece of him staying behind with her as he trudged to the shower.

After changing into fresh sweats, he headed to the kitchen, not surprised to see Charlotte still asleep on the living room sofa, her *not a morning person* his stark opposite. While her problems the night before had seemed so complicated, it was easy to just slip back into banter and playfulness and the light, airy way that they had so carefully cultured over the years.

So, he painted on a smile before he picked up the unused throw pillow and let it collide with her cheek. A groan was muffled under soft cotton and she pulled the blanket over her head, burying her nose deeper into the back corner of the couch.

"Uh uh. Rise and shiny, lazy ass."

He grabbed her by the shoulders, forcing her into an upright position. Her curls were wild, tumbling in all directions like an unruly lion's mane as she squinted angrily into his eyes, her lips pursed tightly.

"Something I can do for you?" There was a chuckle in his words as he took in the sight of hangover ridden Charlotte Murphy. The older they got, the quicker she seemed to hit the wall.

"Yeah. Turn the lights off."

"The lights *are* off, slick. That's the sun."

"Well why is the sun so *loud*?" she groaned.

"C'mon. Let's get you carbo-loaded."

He pulled her up by both hands, a groan coming from somewhere deep in her lungs as she caught her balance. She was still rubbing the sleep from her eyes, still on the edge of her dreams, but remnants of the night before, those words and frustrations and tears, still lingered. He re-positioned his hands to rest firmly on her shoulders and dipped his head to meet her eyes with his own expression stern and serious.

"Hey, you okay?" His tone was lower, edged with sleep still, but his eyes narrowed as he sought the changes in her expression, the way fear twitched for only a moment before she relaxed into a somber state.

"Yeah. Yeah, I'll...I was just being dramatic last night." She rolled her eyes, hoping that his grip would lessen, when in fact, his fingers tightened on her shoulders, his brows squinting closer together.

"Hey. Seriously."

She sighed, her hands coming to rest flat against his chest, doing her best to convince him with a smile that was more forced than not.

"Seriously, Jimmy. I'll be fine. I just need to sort some things out for myself, okay?"

She'd caught him off-guard with the *Jimmy*, which was entirely part of the plan. But as his features relaxed and he squeezed her shoulders twice before letting go, she knew she was off the hook for at least a little while.

Charlotte sat at the kitchen table, watching the way James's shoulders stretched the back of his t-shirt while he flipped French toast in a pan. She'd seen this view plenty before, but there was always a moment when her breath would catch just a little and her heart would beat just a bit faster. It was usually when he would take a second to glance over his shoulder, catch her eye, smile that crooked smile, and go right back to flipping. His French toast was always mediocre at best, but her taste buds certainly gave it much more than it was worth.

"I'm never drinking again," she muttered in-between syrup-loaded bites. James laughed, poking his fork in her direction.

"You said that when we all went out for Easter brunch and you forgot that the mimosas were bottomless."

"Right. And you decided not to remind me of that because…?"

"Because hungover Charlie Kate is in my top three favorite Charlie Kate's, next to Super into a Red Sox Game Charlie Kate and Gets Excited When She Sees a Puppy Charlie Kate."

"I really hate you sometimes."

"Yes, but you also love me way more than you hate me."

"Debatable."

The front door opened, presenting a scrub clad, exhausted Vanessa. She hung her purse on the hook by the door and kicked her shoes next to the mat. It wasn't until she cleared into the kitchen that either noticed her.

"Oh, hey babe. Breakfast?" James asked with his mouth full, his attention split halfway between the two women.

Under tired eyes, Vanessa absorbed the scene in her kitchen of her boyfriend and his best friend sharing laughter and the new bottle of syrup she had just purchased.

"Thanks for the offer, but I think I'm just going to head to bed."

Vanessa passed a tired smile, lingering one moment with her eyes on James hesitantly before heading down the hallway.

With Vanessa's presence now looming, Charlotte felt the whispers of *intruder* creeping in, and she finished her breakfast quickly and without much fanfare.

"So," James began as he and Charlotte headed towards the door, his hands in his sweatpants pockets as he watched the ground where she was sliding on her shoes, "got any big plans for the rest of the day?"

"Oh, absolutely. I'm going to nurse the rest of this with a mega bottle of Gatorade, a tub of ice cream, and some Netflix."

She finished tying her shoes while he let out a breathy laugh, standing upright before she asked, "What about you guys?"

"Oh, uh, I'm not sure yet." He rubbed his hands along the back of his neck, a nervous tick he'd had all his life, one she had seen many a time when he was on the verge of admitting that he had a date coming up. "I think Vanessa's going to try to catch up on sleep. We might just order in and watch a movie."

"Wow, Rango, look at you. So domesticated."

He chuckled, both at the old nickname, as well as the sarcasm that enveloped her taunts. "Yeah, absolutely. I'm totally tied down now."

She didn't miss that his tone dripped with sarcasm, or when his hand rubbed a little harder at the skin just below his hairline.

"Well, enjoy it while you can. First comes love, then comes marriage, you know."

Her brows waggled jokingly, but his eyes bulged, a thick, ironic chuckle spurting past his lips.

"Ha! Oh-kay, that's enough out of you."

She laughed over her shoulder as she cleared the threshold of his front door.

Hours later, Vanessa emerged from her cocoon to join James in the living room; her tired eyes contradicted the sleepy smile that played at her lips.

"Hey there, Sleeping Beauty." James's voice was soft and sugary as he crossed the room to close his arms around her. "Did you get enough rest?" he mumbled against her hair.

"I never do." She chuckled, letting herself melt momentarily into his broad chest and his warm embrace.

"Well, how about a night of absolute vegetation then? Our butts won't leave the couch. I'll make the Uber Eats guy feed us."

"That actually sounds wonderful. I'm sold."

"Perfect. Now, change into your pajama-est pajamas, grab your comfiest blankets, and meet me on the couch in ten. I'm in charge of snacks."

Despite the jet lag feeling that still consumed her, Vanessa allowed her lips to curl up as she headed to their bedroom to heed James's instructions. When she met him in the living room, he was wearing his high school baseball team sweatpants and a t-shirt whose text was so faded she couldn't make it out. He had bags of chips, soda cans, and a bottle of wine on the coffee table.

She giggled as he bowed at the waist, exclaiming, "Your throne, m'lady," his arms presenting the nest he'd created with their blankets and pillows. There was just enough room for her to recline against his chest but still be surrounded by cotton and fuzz.

It was a thought that hadn't crossed his mind for over two years, since Vanessa officially became a part of his life. But as she snuggled against his body, giggling softly at whatever it was that was on the television, he noticed something different.

It wasn't that her body didn't fit or didn't belong. But now, here he was, comparing.

While Charlotte had always curled against his body in a way that seemed like she fit in his pocket, Vanessa was petite in a different way, her bones jagged if she leaned more one way or the other.

When Charlotte laughed against his chest, her breath puffed like clouds. Vanessa's tones were sharp and harsh.

Charlotte's hands were small and soft, whether she was grasping his in excitement or slapping him across the chest for taking his sarcasm too far. Vanessa's touches were always organizedly purposeful, to a point where he wasn't sure when and where he could put his hands for the first months of their relationship.

He coughed into his fist, twitching his legs to shake the restless thoughts as he did his best not to think about how Vanessa's straight blonde hair did *not* smell like lavender and vanilla.

True to her word, Charlotte stopped at CVS on her way home to pick up a bottle of Gatorade and extra strength ibuprofen. But as afternoon blended into evening and she reached her seventh straight episode of a *Grey's Anatomy* marathon, the headache that persisted, that mocked her from her fifth beer the night before, stemmed less from the alcohol entirely.

She didn't often let herself get like this.

It was fun to speculate the future when she was at work and all of her coworkers were bringing treats into the breakroom to celebrate weddings and babies and retirements and asking when it would be her turn. But in the darkness of her apartment, typically with a bottle of wine as her confidant, it wasn't fun and games. It was her life, and the uncertainty hung over her like a cloud threatening to break open.

It was one thing to watch all of her friends graduate college straight into jobs from internships and marry the guys they met freshman year. But the changes she thought she would see when she was next on the list to make a drastic life change, when she and her partner in crime had picked up and moved to the opposite side of the country, failed to come.

The natural struggles of being a real adult hit them hard, but together. It was one of her greatest blessings in life, to go through the tough steps with her best friend. But now, as they continued to grow older, he was moving up. He had been through several promotions, bought a condo, moved in with his long-term girlfriend. He didn't buy off-brand snacks anymore, because he didn't have to now. When they flew home for the holidays, he had airline points to spare while she often considered asking her brother for help, always with the asterisk of *Please don't tell mom and dad* attached.

James seemed to be climbing, and she couldn't help but feel left on the ground. Of course, he was with her every step of the way, but as the gap in their steps grew, so too did the elephant on her chest.

Stagnant.

It had been written on the board in the classroom of a friend who taught fifth grade, a "Word of the Day" exercise that the students would participate in when the bell rang. As they exchanged qualms about standardized testing over pre-student coffee, Charlotte's eyes wandered, tracing the letters of the word in equal parts sharp lines and soft curves.

Stagnant (adj.): Showing no activity; dull or sluggish

Synonyms: Still, inactive, unmoving

*Example: Timmy was **stagnant** in the mornings. It took a lot of effort from his mother to get him out of bed!*

Write your own sentence! Be creative!

It was sure to make the students laugh, to think, to expand their vocabulary for all of the five minutes it took to copy into their notebooks and forget about when the word was wiped away and replaced the next morning.

But despite the warm coffee cradled in her hands, Charlotte was suddenly cold.

The word clung to her throughout that day, crept into the small nooks and crannies like *Helping Cullen open his applesauce at lunch* and *Tying Emerson's shoes before gym.*

Stagnant.

She hadn't been looking for a label to all of her conflicting emotions, but suddenly, one had slapped her in the face, and attached itself to her forehead like a scarlet letter.

She had been teaching in the same building since her career began. She had lived in the same apartment since James started dating Vanessa and the conversation of *Maybe we need our own space?* all but broke her. It had the same furniture that they had purchased as odds and ends pieces: the lamp from her college dorm, the kitchen sink whose hot and cold knobs were wrong but maintenance refused to fix because it *wasn't a pressing issue* and *it worked just fine, anyway.*

She took her same paycheck every other week and allocated her funds meticulously. It wasn't often that she ate out, rationalizing instead that *the ten dollars I spend on one meal at McDonald's could buy me X-amount of groceries.* She worked during the summer at a job that wasn't the worst thing in the world she'd ever done but was frustrating all the same.

There was a comfort about those things when she was home in Newton, Massachusetts, about going to the same grocery store every

Tuesday and Friday with her mom and siblings, and seeing the same neighbors and friends at the community park when they played sports, and always getting her new back to school shoes at the Chestnut Hill Mall. But those things were done with her family, her mom-dad-brother-sister-unit, one that was stable and thriving.

Here though, on her own, she failed to see the beauty in shopping by herself once a week and driving the same congested streets to two different jobs.

Here, on her own, with everyone around her moving, she was restless to change her ways.

Despite the complaints and worries that she was letting herself drown in, Charlotte did her best to push them down and actually enjoy her summer days. While she spent copious hours in the office with Ginny, and more still in her car for a back and forth to Starbucks, the weekend conversations with James buzzed in her brain. She was going to make the most of this summer if it killed her.

She caught up on reading that didn't revolve around Dr. Seuss characters or *Pete the Cat*, enjoyed the Farmer's Market, and visited the beach with some of her teacher friends. Friday nights were still reserved for James, which worked well since Vanessa worked overnights on Fridays. Despite the fact that James and Vanessa had been dating for two years, Charlotte heard about Vanessa almost more than they actually interacted.

Friday after lunch, Ginny asked Charlotte about her weekend plans with James before Charlotte could even utter her sanctioned, "It's Friday, so James is coming over."

"C'mon, Char," Ginny egged. "You act like your life has drastically changed since college—Christ, since you two moved out here. I know the drill."

Charlotte rolled her eyes as she put her purse away.

"You know what would be a fun experiment though? Get him drunk, confess all of your undying feelings towards each other, and get in his pants. Now *that* would be a not-boring story to come back to on Monday morning."

"Virginia. Charlotte. I see we're enjoying our after-lunch break."

Ginny hopped off of the corner of Charlotte's desk, watching as their boss crossed his arms over his plump belly.

"Sorry, Mr. Robertson. We were actually just discussing an idea for a new episode," Ginny replied quickly.

"Oh really? Excellent. I'd like to hear it, then. My office, ten minutes."

As he plodded down the hallway, Charlotte found her eyes protruding from her head for a brand-new reason, communicating

What in the fuck do you think you're doing? through her expression.

Reluctantly, they found themselves in Dean Robertson's office, exchanging volatile glances as they seated themselves opposite the pudgy man.

"Mr. Robertson, I don't mean to disappoint, but we don't actually have—"

"Edley, do you think I'm an idiot?" he cut her off quickly.

"Wha—no—"

"I really couldn't care less about your plans to get laid this weekend."

The glances exchanged were intentional, direct this time. Charlotte was as red as the lipstick that Ginny reserved specifically for nightclubs.

"You were the only two back from lunch and I had to share the news."

His smug smile waved into Ginny's raised brows and wide eyes, her head snapping from Dean to Charlotte and back to her boss as he crossed his arms over his chest and leaned back in his desk chair.

"The show got picked up?"

"The show got picked up."

In all of Charlotte's years as a summer assistant, the shows whose writing staff Ginny had been a part of had gone to the wayside, leaving much frustration, tequila, and a lot of *back to the drawing board*, with a few indie college flicks sprinkled in between. As her own life seemed to be faltering around her, Charlotte pushed it down, wanting to be happy for her friend for finally getting to where she wanted to be in her career.

They shook hands, the women positively gleaming as they began to exit the office.

"Oh, and Charlotte?"

"Yes, Mr. Robertson?"

"Good luck this weekend."

She nodded at the man whose eyebrows were still sky high, blushing as she ducked her head and turned to leave.

Charlotte grabbed Ginny by the hand and dragged her around the corner, waiting to be out of their boss's earshot before they let the squealing and giggling escape.

"Oh my god," Ginny began, her emotions so out of character in the way she had suddenly transformed into an excited little girl. "Charlotte. It's happening. It's really happening."

With smiles a mile wide, Charlotte proclaimed, "This calls for a celebration."

Throwing his keys onto the table in the front entryway and kicking his shoes aimlessly into the living room, James made an immediate beeline for the refrigerator. As cool liquid ran from the beer can down the back of his throat, the tension from his work week oozed from his pores. He breathed a contented sigh, relishing in the fact that the next sixty hours were his. The relaxation coursing through his body only warmed when a pair of hands snaked their way around his chest, coming to rest on his pecs. A wide smile stretched across his cheeks as he turned in Vanessa's embrace.

He leaned forward, meeting her halfway for a soft kiss.

"I didn't know you were coming home early tonight. This is a nice surprise."

Still clad in her navy scrubs with bags tugging at the base of her eyes, she offered him a tired smile.

"They actually need me to fill in for a Saturday shift, so they sent me home to rest for a couple of hours before I have to go back in."

His head dropped, lips pursing into a pout.

"So, I guess that means no dinner plans tomorrow, huh?"

"No, baby, I'm so sorry. I'll make it up to you. I promise."

"You could always make it up to me right now."

With hooded eyes, he bent down to gather her lips once more and scooped his fingertips at the hem of her top, but was stopped suddenly by her firm hands against his chest, this time ceasing rather than inviting.

"James, baby, I would love to, but I just got off of a twelve-hour shift, and I have to go back in another four for eight more. Honestly, I could really just use the rest."

"That's okay. I'll come lay with you until you have to leave."

He kissed her on the forehead, his smile genuine as she turned and headed towards the bedroom.

"You sure you'll be alright by yourself tomorrow?" her voice echoed down the hallway.

"I'm sure I'll find something to do," he called back.

As he slugged back the rest of the can before heading down the hallway towards their bedroom, he felt his cell phone buzz in his pocket, Charlotte's name lighting up the screen. A grin crept up the side of his face as he let the text message seep in.

Eyes wide and smiling, phone still cradled in his palm, he perched on the edge of the bed, having to twist his torso to see Vanessa, as she was already curled under the covers.

"Are any of the guys from the office doing something tomorrow? I'm sure they'd let you tag along."

He heard her briefly, eyes still glued to the cell phone in his hand. "What is it?"

"Oh, it's Charlie Kate. Ginny's show got picked up for this fall. They invited us out for drinks to celebrate."

Vanessa's exhausted expression turned sullen.

She knew he would insist that he stay and lay with her. He would wrap his arms around her and cuddle her in overcompensation for the fact that his mind was elsewhere. In the end, she wouldn't let him, though. Because she knew that, even if he stayed, his heart wouldn't truly be with her, lying in that bed.

It would be with Charlotte.

With sad eyes, she sat up, knees tucked underneath her weary body.

"Well, don't let me keep you here. Go ahead. Have fun."

Her smile encouraged happiness, but her eyes spoke her sad truth. His lips were moving, but his eyes were already searching towards the door.

"Are you sure? 'Cause I could always show up late—"

"James, it's fine. Go. Have fun."

She wanted him out of the room so that she could sleep. But if she was being honest with herself, she truly wanted him out of the room so that the guilt wouldn't pile and add to her already mounting exhaustion.

His eyes asked *Are you sure?* and with her persistent nods, he cupped the back of her head and placed a tender kiss to her forehead before losing himself in their closet to change into something more comfortable.

"So, I'll see you tomorrow when you get home?" he asked, tying the laces on his shoes.

"If I'm still conscious at that point." Her chuckle was less in good humor and more in serious mockery. Empathizing more with the former, he returned a sympathetic chuckle before edging purposefully towards the door.

"James?" Her voice was small, already on the brink of unconsciousness.

"Mhm?"

She took a deep breath, her eyes wandering up and down his profile, afraid to meet his deep, green eyes.

"I love you."

His sheepish smile softened his cheeks and brought him back to boyhood.

"I love you, too."

"Oh, and James? Tell Charlotte and Ginny I said congratulations."

"Will do. Have a good shift."

He patted the doorframe twice and was gone.

Whether her body caved under the guise of exhaustion or a sudden pang of sadness, she never had the time to find out.

The stereotypes of the booming Los Angeles bar flooded Charlotte's senses: sights of scantily clad women dancing with friends, chasing off the preppy boys who slugged back beers before they made advances. Synthesized beats pulsed in her ears and flooded her bloodstream. She felt the fingers of the bartender skim past her own as the already sweaty margarita glass made its way from the bar to her upturned lips.

Her grin widened when she saw his haphazardly styled floppy hair approaching from across the room.

"Hey! Congratulations, superstars!"

James's side hug to Ginny did little to rival the embrace that he pulled Charlotte into as she stood, her soft curls tucked under his chin, his arms protectively crossed around her body.

Her drawn out, "Thank you!" was muffled by the way her lips were pressed into his chest.

As he pulled away, turning to flag down the bartender, Ginny's raised eyebrows expressed all of the words she had uttered earlier that afternoon.

"Hey, where's Vanessa?" Ginny asked, swirling the straw around her drink, eyes searching behind him for any sign of his girlfriend.

"Uhh, she had to work late. But she told me to pass along her congratulations."

As James turned to place his order, Ginny waggled her eyebrows at Charlotte before attending to the group of her coworkers who had just joined them.

James paid for the first round of shots, the celebration leading to several more rounds of assorted drinks and a lot of sloppy dancing. As her body was warmed with the buzz of alcohol, Charlotte began to truly let go, the pile of anxieties that she'd been sitting on dripping from her with the sweat and laughter and carefree manner that her body swayed. Though she had known these people for years, she still considered the writing staff more "Ginny's coworkers" than her own. So, when the dancing began, she gravitated towards comfort. Towards James.

She considered herself a terrible dancer, so it was in full character that James grabbed her by the hand immediately and began to twirl her around the sticky floor, seeing laughter flood her cheeks.

As they continued to sway and bounce and make fools of themselves, Charlotte felt herself opening up more, ditching the sprinkler and the robot for hands on his shoulders and bodies held closer. Ginny's words rang in her ears like warning bells, but as they continued to drink, and the heat swirled around their dancing bodies, she felt their eyes pulling them together like magnets.

It started out slow, at least, reminding her of the way that they would move in middle school dances, with hands on shoulders and enough room for Jesus and the principal in between. But then, his large hands snaked their way sensually down her sides, skimming her body with just enough pressure for her to pull her bottom lip between her teeth as she glanced up to where his eyes were lazily closed. She could see the alcohol humming through his body in the slight bounce of his head.

Her own arms raised slowly above her head, swaying aimlessly as she turned in his. James's hands were hot as they skated effortlessly across her abdomen to switch hips when she turned around. With her back pressed against his front, his long fingers spanning her waist, his breath warm on her neck, it was easy to lose herself, to let one hand fall to the top of his head, curling around the back of his neck, to let him pull her closer against him as they closed their eyes and let the music control their bodies.

When she turned again to face him, his head was bent, eyes hooded, as his fingers gripped at her waist tighter and pulled them together so that their foreheads touched. It was the ghost of a familiar place, one that hadn't crept up for quite some time. But here, his eyes black with intensity, with his lips in a straight, serious line, with the tip of his nose brushing hers just slightly, her fingers tangling up into his hair were moving of their own accord.

She felt his breath dance against hers, felt the sticky heat of his lips in a soft puff, before Ginny's high-pitched squeals pricked her ears. Immediately, James's eyes were suddenly wide discs, his hands held in the air between them as if she was hot to the touch. Charlotte vaguely heard Ginny say something about *watching that hot guy do a body shot off of me!* but her eyes were glued to James's, their doe-eyed expressions a mirror image before he disappeared down the back hallway.

When she saw him again, his skin was flushed and wet, as if he'd just dunked his face in ice water. He nodded across the bar, signaled to the bartender for his tab and Charlotte's, and cocked his head towards the doorway until she and Ginny followed.

The cool breeze was a warm wake-up call as the trio stumbled down the sidewalk. When they walked through the doors of a hole in the wall karaoke bar a couple blocks down, Charlotte felt so much more at home. The scents of whiskey and tequila, beer cheese and deep-fried goodness, hung in the air and wrapped around her like a weighted blanket.

James asked for three waters and followed Charlotte and Ginny to a booth near the karaoke stage. Since their first dinner together at Charlotte's sixth birthday, James had always sidled next to her in any restaurant booth. But now, with his skin still pulsing, he was deliberate in the way that he sat across from her. Charlotte pretended to miss Ginny's wondering stare.

"So, ladies, how's it feel to be heading to the big leagues?" he began, his voice raised to overcompensate for the loud music and his own hypersensitivity.

"You guys," Ginny began, words slurred and thick, "I know that I'm always being snarky and shit, but can I be serious for a minute?"

Charlotte and James shared a nervous nod, eyes still wavering as the blood in their heads continued to race.

"I'm just so happy that my work is finally being noticed."

Ginny's head fell to the side, her eyes actually soft and her tone as serious as it could be after that amount of liquor.

"I mean I just...I've worked so hard and like...I finally get to share what I do with other people. It's just so *great*."

Charlotte and James nodded in agreement as Charlotte did her best to push down her own insecurities and emotions, ones that had been slowly trickling back into her bloodstream.

Somewhere in the background, Ginny continued on, but it went unnoticed as the nervous pair played eye contact tag, catching and releasing each other's stares as they did their best to simultaneously figure out what had just happened and push it away as though the moment was a falsity.

Their game was interrupted by off-key screeching coming from the karaoke stage.

"God, you'd think they'd make these people blow before they put them in front of a microphone. There should be a legal limit to sing karaoke." And Ginny was right back at it.

"Or they should at least have some caliber of talent," Charlotte offered, sipping at the straw of her water glass.

They passed a chuckle around the table as the clearly inebriated man on stage stumbled to the edge, losing his balance as he threw one foot down.

"If that's the case, why don't you go up there, Charlie Kate?"

Her eyes screamed *Absolutely not,* bugging and wide, her jaw protruding at James's suggestion. Ginny's eyes sparkled with something else entirely as Charlotte began to protest his encouragement.

"No, no no *no.* There's no way in hell I'm embarrassing myself in front of all of these people," she rattled, eyes closed, waving both hands in front of her in protest.

"Come on, it'll be fun! Put those years of high school choir to use for once." His eyes pleaded with Ginny to back him up, which she promptly did.

"Come on, Char. At least you'll be better than this asshole." Without turning her body, she hitched her thumb behind her towards the stage, where the man from before was drawling on incoherently.

"No. Absolutely not. Final answer."

With a shared gaze and a curt nod, James and Ginny grabbed Charlotte and effectively dragged her the ten short feet to the stage as the country twang from the previous song began to fade out.

"How 'bout a big round of applause for Tim and his rendition of 'Honkey Tonk Badonkadonk!'"

A few choice claps and whistles, buried by several boos, rang silent to the anger that was furiously burning out of Charlotte's ears. She struggled against the hands clenched at her shoulders.

"Any more takers?"

"This hot lil' mama right here!" Ginny shouted over the crowd before heading to a high table that was front and center. "You'll thank me for this later," she mouthed as she sipped victoriously at the martini that she had exchanged for her water.

Charlotte's face paled, in stark contrast to the quick heat that rose from her toes to her cheeks. James began to release his grip, but as the host was asking for her song of choice, Charlotte clamped onto him, refusing to let go.

"Stop being such a worry wart. Try to have a little fun," he laughed, covering her fingers with his own to loosen her grip.

"And what's your name, pretty girl?"

"Her name is Charlotte," Ginny shouted with one hand cupped around her lips.

"Alright, everyone, let's give a warm welcome to Charlotte!"

"And James!"

The words slipped past her before he even got the chance to leave the stage. Lips parted in shock, he widened his eyes at her, mentally portraying his feelings of absolute disapproval.

"If I have to be up here, so do you," she retorted, her eyes shooting daggers.

"A duet, then! Charlotte and James, everybody!"

It took several minutes to find a duet that they both agreed on, which was plenty of time for sweat to collect in her palms and bile to rise several times at the back of his throat. By the time the music began, her eyes closing with the guitar's intro to "Falling Slowly," she was running on autopilot.

Despite their feigned attempts to start a rock band when they were in elementary school, James's voice shook with the words of the first verse that had them alternating lines before joining together in a mostly in-tune harmony. Charlotte's hands clung hard to the microphone, her once free and floaty demeanor contrasted boldly by the way she was standing stock still and unmoving, save for her lips. As the words continued to pass between them, the implications of the lyrics pulled their heads towards the middle like magnets, eyes wide and still as they breathed the final *time*.

Time seemed to jump then to the backseat of an Uber, James and Charlotte occupying opposite ends, their bodies nearly pressed flush with the doors. Thoughts swam, their heads too stuffed with *dancing* and *implications* and *those goddamn song lyrics* for conversation other than a hello to the driver. James clicked through his Uber app, making sure that he paid for Charlotte's portion of the ride as well.

With a curt nod goodbye, he lingered tentatively at the door to the car, not wanting to go inside, but not quite wanting to stay either. Eventually, he padded up the sidewalk with his hands shoved into his pockets, his head down, resembling a puppy who peed in the house and was being forced to sleep in the yard for the night.

He paused at the front entryway to watch the taillights as the horizon swallowed them.

Once inside her own apartment, Charlotte moved fluidly, dreamlike almost, her hands knowing exactly where the shoebox sat dwelling in the back of her closet. Tossing friendship bracelets, a wilted flower crown, and movie ticket stubs to the wayside, she found her target, running her fingers softly over the tattered purple notebook to trace the letters in the primary inscription that read *Charlie Kate's Songs*.

As she thumbed slowly through the dog-eared pages, a wave of memories flooded over her like the surf at high tide. Amidst games of hangman and mediocre sketches of herself and James in a rock and roll band, her own words pricked behind her eyes. Reading her own loopy script, the words she'd scribed as song lyrics jumped off the pages, taunting her with years of love and letdown. Before she had the chance to absorb the years of thought put to paper, a Polaroid photograph fell from the pages of the notebook and into her lap. Staring at the photo, memories began to flood her consciousness, thrusting her suddenly into her childhood.

Eleven-year-old Charlotte flipped through the pages of her brand-new notebook—at least 100 pages, James had insisted—the Rite-Aid bag discarded on her bedroom floor. With a Sharpie marker in hand, she scribed "Charlie Kate's Songs" on the cover and beamed, the potential in the crisp, white pages making her buzz with anticipation.

James sat on the edge of her bed with a shiny new acoustic guitar balanced across his lap. They had spent three summers running lemonade stands, and now they finally had the money. It wasn't top of the line by any means, but it was his. She watched his fingers as they fiddled with the strings, his ear perched near the sound hole as he tuned the instrument as closely to perfection as he could manage.

She was shaken from her admirative gazing by the flash and click of her brother David's Polaroid camera.

"Hey! David!" she yelled, her brows knitting together in anger and annoyance.

"What? I'm bored. And since you won't let your boyfriend *over here leave for twenty minutes so we can go play catch, I don't have anything better to do."*

Her cheeks were burning, but not from the sticky Massachusetts summer air.

"He's not my boyfriend," she replied, her voice far away, almost as if trying to play keep away from the boy with the moppy brown hair. Her eyes shot casually to James, who was still lost in the sounds of his brand new six-string, the songbook that came with it now open as he attempted to teach himself the first chord.

It was then that Charlotte noticed a baseball glove tucked under her brother's arm, remembering James's earlier promise to practice with David. She never thought she'd have to share James. He was hers. But the second he had been introduced to David, she knew that the lessons they had learned in kindergarten would often be heavily practiced. She would always be James's number one, but sometimes, Charlotte really hated her older brother.

"Just let me figure out one song and I'll meet you in the yard," James called, the book propped up on his feet, his gaze not wavering from its pages.

"Fine." With a defeated tilt of his head, David disappeared down the hallway.

Charlotte finally relaxed, gathering her notebook and a purple gel pen before joining James on her bed.

"Do you really think we could be rock stars one day, James?"

His lopsided half-grin met hers, those green eyes shining with hope as he brushed his long locks away from his face.

"We can be anything we wanna be, Charlie Kate."

She returned his smile with her own toothy grin and scooted closer, observing how awkwardly he held the large, wooden object. It was a full-sized guitar, but James was far from full-sized. He frowned, frustrated by the temporary setback as he struggled to maneuver his fingers across the frets.

"I should've waited until we had enough lemonade money to buy a guitar and *a strap," he said, trying his hardest not to succumb to defeat.*

"I think Kelly might actually have an old one. Hold on."

She returned from her sister's room minutes later with a lavender strap clutched in her hand.

His disgust wasn't fabricated, and he backed away quickly, bumping against her headboard with a thump.

"Purple? Really, Charlie Kate?"

"It's all I have! It's better than nothing."

She gave him that wide-eyed shake of her head that said I'm doing my best here, pal, *as she thrust the nylon strap towards him once more. When he didn't take it, she took matters into her own hands, fastening it to the nub at the bottom of his guitar and pulling the strap up and around his shoulder.*

"But it's girly*," he protested, acting as though the strap was searing his skin while his mouth twisted in disgust.*

Her expression screamed Really?

Thinking quickly on her feet, she knelt to grab her backpack that was riddled with an assortment of buttons—the cool thing to do now. Plucking one from the canvas, she gave it a new home on the part of the strap that rested over his heart.

"There. Now it'll be a little less 'girly' until you can get a new one."

He gazed down the strap, eyes resting on the Green Monster button before meeting her gaze, apologies written in his own.

"I guess it's better than nothin', right?" He shrugged then, accepting her nod as forgiveness before diving back into his book.

Knowing that Vanessa would be long gone by the time he arrived home, James dove straight for the hall closet. Now, laying on his bed, his shoes untied on feet that were crossed at the ankles, his fingers strummed aimlessly, muscle memory plucking chords in a simple pattern.

The guitar strap, covered in far more buttons now, still had undertones of lavender that he had never gotten around to covering. Over the years, anytime Charlotte saw a button that reminded her of James, it was added to the mass. The latest, still around ten years prior, said *I'm not antisocial, I just hate you*. He had rolled his eyes when she had exclaimed through laughter that it was, "*So* James!"

The solemn expression painted over his eyes matched the minor chord of the song still stuck in his head that his fingers absently plucked once he had figured out which sounds matched up with the lyrics that were still swimming around his thoughts. It wasn't a sad song. It was one filled with hope, belief, love. But tonight, as thoughts wound tightly around his congested mind, he let himself get lost in the pensive glumness of the lyrics.

Do we still have time?

June 2018

"*YOU.*"

It was 7:54 AM. Charlotte had barely stepped foot in the office before an unusually early Ginny flagged her down. The sunglasses and Venti coffee this early on a Monday were expected. The interrogation? Not so much.

"Good morning to you, too," she quipped back, not yet in the mood for socializing.

"Oh my god. You disappeared before I got the chance to find out the dirty details. What the hell happened on Friday night?"

Ginny pushed through the door to their office suite, shoving her sunglasses onto her head.

Today was the first day back at the office since finding out that the show had been picked up, which meant an early morning and a lot of preparation. Charlotte was equipped with a charged tablet and laptop, a fresh notebook, and a new set of pens, almost as if it was the first day of school.

The lack of response was meant to be her entire response, as *I honestly don't even know* hammered behind eyes that were still a touch red from both hangover recovery and restless nights of captured thoughts.

"Umm...a lot of tequila?" she said with a guilty shrug.

"I gathered that," Ginny replied, leading them past the office mailboxes into the conference room where they found empty seats among a crowd of several others. "So, did you guys do it?"

The words rolled so effortlessly off her tongue that Charlotte almost wondered just how invested Ginny was in her love life.

Charlotte's eyes were half lidded as she stared annoyedly at Ginny until her friend broke and gave in.

"I'm just saying, you two looked *pre*tty hot and heavy on the dance floor. Could've led to something."

With a shrug of her shoulders, the conversation was done, and Charlotte set to work preparing the writer's room, double checking coffee orders, and taking one final breath before chaos ensued.

It wasn't often that Charlotte and James went a day without talking in some capacity, but since Friday night, and in the midst of a hectic office environment with Ginny, Charlotte buried her creeping feelings—about James and life in general—losing herself in the work instead of in James. It wouldn't have mattered if he had tried to get in touch with her, anyway. Her phone was an umbilical cord to Ginny now.

So, when an oddly quiet afternoon delivered a text that said ***You around for lunch today, or is the boss feeding you biscuits while you work from the doghouse?*** she found herself walking two blocks to meet up with James at In-N-Out. It wasn't until she could see the red and yellow sign that she noticed her stomach flipping, and not at all from hunger.

Awkward wasn't the appropriate word, and neither was *weird*. It was just that the tension was so far away for them, so distant and understood but still unresolved after years of ignoring and skirting and dodging and brushing it off. Now, into adulthood, the tightness in her throat told her that those days of ignoring it were far from over.

And on top of everything else—her worries and the new pace of her job and life in general—the last thing she needed was for those feelings about James to resurface and blow it all to hell. The turmoil that they'd put each other through over the years had been anguish enough. Now, with his life so stabilized, and with her own mind finally at peace with what his choices had been and where their relationship had finally ended up, she couldn't bear for the past to happen all over again.

The past was in the past for a reason, wasn't it?

He was happy. She was moving forward.

Although they'd never truly hashed everything out, this wasn't really the time anyway. He wouldn't bring it all up in the middle of a fast food restaurant, would he?

But in true James fashion, he was already in line, his hair a little out of place of its corporate gel and style thanks to his walk over in the scorching sun. Before she could step in line, he was already making his

53

way to a table with one red tray and two orders. His lips spread into a wide grin as soon as he saw her.

It would be okay between them. Somehow, it always was.

"Are you excited?"

"Hmm?" She was buried in her milkshake, distracted by the whispers in her head that still said *You two need to talk about what happened* that she'd missed his words entirely.

"You all here today, pal?" James chuckled, tapping the table in front of her. "Come on, Charlie Kate. School's out for the summer and you're literally going to be working on a television set. You can't tell me that you aren't excited."

She hung her head, a mixture of laughter and sighs peppering her words.

"First of all, I don't get to work on the actual *set*, Rango. I get to sit at a table and like, take notes for Ginny and go on coffee runs and handle all of her appointments for when *E! News* wants to interview her about the show."

"Okay, but still. That's kind of amazing. How many people do we know that get to kind of contribute to, like, real television?"

"Kevin Kowalski from college ended up on a season of *Big Brother*."

"I'm going to pretend you didn't bring that up."

She shook her head, sharing in his laughter before being brought back to the present.

"I don't know, James. I mean, I *am* excited, don't get me wrong. I just...does it ever end?"

She hung her head like a heavy depletion, watching as he dropped his in a different manner, his eyebrow cocked in indignation as he finished the fry in his hand.

"Seriously, Charlie Kate. You have *got* to lighten up a little." When she gave him a sideways glance, he added, "You get to pick your attitude, kid. Maybe try choosing a different one."

The blush in her cheeks matched the red in her tray as she stared wide-eyed at the almost empty sack of fries, her stare blank and embarrassed. When she peeled her eyes away from the table, her grin was sheepish.

"You...might be right. I have been complaining about this lately, haven't I?"

"Only a lot," he joked, bumping her shoulder and stealing ketchup from her tray. "But that's what I'm here for."

"Really? I thought you were here to feed me and tell me I'm pretty."

It was a running joke that had transpired somewhere around their freshman year of high school that rolled so effortlessly off her tongue that she had no chance to stop it. She wanted so badly to reach out into the open air, to grab the words before they hit his ears. But by the way the tips of his ears were reddening and his head was snapping forward, down, suddenly very interested in the contents of the almost empty tray, she knew his head was swimming just as much as hers was.

He shut it down in such a James manner. A subtle shake of his head, a smile that began strained but quickly warmed with his words.

"Last I checked, I just *did* feed you. And you are pretty. Pretty psychotic."

He gave her a soft shove on the shoulder, stood with their tray, and took a walk to the garbage can.

If she hadn't been staring at his back, she'd have seen the slight tilt of his chin towards the ceiling, the extended pause and close of his eyes, the sharp exhale. His eyes swam, tense with memories of the past weekend and everything in between the *then* and *now* that had still gone unanswered after all this time. When he returned to the table, he tried not to make his smile seem so forced.

It was easy to let him drag her back into baseball talk, to argue about statistics and MVP runners for the Sox that year, rather than slipping backwards and owning up to the near cataclysmic explosion that had almost doomed them that weekend. But when they parted ways shortly after, with her schedule now dictated down to the minute, he pushed the air from his lungs in a heavy expulsion.

I don't need this, he decided, his feet clapping quickly along the pavement. *Not now. Not again.*

They were doing so well, too. In the midst of it all, he had moved on. Vanessa was his future now, wasn't she?

No, he shook his head. *I'm not going back there.*

And for the rest of his afternoon, he took on a rigorous workload that had even his assistant questioning his well-being.

April 2004

James had a *date*. James Ramsey, her best friend in the whole wide world, had a *date* with a *girl*.

A girl that wasn't her.

Fourteen-year-old Charlotte didn't know whether to feel happy for her friend, or sad that he had cancelled their Friday night plans for the first time in their eight years of friendship.

Or *jealous* for the fact that he was going on a date with Hannah Thompson.

Hannah Thompson was brand new to Oak Hill Middle School, but her popularity was quickly spreading. Her stick straight blonde ponytail was always adorned with a new, brightly colored bow, that Charlotte was sure was about the size of her head. The girls thought it was *so trendy,* and the boys thought it was *super cute.*

Charlotte thought it was obnoxious.

But apparently James did not.

On their walk home Thursday afternoon, he was ten minutes late to their meeting point. He used the excuse that Mrs. O'Brien had held him back a few extra minutes in math. But she saw right through him. James was the top math student in their grade. And besides, his math class was during third period.

He had never been very good at lying when it counted.

On top of it all, she had watched his tall, gangly body, the muscles in his arms just beginning to protrude through his skinny form, as he leaned against the brick overhang at the front of the building. He had one of those fancy new Sidekicks in his hands and was punching something into it awkwardly. Only when it slid back into the fingers of the cheerleader standing next to him did Charlotte realize what was going on. He was more than likely putting his phone number into Hannah's cell. Charlotte knew it would be his home phone number. Their parents had decided that they would both have cell phones next year, once they were in high school.

He wouldn't have had to give Charlotte his phone number. She'd had it memorized since she was six years old.

57

Once James eventually caught up to her, Charlotte was struggling to mask the red tint that had crept into her round cheeks, yanking her curls to hang in front of her face instead of behind her ears.

He didn't confess his plans until they were in her kitchen, exactly one block and four houses from his, choosing instead to make small talk that seemed like an overcompensation for the news that she already knew he was trying to cover. She didn't get a word in edgewise, but it wouldn't have mattered. She wasn't sure she could say something without crying anyway.

He always dropped her off first, more than occasionally staying for a cookie or two, or for help on English homework. Today, Mrs. Murphy had made her special "garbage cookies," loaded with all kinds of sugary goodness. James was always good for enough to ruin his dinner appetite. As he shoveled the fifth cookie into his mouth, his words conveniently hid between bites of chocolate chips and rainbow jimmies.

"So, um, about tomorrow…"

Milk sloshed down his throat in a hearty gulp. She could let on that she knew or let him confess.

She chose to play dumb.

"Oh, I'm so excited! Mom said she'd even let us order stuffed crust from Pizza Hut since it's the end of the quarter."

"Dude, score!" His hand, poised for a high five, made her momentarily forget about the afternoon that was about to turn into a string of disappointments. But as he pulled away before she was able to connect her own hand, her stomach churned in anticipation.

"But, actually, could we maybe move it to Saturday?"

"Saturday?" She hadn't intended for her voice to be so small, to ooze sadness and disappointment; it came naturally.

"Y-yeah… I, uh, I kind of have plans for Friday night."

She didn't want to meet his eyes when he answered her next question, so she focused instead on picking the jimmies out of her own cookie as she asked, "What kind of plans?"

He watched her intently, trying to read the reaction that she was intentionally masking as he fiddled with his fingers.

"Well um, I kinda, sorta, have like, a…date thing or...something, with uh, with Hannah Thompson."

Closing her eyes, willing the tears to remain inside her head, she took a deep breath.

"A date?"

Her voice rang so silently, he thought he'd imagined it.

"Yeah...yeah, I think...I guess." She saw him shrug out of the corner of her eye, heard the way his voice was now barely above a whisper. "She passed me a note in math today and... well...now we're going to the movies with a bunch of her cheerleader friends and their boyfriends. So, I guess it's *sort of* like a date. I don't know."

"Oh."

It was the only syllable she could manage, as images of James and Hannah—the perfect couple, hand in hand at the movie theater, probably sharing popcorn—choked the rest of her down. Would he use the move that her brother David had taught him, where you pretend to yawn and then put your arm around the girl's shoulder? The one that he had practiced on her, when she overcompensated on giggles and *Ew's!* to hide the blush in her cheeks. Or would he not need that silly trick, because he was James, and he was all confidence and charming now that his hair was getting longer and his body was growing taller?

James fidgeted in her silence, wishing, hoping she would say something, *anything.*

"I mean, I don't even know if it's like, a *date* date," he continued, his volume now rising. He needed to fill the silence before he physically turned her in her chair to gauge just how much of the sadness in her voice was etched into her rosy cheeks. "Like, a *bunch* of the basketball guys are going with a bunch of the cheerleaders, and, like, she didn't have anyone to go with, since, you know, she's like, *new*, and since we sit by each other in math, we talk a lot."

A crime scene of cookie bits collected on the counter, which was sure to drive Linda crazy once she returned from folding the laundry. Without a response from Charlotte, James continued puttering on, cocking his head as he blathered.

"And like, I'll probably mostly be hanging with the guys anyway, ya know? We're seeing *Bend it Like Beckham*, so it's not a chick flick. And it's about soccer, so I'll probably be bored out of my mind."

He did this often: rambled when he was nervous. He was a nervous rambler and a nervous fidgeter, which was evident by the bits of napkin that were now being shredded all over her mother's clean kitchen countertop in the absence of another cookie for him to destroy. Still, Charlotte refused to speak for the sole purpose of keeping the sobs that were stuck in her throat right where they belonged. She knew that if she so much as opened her mouth to take a deep breath, that would be the end.

"So, Saturday then? I can't miss out on stuffed crust night."

He cocked his head more, his cheek now parallel to the countertop so that Charlotte could see him making a conscious effort to get her attention out of the corner of her eye. He knew that his mouth could go a mile a minute when he was nervous, but why was he so nervous to tell her all of this? Charlotte had been his best friend since he had moved to Newton the summer before kindergarten began. She knew his life backwards and forwards. Why was it so hard to admit to all of this?

He observed the way her head nodded up and down twice, enough to signify that they had plans on Saturday night. But he couldn't see her face. Her rich, honey curls, framed by frizz this late in the day, hung around her eyes today rather than being tucked behind her ears. He'd have to press his nose into her personal bubble to see what was going on under her bowed head, but he knew better.

Masking his own nerves, he grabbed a sixth cookie, preparing for the battle his mother would have with him come dinner time, and threw his backpack over his shoulder.

"Alright, Murphy. You'd better bring your A-game on Saturday night. We'll have a lot of ground to make up for."

One last time, he tried to angle his head enough to see past the walls that she had put up, but like a locked gate, she wasn't letting him in. Shoulders dropping, he offered her a tender hand on the shoulder.

"I'll see you in the morning, Charlie Kate."

"Yup," was all she could muster as she finished dunking a now soggy and crumbling cookie into a murky glass of milk. As soon as she heard the distant, "Thanks for the cookies, Mrs. Murphy!" and the click of the front door, she let her tears fall.

It wasn't until sometime after dinner, when the chores rotation had Charlotte drying the dishes as Kelly washed, that the subject was brought up again.

"What's up with you, squirt? You usually put up an argument whenever you have to dry. What gives?"

With a silent shrug, Charlotte wiped the moisture from a plate before placing it on the dry stack. Suddenly, the water in the sink was off, and Kelly turned to face her younger sister with arms crossed over her chest.

"Seriously, Charlotte. Do I need to pummel an eighth grader or something? You're *never* this sad."

"I don't wanna talk about it, okay?"

The red in her cheeks crept up like embarrassment and anger were battling, and in the absence of her sister's cleaning, Charlotte reached forcefully for the wet rag in the sink and began scrubbing angrily at a spaghetti sauce stained plate, anything to get the job done more quickly so she could retreat to her bedroom for the night. It wasn't until Kelly snatched the plate from her hands that she snapped out of it, startled.

"Listen. I get that middle school is tough, but this little tantrum that you're throwing is out of line. Tell James you like him already and stop sulking about the fact that he's going on a date this weekend without you."

Kelly was red cheeked now too, scrubbing harder than necessary at the remaining dinner dishes while the sisters finished their chores in silence. As the water in the sink drained and they wiped down the counters, Charlotte's *How'd you know?* was a whisper that followed the water down the drain.

"Mom told me," Kelly replied without lifting her eyes from the task. "She heard you guys in the kitchen after school. I could've given you *actual* advice if you weren't being so stubborn."

It was Kelly's way of apologizing, and after years of practice,

Charlotte knew that was the closest she was going to get from her big sister. With her eyes still trained on the now sparkling granite, she asked, "What do I do?"

Kelly sighed, folding the dish rag over the edge of the sink before resting the small of her back on the counter.

"You know, squirt? He's your best friend. You have to talk to him. You guys have known each other forever, so it's not like this little crush is totally unfathomable."

Charlotte's cheeks pinked as her eyes found the tile floor.

"Just tell him how you feel. He can't read your mind."

"But he's my best friend, Kelly. What if he gets all...awkward and stuff?"

"That's a risk you're going to have to take."

With a shrug and a rough pat of Charlotte's head, Kelly headed out of the kitchen.

Charlotte heaved a huge sigh, her back trickling down the cabinets of the kitchen as she sunk with the weight of her options.

She did her best to be as normal as possible on their walk to school the next morning, but the words *Are you ready for your date tonight?* and *I wish you were going on a date with me tonight* were all her brain could fathom. Instead, she chose silence over honesty and let James blather on for the entire twelve minute walk about something his little sister Abby had done the night before at dinner.

School dragged on, and it wasn't long before she was sitting cross-legged on the couch, clutching a pillow in her lap with her chin resting atop its cushy foam. Her neck was growing tired from the crouch in which she had been sitting for the past several hours, refusing to do much more than succumb to the mind-numbing powers of Friday night television. In her own defense, she truly knew no other way.

For the past hundreds of Fridays since she was five years old, she had only known time spent with James. When they were younger, it was play dates until they inevitably fell asleep on the foam mats of the playroom floor while their moms chattered away in the kitchen. As they grew older, Julie and Linda had extracurricular activities to rush their other children to, but Charlotte and James kept the tradition alive. Whether it was venturing through the neighborhood, spending time in the treehouse, or watching every Red Sox game together during the summers, Friday nights were sacred. Even when James and David's baseball team had games or tournaments, she was always there to cheer him on, an inevitable sleepover happening at one of the two households (after a thorough shower, of course).

Without him, she wasn't just at a loss for entertainment, but direction. She watched the recap of the Sox spring training game. They'd bested Cincinnati 8 to 5. Kevin Millar had even hit a home run. But she had no one to celebrate with. She had aimlessly ended up on a random show when there was a sudden commotion at the front door.

"I know the rule about hanging out after eight, Mrs. Murphy, but I just...could we please make an exception, just this once?"

Charlotte peeked over the half-wall that separated the living room from the foyer. Her mother was standing at the front door, a gentle spring breeze chilling the air. Linda's arms were folded across her chest, holding a checkered dish towel in the crook of her elbow.

Charlotte heard her mother respond, "I suppose just this once. Did you call your mother yet?"

"No. I was also hoping to borrow your phone. She thinks Hannah's parents are dropping me off after the movie. I'd like to let her know where I am before I come in."

"That sounds like a good idea, James. I'll grab my cell."

James.

Charlotte's heart thrummed against her chest. She fought the separate urges to pop off the couch and simultaneously fold herself deeper into it. She counted the minutes on the cable box, those two-hundred- and forty-seconds lasting hours in her mind, until his Converse made their familiar *clod* against the hardwood in the entryway.

She kept her eyes facing forward, waiting to make sure that this was all real before she even tried to let herself acknowledge what was happening. It was only when his arms draped over the back of the couch, his chin finding a home in the indentation of the polyester, that,

"Hey Murph," rolled like silk off his tongue, and she finally let the smile erupt through her cheeks like a crack in the fault lines.

"What are you doing here?"

Her body immediately flipped around as she faced the boy who leaned against the couch behind her. His goofy, lopsided grin, one he hadn't worn all night, was brighter than any light on in the Murphy household.

"Eh. Got bored. Came back early. Wanted to see my friend."

As the last part of his confession trickled off his tongue, she saw the twinkle in his eyes, the heightening of his smile. She matched it in her own, and he took that as permission to take his spot on the couch.

It was awkward to start, she realized, as they both stared around the living room. James's hands were clasped between spread knees, and his chin tipped back as his gaze wandered around the room. His eyes finally landed on the cardboard box that sat atop the coffee table, containing a mostly untouched pizza.

"Charlie Kate, what *is* this?" he exclaimed exasperated, lifting the lid to reveal seven pieces of still in-tact pizza with one half-munched slice taking up the last space.

She shrugged. "I guess I wasn't really hungry earlier."

"Oh my god. I'm disappointed! I will *not* stand for this!"

Immediately, he made himself at home in the kitchen as he found a plate, stacked it with pizza, and slid it into the microwave.

She giggled, standing across from him in front of the microwave as the seconds ticked down, cheese bubbling and popping with the whir of the machine. James was drumming his fingers on the counter, watching intently as the numbers on the display crept closer to zero and pulled the door open as it flashed *00:01*.

With the warmed plate in hand, he flashed a large grin towards Charlotte before they returned to the living room.

"So... how did the Sox do today?" James asked, his mouth already stuffed with pizza and his eyes trained on the slowly disappearing pepperoni.

"They won 8 to 5. Millar hit a homerun."

He nodded as he finished off his slice and reached for another.

"We should see if we can convince our parents to get tickets for the home opener this year."

"Hey, it was *your* fault that we couldn't go last year," Charlotte teased.

James's shoulders slumped.

"I hate English. Mr. Mareck had no right to fail me on that paper. I spent all of Opening *Weekend* doing homework. I should've been at Fenway."

"Uhh, he failed you because you didn't turn it in, *dork*."

He shifted on the couch far enough to lightly ram his shoulder against Charlotte's, rolling his eyes at her smug smile.

"Yeah, but writing comes *easy* for you, Charlie Kate. I wish you would just give in already and write all of my papers for me."

She giggled, rolling her eyes as she finished off her own piece of pizza.

"You wanna watch a movie or something?"

She nodded, watching as James slid on his knees to the Murphy's movie stand, plucking a favorite from their VHS collection, and popping it into the machine.

They spent more time quoting *The Sandlot* than actually watching the movie, which was typical with many movies that they'd watched over and over again.

"Hey, could you grab me another Coke, *Smalls*?" he chided, his nickname for her stolen from the movie long ago.

"Ugh, why do you have to call me that?" Her groan was tinged with laughter as she bent doubled over the pillow that she had clutched in her lap.

"Because you're small," James shrugged, as if stating a fact. "I could fit you in my pocket. *Smalls*."

She eyed him with warning, and when he waggled his eyebrows back, the throw pillow that she had in her lap collided with the side of his head. A pillow fight ensued, ending very quickly when Linda called from the kitchen for them to settle down.

With faces flushed and heavy breathing, the pair settled back into the couch with wide smiles. Charlotte cocked her head and giggled, noticing a ball of puff in James's hair.

"Are you saving a little snack for later, Ramsey?"

"What are you talking about?"

She plucked a popcorn kernel from behind his ear, holding it between her fingers with a smug smile on her lips.

"Why on *earth* do you have popcorn in your hair?"

Instantly, his face turned the color of the pizza sauce that dotted the corners of his lips. He chewed the side of his mouth contemplatively for several seconds before responding.

"Well, umm...I, uh...I kind of got a bucket of popcorn dumped on my head tonight." He rushed his words, burying them in his lap as he let his head hang.

"James!" She was wide-eyed, fingers covering her mouth as the giggles escaped her. "Spill!"

"Okay, you can't laugh at me. Promise?"

His expression was serious and a tad embarrassed. When Charlotte nodded twice and nuzzled her chin into the pillow, he took a deep breath.

"So, I guess this whole night was supposed to be, like, 'make out night' for the basketball guys and the cheerleaders. All of the guys were going to kiss their...the girls they brought at the end of the night. It was this whole set-up. I had no idea, Charlie Kate. And Hannah thought I was going to kiss her too. But the thing is..." His eyes fell to his lap, studying his fingers as they twisted together, and remained there as he finished his sentence with a halfhearted shrug. "I don't know. I didn't want to."

Her ears were suddenly hot, the feeling seeping into the rest of her face and down her chest, as the silence became suddenly overwhelming. She was acutely aware of the ticking of the clock on the wall, the buzz of the blue screen after the movie had ended, the television in the basement where David was playing video games. She desperately wanted to know why, but the single syllable stuck in her throat, so she settled for listening to the rest of the story as he picked up several moments later.

"The more she pestered me about it, the more I turned her down,

66

and the madder she got. Took my whole popcorn and dumped it on my head. I paid for it, too. What a waste of an allowance!"

Her laughter was more nervous than reactionary, as *Why why why* hammered against her cranium just begging to escape.

"I'm gonna have to cut the grass again this weekend to make that money back. I mean, how dumb, right?"

"Yeah, right."

She flipped regular cable back on in an attempt to direct her nervous energy *somewhere*, and though he was *here* despite the plans for him to not be, she was chewing the inside of her lip, the contented silence still making her ears buzz.

It was close to eleven when she caught herself dozing, shaking her head with a twitch before looking dazily to her right to see James smirking, shaking his head, and stretching his arms above his body before standing.

She followed him to the door, her arms wrapped around her against the sudden chill as he slid his shoes back on, not really bothering with the laces.

James glanced around the foyer, following the curve of the vaulted entryway as he let *So* whisper into air that was now thick.

"Yeah," Charlotte followed, tracing the hardwood floor with her eyes in a similar path. "Umm, I'm really sorry that your date didn't go so well, but thanks for...I'm glad you stopped by."

"Me too," he agreed with that lopsided grin of his. "Couldn't pass up a Friday night hang out with my best girl."

Suddenly, his eyes widened, and his cheeks flushed red in the instant that it took her to bite the inside of her mouth and dart her eyes to the side.

He mumbled something incoherent, his eyes at his shoes now.
"Huh?"

"Oh, uh...I said it wasn't really a date anyway."

She heard him this time, though his words still seemed to be spoken underwater. Now though, with his hands shoved in his pockets, he met her eyes, the usual forest green now piercing as he bit his bottom lip.

"Oh?" was all she could push out, her eyes timid and wide as she peered up, his body now seeming to tower over her.

"No," he shrugged. "Can't be a date if you didn't wanna kiss the girl in the first place."

He shrugged then, and as her body began to grow tingly and hot, she somehow pushed out more syllables that formed the words, "You didn't?"

"Nope," he shrugged again, his feet sliding across the distance between them. "Would've been a *waste* of my first kiss."

He had to bend his body to reach her, the growth spurt bug having bit him hard. She could hear their bodies buzzing between them, could see the heatwaves in the air when his lips pushed against hers.

The stereotypes that you *saw stars and fireworks* were kind of true. He tasted like pizza sauce, and his lips were a little chapped, but her shoulders were burning under the shaking palms that held her there. She had her eyes clenched shut, because that's what Kelly had said to do, and Kelly had a boyfriend, so she knew, right?

When he pulled away, their lips made a little popping sound, and suddenly she had the urge to pull him by the cheeks and make him do it again, just to be sure it was real.

His cheeks were beet red, his lips still parted, when she opened her eyes. She could feel herself blushing though, too.

"See, now *that* wasn't a waste of a first kiss at all."

June 2018

Charlotte was grateful for the opportunities. Truly, she was. But on hour nine in the writer's room taking notes, she was bored. And hungry. And a little bit exhausted. The work was fascinating, watching the professional writers huddled around the table tweak and change the scripts they'd been working so furiously on to make shooting deadlines, but they'd been stuck on the same plot point for the past ninety seven minutes (but who was counting, really?), and all Charlotte wanted to do was put her feet up, pour herself a glass of wine, and watch a few episodes of the trashiest trash that reality TV had to offer.

But not until the people around the conference table could figure out how "Todd" was going to convince "Rachel" that "moving in together now was too quick," but, "that didn't mean he didn't love her." They'd truly run the gambit of different boneheaded things he could say to piss her off, but it wasn't connecting the rest of the plot together, and the episode depended on either getting this right, or rewriting the entire first half. At this point, Charlotte was starting to wonder which was the lesser of two evils.

The showrunner, Dan, called for a ten-minute break, at which moment everybody in the room either slumped back in their chair, ran fingers through already tousled hair, or bolted out the door altogether. Charlotte, checking the messages on her phone, glanced over to see Ginny rest her forehead in her palm momentarily before drumming her freshly manicured nails on the tabletop.

"Riveting first week, huh?"

"Yep. I can see why you drink so much," Charlotte chuckled.

"This should be the easiest fucking thing in the world to figure out. I'm surrounded by morons," she quipped with no regard for the people still seated around the table.

"Well, he doesn't want to move in with her, but they still have to make it to his parent's place for dinner that night, right?" Charlotte began recounting the outline of the episode thus far, continuing after Ginny's curt nod and purse-lipped stare. "So, why not have him make some big declaration then? Why does he have to say something demeaning? You guys keep focusing on painting him as the bad guy and trying to find ways for him to make some, I don't know, asshole comment, and it isn't working out. They'll already be tense enough as it is, with Rachel upset that Todd doesn't want to move in together. Stop trying to add fuel to the fire and keep it simple. She'll let it stew in her head enough to make the pot boil over and explode at dinner later."

"Keep talking."

Charlotte felt her cheeks flush and her body tense as the two other pairs of eyes still inhabiting the conference room were drilled in her direction.

"Um, I don't know…you guys have given all of these ideas of like, stupid things for him to say that will just make her even angrier. Give him a leg up and make him say something sweet instead, something like, 'I don't want to just play house with you,' or, 'I think this will be so much more special if we wait.' That way, *he* thinks he's being genuine, but *she's* still able to find loopholes that can lead to the argument you want them to have at the end. Trust me, the 'male versus female thought process' will have them both fuming on opposite ends of the room by the end of it, giving you that dramatic fight that you're looking for. They both think that they're right, when really, it's a huge misunderstanding with no true right or wrong."

By the time the ideas had tumbled past her lips, everyone was back in the conference room, eyes and ears perked towards her in a fury of intense stares and cocked eyebrows.

"I-I'm sorry, I'm just supposed to be taking notes, I—"

"Write that down."

Dan, the showrunner, a man in his mid-sixties with flour-white hair that stuck straight up, his wide eyes shining through large, square frames, pointed at the white board where the writer's assistant was already furiously scribbling as he took his seat in front of his computer. Charlotte's tentative eyes met Ginny's under a raised eyebrow. Ginny's return smirk was curt and simple, a shake of her head before she snapped immediately back into her zone, that Charlotte learned early on was business strict and cutthroat.

Charlotte watched in awe as her idea sprang to life in words and Expo marker, eventually flying under her own fingers as parts to the script that was finally beginning to solidify. Forty-five minutes later, she received a few pats on the back as the writing staff filed out of the room, leaving her alone with Ginny as Charlotte double checked notes that still needed to be organized for the next day.

"So, what the hell was that?"

Charlotte glanced up from winding the cord of her laptop charger, her eyes bugging as Ginny's crossed arms and cocked head froze her to the spot.

"Hey, I'm sorry. I didn't mean to be out of line. I sincerely thought that you and I were just talking—"

"You saved us back there. Stop apologizing. Apologize when it gets my ass in trouble. Come on. I'm buying you alcohol."

"So, where did that even come from?" Ginny probed over margaritas that Charlotte insisted stopped at one. "Is this why you and Scotty broke up? You were trying to force him to move in with you and he was dragging his ass about it?"

Charlotte chuckled, taking a sip of her drink.

"No. Absolutely not. Scotty and I had no business being together in the first place."

"He was definitely out of your league."

"Ginny!"

"What? I'm only trying to help here." She raised her eyebrows, taking another sip of her drink. "So? Talk to me. Where'd you all of a sudden get a knack for solving our character conflict in the blink of an eye?"

"I don't know," Charlotte shrugged. "I've kind of always enjoyed writing. I did it a lot when I was a kid. I actually started a few children's books back in college, but they sort of fell to the wayside."

"And you decided not to tell me this because?"

"Because it's just a hobby, Gin. A little escape I used to take, I guess." Her eyes drifted for a moment, to days holed up in her bedroom with a pen and a notebook, her lips quirking as she continued.

71

"When we were little, James would write these dumb guitar melodies and I'd give him the lyrics. Nine out of ten times he called them too sappy, so I'd just turn them into short little stories instead."

"Oh? Were any of them dirty?"

Charlotte rolled her eyes at the less than subtle sarcasm as Ginny's lips curled up around the edge of her glass.

"Either way, you'd better dig them up for Monday. We might need your expertise if my team of bozos keeps this up."

When she returned home after a few drinks, laughs, and failed attempts by Ginny to send her home with any random stranger, Charlotte was restless. She'd gone through her nighttime routine, even taking extra care to floss which she never did, but around one o'clock in the morning, with her eyes following the blades of her ceiling fan around in slow circles, she couldn't lie awake any longer.

Dragging herself out of bed, she found the notebook that she had unearthed days before and flipped to the back. About a quarter of the way through the wrinkled pages, "Charlie Kate's Songs" turned into "Charlie Kate's Stories."

What began as a short adventure into attempted songwriting with James eventually transformed his vented words into wandering plotlines.

Like when his mom and dad made him share a room with his older brother Kyle upon the arrival of their baby sister Abby, it was a tale about prank wars and dueling siblings.

When she watched him take the mound for the Newton Sox in the little league championship, her works took the point of view of a determined baseball player, getting inside his head as he pitched for major league scouts.

When she spent time watching girls in middle school throw themselves at the Jimmy Ramsey who had suddenly grown his hair out and sported muscles on his scrawny arms, her words became reminiscent of the plots to *She's All That* and *Never Been Kissed*, the narrator's voice always the haunted, shy girl who watched from afar.

She sighed, laughed, and cringed at her own early writing, lingering on some works while quickly passing others by, toying with the idea of bringing them to the next beach bonfire. Most were unfinished plots begun and quickly forgotten. Some were FanFiction of shows she'd become obsessed with in college, shows whose endings she didn't care for, so she'd written her own.

When she came to the end of the first notebook, she dug around her closet on hands and knees until she pulled out her old college binders, finding notes about curriculum riddled with ideas for children's books that had all started with an assignment from her children's literacy class.

She hadn't been lying to Ginny—writing truly was just a hobby of hers, something she did to unwind or express thoughts in her head that she couldn't quite work through without penning to a page. Granted, writing was something she was *good* at, but she was always humble about it, secretive even, without ever giving her talent a chance. But as her own print jumped off the pages in her hands, the character she had based off of her newborn niece so long ago suddenly began to fly.

Her position on the floor changed from lounging on her knees to cross-legged and looking for a pencil. Early morning light was peeking through her windows by the time she had pulled herself from the immersion of her make-believe world.

The rest of the week went by without much fanfare. Although Charlotte's input had been more than welcomed during crunch time, she tried to remain a wallflower during the next several days in the writer's room, burying herself in typing notes and making sure that her duties were fulfilled above and beyond. She was commended for her timeliness, organization, and thorough fulfillment of Starbucks orders. Though the work had her flying by the seat of her pants, the buzz of excitement that coursed through the writer's room on a daily basis was definitely seeping into her veins.

Around the middle of the week, a text from James had her simultaneously smiling and realizing just how exhausting her new position really was.

You alive out there, Murph? Am I going to have to turn on TMZ

to ever hear from you again? What happened to not forgetting the little people?!?

That night found them on towels at the beach with a pizza box between them.

"So, tell me: better or worse than sitting in the office and making copies?"

"Depends on how you look at it," she began. "I've changed my receptionist duties from binding papers to taking diligent notes all day in meetings, so I *do* have to actually pay attention." They shared a chuckle as she continued. "But, way more interesting to watch Hollywood bigwigs bicker over how their next 'it couple' is going to break up than removing staples and highlighting production dates," she said with an over-eager nod.

"I'll bet. Do I get a scoop? What's the show even about?"

"No can do," she said, shaking her head. "But I *can* tell you that, umm, some of *my* words might make it to your TV screen later this fall."

She stared at the tops of her knees as she spoke, suddenly interested more in her uneven tan lines than in watching James's reaction. But no sooner were the words out of her mouth than his head was hanging sideways, his chin jutting into her personal space to pull her attention back to him.

"Oh my god, *what*?"

She was biting her lip, whether to stop from smiling or to hide her chagrin, he couldn't yet tell.

"Dude, you can't leave me hanging like that." He was reaching for her now, tapping rapidly on her kneecaps with two fingers to get her attention. When their eyes met, hers were shining.

"So, uhh, I *might* have accidentally helped finish a script on my second day on the job."

"Charlie *Kate*!" His voice rang with excitement and pride, the skin of his face stretching with his smile. "Details!"

As she recounted her first evening at the round table, James's eyes swelled with pride, his smile flashed with teeth and pure joy for the woman he shared a beach towel with. He was always her biggest cheerleader, but never out of necessity, always because he truly thrived on her happiness.

"That's amazing. I am *so* proud of you. It sounds like all of those little secret stories of yours have finally paid off."

He waggled his eyebrows, reminding her of all the times he had not so subtly teased her about keeping her notebooks under lock and key. Even in a world where they shared every thought, every word, Charlotte's stories had always been her own.

"True, but when it comes out, I'm still not going to tell you what parts are mine."

"Aww, come on!"

She giggled, kicking at the sand with her toes as she attempted to bury them beneath the warm grains. Her smile was radiant against the sun that lowered in the sky, bouncing off her curls in a way that made them rich like shimmering gold.

"Seriously, Smalls. I'm really proud of you. Maybe this is your breakthrough or something," he said, his clasped hands hanging loose between his tented knees as he stared at the sand between his feet. He was doing his best to restrain himself from letting his pride tackle her to the ground and hug her silly, because he knew that if he let the returning comfort overtake him, he might not be able to turn away.

She sidled into him with her shoulder, her groan almost masked by the breaking of the waves.

"Why do you have to call me that?" she chuckled, rolling her eyes as she toed sand in his direction.

He smirked, trapping her bare feet beneath one of his to stop the impending torrent of sand.

"Because you're so *small*," he reminded her, leaning across the sand to wrap her in a big bear hug, giving into his urges anyway in a defeating sucker punch to his subconscious. "You fit right into my pocket."

She giggled as he slid her small frame easily into his strong embrace, and it took every ounce of willpower within him to ignore the metaphorical locking sound as her body clicked into place with his own.

His nose, buried in her hair, was eased by the lavender scent, the touch of vanilla, the hints of espresso bean. Instead of letting her go, which really he should have, he held on just a little more tightly as they watched the waves lap slowly along the shore.

It followed him home, the sound of Charlotte's laughter and the feel of her head on his shoulder, the way that she really did fit right into his pocket. Rather than rolling down the windows and trying to shake it off and let the wind carry it all away like he should—like he *knew* that he should, because he was on his way home to someone else—he closed up the windows and breathed it all in. It was a private moment to himself, to pause and absorb the warmness that Charlotte brought, that sense of home that had been absent from his life for so long.

But as he continued home—home to Vanessa, because Charlotte had driven off in the opposite direction—he realized that maybe, maybe that feeling of *home* that he left with Charlotte on the beach hadn't really been *absent*. As his car idled to a stop in his driveway, and he stared for a long, almost guilty moment at Vanessa's RAV-4, he thought that maybe his heart had just been falsely filled for too long under the guise of something temporary.

June 2018

Charlotte had spent enough time sitting around the conference table and had plenty of experience people-watching in her lifetime of timidness to categorize each and every person on the writer's team without much more than a polite *hello*.

Dan, the showrunner, reminded her of a grandfather who hadn't quite yet gotten the memo that he was "old." His physique was that of a man in his forties, but he was well respected in the world of sitcom television. Heidi, Mark, and Jenna were all on the same level of intensity as Ginny when it came to writing, but outside the room, Heidi was reserved, Jenna was incredibly quirky and often in her own world, and Mark was just downright rude. It was Jack who intrigued her the most.

Calm and level-headed, Jack McKinney was the one who focused the group, kept them on task, and made sure each voice was heard. He reminded her of her favorite teacher back in elementary school, Mrs. Wilson, who regardless of intelligence or behavior, made every single student in the room feel respected. When Jack dismissed an idea, it was done in a redirective form, for the good of the group, so similar to the growth mindset tactics that she used with her kindergarteners: *Mistakes make us grow. What can we learn from this? We don't have it* yet. *How do we keep moving forward?*

Not to mention that it surely wasn't the worst thing to have to look across the table at him all day. His handsomeness was subtle and understated, with neat chocolatey brown hair and soft eyes to match, a strong jaw that gave hints to his confidence. He carried himself not with an air that dictated his good looks, but that was warm and kind, always putting her at ease amidst the chaos of the days.

As most of the crew filed out of the conference room for lunch that afternoon, Charlotte switched tabs from the note taking she had been doing for Ginny to the story she that had recently unearthed from her closet notebooks and had begun to transfer into a Google Doc to work on. She pulled a yogurt from her backpack and used her break to delve right back into the world of fiction.

There was something liberating about seeing her untouched story with a fresh perspective, and being surrounded by the likes of creative genius for more than eight hours a day certainly didn't hinder her own flow. A grin peeked out around the spoon between her lips as her fingers flew across the keyboard, letting her story take shape.

"You know, when they call for lunch, people usually take a *break* from writing for a few minutes."

His rich voice startled her, but the soft smile brought her back to earth. She watched Jack's fingers delicately pluck his forgotten water bottle from its spot across from her at the table, a ring of warm condensation left behind in its wake.

She returned his smile with a shy one of her own, blush creeping up her cheeks.

"See, as tempting as that sounds, I *really* enjoy the pain that comes from making myself slave over a hot computer during my off time. It's thrilling."

"Oh really?" he returned with a smirk.

Suddenly, he was gliding around the table, his broad body pausing behind her chair as he peeked over the top of her computer.

"So, Miss Masochism, what are you working on? More ideas for when my team has another collective brain fart?"

It was strange, how easy this banter seemed to immediately slide between herself and a man with whom she was only now having a first, private conversation. The thrill made her stomach flip in anticipation as he bent forward a little at the waist. When he peered over her shoulder, she was quick to switch windows, revealing to Jack only the notes from their last meeting.

"Oh, it's uh…" she stumbled. "Sorry, Jack. I don't mean to be rude, but I really don't share my writing with people."

She bit her lip, preparing for intrusion, or at the very least, for that pretty face of his to furl into an offended frown. But his eyebrows stayed smiling, his expression softening from kidding to kidding aside.

"That's perfectly okay. I respect that," he said, passing her a reassuring smile. "To return your honesty, I used to be the same way. In fact, my own *mother* wasn't allowed to read my plays until they were performed on stage back in high school."

Her body was relaxing again, the tension dissipating visibly as her shoulders dropped from their stiffened state.

"Wow, Jack McKinney, I didn't peg you for being the secretive type," she returned with the cock of an eyebrow.

"Oh, that's only just the beginning," he replied with a wink. "Just wait until I show you what I keep hidden in my closet."

They shared a laugh, and Charlotte could feel her cheeks warming as she glanced down to the table, doing her best not to get caught up in how nice his laughter sounded against her eardrums.

"Well, I'm gonna run. But, Charlotte? If you ever *do* want a second pair of eyes, let me know. I'm more than happy to help. I know first-hand how much another's opinion can help open your eyes to a break in a story. And, as of last week, apparently so do you," he offered with a smile.

While she felt the word *Okay* whisper past her lips, she wasn't sure if its decibel had registered in his ears as Jack smiled and turned to walk out of the room. She watched her cursor blink in the same spot for the last twenty minutes of her lunch break, a giddy grin plastered across her lips.

The script for the first episode was finally complete, and with Ginny's name plastered across it as lead writer, Charlotte found herself on the set of a real television show.

She wasn't the most diehard of late-night drama or comedy fans like she had been in high school, but as familiar actors traversed past her to get to their set places, her body was full of star struck tingles.

"Pretty cool, huh?" Ginny said, sidling up next to her with a bottle of water pursed against her lips.

"Alright, this *is* kind of awesome."

It was so fascinating to see Ginny in her element, taking command in a way that was so different than controlling Charlotte's outfit choices before they went out for the evening. Ginny's presence in the writer's room echoed the way that she worked with the actors, in a way that showed respect for the rest of the people on set. She was one cog of a giant wheel that couldn't flow without each and every person doing their part.

Charlotte mentally thanked herself for her choice in shoes that morning after she had done several laps back and forth across the Hollywood set to make extra script copies, refill coffees, and run equipment when extra hands were needed.

She had fleeting moments of freedom throughout the day when she was able to take a breath, poised next to Ginny behind the camera crews as the words that had been discussed around a conference table just yesterday came to life with diction and emotion. It surprised her to truly understand how much went into making one episode of a television show, as lunchtime approached, and the actors were still working on the same scene with which they had started.

If she had to hear the lines, "I'm not fighting *with* you, Rachel. I'm fighting *for* you," one more time, she was going to make another Starbucks run just to get out of the room.

When everyone broke for lunch six hours after shooting began, Charlotte took her chance to sneak back towards the vacant writer's room, itching to use any of her spare time to continue working on her own writing.

"Man, look at you. One day of working with the big dogs and they're already letting you onto the set? Big time, Murphy. Next thing you know, I'm going to be watching over my shoulder for you to steal my job."

She was stopped in her tracks by Jack McKinney not ten feet from her destination, but her eyes were smiling when she turned to face him.

"I'm not going to lie. This is kind of insane."

He returned her smile and nodded, then hitched his thumb over his shoulder.

"You do know that lunch is that way, right?"

"Oh, yeah, I know. I just thought I'd take a minute to myself to breathe."

"Wow, one day on the Hollywood scene and she's already too good for us little guys?"

Jack turned his body towards the doorway, leaning his broad

shoulders against its frame as his arms crossed over his chest.

"Absolutely. You lowlifes are only here to drag me down. You may refer to me from now on as Ms. Murphy."

She kept her expression serious, and although he saw through her tone, he continued playing along, knitting his eyebrows together and drawing his lips into a straight line.

"Well then, *Ms. Murphy*, I'll let you get back to your very important work. I won't bother you with the *trivial* information that craft services has ice cream for us today."

"Trivial. Absolutely trivial," she replied, continuing the charade. "However, as head honcho in charge, I should probably check it out to make sure it's okay for everyone. You know. For the well-being of the rest of my lackeys. Standard procedure."

She turned on her heel, deciding that penning her fictional adventures could wait another fifteen minutes.

"So, first day in the big leagues on a scale of one to ten: go."

They joined the line of crew members, conversation buzzing around them along with the sounds of the food service line.

"Well, my feet are killing me, and I don't think I've actually put my butt in a chair since I got out of my car this morning," she began, eyeing the dessert buffet that they had skipped to in favor of an actual hot lunch. "But the fact that there is *cookie dough in the ice cream*—oh my god—is bumping it up to about an eight and a half."

Her eyes bulged like a kid in a candy store as the craft services workers poured toppings galore into her bowl of ice cream, and Jack could only laugh, shaking his head in amusement as he loaded his own bowl. They wandered towards the lunch tables, winding up amidst several semi-full tables of their cast and crew.

"So then, Ms. Murphy, why'd I find you alone heading for the conference room? This seems to be a recurring trend with you."

As she poked at the soft serve with a plastic spoon, she focused her eyes on the cookie dough in her bowl.

"Honestly, Jack? I'm kind of very, very introverted," she began with a nervous laugh. "I mean, don't get me wrong, this job is insanely cool, but sometimes I just need a break from people for a minute."

She met his wide and apologetic eyes as she lifted her spoon to her lips.

"Oh, hey, I'm sorry," he said quickly, his eyebrows knitting together. "I can leave you alone. I know first-hand how that is."

She jumped in quickly herself, waving the spoon between them before he could get up out of his chair more than he had already.

"No, no you're okay. You're normal. *You* I don't mind."

He grinned then, burying his eyes in his own bowl of ice cream as they continued to munch.

"How's the book coming along? Have you been getting time to work on it with this crazy schedule?"

"Yeah. Or, I guess I'm *making* time. I think I've gone to bed past midnight at least twice this week."

"Wow, dedication! It's refreshing to see."

She braced herself. This was usually the point in the conversation where people would begin to push for information, to pry her ideas from her head and offer advice or criticism. But she wasn't in the business for prying eyes just yet.

She bit her lip in anticipation, waiting for the first red flag on her Jack radar to pop up, the first brick in the wall that would ultimately put a safe distance between herself and getting hurt.

But as she mixed soggy toppings in her slowly melting bowl of ice cream, the intrusion never came. He was making a joke about one of the other writers on staff, pointing across the cafeteria with his spoon, and flashing the smile that was equal parts confidence and shy.

Then, he was asking if she wanted a refill ("because we deserve it"), and she followed him blindly back to the ice cream.

"Now, are we going for the same thing? More cookie dough? New toppings? Being adventurous or staying safe?"

There was a burn in her chest that was unfamiliar, but somehow, she knew it was a good burn. So used to almost always having cookie dough in her ice cream, so used to playing it safe and being predictable, she surprised herself by asking for nuts and hot fudge instead.

"Adventure! I like it," Jack replied.

He offered her a smile and a wink, and she turned her head towards the craft services worker to hide the blush in her cheeks.

"So, I have to say, we've worked together for a few weeks now, and I don't know much about you, Charlotte Murphy."

They sat in the same spots, scooping ice cream more slowly this time as the conversation seemed to pick up.

"Oh. Well, you know that Ginny basically has me on a leash by now. But during the year, I'm actually a kindergarten teacher."

"No way! That's amazing. My mom was a teacher for thirty years," he exclaimed, his smile bright with pearly white teeth. "I have a newfound respect for you. Mom said that teaching wasn't always easy, but the payoff of helping those kids made it worth it in the end. What's your favorite part about teaching?"

Jack's eyes seemed to light up in tune with hers as Charlotte told stories, trading small tidbits that Jack had tucked away from his mom's experiences. It was floating so freely, this conversation, that she was sad when she noticed several members of the crew and writing team heading back to their respective places.

"You've got your summers off and you choose to spend them here? I applaud that. Really, I do," Jack said as they headed towards the garbage can with their now empty bowls.

She picked at the Styrofoam, her face hot as she realized, in their limited time left, that she didn't want their conversation to end. In the thirty or so minutes that they'd spent sharing ice cream and stories, there was something warm and kind and *safe* about this man that she wanted to know more about.

"Well, I suppose there are worse places to spend your summer," she replied, doing her best to hide the shaking in her hands. "And besides, working in a room full of professionals gives me a lot of fresh insight for when I go home to work on my own book."

The nerves bubbled inside her like carbonation as she clasped and unclasped her hands, the jabbing of her fingers adding heat from the friction of her movements.

It was an intentional bait, and she wanted so badly for him to take a bite, just the smallest nibble. With his kindness over the past half hour, he had broken through a crack inside her, and the heat in her body had her begging him to ask about her story, to take more interest, to continue wanting to know more, a thought that both thrilled and terrified her.

But there he was, smiling shyly and nodding, adding, "I'll bet what you do at home with your own story is a lot better than what any of these yahoos can come up with here."

He winked then, extending his hand to take her empty bowl and throw it into the trash.

As Jack skirted directly around her trap, she took a breath, realizing that she was actually going to have to be direct for once, something she didn't do very often. It had gotten her into so many predicaments throughout her life, this pattern of wishful thinking and *hoping they would catch on* that usually lead her to a dead end with no answers and more of a stuffed up heart than she had begun with.

It had happened with James so many times, she had lost count.

But in this state of being so *stagnant*, she was beginning to realize that maybe, in order to move, she was going to have to actually pick up her own two feet.

Mustering all of her strength, she took a deep breath before, "Yeah, but, just in case, do you think you might want to, I don't know, take a look at things for me?" ran together in one disjointed string.

It was refreshing to see the tips of his ears sprinkled pink, his teeth white behind a widening smile.

"Really?"

She bit her lip, suppressing her smile from splitting at his reaction that was nothing short of adorable, as she nodded in affirmation.

"Well, are you free tomorrow night? We could head to Starbucks or something. Or, I mean, I could just take a look on our breaks, if you want. It's up to you."

Something about his calm and collected nature was suddenly missing, as she noticed his eyes scanning the floor while his words quickened, his eyes avoiding her. He was nervous. And it made her feel better all of a sudden that the she was choosing to put the label *giddy* on her own emotions.

"Yeah. I mean, sure. Maybe we could...do both?"

She was biting her lip, doing the eye-avoiding thing too, as he finally met her gaze with a shy *Awesome* before he went back to smiling goofily at the ground.

It was only once, but while things were at a lull during conversation in the writer's room that afternoon, Charlotte's eyes were drawn across the table. When she found Jack, it brought heat to her cheeks to find that he had been looking for her, too. They held eyes for just a moment, before shy smiles blinked them back into focus.

She didn't sleep much that night, partially because she was nervously trying to ready her story to a point where she was comfortable sharing it with Jack. The other part was because every time she closed her eyes, his smile was suddenly there, keeping the butterflies in her stomach awake and fluttering.

Charlotte Murphy didn't typically do much to make her appearance more than *office presentable*. The writer's room was usually cold, so after a quick shower and hair product run through her curls every morning, it was typically a hoodie and leggings with a slapped-on coat of powder so that those around her couldn't read the tired under her eyes. This morning, however, found her awake earlier than normal.

The curling iron had dust blown off of it to add a bit of definition to her otherwise tight curls. Her eyes were lined with a bit of natural shadow. Her hoodie was traded in for a cardigan and a form fitting V-neck. It wasn't much more effort than her normal standard of office comfort. But in the back of her mind, she hoped that Jack might take notice.

She arrived to work early after a coffee run, suddenly nervous and giddy and bubbling with this new anticipation that she hadn't felt in God only knew how long. She took the extra time to polish the newest section of her story, fumbling with a metaphor that she couldn't quite tie up.

As bodies began to filter into the room, she noticed a scent that had bridged the gap between them over ice cream the day before. It was a clean, Irish spring, with the subtlest bite of spice. Her head snapped up almost immediately.

He had shaved.

It was just the stubble that had collected over the course of that week, but *today* it was gone, and the smoothness that reflected from ten feet across the room had her fingers aching to feel it.

She had a passing thought that her makeup was wasted today as she felt the red in her cheeks surely sneaking past her foundation every time she looked up to find him staring in her direction, passing her a small smile or a nod, or the occasional eye roll when someone else in the room would say something incredibly outlandish.

She was counting down the minutes to lunch. Unbeknownst to her, he was doing the very same.

June 2018

Her body was a bottle of nerves waiting to burst at any second from more than several different variables, Ginny's own anxieties being the first.

The actors on set, "weren't conveying her words right," she claimed. It was a constant creative battle, one that no one could seem to win. The standoff had steam boiling from so many heads that Charlotte was beginning to wonder if she actually needed long sleeves today.

Charlotte was running back and forth with the writer's assistants to make edits, run copies, and bring them back to set quickly enough for new lines to be developed and learned and shot on camera.

In the back of her mind, she was reviewing her own story over and over and over again, sitting abandoned in a Google Doc, still not up to her liking. Her inner mantra was a constant string of *This is why you're getting help* and *He's here to help you make it better*, but unhelpful regardless. She'd be embarrassed to share her words even if they were completely polished to her own liking.

She spilled coffee across the conference room table in her own state of jitters, earning a mixture of sympathetic and aggravated eyes thrown in her direction.

Of course, Jack's had been the former, and when she ran off to the bathroom to take a breather, she was surprised to find him on the other side of the door with a fresh refill and a soft *Don't worry about it, happens all the time.*

But then, there was Jack himself, all clean shaven and handsome. It didn't help that, in the midst of high tension over script rewrites, he was the one to calm the storm that was Ginny's and Dan's frustrations coming to a head. His commanding presence had bubbles rising in her stomach.

Lunch was called, and the tension melted from the room as quickly as bodies flung from the doorway in an effort to clear the air, leaving only Charlotte and Jack behind. She was surprised, but then again not so much, to see his head hung and his hands in his pockets.

He was nervous too.

"You ready?"

It was a simple question, but ambiguous all the same.

Was she ready for lunch? Absolutely. The granola bar and banana she'd shoveled into her mouth between jobs this morning were both long gone by now.

Was she ready to share her story? Yes and no. She didn't really share with anyone. But she was warming up to the idea.

Was she ready to spend quality time alone with this man who had her stomach flipping inside out in a way she hadn't felt in a long time? To let someone into such a private part of her life for the first time? To take the proverbial plunge into *forward motion* that she'd been fighting for so long?

Absolutely not.

But all the same, she watched him hitch his head towards the doorway, heard him mumble something like, "Maybe we get out of this room for a little while," and let him lead her to a vacant and smaller conference room down the hall.

This room was much more inviting, she realized, with a couch along one wall facing two stuffed armchairs and a round coffee table situated between them.

Her breath hitched when he chose the couch and gestured for her to take a seat next to him, realizing the close proximity. But she sat anyway, propping her MacBook open on the table as she focused all of her energy on entering her password, pulling up Google, and taking regular breaths, not at all thinking about the slowly decreasing space between their knees when he spread his open.

"So, I'll give you an overview first," she began, pulling the machine to her lap and facing it away. "The goal was for it to be a children's picture book. The main character is Emma, and she lives in this colorless world. All of the kids around her have this pessimistic energy, and she makes it her duty to get them to see the best in life."

She took a breath, checking Jack's expression for any sort of giveaway before continuing.

"I based it off of something that I've talked about a lot with my kindergarteners. We try to have this 'best day ever' mindset when they come into the classroom each morning. Basically, yesterday is over and you can't change what happened, and tomorrow hasn't happened yet. So why not make *today* the best day ever? Kind of corny, I know."

She trained her eyes on her lap, biting her lip and drumming her fingers anxiously against the metal of her computer as visions of *Totally cheesy, I can't believe I'm actually about to waste my time reading this* and *God, Charlotte, I thought this was going to be a serious work time. See ya!* danced in her head.

"Wow. That's kind of deep, Murphy. But the fact that you can have kindergarteners opening their mind to that kind of positivity is really inspiring. I really hope we can make the rest of this work so that more kids can see that, too."

It was then that she finally turned to meet his eyes. His chocolate irises were warm and hopeful, and the close-lipped grin that stretched along both sides of his face had her suddenly beaming, her anxieties melting away little by little.

With his palm up, he gestured toward her computer, and she passed it over to his awaiting lap.

The wait and see game returned some of her nerves. Her story wasn't finished, by any means, and though it was a kids' picture book, it wasn't entirely long, either. She bit her lip as she studied his face. His eyes had been trained in concentration for some time now, and he bit his lip every so often. Sometimes he would shift his knees underneath the laptop, causing it to bounce.

At one point, she wanted to scream, "Just tell me it sucks already, okay?!" but instead, she picked up her bottle of water and distracted herself with a wash of coolness, focusing instead on bringing her body temperature down a few degrees.

She was counting the tiles in the ceiling when the couch sagged to her right, a large breath expelling from Jack's lungs. She twitched, turning to see him place the computer on the table as he faced her.

She braced herself, pinching her eyes closed, soaking in the last fleeting moments that held the opinions about her writing solely inside her own mind.

"Charlotte, this is great."

When she peeled her eyes open one at a time, turned her own chin in the direction of his soft words, she found a shy smile and wide eyes peering back at her.

Still not entirely sure she'd heard him correctly, she mouthed a whispered, "What?"

He chuckled; his eyes trained down before quickly pulling back up.

"I said it's great. The start that you have. It's really awesome."

She was smiling now, but more in relief than anything else. It was fear that drove her to keep her ideas so secretive. Fear that had been instilled by her brother at a young age, but also fear of criticism in general. Her stories were perfect in her eyes. Each and every one held a special place in her heart. To hear them torn apart would quite literally strangle the intricate parts of her.

It was that fear that homed all of her stories to notebooks shoved under her bed and snapped laptop lids closed when so much as a stranger would walk by while she was at the library. The fear kept her from taking a chance, from opening her eyes to what could be.

But now, with her body awash in his smile, in *Great, great, great*, she was on top of the world.

"Hey, we've only got about a half hour left before we're back at it, so what do you say to finishing this conversation with a little bit of fuel?"

She nodded in agreement and followed him blindly to the cafeteria where most everyone was already situated over hot plates, which made it easier to jump through the line quickly themselves before sneaking back to the conference room with their meals.

Over potato salad, turkey on rye, and steaming bowls of chili, Charlotte mustered the first true sentence she'd said since they broke for lunch.

"Seriously McKinney. Don't hold back. What do you really think?"

It may have been the praise bug that had bitten her in that conference room, but suddenly she was dying for more, for more words of affirmation and *keep doing what you're doing*. And, if she was being honest, more of that smile that seemed to go along with it.

"I'm not holding back," he chuckled between bites. "You have a really nice start, and the premise has a ton of potential."

The word *potential* stung, but rather than locking herself away, she let him continue.

"I was really impressed with the color metaphor that you have running throughout the story, too. The way that little bouts of color are popping up as characters start to realize what they're capable of. It's really going to connect with your audience."

It was so commonplace for her to stare at the table or the ground, avoiding the conversation by letting it float above. But now, under this newfound confidence, she jerked her gaze away from her slowly disappearing lunch and met his eyes.

"Thanks," she began, slowly finding her footing. "I started the whole thing in college, but the color part was honestly what kind of got everything going again a few years later. After meeting and holding Emma for the first time, I don't know, it was like my world was suddenly brighter, more colorful. I wanted to share that with the world."

He frowned now, and she edged back in her seat, before, "Sorry, what do you mean, *meeting and holding Emma?*" eased her worry.

"Oh! Sorry. I didn't even tell you: my niece Emma was kind of the one to inspire the story. She brought it all to life."

His eyes softened then, his brows pinching upwards.

"That's awesome," he replied, his voice softer now, as she watched his eyes drop to his empty bowl of chili. "It's actually kind of adorable."

After a lull of silence, he continued, "How old is she now?"

"She turns three in August, actually. Do you want to see a picture?"

Though she lived back in Newton with Charlotte's brother and sister-in-law, Emma was still the pride and joy of Charlotte's existence. So, when her smile widened and her cell phone was already coming out of her pocket, Jack's *Absolutely* was inevitable.

She scrolled through the album in her phone labeled *Emmy Bear*, starting at the most recent photos that Marie had sent her of Emma in a purple sparkly leotard doing forward rolls down an inclined mat at her gymnastics class.

"She's so cute," Jack breathed, inching closer on the couch to see the photos better. Charlotte's breath halted when his knee touched hers, resuming a little heavier when she noticed that he wasn't going to move away.

"I know I'm a little biased, but she totally is," she returned, sliding her thumb across the screen to show him photo after photo of the little girl with soft, curly brown hair. It was a Murphy trait, but she always teased David and Marie that Emma was more *her* twin than either of her parents combined.

She arrived suddenly at a photo from Christmas, of Emma poised half on Charlotte's lap, and half on James's. They were sitting in the Murphy's living room, the tradition of matching Christmas Eve pajamas taking on a candy cane theme that year. Emma's lips, caked in sticky red and white from the candy in her hand, were the perfect accessory.

Charlotte's breath hitched, her chest now tight with nerves as her thumb continued to scroll quickly past pictures. The next several, however, were more renditions of the last. Emma, still in their laps, transitioned quickly from sitting nicely with a bright smile, to shoving a candy cane in James's mouth and eventually climbing on his head. Charlotte's smile was wider and her head was thrown back further with every picture she scrolled past.

"Is that your boyfriend?" Jack asked before she finally came to the end of the string of *Charlotte and James and Emma* photos, landing them on the picture of Emma at the mall with Santa.

"Um, no," she began slowly, her face hot again for a new reason altogether.

It always happened like this.

When she was finally comfortable somewhere else, with someone else, before she could settle in too much, James was always there. It wasn't like she was *cheating* though; he was in a committed relationship, for God's sake. But it was inevitable, this feeling of introducing someone else to James, of knowing that part of her heart was always going to belong to another, that had her pulse beating in her ears.

Scrolling back to the previous photo, where Charlotte was on James's back, and Emma on hers, their heads stacked like a snowman, she sighed heavily.

"This is James. He's my best friend. And we're Emma's godparents."

A breath whizzed past her lips as she shut her eyes in anticipation.

"Oh. That makes sense."

When a breath pushed past Jack's lips, she opened her eyes a little, eying him cautiously from the side.

"Yeah. He's...we've been, like, best friends since we were six. Our families are super close."

It sounded like excuses, the way she was defending the relationship that Jack hardly knew, but he saved her from tripping over more rationale.

"Yeah, it looks like it. How'd you con him into the candy cane onesie?"

She laughed, more in relief than anything else, as she explained the tradition that the Murphys and Ramseys had adopted when she was in first grade and James had gifted her a set of pajamas that matched the very same ones that he planned to wear while he "tried to capture Santa and Rudolph" that year.

"Oh man, Murphy. So, did you do it? Did you bag up the big man?"

"No," she chuckled, a snort sneaking through that made her cover her nose. "I believe, if I remember correctly, he slept on the couch and woke up to the dog eating the cookies and knocking over the milk."

It wasn't *If I remember correctly* at all, but more *I was there because we begged my mom to let me help him set the trap* and *The milk spilled onto me and ruined the pajamas* and *I cried the entire time they were in the washer and dryer because they were a present from James*. But those details remained in her mind, much like the fictional stories that she was only just beginning to share.

"Rough day for a seven-year-old," Jack replied with a chuckle of his own and a shake of his head.

The awkward silence was back as she locked her phone and tucked it back into her bag, turning her body again to face him with a wipe of her hands along the legs of her pants.

Their *So's* tangled together, and after a short and awkward laugh, he picked back up.

"So, I'd love to actually *talk* with you about your writing more than just sitting here and praising it. I know we had said something yesterday about hitting up Starbucks after work. Would you, uh...would you still want to do that tonight? Or another night?"

She wasn't used to this, to men stumbling over words as they invited her somewhere that wasn't work related. But suddenly, she found herself soothing *him*, nudging him with her knee as she passed him a smile.

"How could I turn down an offer for you to sit and shower me with more praise about my obviously brilliant work?"

He smiled too, cocking his head to his lap while his smile crept up his cheeks.

He nudged her back, their knees remaining pressed together as he retorted, "God, are you already letting this all go to your head? I might have to knock you down a few pegs."

As Jack stood, he offered his hand to help her up. Though she was only getting up off the couch, she slid her palm into his. Warmth radiated up her arm for those fleeting seconds, and it dawned on her momentarily that she should keep her hand here, should let him hold her for longer than he really needed to.

His grip was warm, and she felt the slight nudge of his thumb along her wrist as she stood, her eyes falling at his neck before she felt the courage to meet his eyes.

They were wide and darkening, the usual milk chocolate brown dripping quickly into mocha.

His lips were parted when she dragged her eyes down for that split second, pondering if she really was seeing the breath expel past them.

But then, the pounding feet and shouting of directions outside the door jogged them both back into reality, fingers slipping against skin that was now suddenly cold.

The same hand that had just been clutching hers was suddenly at the back of his neck, rubbing softly back and forth as his gaze met the floor.

"If you knock me down, I'll just get back up with twice the force, McKinney."

Her own words startled her even as they bounced from her tongue, so sharp and bold and uncharacteristic. She watched his head snap from where it studied the blue-green of the carpet, and as he raised an eyebrow in challenge, she could swear that he was smirking, too.

She was grateful for the chaos to resume, to have a distraction that demanded all of her focus for the remainder of the afternoon. She couldn't afford to get lost in those eyes again, for fear that she might drown and never resurface.

As things in production finally clicked into place, and the scene was finally shot in a way that pleased everyone, Charlotte found herself packing up shop close to seven thirty. She was working on readying a few odds and ends for the next morning when she heard his throat clearing from across the room.

"You're not going to stand me up, are you, Murphy?"

His words, typically so soft and inviting, warm and kind, were suddenly low with a gravelly texture that she felt in her toes.

She paused her fingers above the keys of her laptop, met his eyes directly, and replied, "Wouldn't dream of it."

Charlotte followed him out to the parking lot where they agreed to drive separately. She blasted the air conditioning, duly because of the temperature of midsummer Los Angeles even this late in the evening, but also to quell the heat that was still pooling in her belly.

When they arrived at Starbucks, he held the door for her, and scoffed dismissively when she offered to pick up his drink, *Come on, it's like payment for helping!* going dismissed with a wave of his hand and *Not a chance, Murphy.*

It was over coffee and cake pops that she saw the Jack McKinney of the writer's room, his diligent and serious demeanor coming out through waving arm gestures and quick scrolls of her keyboard. In the moments that he gave her suggestions and helped her to edit her work, to connect disjointed pieces together, and fumble through mixed verb tenses, her body absorbed every bit of this business conduct, thriving on the way that they could transition so quickly from *Making nerves stand on end* to *working professionally*.

When the barista readying a mop bucket warned them of the store's closing in fifteen minutes, the bubble of professionalism popped, and brought Charlotte to the stunning realization that she didn't want her time with this man to end.

They relaxed against the plush armchairs, Jack rolling his shoulders out from his hunched position as Charlotte cracked her neck from side to side.

Over now cold beverages, they blinked their eyes a few times and took solace in the quiet, the grungy coffee shop soundtrack helping to ease the tension in shoulders and legs.

"How are you feeling now?" he questioned, sipping at his cup. "After we've kind of gone through and polished some things up, I mean."

She nodded, finishing off the last of her drink before setting the cup back down.

"A lot better. I think I know how I want to move forward. You were a really big help today, Jack."

His smile was small, but grateful all the same, as he relaxed more deeply into the chair.

Dark shades of navy dotted with the glow of the horizon layered the parking lot in deep shine as they walked out to their cars. Jack lay his palm across the top of her car, peering down at dark asphalt before bringing his eyes up.

"I uh...Charlotte, I'm not gonna lie, I've really, really enjoyed spending time with you."

The smile that crept up as she muttered back, "Me too," as she bit her lip, as she tried her best to not bounce up and down on her toes, was persistent as it widened along her cheeks.

"Would you...I mean, are you free on Friday night? I would love to get to see you in a setting that doesn't involve a computer."

His words came out in that nervous manner that she had begun to admire as he chuckled and stumbled over his own proposition.

"Actually, my Friday nights are kind of booked solid," she admitted, watching his face fall and catching it before it hit bottom with, "But I'm not doing anything on Saturday."

Just like that, his lips were upturned again, the fingers in his pockets unfurling.

"Awesome."

After plans were exchanged to *go to the boardwalk instead of just dinner* because *dinner sounds so stuffy and boring* and *let me get you my number, just in case,* she turned to leave, stopped by his hand on her wrist, by his body effectively pinning her between his and the driver's side door.

When his lips pressed softly into her cheek, her entire body stiffened at first, but when she finally relaxed, she could feel the rollercoaster in her stomach, the way that her nerves were standing on end. She let her eyes close, absorbing the feel of his fingers relaxing around her wrist as they reached further down to squeeze her hand.

"So, I'll, uh...see you in the morning?"

"Bright and early," was the only response she could muster before watching him saunter back to his car.

Per his request, she sent him a text when she arrived home safely.

With her body warm and tingly under so much more than the Los Angeles heat, she closed her eyes, replaying the moment over and over, letting an odd contentment wash away all of her worries, if only for that moment.

Amidst the chaos of her job, and despite her typical tendencies during the summer to use any and all free time that she had to relax and enjoy all of the warm and sunny reasons she moved out to California in the first place, Charlotte found herself glued to a computer with every chance she got. Penning her children's book seemed to consume her every free moment.

It was liberating to watch her ideas spring to life at her fingertips, for the spark and motivation to almost pull the words from her body at a forceful insistence each time she sat to write. Of course, she couldn't help but think of Jack, and the way that his assistance helped to boost her confidence, to surge her forward with a newfound boldness about her own talent.

So when James showed up unannounced on her doorstep later that week, he seemed to pop the bubble, the thick vat of concentration that Charlotte had buried herself inside.

"Oh my god. They've finally done it. The Hollywood bigwigs have turned you into a zombie."

James grabbed her by the shoulders, shaking her jokingly with his green eyes bulging in mock surprise.

She chuckled, swatting him in the chest as he pushed past her to toe off his shoes.

"I'm so sorry. I should have come sooner. I knew something was wrong."

Rolling her eyes, she motioned for him to join her in the living room while she paused to check her appearance in her hall mirror that he had so lovingly mocked.

Wearing an oversized sweatshirt, no makeup, and her curls piled high atop her head into a messy knot of a bun, it was no different than Saturday afternoon study sessions in college or Sunday afternoon hangovers. When she joined James in the living room, he had made himself at home on the couch, and was sliding her laptop to his own thighs.

"They've got you working at home? Seriously, dude, you aren't getting paid enough to do this job."

But she was across the room in a flash, snapping the MacBook closed in the same motion that it took her to cradle it under her arm. James's hands flew up in front of his body in surrender.

"Whoops, sorry. I forgot that the corporate mongrels at ABC will strip me down and bury me six feet under if I catch a scoop."

"Right, yeah," she chuckled, tucking the laptop on the bottom shelf of her coffee table. "Actually, I was working on something of my own."

He relaxed his tall frame into her old couch, one arm stretched over the back while he spread his legs wide, taking up two-thirds of it, while Charlotte tucked herself into the reclining chair.

"Oh, really? Well, why'd you snake the computer away so quickly? Pass it over here, Smalls."

James stuck his large hands into the space between them, his eyes lighting up in anticipation, but the computer remained rooted to its spot.

"Not happening," she chuckled, bracing herself to grab the computer if he tried to go for it again. She watched his eyes turn down, his mouth agape and following suit in one fluid motion.

"Why not?"

"You know the rule, James: You can read it once it's published. It's not quite ready yet. We still have quite a bit of work to do, but you can be my first official reader once it's done. You can even have the first signed copy."

She tacked on a grin to the butt of their running joke, but the usual twinkle in his eye, and the typical, "Fine. As long as you make it out to *My Number One Fan*" didn't follow suit. Instead, his eyebrows pinched together in the middle, his head cocking to the side as one syllable ripped through her.

"*We*? Who is *we*?"

The guilt that suddenly ran hot through her body was immediate, like she'd been caught in the act, the same heat that had presented itself amidst the butterflies and good feelings that she had when she spent time with Jack.

99

But this wasn't adultery in the slightest. As the past weeks with Jack came to mind, she recalled several times where the same feeling had spiraled in her gut. When she realized that the look on James's face was more confused than accusatory, she found it within herself to shove the brewing guilt aside, testing the waters of her newfound bravery.

"Yeah. One of the other writers on the show is helping me with some of the finer details. It's a work in progress, but it's really coming along."

James was usually her biggest fan, the cheerleader that encouraged her no matter what. But something about not being the only one in this corner of her life was clearly putting creases in his forehead, and an empty feeling in the pit of her stomach.

"You're really going to love it, J. You're going to be so proud of me."

His face softened, seeming to be tugged on by her words, and he offered her a smile that was largely warm, but with a small hint of defeat.

"I always am."

They played catch up conversation, filling in the blanks of time spent apart, letting the background noise of the Red Sox fill in the silence before the gnawing in the back of James's head caught up with him.

"So... this other writer that you're working with...how'd that come about?"

The part of her that wanted to apologize, to let him just read her book and say that the whole situation wasn't so big of a deal, nagged at her. It would be so much easier than telling him about Jack, about the feelings that were painting puppies and rainbows in her head. But in the end, on the string of confidence and speaking her mind, she pushed old feelings down in place of this new forward movement.

"I kind of picked up an old piece that I'd started, like, way back in college, and I was working on it one day during lunch and...I don't know, Jack and I just sort of clicked. He offered to help, and here we are."

She shrugged, letting a small smile creep up her cheeks.

"I was kind of stuck on some plot points moving forward, but Jack has been really helpful. I've been on a roll lately. He thinks that I could be ready for professional editing by the end of the summer. It's really nerve-wracking, but I'm excited."

James mulled over her words, sliding his fingers back and forth along the arm of the couch. With his eyes trained on the TV, he mulled over his words carefully before he spoke.

"So, this...Jack guy...is he legit? I mean, I don't want you being taken advantage of here, Charlie Kate."

"What are you talking about?"

Her brows knit together now, her body facing the television while she turned her head to face James whose eyes were still on the game.

"Well, you're literally working in the middle of show business now. Are you sure he isn't going to take your idea and run with it?"

"You mean my idea for a *children's book*?" she scoffed, the annoyance now twisting her features. "Yes, James. He's going to steal my silly little idea for a picture book and plaster it all over the big screen."

"Well I don't know," he shrugged nonchalantly. "I mean, you've known this guy for what, like, a few weeks, and he already knows more about this whole other part of your life than I do?"

"Where is this coming from?"

He let out a huffy breath, ignoring her comment, but not quite knowing where to go from there. They sat in terse silence then, watching the baseball game, but barely paying any real attention as Chris Sale struck out the side.

"What do you mean, *where is this coming from*?" he asked, finally turning to face her. "It's coming from the *I don't want you getting taken advantage of* part of me that's always been here. I just want to make sure that you're being safe about this, that's all. I don't want you turning into one of these stories about people getting taken a ride for in Hollywood, Charlie Kate."

His concerns were legit as she tossed the words around in her head. But at the same time, she was working with professionals. He saw that, didn't he? Didn't he trust her to take precautions and understand right from wrong?

"While I appreciate your concern, I'm sure I'll be fine. I'm a big girl. I can take care of myself."

Although he let out a loud sigh that made his shoulders hunch up and down, the tension clearly wasn't dissipating anytime soon.

"Good. Just as long as he keeps it professional."

He seemed to be all eyes on the television then, his mind wandering elsewhere, but Charlotte was suddenly at a crossroads. They told each other everything. Always. And as hard as that could be, dates were always included. Taking a deep breath, she let the truisms continue to tumble.

"Actually, James, he...we have a date this Saturday."

She held her breath, her entire body stilled as she braced herself for his reaction. His face, once twisted in anger and offense, now fell into something else entirely, like he was physically panged in the way his mouth fell down at the corners and his eyebrows peaked up on his forehead. That look on his face caught all of the air in her lungs.

It was like his entire body had been knocked down a peg, the way his shoulders drooped, and his knees rose to his chest as he sunk deeper into her couch. If he was trying to hide his reaction, he wasn't doing a very good job of it.

But all too soon, his eyes began to pinch together again, his lips widening into something like a grimace.

"I... really?"

"Yeah. I, um...I told him that my Fridays are reserved, so..."

She covered her nerves well, hiding them in the shrug of her shoulders that masked the shakes, in the giggle in her throat that stopped her words from trembling. There was no reason to be nervous. Why was she so nervous?

He took a minute to absorb the new information, to process exactly what would be happening in just a few short days, before speaking.

"Yeah but, you barely even know this guy."

Her body ran hot, but now for different reasons, as James continued to let it pour.

"You met him, what, like a few weeks ago? He *all of a sudden* has interest in your writing, and now he wants to have dinner with you? Something about this sounds off."

"We're going to the boardwalk, actually," she replied, clenching her fists and grinding her teeth, doing her best not to explode at him. "And what the hell sounds *off* about any of this? Of *course* I barely know him. How else are we supposed to *get to know each other*? That's kind of how dating works, James."

"Oh, you're *dating* now?"

His voice was rising as his body turned, anger clear in the pink that rose up his collar.

"I... I don't know! We haven't even gone out on *one* yet, but...why are you getting so angry about this? What the hell?"

"Because I'm looking out for you, Charlie Kate!" He exploded now, his long arms wavering to either side as he let it all rip from his lungs. "You have this track record of picking out real shitty guys, and no matter how much I try to point it out to you, you always end up coming to me to cry. I'm just trying to stop it before the tears this time."

It wasn't the truth that stung. He was entirely right. She didn't have the greatest history when it came to picking men. He *did* often try to point out their flaws. Of course he was always there to pick her up when she fell.

But it was the harsh nature of his words, the way he was saying *I don't want to have to do this again* and *Get yourself together* and *Do I really have to keep piecing back the shambles of your life?* that had her jaw set, dual parts in anger and to hold down the knot in her throat that was ready to rip open the floodgates.

She could see it in his eyes though. The clarity of the words he'd just said hitting him square in the face. The way he absorbed the pain in her eyes. The way it seemed as though, just for a moment, he wanted to take it back. But she was done.

"You should go."

Her words were hollow, almost dead, with no trace of emotion, the same as her eyes.

"What?"

"I think...you should just go, James. I want to be alone. I have a lot of work to do. Can you just...I think you should go."

It all stuck in his throat.

Oh my god, I'm a grade-A asshole.

I didn't mean a goddamn word of it.

Let me know how your date goes.

I hope you have fun.

If you need me, for anything, call me, no questions asked. You know I'll always be here for you, no matter what.

But by the time it collided with, *Don't go on a date with him,* and *I don't want to see you with other people,* and *I think I'm falling in love with you all over again,* his words amounted to nothing but puffs of air that he couldn't even justify as grunts.

Instead, he palmed the back of his head, stood awkwardly, and made his way slowly to the front door. She usually stood to walk him, never minding the fact that her couch was but ten feet away from the front door. Tonight, she stayed on the recliner, her body wrapped in a ball with her knees tucked into her chest and her arms wrapped around her legs. Her chin rested between her knees. Her eyes stayed on him.

The burning in her irises as they singed holes straight through him caused bile to rise in his throat and scald every word he hadn't had the courage to say.

May 2008

Despite her constant refusal to participate in social norms when it came to high school, Charlotte was really, *really* excited about prom. Even more so, she was excited about the prospect of going to prom with James. She hadn't yet opened up and told him about the mounting feelings that had been growing since childhood. He hadn't asked her outright with flowers and a string quartet. They weren't about to be voted "Cutest Couple" in the senior superlative awards. But in the back of her mind, she was secretly hoping that he wouldn't have a date, and that they would just go together, best friends finally trekking down the road into something more.

At the front of her mind, she played endless scenarios in her head about him professing his love for her and begging her to be his prom date. But those she reserved for late at night when she was trying to fall asleep, her thoughts protected by the blanket of night.

Over the course of their high school careers, she'd watched him date exactly five different girls, and with each one, she let the jealousy and the hurt fill a little more closely to the brim.

Ashley Sullivan was by far the bitchiest, some fluke of her being a cheerleader and James being the only freshman on the JV baseball team that put them all through two months of torture.

Jessica Anderson only lasted three weeks, because she had a history of cheating, and despite Charlotte's warnings, he refused to see past the blonde hair and cleavage, and twenty-two days later, he was on her couch nursing his broken heart with a pint of ice cream, a pout, and an *I told you so*.

Bianca Esposito wasn't terrible, actually. But her father had scared the living daylights out of him, and half the block, when he'd caught them making out in the front seat of James's car before he dropped her off. That relationship was parentally ended, and maybe for the better.

Quiet Emily Abbott was probably Charlotte's favorite of the bunch. She was nice, and incredibly shy at first, until she began to warm up to the idea of her boyfriend essentially having two different families on the same block. Once she warmed up to Charlotte, the two

105

would trade secrets until James walked into the room, and Emily would grow quite red in the face and stiffen up. They broke up because Emily was insecure about Charlotte, in the end. It was never something she quite understood.

His latest, Taylor Jernigan, had stormed out of the Ramsey house exactly 19 days ago, upset with James for picking *something* over her *for the last time.* According to James, it was the Red Sox. Later that night, when Charlotte was on the couch in the Ramsey's living room waiting for James to return from the bathroom, Abby had sidled up next to her and whispered, "It wasn't about the stupid game. They were fighting about you," before disappearing as quickly as she'd come.

Now, at the beginning of the end of all things *childhood*, she had a vision in her head, one that had been brewing since she was fourteen years old and his eyes were shy behind the mop of hair that she thanked God everyday his mother had made him cut, and he was kissing her in her front hallway. This was *right. They* were *right.* And prom was the perfect time to let him know.

"So, do you have a date for prom yet?" James asked, his mouth full of French fries as he dipped yet another into their shared ketchup.

"You ask me that like I keep secrets from you," she retorted with a snort and the cock of an eyebrow. She was right. They told each other everything. "But no. I don't."

Her shoulders drooped, her eyes focusing now on the table as she asked him, "What about you? Have you decided which of your hundreds of suitors will be the lucky winner of *Win a Prom Date with James Ramsey?*"

It was his turn to snort as he watched her draw lines on her plate with ketchup and fries.

"Very funny," he trailed off. "Actually, I, uh...I don't think I'm going to go to prom."

"James Ramsey! You *can*not be serious! You're *going* to prom." It was the most expressive she had been since they sat down to lunch. When they had first arrived, she'd put her head down flat and whined for at least ten minutes about how her calculus teacher was *out to get* *her.*

"Oh really?" he quipped, wide-eyed. "Is that so?"

"James, come *on*. It's our senior year. We've been waiting for this moment, like...since we were five!"

"Correction, Charlie Kate. *You've* been waiting for this moment, like, since we were five."

She scowled at his mockery, taking only a moment to hold the grudge before pressing on.

"You can't *seriously* be considering *not* going to our senior prom. Come on, you aren't really going to leave me hanging, are you?"

When her lips curled into a downward pout, he dropped his head in an attempt to hide his smile.

She was so damn cute.

He picked up his head and sighed.

"C'mon, don't do that. You *know* I'm not into the whole *dress up in a stiff suit to awkwardly dance with a bunch of sweaty people in the middle of a banquet hall* thing. I can see how it's fun for girls, but for us guys? It's downright *torture*."

She rolled her eyes with a smile and stole a fry from his tray.

"Unless, I guess, you're spending the dance with the right person, that is…."

His words trailed into the bumble of the cafeteria, his gaze avoidant as he cradled his cheek in his palm again. When he gazed into her eyes, he was hoping that she could read him, would see past his ploy of *Maybe we could spend it together, but we've never done this before, so I don't know how to tell you how I'm feeling.*

But her response had his heart sinking, his lips faltering if only slightly.

"James, is that what you're worried about? That you won't find a date?"

He shrugged and stared down at his empty plate.

"Come on, Rango. You know you can get *any* girl in the state of Massachusetts to go to prom with you. Who can resist the Ramsey charm?"

He chuckled and raised a wary eyebrow, clearly impervious to the

107

charm she spoke of.

"Oh, is that right? You think I'm cute, don't you, Charlie Kate?"

When he waggled his eyebrows and moved his face closer to her across the table, she widened her gaze and shoved him playfully on the shoulder.

"Stop it," she giggled, rocking back to her own seat. "James, come on. You *have* to go to prom. This is our last big moment before we're done with high school and like, out in the *real world*. I can't even imagine not having you there with me."

Underneath his budding feelings and his pain of assumed rejection, this was still *Charlie Kate*. She was right. He'd kick himself if he missed this, if they didn't get to do this together.

"You don't even have to have a date," she continued, pleading her case. "We can just, like, go to make fun of all the losers who spent a ton of money on slutty outfits and stretch limos and had to take awkward pictures on their front lawns."

"You say that like Linda and Julie *aren't* going to insist that we take awkward prom photos together on your front lawn," he chuckled.

Her eyes widened with a shake of her head.

"Oh my god, you're right. They totally will."

He rolled his eyes, a *Duh* clear in his expression.

"But I'd rather do something like that with *you* than with, like, some rando."

He sighed, picking pieces off of his Styrofoam plate.

"Yeah, but, come on Charlie Kate. You can't sit here and tell me that you *don't* want all of that."

When she scrunched her eyebrows in confusion, he took a breath and pressed on.

"You *want* the fancy dress and the pictures down by the pier. You *want* to have to beg your dad for money to go in a limo instead of taking your crappy car. You *want* to slow dance to 'Don't Wanna Miss a Thing.' Convince me that I'm wrong."

He sat back in his chair, leaning on the two back legs, while his arms crossed his chest and his eyebrows shot up, screaming *Try me*.

She frowned, first in frustration, but then in sadness. He had pegged her, alright. She blew out a breath and shifted her gaze from one side of the table to the other.

"What I *want* is one last night to spend with my best friend where we can just be stupid kids and not spend time talking about college or moving out or being in the real world. I just want one more night of us being *us* before we...I don't know...grow up."

He could sense the pleading in her voice, but also hesitancy about the list of fears she had just bulleted. So, shoving his own frustrations aside, he grabbed her shoulders from across the table and donned a serious expression.

"Hey. Just because we're graduating high school doesn't mean we're going to stop being *us*. Charlie Kate, we'll *always* be best friends. We'll always be there for each other. Sure, we're going to change along the way, but I shot up four feet between fifth and sixth grade, and I'm still the same old James. Nothing's going to change."

She shrugged, offering him a small smile, but he could still see the reluctance in the pull of her eyebrows.

"I'll tell you what. Let's make a deal: If neither of us can find a prom date by Friday, we'll go together."

It was like the flick of a switch, the way her head snapped, and her eyes lit up, and her smile was positively beaming.

"Really? You'll go? You promise?"

"Scout's honor."

He held up his fingers in pledge, crossing his heart with his free hand.

At this, Charlotte stood, rounded the table in a quick, swift motion, and pulled him into a tight hug, one that had his nose pressed into her shoulder so hard that it scrunched and hurt just a bit. But he didn't mind.

With the heat in his chest rising, he held on just a little bit tighter.

When she pulled away, her eyes were still shining, her teeth flashing, as she asked, "You know what this means, right?"

He found himself stranded outside of dressing rooms in the Chestnut Hill Mall well into the late afternoon. But as Charlotte paraded around in dress after dress, he realized that there was no place he'd rather be.

He offered suggestions, often pulling things that were either too gaudy or too obnoxious or way too skimpy—things that he *knew* her father wouldn't let her out of the house in, anyway—and it turned into an afternoon filled with more laughter than words.

Once she began to model serious choices, he saw the timidness creep into her cheeks, the blush of embarrassment when her body was on display in long cuts and necklines that weren't her everyday style. But it took his breath away, and continued to do so, as she tried on one dress after another.

The blue was a navy shade, not shiny and loud like royal blue, but more muted, still rich and deep and everything right to bring out her skin tone and the sparkle in her eyes. The way that her hair fell had her curls bouncing on shoulders that were bare aside from a thin spaghetti strap. The silver accents along the V-pattern down the front made him think about the stars against a clear night sky over the lake house during the summer.

He must have looked like a stunned idiot, sitting on a bench with her purse next to him and his jaw in his lap and his eyebrows in his hairline. But she was so, so beautiful that he couldn't think of anything else to say or do.

When her lips curled up, still shy under timid eyes, he did the same, his gaze telling her everything she needed to know.

By the time she had shoes and earrings, it cost half of her Cabot's paycheck, but it was all worth it.

"I could've bought us tickets in the grandstand at Fenway for the same price," she tried complaining as he drove them home.

"While I'm not about to *argue* with that," he began, giving her a sideways glance, "I will say that you're going to enjoy this purchase a lot. So... stop complaining."

She rolled her eyes and adjusted her purse on her lap.

"You look really, really pretty in that dress anyway."

His voice was so quiet, she wasn't sure if she'd heard him correctly. But the way his cheeks were blushing when she glanced in his direction affirmed it.

Her *Thanks* was equally as small. His voice only grew when he tacked on, "And it would look pretty silly if you wore a ball gown to Fenway anyway. So."

She chuckled, rolled her eyes again, and turned up the radio.

By Wednesday, she was still dateless, and curious about James's plans for the upcoming dance.

"So, have you decided who you're going to ask yet, or am I going to have to pick someone out of a hat for you?"

He shrugged, recoiling a bit at her suggestion that he *actually take someone to the dance* when a free ride with *her* was still on the table. He only had to make it to Friday.

"I don't see why I even have to ask anyone at all." He swatted her hand away as she tried to snag a fry from his tray. "Besides, I don't see *you* walking around with a free ticket yet."

"That's because no one has asked me," she shrugged, sneaking a fry anyway.

"So? Who said you can't ask a guy?"

"I'm the *girl*, James. *I'm* not asking *anyone*."

"Well, two can play at that game," he retorted, watching her arch her eyebrow. "If *you're* not going to put yourself out there, then *I'm* not going to try, either. I guess we'll just have to go together."

His smile was small, hidden behind his burger. But too quickly, it was wiped away, cut off by her challenging words.

"What, you don't think I can get a date by Friday?"

He scrambled for an apology, but was shot down by her waving hands, and, "Hey, at least I'm actually *trying* to put myself out there instead of sitting on my ass and settling like you are. Just because we have a deal doesn't mean you get to be lazy, James."

"Oh, you're *trying* to put yourself out there?" he scoffed.

"I am." Her voice was smaller now, her eyes avoiding his stare before her words were quicker, more frantic. "I don't know, James. I don't want to, like, *proposition* somebody. I think it would be…" she trailed off, picking at her fingers, seeming to debate the words in her head before her scared eyes met his. "You can't laugh, okay?"

He gave her a small smile, a promise to treat her with respect, a simple nod that said *Go on, I'm listening.*

"I just want to, like, be *wooed* once in my life, okay?"

It was a silly way of putting it, and he wanted to laugh at her word choice, but instead he opted for, "Yeah? How so?"

"Well," she started, staring at the table again, taking her time. "I... I don't know. You always see these, like, big, elaborate gestures in the movies, you know? I think it would be cool to...to mean enough to somebody that they would go out of their way to ask me to prom. It's stupid, isn't it?"

His eyes were warm, his smile reassuring.

"No, Charlie Kate, it's not stupid," he answered, his voice soft and low. "Although, after *all* the time I've spent training you on cinematic culture, I was hoping that you wouldn't be so swayed by chick flicks."

She smiled, shaking her head in jest and letting all of her worries float away with it.

"Okay, so, dream world time," he pressed on. "Let's say some dorky guy was to *very cheesily* ask you to prom. What, uh...what would you want him to do?"

She was so lost in her own thoughts that it didn't even cross her mind that James was fishing for information. She didn't notice that, when she mentioned *some chick flick* where *some guy wrote a song about a girl* and how she thought that was *so cute*, that the wheels were turning in his head, that his fingers were absently plucking chords under the table already.

When the conversation faded from her dateless-ness to his, after she'd asked him, "So who are you asking?" he startled back into reality and thought up a quick cover on his feet.

"I can't just *tell you* who I'm going to ask, Charlie Kate. You have a girl code, and guys have a bro code. Under 'prom' it says *never tell another girl who you're going to ask because she will just open her big mouth and ruin everything.*"

"I do *not* have a big mouth!"

"Oh really? Then where did all of my fries go?"

Charlotte gave him a smug grin and stole another fry.

"Come on, lover boy. I told you mine. Isn't it somewhere in the *best friends code* that you have to tell me yours now?"

He grinned at her pleading eyes but gathered his books and began to stand anyway.

"Oops, that was the bell. I'd better get to class. I guess you'll just have to wait until Friday to find out!"

She tried to follow him down the hallway, but gym and US History were on two opposite ends of the building. She watched the back of his head as he blended into the crowd, only turning around once to wink before he disappeared through the doorway.

The last two periods of the day for James had much less *history and physics* and much more jotting lyrics in the margins of his papers. He had come a long way on the guitar from being eleven years old and not understanding what a tuner was. Charlotte was typically resigned to lyrics duty, but in this special circumstance, he was alone.

Settling on *just write what's in your head* was the best method for his current mission. Not everything rhymed, and it didn't flow perfectly, but that made it all the more special and cheesy, he thought, as his final draft flowed under fumbling fingers late Thursday evening.

He barricaded himself in the basement, away from the wary eyes and ears of his parents and the prying of his kid sister. Thank God Kyle was still away at college. He didn't need them poking their noses into his business. Or worse, having to sit through the reaction that his mother would have when he admitted that he was *finally going to ask Charlotte Murphy on a real date*!

No. *That* he could do without for a few more days.

It was odd, the way the lyrics and the music came to him so perfectly when it was all said and done, flowing so freely from his soul like it had been brewing there all along. He thought it would be hard but was proven wrong as his little chorus bounced between the damp walls of their unfinished basement, tugging his lips into a smile as his anticipation grew, the need for her to hear these words increasing by the chord.

He knew she wanted *cheesy* and *romantic*, but in the end, he was just praying that his unbarred soul was enough.

On Friday afternoon, Charlotte sent James a text that she had an assignment to work on, that he shouldn't wait for her in the parking lot, but that she would be over as soon as she was finished. When Julie Ramsey opened the front door, it was evident that there was something different about Charlotte's tone. His entire body went tingly and warm, his nerves suddenly on edge when he heard her voice bouncing off the walls of the front entryway. He clenched the guitar tightly in his fingers, stalling out the chord he had been strumming, reducing it to a hollowed-out *ping*.

But his features softened, his grin wide and excited when she rounded the corner to approach the couch.

"Hey," he greeted her warmly, standing the guitar up next to the couch to adjust his frame to face her, his words scratchy in his throat.

"Hey." When she returned his greeting, his smile faltered, the shake in her voice and the way her smile didn't quite reach her eyes a cause for alarm.

She still wasn't sitting down on the couch or propping her legs up on the coffee table or tucking her feet underneath her body and stealing the remote. She was fiddling with her fingers and looking at the floor.

He decided to push past it. It was Friday, after all. Maybe she was upset that she'd made it through the last day of their deal without a date and didn't want it to show. Which meant he was going to do everything in his power to make this night, this song, all that much more powerful.

"So, what do you wanna do tonight?" he began, scooting across the couch enough that he hoped she would sit, grabbing his guitar along the way. "I know we haven't really done this in a while, but I started playing this chord progression earlier, and I could really use my lyrics partner to—"

"Joey De Luca asked me to prom."

His heart stopped; his hand froze with the guitar halfway to his lap as his smile dropped.

"I... what?"

"Joey De Luca asked me to prom."

114

It was the first time he'd seen her smile since she walked through his front door. But still, it was tentative, almost seeking his approval before she showed the true excitement that was clearly bubbling beneath the surface.

"What...what'd you say?"

The raspiness in his voice was no longer from nerves or jitters, but from the lump that was crawling up his throat; the heat in his cheeks was nervous for a brand new reason entirely. When she answered, "Are you joking? I said yes!" he felt his body physically sink into the couch, his shoulders pulling down at the same rate that his eyebrows peaked upward.

"James, he's like, the *hottest* guy on the baseball team—no offense—and he's *so* charming, and I...no one has ever...come on, you're my best friend, why aren't you more excited? Be excited with me!"

She was sitting now, her hands warm as they clasped around his cold digits, shaking them in her grasp as she tried to force his mood to change.

He shook his head, doing his best to wipe the utter defeat from his eyes; he couldn't be this down when Charlotte was positively beaming.

"No, I... I *am* excited for you, Charlie Kate, I just...Joey De Luca is kind of an asshole."

Her eyes fell to where their hands were joined, noting the way that his gripped a little tighter.

"Are you sure you want to go to prom with him?"

She pulled her hands slowly from his and rested them heavily on her thighs, her eyes following.

"Are we talking about the same Joey De Luca? The captain of the baseball team? The one who volunteers with the Buddies program in the off season? The one who *put my name into a Shakespearean sonnet* to ask me to prom today?"

"We are talking about the same guy. But you're talking about the suit he wears for the public. He...you girls haven't seen what he's like behind the scenes. The way he talks in the locker room."

He shuddered as post-game talk floated in and out of his ears, doing his best to clue her in without making her want to throw up.

"He's looking for the quickest way to add a notch to his belt, Charlie Kate. The way he talks about...I mean he calls girls his *conquests*. It's disgusting. I don't want you getting wrapped up in that."

She stood, her eyes knit and defensive, her jaw set firm as she formed her retaliation.

"It's *locker room talk*, James. You've never told me about it be*fore*. Why is it all of a sudden relevant *now*?"

"Because *you're* involved now." He was standing now, too, his arms flailing as fury bubbled in his eyes. "I'm not about to let you get mixed up in his sick games. He's a *dick*, Charlie Kate. He doesn't care about *you*, and he never will. He asked you out for his own self-interest. He knows that you're oblivious to his playbook. There's obviously gotta be something wrong with him if no girl in the school has taken him up on his offer this late in the prom-game and he's using you as his last resort. You must be the only naive one left."

He regretted the words as they bounced off his tongue, jerking forward in an effort to stop them from hitting her ears. The look in her eyes, in her face, as she blew backward and clenched her lids shut told him that he was too late.

His, "Charlie Kate, I didn't mean—" did absolutely nothing to cushion the blow of devastation that was etched into the lines in her face, the few tears that made it past her clenched eyes.

"No, James. That's ex*actly* what you meant."

Her eyes were glassy and clouded when she finally opened them, her fists clenched at her sides as she stared right through him.

"No, no, I didn't, I—"

"You know what, James? Maybe next time, instead of being a little bitch about all of this and ruining my *five minutes of happiness,* you could just try being happy for me for once."

Her words were biting, a tone that he typically only heard when she was spouting off about her parents or her siblings. He knew that he had no right to flinch. Instead, he absorbed the blows, taking each punch as it came.

"Or maybe? Maybe you should have just grown some balls and *asked me first* instead of trying to beat around the bush."

She spat the last of her words through a hard line of teeth, spun on her toe only after she watched her words slam into him, watched the realization dawn in his eyes, and moved swiftly to walk right back out his front door.

By the time he was able to react, to grab her by the bicep and say, "Hey, wait," she was yanking her arm from his grip and moving her legs more quickly down his porch steps.

He called her name once more, with his hands clasped behind his head as he saw her move swiftly down the sidewalk, the backs of her hands wiping at her eyes.

Still, he waited to see her disappear around the bend towards her own street, waited the four and a half minutes he knew it would take her to get home before sending a text that said, *I'm so sorry. I know you don't want to talk to me right now, but can you at least just let me know that you made it home?* even though their neighborhood had no plausible threats, especially at five o'clock on a Friday in April.

Her *I did* came shortly after, adding one final blow before his own angry tears pricked his cheeks.

He stormed inside the house, slamming the front door on his way up the stairs, ignoring his mother's qualms of *Be careful with my doors!* before she followed him up the stairs, standing outside his slammed and locked bedroom door with a quiet *Sweetheart, are you okay?*

He didn't answer, his face buried in the pillow that he had his arms wrapped tightly around. He screamed his frustration and stupidity and jealousy into the cottony fabric.

Charlotte waited until she crossed the threshold of the Murphy house before the angry tears turned fat and sad. The sob that hitched in the vaulted ceilings of the entryway gained the attention of her mother, who followed her up the stairs, similarly coming to a locked bedroom door.

Her excuse of *I have a lot of calculus homework* and *No, James and I are just going to hang out at the dance tomorrow* didn't fool

117

Linda Murphy though, who waited outside of her daughter's bedroom door, her heart breaking with each muffled cry.

Charlotte pulled a picture off of her nightstand, one of herself and James from the regional baseball tournament two seasons ago. She was on his back with her head resting on his shoulder, their faces touching at the cheek in their signature pose. He was covered in dirt from head to toe, a day full of diving across the field to knock down balls and sliding into bases sure to annoy his mother come laundry time. He was holding her up underneath her thighs; her arms were wrapped tightly across his chest, almost obscuring his first-place medal.

Glancing at the photo, she bit her lip, choked back another sob, and hurled it angrily across the room. It landed on the carpet with a soft *thud* that wasn't at all satisfying, so she began to chuck the various stuffed animals on her bed along with it. When she got to the bottom of her pile, a plush monkey halted her throw. It was rainbow patterned, and the hands connected with a square of Velcro. Attached to its ear was a gift tag that she had yet to remove from her 13th birthday, when she'd begged her parents to take her and a few friends to Six Flags. Despite being the only boy aside from David, James had had a pretty good time.

He spent all of the cash his mom had sent him with trying to win her that monkey.

She read *Happy Birthday, monkey! Love James*, hugged it to her chest, and let the tears pull her into a restless slumber.

Some hours later, with her head throbbing and her eyes burning and dry, she awoke to a ruckus outside of her bedroom window. She overlooked the front door and snuck, still half asleep, to the window to pry.

"Mrs. Murphy, can I please go up for five minutes? I just need to see her. I want her to know how sorry I am."

"I think you should go home tonight James. You're both upset. You can talk to her tomorrow."

From her perch on the windowsill, with her nose scrunched to the screen, she saw his head fall, his hands fly to the back of his head the way that they always did when he was uncomfortable.

She had to strain to hear his next words, so small and defeated.

"I just...I care about her so much. I was just trying to look out for her. I'm really sorry, Mrs. Murphy."

She saw her mother's arm extend from the doorway and reach out to squeeze his shoulder.

"I know, James. I do."

He turned to leave then, trudging down the front steps with his head still down. But when he got about halfway down the walkway, he stopped, turned his head, and directed his gaze to her window.

It wasn't hard to find. She had a Wally the Green Monster cling suctioned to the glass.

Her eyes were peeking through the blinds, her fingers poking through the slits to hold on.

Their gazes locked in heat, surprise. Finally falling to sorrow and regret, she blinked, adjusted herself at the window, and watched him go.

The truth was, she *didn't* want to go to prom with Joey De Luca. She wanted to go with James. Maybe the thought of someone else asking her would egg him on or something. But that plan had failed, shattered into a million pieces along with her heart and her head and everything she thought she had pegged about him and his feelings for her.

It was rounding on nine o'clock before she made her presence in the kitchen, donning pajamas. Her mother was predictably asleep on the couch, her father tuned into the evening news. She warmed up a plate of pizza, leaning against the countertop as she sighed into the tasteless melted cheese.

"So, you gonna tell me what's going on?"

Her older sister Kelly, home from her senior year of college, had snuck up on her.

So much for getting in and getting out without being noticed.

Charlotte sighed, putting her plate in the dishwasher and fishing in the refrigerator for a can of Sprite.

"Come on, Charlotte. You can't keep it inside forever. I could practically hear him sniffling as he left the house."

Kelly was more forward than David, usually getting right to the point rather than beating around the bush. It wasn't an approach that Charlotte responded to. She needed time to process, and she just wasn't there yet.

"I'll get over it, Kel," she said, rolling her eyes. "Just...we need to cool down."

"You know what you need to do?" Kelly pressed on, crossing her arms as her sister crushed the can and headed to the recycling bin. "You need to tell him you like him already. Enough of this little dance that the two of you have been doing since the fourth grade. Rip the Band-Aid off, Charlotte. Or," she paused, the shock in Charlotte's eyes enough of an indicator that Kelly needed to stop, "decide that it's never going to happen and *move on*. Go to prom, have fun with this *hot guy* that asked you, and forget about it."

With that, Kelly grabbed a beer from the fridge and disappeared to the den.

After returning to her room, Charlotte hugged her knees as she sat atop her comforter, leaving four different texts from James untouched.

4:53 PM
I'm an asshole, Charlie Kate. A royal asshole.

5:47 PM
I deserve the silent treatment. I just want you to know how much I hate that I'm the one who made you sad this time.

8:32 PM
Listen, I'm on my way over. Can we talk? I just need to tell you how sorry I am.

9:22 PM
I know this is wasted by now, but I hope your night got better. I hope you don't go to bed upset. Not even because of me. I hope I'll see you tomorrow.

The two options that her sister presented were suddenly blinking, looming in the empty space between the floor and the ceiling.

Rip the Band-Aid off or move on.

She wasn't sure which would hurt less.

The next day, as Charlotte stared at her reflection in the vanity mirror, with Mom doing her best to tame her curls with a hot iron, her smile failed to reach her eyes. She should've been giddy with excitement about the night ahead, but instead, after a few texts exchanged with Joey about where his group was taking pictures and what color tie he should wear, she was almost dreading having to put on the dress that hung on the back of her door. In her mind, the only reaction she wanted to that dress was the one that James had given her when she had stepped out of the dressing room.

She glanced around the vanity table, eyeing the foundation and eye shadow her sister had picked out, her eyes eventually landing on a framed photo from their seventh-grade dance. She wore a purple puffy dress, the skirt thick with tulle, her smile large behind braces that matched. James, going through a growth spurt, towered over her by at least a foot and a half, his black shirt and purple tie not quite fitting right. His tongue was sticking out to the side.

Her smile was sad, the constant reminder to *not ruin your makeup* the only thing preventing her from crying again.

It took James all of ten minutes to change into his dress pants and button down, tie on a tie, slap on some cologne, and run product through his hair to tame it enough for the inevitably hot dance floor. Without a date to tend to, his mother settled for pictures in their front yard under the blossoming tree that always served as a background to family photos. One of him and his sister, one of him and his parents, and several of his mom trying to pin on a boutonniere that she had picked up at Wegman's despite his every protest.

He drove over to the house of one of his baseball buddies, opting to tag along with them and their dates in favor of showing up completely alone.

He was sitting at a round table in the banquet hall, swirling cherries around the glass of his kiddie cocktail, when the air in the room changed, pulling his attention towards the doorway.

She looked even more radiant than the day that she had tried the dress on, her curls billowing and smooth, her skin glowing undoubtedly under products from Kelly's makeup bag.

Their eyes met, and he watched hers go wide in shock, her head twitching slightly before she softened. Her eyes were sad. His were full of apologies.

He was about to stand, to cross the throngs of high school students and circular tables and bunches of balloons, to gather her in his arms and apologize until his lungs were blue. But as his long legs stretched his body into a standing position, his teammate appeared behind Charlotte with a possessive arm around her waist. She shrugged towards James, the gesture sort of saying *Really, what did you expect?*

Despite his best efforts to make the most of his seventy-five-dollar ticket, James's attention was entirely warped by Charlotte and Joey. He watched their table intently, scrutinizing every smile and frown and twitch of her face, analyzing from four tables over if her smile was meeting her eyes, or if her laughter was genuine or forced. He was on his seventh kiddie cocktail when dinner was wrapping up and ballots for homecoming king and queen were being collected and tallied.

When *Joey De Luca and Charlotte Murphy!* were announced, his heart simultaneously burst and pulled inside his chest. The only thing to catch him, to make him stop biting the inside of his lip and feeling sorry for himself, was the glow in her eyes, the way her smile stretched to her ears. It didn't take much. He would always thrive on her happiness.

As per tradition, the king and queen shared the first dance before the rest of the patrons joined them on the dance floor. When he saw her gazing up into Joey De Luca's eyes and laughing and playfully shoving him while he hugged her more tightly, he forced himself to look away, to go and grab another kiddie cocktail and add to the graveyard of empty glasses and cherry pits that he had already collected throughout the night.

As the music changed over to upbeat pop and hip-hop beats, he joined a group of friends and did his best to have fun, despite his lack of dance coordination. It was a nice distraction until he realized that

Charlotte and Joey were missing from the dance floor. When he turned to face the banquet hall, he noticed them over by the fondue table, evidence of an argument in their expressions, in the way she was crossing and uncrossing her arms and yanking her body backwards the longer that Joey spoke.

It was pure instinct for him to immediately cross the room, to push past people as he began to hear the blood rushing in his ears while his face ran red. The clips of the conversation that he heard as he crossed the distance between them made his blood boil.

"I *said* I'm not leaving, Joey."

"Listen, princess. After all I've done for you tonight, the *least* you could do is pay me back. Let's get out of here."

Joey's arm wrapped around her bicep tightly, and she yanked with her whole body to free herself from his grip.

"I said *no*."

"God, I have every right to knock that pretty little crown right off your head. Do you think anyone would've even paid a *bit* of attention to you if I hadn't brought you here tonight?"

"Get your hands off of her, De Luca."

It was a tone that chilled her bones, froze Joey to his spot and caused him to loosen his grip enough for Charlotte to wiggle free as James came up beside her and gently pushed her behind his outstretched arm.

"Well, well, well. Look who finally decided to show up. Is Princess Pussy here to rescue his damsel in distress?"

"Just leave her alone. This conversation is done."

"Actually, Ramsey, for once in your life, someone *else* has claim to Charlotte Murphy. So I suggest you back off. Let's go, Charlotte."

Joey reminded James of a greaser with his dark hair slicked back and his thick accent making him sound slimy. When Joey tried to move around James, his hand reaching towards a cringing Charlotte, James pushed his body between them even more.

"I don't think so. She isn't a piece of property, Joey. No one has 'claim' to Charlotte except *Charlotte*. And she said no. She doesn't have to go anywhere with you."

"She ain't your date, Ramsey. She's *mine*, and I—"

"What the fuck is your problem, man? You treat girls like shit just to add notches to your belt. News flash, asshole, they're finally starting to catch on. I know it's hard to get denial through that thick skull of yours, but she said *no*. Now back off."

After several shoves of palms on chests, and one or more *You back off, asshole*, the room began to spin.

It was all so sudden, so out of character for James, that it took Charlotte the aftermath of screams and grunts and blood on the floor to realize that he had actually cocked back and punched Joey De Luca in the nose. No sooner was James shaking out his fist in momentary pain than he had Charlotte gently by the shoulder, his words *Come on, I've got you* heavy and deep in her ear as he led her through the backdoor of the banquet hall.

They were barely seated on a stone bench before she was clinging to his shirt front, letting her tears stain the deep blue of his new tie. As she cried, let the firm strokes of his hands reassure her that she was safe, absorbed the way he whispered *It's okay, Charlie Kate, I've got you* and *It's okay, you're okay,* she noticed that his tie matched her dress better than Joey's ever had.

"I'm so sorry, James," she eventually choked out, pulling back enough to look up into his eyes that were nothing but concerning and protective. "I should— I should've lis—listened to you—"

"Hey, hey, stop that." He cut her off, claiming her cheeks in his palms as he tried to steady the way the sobs were making her entire body shake. She latched onto his forearms, her grip tight as his thumbs brushed across her cheeks. "You have nothing to apologize for."

"Y-yes I do. You tried to tell me. You tried...I just *yelled* at you and... I was so selfish—"

"Hey. Stop. Listen to me." His tone was warm, but more firm now, matching his grip. "You didn't listen to me because I went about that whole situation *so* wrong. I... I let myself get jealous and spiteful and I said a ton of things that I regret. You didn't deserve *that* any more than you deserve *this*. I... if anyone should be apologizing right now, it's me. I'm so sorry, Charlie Kate. This...if you're going to blame anyone right now, blame me."

She let out another sob, this one coming through an attempted smile as she squeezed his arms tighter, then wound them around his neck and buried her face in his shoulder. He wrapped his arms around her back and held on for dear life.

"God, I don't know what I'd do without you, James Ramsey."

"Good thing you're never going to have to find out," he whispered back, his lips close to her ears as they reluctantly pulled apart.

Their hands found each other's in his lap, their eyes trained on where their skin met, heat pulsing between them.

"You look so beautiful tonight." His words were low and raspy, though he continued to avoid her gaze. "Just like the Disney princess you always wanted to be."

It was then that he allowed himself to meet her eyes, his smile small and shy and on its way to getting back to being *them*.

She chuckled at the irony of the situation, reaching up with one hand to pluck the crown from her head as the other stayed wrapped in his fingers.

"Yeah...too bad I don't want anything to do with this stupid crown anymore. The one time I'm supposed to be the fairest of them all, and my Prince Charming turns out to be a total asshole."

Gazing out at the small koi pond in the garden where they sat, she flicked the plastic crown and heard it land with a satisfying *plop*. She sighed, watching it bob and eventually sink to the bottom.

"Here, hold on, I have an idea."

Suddenly James was up and moving frantically, plucking flowers from the surrounding area. His fingers worked deftly, and before she knew it, he had tied together a circle of daisies, placing it on her head triumphantly, softly, as he returned to his seat next to her on the bench.

"Still a princess."

His fingers trailed down her cheek softly, his thumb brushing her blushing skin as he lingered there, cupping her face. At that moment, the music inside changed to a slow song, and though it was muted, he stood and extended his hand, bowing at the waist as he said, "Charlie Kate Murphy, will you honor me with a dance?"

"The pleasure is all mine," she replied, her smile small and shy as she curtsied in his direction.

Her head lay on his chest, resting just above his heart, as they swayed gently to the music. His hold around her waist was firm but comforting, his hands clasped at the small of her back. His cheek lay against the top of her head, with her fingers woven around his neck. She could feel his heartbeat quicken under her cheek, could feel her own temperature spike, as she pulled back to see his gaze so intense that his eyes were black as the night sky above.

His eyes flicked downward to her lips at the same moment that she was leaning forward, their breath hot between them. She didn't know if she should keep her eyes open or closed, or if she wanted to grip onto the lapels of his suit jacket like she'd seen all the women in the movies do, or kick her heel up behind her, but she was about to kiss James Ramsey, and she was pretty sure that her heart was going to beat out of her chest before she got the chance to do so.

"Ramsey. Here. *Now*."

It was the principal, Mr. Williams, that ultimately ceased the gesture, cut the tension between them, and left her on edge for the rest of that night.

Both the Murphys and the Ramseys had their nights interrupted by the disciplinary hearing, Charlotte's parents picking her up because of harassment, and James's for fighting. The night ended early, but Charlotte didn't go to bed upset this time.

On Monday after school, Charlotte headed straight for James's house, letting herself in the front door with his homework in tow. He had an Xbox controller in hand and his socked feet propped up on the coffee table when she plopped down next to him.

"I'm sorry I got you suspended." She shrugged, watching his lips curl up, the game on pause as he turned to face her.

"You got me out of school for three days, Smalls. I should be *thanking* you."

She giggled, remembering the text he had sent her on Sunday after talking with his parents and the principal and the athletic department heads. Despite the circumstances, his actions were still violent. But compared to Joey's week of suspension, sensitivity counseling, and indefinite suspension from the baseball team, this was a cake walk. His mother didn't condone violence, but his father was proud of the way he'd stood up for Charlotte. All things considered, three days of house chores wasn't the worst punishment in the world.

"And besides, I wouldn't take back what I did to Joey for a second. He deserved everything he had coming to him. More, probably."

Her expression changed from light giggles to serious lines as she thrust her body across the couch and wrapped her arms around his waist.

"I love you, James."

He gulped as he instinctively wrapped his arms around her, holding her to him tightly. When he said, "I love you, too," it meant so much more than he was letting on.

They pulled away slowly, the same way they had two nights before, with hands tickling down one another's arms until they were clutched between the pair. He winced a little, and Charlotte's brow furrowed in concern as she took his right hand gingerly in her palm and lifted it to her face.

"This looks like it hurts," she began, doing her very best to keep her voice steady.

James gulped again, his fingers shaking in her grasp.

"Uhm, it's not too bad. Coach is just happy it isn't broken," he replied, his voice thick and raspy.

She brushed her thumb over the raised red and purple skin of his knuckles, taking her time to inspect the injury he had incurred to defend her honor. She was brought back immediately to the way he held her as they danced, the look in his eyes when they'd pulled back, the buzzing between them when his lips had been so close.

It was her turn to be brave now.

She lifted his hand slowly to her lips, taking her time to kiss each knuckle softly, enough so that he could feel it without causing pain. But indeed, his skin was on fire, burning underneath her lips as she moved from one finger to the next. When she got to the last one, she lifted her eyes to meet his that were now glassed over in a daze. As she let his hand fall to his lap, she used her fingers to push the unkempt hair from his eyes, her thumbs running down his jawline, before angling her body towards him.

They met in the middle in a shower of sparks, despite how gentle the kiss was, how timid they were being as their lips finally touched. It wasn't until they pulled away, recognized the fire in one another's eyes, that they were diving back for an unquenchable fill of lips parting and meeting, sighs beginning to fill his living room, hands on cheeks and shoulders and clutching around backs in a fury.

When she began to shift, to hook her bent knee over his lap, he finally pulled away, opened his eyes to truly *look at her* for the first time. Her face was flushed and pink all the way down her neck, disappearing past the cotton V of her collar. Her eyes were large and dark. It was the fact that this desire in her eyes was all for *him* that made James close his eyes and think for a second.

With his fingers running through the curls on either side of her head, his eyes blinking under hooded lids, he somehow managed to form the words, "Hey, we're uh...we're kind of in the middle of my living room."

Though both of his parents worked, and his brother Kyle was away at college in Colorado, and his sister Abby had soccer practice until 6:30, there was still that thought in his head that *somebody* would walk in. He didn't want to stop by any means of the word, but he had to be the one to think clearly, as she was already trailing her fingers up and down the front of his T-shirt in a way that made him want to carry her far, far away, where they were the only two people in the world.

"Yeah...right," she began, clearly struggling with speech, her fingers dipping dangerously lower on his abdomen. "I... can we...go upstairs?"

They were the words he hadn't wanted to make out of fear that she would pull away, but his chest swelled then, his face heating at her request. He nodded slowly as he leaned in to kiss her once more, tenderly, before pulling her up softly by the hands.

She had been in his bedroom more times than she could count, had seen it transition from boyish cartoony baseball wallpaper into something more modern-day-teenager. But as she crossed over the threshold and was greeted in the mid-afternoon daylight to the bedspread with different shades of blue and the sports and rock band posters and the hamper overflowing with dirty laundry, something about the air felt different.

He sat on the edge of his bed, gently pulling her with him so that they sat next to each other. He ran his hand over her curls, traced her jawline, and then pulled her softly by the chin until their lips met again, this time back to that slow wave of exploration. It was some time before he let his hands dip to her waist, pulled her towards him, shifted her legs so that they were flung over his lap. Her fingers closed more tightly around the fabric of his T-shirt when his tongue touched her bottom lip, a gasp opening her mouth to him as they began to explore more of each other.

It was Charlotte who tugged them down, lying next to one another. Her fingers tangled in his hair, scratching and massaging lightly, a gentle hum buzzing in his throat.

He stopped each time his fingers wanted to go further, their communication all eyes and looks and frantic nods of the head as he dipped underneath her shirt, tickled up her spine. When she clawed at his belt, he put a sizable distance between them, their lips parting with sighs and a distinct *pop*, wanting so badly to give into the chase that she made when she crawled immediately to him and claimed his lips.

"I... I don't want to make you...do you want to slow down?" he managed between the assault of her lips, her fingers still reaching for him.

She was shaking her head, but he needed to hear her say it, to vocalize the want that he could see in her eyes.

"No. No, I don't want to slow down. I want...*James*."

His name was a pleading cry on her lips, and he bit back a moan as he covered her body with his and let his tongue dip past her lips in a new wave of hunger. As her hands became more frantic, ridding him of his shirt and jeans, leaving hot trails along his bare skin, he had to play catch up, tossing her shirt off when it was interfering with the skin that his lips could reach.

When she was moving beneath him, twitching almost impatiently, he pulled his lips from where they had been ravishing her neck, and kissed her eyes, her cheeks, her nose, before forcing her to look at him.

"I...do you want this?"

Her immediate *Yes* was all it took for him to fumble in the bedside table drawer, cover her body with his, and show her how much he loved her with every fiber of his being.

She lay in his arms after, her damp hair stuck to the sticky skin of his chest, as his breathing began to resume its normal rhythm under her cheek. Her fingers roamed the tufts of hair along his chest that she hadn't seen since their annual trip to the lake house the past summer. But even then, she failed to notice the way the hair was just beginning to curl, how it stopped halfway down his abdomen and picked back up around his naval.

Her body, still buzzing and sore, clung to him where her leg was draped across his thighs, where her chest pressed into his side under the weight and force of his grip. While she still wasn't ready yet to meet his eyes, her gaze drifted to the bedside table where the box of condoms was spilled on its side. Chewing her bottom lip, she let her mind wander before his voice, low and gravelly, interrupted her train.

"So, umm…"

She filled his silence with a, "Yeah," of her own, not quite sure where he was going with all of this. He surprised her still when his words were a whisper of concern painted along her ear.

"Are you okay? I didn't...I didn't hurt you, did I?"

His words not minutes ago echoed so similarly, the careful way in which he had told her time and time again, *Let me know if I'm hurting you,* and *Just tell me if I need to stop, okay?* at least a hundred times in a hundred different ways before she was anchoring her feet behind his back and pulling him closer, on the verge of begging.

At this, she pulled herself up so that she leaned on the arm that was tucked around him, using her other hand to cup his cheek and stare, for the first time, into eyes that were knit together in concern, tinged with threatening tears.

"Stop that," she warned softly, her fingers tickling the stubble that he had foregone shaving that morning, stubble that would no doubt leave marks on her skin for her to find later. "You uh...definitely made up for it."

She smirked then, doing her best to squash the rising blush in her cheeks as a wave of embarrassment washed over her and she attempted to bury her face in the crook of his arm. But when she averted her eyes, his strong hands were pulling her right back to him, a sly smirk of his own sending tingles to her core that she wasn't sure she could handle so soon again already.

"You sure?" he asked, smoothing his fingers over her jaw, her cheeks, as he pulled them together so that their noses touched.

"Yes," she breathed, bending lower to kiss him softly, nothing more than a slow peck, before she found her spot nestled against his chest again.

It was some time in their content silence before she found the courage to ask him the biting question.

"So uh...you seem to have been...prepared."

She could feel his head cock, knew that when she glanced up, she would find his eyebrows tented and his lips pursed like a duck. So she lifted her head, angling it towards the toppled over box on his bedside table.

His cheeks flushed red, and she felt his body grow stiff in their embrace as his words tripped over one another on their way past his tongue.

"Oh, that, I...my dad...it was *really* awkward, and he...just in case, you know? But I..."

Suddenly, he was taking a deep breath and adjusting their bodies so that they were laying side by side facing one another. His eyes started at her stomach, flitting up at a tantalizingly slow pace before they met his hands at her cheeks. His touch was so soft that it was barely there, much like his next words that tickled her down to her toes.

"I haven't...with *anyone* else. Charlie Kate, you were..."

She saw tears threatening his eyes again, now such a deep green that it reminded her of a rainforest, calm yet fiery within. She cut off his sentence with her lips, but ultimately let him pull their bodies together, laying in an embrace that was so tight, she wondered if these bruises would be more prominent than the ones left by his lips.

It was a mad dash for clothing when the garage door rumbled underneath his bedroom window, but they were downstairs at the kitchen stools sipping tall glasses of water before Mrs. Ramsey was even unlocking the inside door.

She was always invited to stay for dinner, but after an excuse about homework, Charlotte put her glass in the dishwasher and headed towards the front door, hearing Julie ask James to set the table for dinner.

"I'll be right there mom, I just, I'm gonna walk Charlie Kate out."

His hands were shoved deeply into his pockets as they walked with heads down, seemingly smiling at concrete. When they reached the edge where the pathway to his front porch met the sidewalk, their toes turned to point at each other. When their eyes finally met, their twin grins were smug, a little shy, their skin tinted pink.

"So, uh…"

"Yeah, um, I'll…see you tomorrow I guess?"

She laughed silently, like pushing air out of her lungs, as her gaze fell to where she was toeing the crack between slabs of concrete.

"Yeah, yeah, I'll, uh…I'll bring you your homework after school."

She bit the inside of her cheek, staring up at him again. As she turned to go, he reached out, grabbing her by the bicep. Shock was written in her expression, but it was the hope, the longing in her eyes that gave him the courage to cradle her cheek with his other hand, to run his thumb along her soft skin.

"I'm really glad it was you."

Her smile grew into his hand as she leaned into his touch.

"Me, too."

Now, with both hands cradling her cheeks, he kissed her softly, lips tender and really unmoving as they lingered. He could feel her smile growing underneath his lips.

When he pulled back, just enough to see her, he whispered, "Text me when you get home, okay?" into the space between them. He saw her lips form the word *Kay*, but wasn't quite sure he had heard it as she bit her lip to keep her smile from splitting her sides.

June 2018

He was worried, scared, frustrated. The feelings for Charlotte were overbearing, piling higher by the minute.

The concern filled his days, consumed his thoughts. It also had his girlfriend upset because *James, if you don't tell me what's bothering you, I can't do anything to help!* which, ironically, wasn't doing much to help the situation anyway.

He focused half of his attention on *Charlotte's* worries, on the constant and racking expression that *something just wasn't right in her life.* She was uncomfortable, searching, grasping at straws that just didn't amount. He hated seeing her like this, grappling with life itself for a purpose, when all this time, he thought he could be there to protect her, to be the cog that made the wheel at least move forward.

The rest of his thoughts were swimming in the past, of a different set of hands exploring his skin, a different set of lips telling him for the first time what it was that he liked and didn't like, a different body reacting to his tentative touch, encouraging him to keep going and trusting him entirely.

A different life, one experienced with someone else. One in which, despite every twist and turn, somehow found him back in her arms in one form or another. So why, now, was he over two years into something that wasn't her? What had changed? What had happened?

After that night at the bar, it was the dancing and the drinking and the goddamn *song* that had him waking night after night with a clouded head that wouldn't seem to clear. He was going on two weeks now and his skin still burned where she had touched him, still hummed whenever he closed his eyes to the feel of her body moving against his.

Still sent him back to that summer before college, those summers in between, the nights in their first apartment together when one of them was lonely and the other was an unspoken body to lean on.

Those nights, not weeks ago, when her head on his chest felt like a weight being lifted from his body. Her body moving against his on the dance floor, like they were the only two people in the world, was a breath of air that hadn't been fresh in some time now, despite the life he'd been working so hard to build for himself. Suddenly, it was beginning to feel like a sham, a cover for everything he'd never said.

It only made things worse that she was actually working this summer. He'd become so dependent upon her availability during the summer months, her hours more fluid, making her constantly available to him. But now, with Ginny's team of writers actually on a live set, he was lucky to get a text from her once a day, usually only after he sent something first.

And of course, the big fat cherry on top was the news she had just smacked him square in the face with: She was going on a date.

Part of him wanted to yell, "So what, man? You're in a relationship. She can date other people. You *obviously* are."

But the greater part that always out shadowed his rationality, the counterpoints of *It's always been us against the world* and *No guy is going to treat her like I can* and *I don't want to see her get hurt* caused the sensible side of him to roll its eyes and stomp away in defeat, mumbling something like *Arguing with a stupid person is useless* as it gave up and retreated back into his subconscious.

It gnawed at him, the feelings he had left her apartment with, and left *her* with. They didn't typically leave things on terms this badly, but with all of his feelings being shucked into a blender, he didn't know what else to do, aside from his growing need to see her, to talk things out, to maybe lay it all out on the table.

It was something he needed to do himself, first and foremost, to sort out his own priorities, to dump his brain out in front of him and align all of the pieces. But the ache in his chest was insistent that he dragged her into this, that he ask her why his feelings were turning upside down and sideways all of a sudden, as if she held all of the answers.

It's coming back.

I know I'm with Vanessa, but I don't want you to be with him.

Do you think I should still be with her?

What are we supposed to do?

It was pathetic, really. He was turning into a stage five clinger, anxious to the point of sending her a text and throwing his phone in his drawer, making deals with himself like *Once I finish this expense report, I'll check my messages* and *Make it until lunch, then you can have your phone back, loser.*

It was the same shit he used to pull back in high school with Charlotte, but she was on the receiving end. When she had boy issues, and he would do things like sit on her phone and hide it in the couch cushions to prevent her from checking to see if some nobody had texted her or not.

But then, something would make them forget about their relationship drama, and cell phones would go forgotten long into the morning, when she had her hair piled high on top of her head and syrup all over her face, and he wanted to take a picture, telling her *You look like a dork,* but in reality, knowing that he was taking the picture because *She looked so goddamn adorable.* The *Hey, where's my phone?* would be followed by giggles, pink tinted cheeks when he remembered that she'd shoved her phone in a box of Christmas decorations the night before so that she wouldn't think about *texting Johnny Perrault back again.*

As he fished his phone from his desk drawer and stuffed it roughly into his pocket, he whispered *Get ahold of yourself, you asshole*, and did his best to pay attention to the shareholders meeting that took up most of the afternoon.

But then, someone was comparing a strong sales staff to a pitching staff, and suddenly it was Charlotte, on his couch, with her baseball hat turned backwards as she yelled, "Get Pomeranz out of this bullpen, you assholes!"

Sales numbers, drawing in more investors, *the new guy looks like Sawyer from Lost.*

Charlotte's fists clenched under her chin, a steady stream of fat tears rolling down her face as Jack Shepherd closed his eyes one last time. The moment that a sob finally escaped her lips, he was pulling her to his chest, smiling against her hair as he let her cry, cling to his body, his "It's okay, Charlie Kate's" undertoned with laughter as he held her tightly.

Two men from upper management bickering back and forth.

"If we make this move, it's not going to change our numbers for the better—"

"But it *will* change them for the *good* of the company."

For Good.

"Mom, do I seriously have to wear a tie?"

"Yes, sweetheart. You're going to a musical. Now stop that, you look nice."

Charlotte's twelfth birthday.

Tickets to Wicked *at the Boston Opera House.*

But the smile on her face when she came out dressed in all green, a green that matched his tie and brought out the color in her eyes, made the tie suddenly tighter around his neck.

To this day, he still knew all of the words to "Defying Gravity" and would belt them at the top of his lungs without question when the song came on shuffle.

When they took a short recess, he stood abruptly, taking large strides to find water in the kitchen and run it through his hair, to gulp it by the bottle. His cell phone was barren, the background photo of Vanessa and him from a photoshoot that she'd dragged him to after they had reached two years seeming to mock him.

He gave a curt nod, frustration in his eyes when one of his coworkers had asked, "Hey man, everything okay?"

By the time the meeting was over, he was exhausted from trying to focus on his work while trying at the same time to *not* process everything going on inside his head. He felt bad when he came home annoyed, tired, frustrated, toeing off his shoes and planting his contorted face into his pillow. Because following close behind him was his girlfriend, his wonderful girlfriend, who had the night off because it was Thursday, and wanted to spend time with him.

The double-edged sword running through his mind told the tales of *We'll hang out and I'll be pissed off the entire time, or I'll ignore her altogether*. Neither ended well. But he just didn't have the energy tonight.

He feigned illness, recoiling suddenly when he remembered that *she was a goddamn nurse*, and asked that she just leave him alone. On any other night, he would welcome her warm touch and even enjoy being taken care of. But tonight, he wanted to be left alone.

With his thoughts, if he was being honest.

It was a stretch, but he made some false claim about not wanting to disturb her with his tossing and turning and ended up in the guest bedroom.

With every intention to sit in the dark and sort everything out, he grabbed the blanket from the back of the couch and trudged down the hallway. He was halfway through drawing an imaginary grid in his head of pros and cons columns when he buried his nose against the sheets of the bed and threw his entire stream off course.

She had been the last person to use the blanket, and her soap was still all over the damn thing.

He groaned, loudly enough, apparently, that Vanessa was knocking on the door, asking if he was *sure she couldn't do anything*.

He grunted in response, balling the blanket up and chucking it at the door, pinching his eyes closed with a force that made his head ache even more. But the pain was better than the confusion, he decided, tunneling all of his energy on the pricks behind his eyes, the thump in his temples, the raging pulse in his bloodstream, until he fell into a fitful, restless sleep.

His dreams were more like a cinema of memories, of Charlotte's smile, her wide eyes, her skin beneath his fingertips. But then, it was also Vanessa, her smile warm and her laugh bright on the first afternoon that they had met.

As his subconscious played tricks on him, even Dream James seemed to have a mounting pile of frustration weighing him down like lead.

He awoke early Friday morning to light raps on the door, then light cascading in, the grey shadow of his girlfriend growing menacingly taller as more light flirted with the carpet of the bedroom floor.

"James? Baby, it's six. I'll give you another fifteen minutes before I come check to make sure you're up. Are you going into work today?"

He mumbled some semblance of affirmation but waited until she had closed the door again to reach for his phone.

Nothing.

He scrolled absently through emails and posts on Facebook of people he hadn't spoken to since they graduated high school and college, rolled his eyes at sappy engagement posts, and was finally motivated enough to drag himself to the kitchen to switch on the coffee pot. It was then that he realized it was Friday. Regardless of their long communication drought, he would see her tonight. That made the tension in his shoulders lessen just a little.

After slugging down his breakfast, he drafted a carefully worded text message, one that he deleted and retyped at least four times before finally hitting send.

Hey, Smalls. I'm still feeling terrible about what happened. Let me make it up to you tonight. We can do dinner here, and I'll order in whatever you want. And then I'll put on my best groveling performance. I'm pulling out the big guns, because you deserve them. At this point, I might even end up on my knees.

He didn't quite expect her to text back right away, but as the hours of the morning ticked by, and lunch came and went with no reply, the tightness in his chest grew.

Home was as vacant as his inbox when he returned, and he was slugging back a beer before he was even out of his work clothes, shucking his shirt with half of a bottle gone as it slammed into his bedside table.

When the clock crept past seven, and his beer count totaled four, he dug his phone from its spot between the couch cushions, a new text alert buzzing as soon as his fingers closed around it.

Hey. Sorry for the late response. Been really busy here today. We actually have to stay kind of late tonight to finish a scene. Can I get a rain check? Maybe we can do something Sunday?

It was so unlike her to cancel a Friday night, but even more uncanny for her to be this formal with him. His body, warm and tense and on edge since he'd come home last night, stood from the couch and began to pace. He wanted to call her, wanted to explain himself away and apologize and just *hear her voice*, but he knew she wouldn't answer.

Sunday was far, and he'd have some ground to cover with Vanessa tomorrow night after his less than stellar attitude as of late, but his mind was miles away.

Seven miles away, to be more precise.

It took twenty minutes of chugging water, slapping on deodorant, and changing into something other than old sweats before he was behind the wheel of his car and parked in the visitor's spot in front of her apartment.

He had an extra key. He could let himself in if he truly wanted to. But he felt slimy even thinking of the idea, the word *intrusion* ringing loudly in his ears despite the numerous other occasions where he had done just so.

So he sat, letting alternative rock sift from ear to ear, drumming his fingers to the beat against the steering wheel. An hour passing turned to two, and before he knew it, he was asleep in the front seat.

Long day was a severe understatement, they joked from the parking lot as Charlotte and Jack headed to their cars. It was eleven-thirty, and they were finally getting off after an afternoon shoot demanded extra time and lighting adjustments and mandated dinner because *six hours on set for actors meant legal food breaks*. But they pushed on, finishing the scene long after the sun dipped below the horizon.

Despite the late-night tacos that were brought in by craft services, Charlotte's stomach grumbled as gravel crunched underfoot, and Jack laughed.

"I thought you fed the beast a few hours ago?"

"That was a few hours ago," she retorted with her hand on her hip. "It's a 'round the clock job, taming this one."

She patted her belly, warm despite its cravings, while she watched his head dip down in laughter.

"Well, hey, I'm on my second wind. Wanna swing somewhere and grab a bite?"

"Sure."

It wasn't until she was in her own car and tailing Jack to the nearest McDonald's that guilt began to seep back in.

She'd been distracted all day, her boiling drama with James settling to a simmer in the background while she focused all of her energy on work and keeping up with Ginny. But it was Friday night, and when she awoke to his text message of apology and repair, it took a lot to lock up her phone and ignore it.

The old Charlotte had a knack for running right back, for priding herself on not holding grudges and forgiving everyone. But she was *mad*. She was *angry* at him for making her feel this way, for taking her joy and squashing it like a bug on the windshield. Nowhere in the rules did it state that if your best friend says they're sorry, you have to say "it's okay" right away.

She wanted time. Time to process her anger, to figure out what the hell angle he was coming from, before she really let him back in.

Right now, she wasn't ready to do all of that. She was ready to follow Jack to a late-night snack and enjoy herself rather than spending her Friday night miserable and teary-eyed.

So she pushed the guilt down, and tailed his black Nissan to the Golden Arches.

When the Bluetooth in her car rang, she half expected it to be James in an attempt to make his pleas known despite her claim in an earlier text that they would talk later. But then Jack's voice was filling her car in observation that the lobby was closed, and that they could only order through the drive-thru.

After they both had their meals, she pulled up alongside his car and rolled down the window, giggling at the fact that he already had a handful of French fries.

"This isn't exactly what I had in mind," he chuckled.

"No, me neither," she admonished. "But, hey. I'm not too far from here. Would you maybe want to take it back to my place?"

"I thought you said your Fridays were booked?"

"They were," she began, reaching deep. "But I think I can make an exception."

Her smile wasn't warm and kind, but sly, mischievous. She let *that* feeling bubble atop the guilt and the frustration that James had brewing in her all of a sudden, allowing herself to enjoy the good rather than focusing all her efforts on making sure that James was okay.

But as she pulled into her lot, she was slapped in the face with it all over again.

James's car occupied the visitor spot, the one that she was about to have Jack park in. She noticed that the lights were out, and her face grew hot as she realized that he was more than likely waiting for her upstairs.

On any normal occasion, her heart would beat wildly to see him sneaking in like he lived here. But now, with Jack in tow, she bit her lip both in nervous anticipation and, honestly? A little bit of annoyance.

She'd told him no, for crying out loud. So what was he doing in her apartment?

Upon further inspection, though, as she balanced her soda and food bag on the roof of her car, signaling to Jack to wait, she realized that he wasn't upstairs.

His hair, unkempt and unruly like he'd been digging his fingers through it, stuck to the driver's side window. His mouth hung open, condensation appearing and disappearing in a small oval shape against the glass with his every inhale and exhale.

Despite her frustrations, she couldn't help but shake her head and smile a little.

She rapped her knuckles against the glass, and his head jerked back, eyes widening in confusion as he gained his bearings. As he blinked sleep from his eyes, she crossed her arms over her chest and cocked her head to one side, effectively saying, *What the hell are you doing here?* without so much as opening her mouth.

After stretching his body as far as it would go inside the cabin of his car, he peeled the door open, unfolding his long legs and stretching his arms above his head as his flip-flopped feet hit the pavement.

When his arm stretched behind his head to scratch at his neck, his eyes met the ground, his cheeks reddening in embarrassment.

"Umm...hi."

"Hi yourself." Her tone was edged with annoyance, and she wasn't in the business of trying to hide it tonight. When he didn't respond, she let, "Wanna tell me what you're doing here?" bite the air.

He stalled again, tripping over the strangled sounds stuck in his throat before he finally pieced together a sentence.

"I umm...I just...I wanted to apologize, Charlie Kate. I... I couldn't stand knowing that I had said all of that shit and just...left you like that."

She flinched and blinked as she saw the wide forest shade in his eyes gleaming under true and apparent sorrow. She was so ready to tell him off, to stomp her feet and make this big show of standing up for herself. But something stopped her, this vulnerability in him so raw and open, that her claws retracted.

The anger was still present, but she tampered it down, chose instead to sympathize just enough to ease his pain.

"I... well, thanks, I guess. I mean, I'm still *mad*, James. I..."

She bit her lip, the emotion a sudden onslaught that had tears rushing to her lids. This was the opposite of what she'd wanted, the hitch in her voice and mist in her eyes contrasting the tough front she had been building up for herself all day.

She kicked a rock, staring at the ground instead of looking into that pitiful face, because she knew that if she did, that would be the end.

Instead, she was startled from her thoughts by, "Everything okay?"

Jack's car door closed with a soft *thud* as he approached the couple with a concerned look in his eyes.

"Yeah, everything's fine," she returned with a defeated sigh before realizing the true nature of the triangle before her. She was grateful for the cover of night as her face grew hot. As both men sized each other up and realizations were drawn, she tried to tame the growing nausea in her gut.

"Umm, Jack, this is James. James, Jack."

Her arms waved between the two men before wrapping around her middle, trying her best to hold in her churning stomach. There was a silence, a discernment, before both men extended arms to shake hands.

"Nice to meet you, man," came from Jack, as, "Likewise," came from James, both tinged with a wariness that had Charlotte wanting, momentarily, to swear off men forever and take off running in the other direction until she hit a convent.

"I, umm...I should probably get going then," James said, tripping over his words as he stared at the ground.

"Yeah, okay," Charlotte replied. "Hey, I'll call you tomorrow morning, okay?"

"Yeah, sounds good. And uh, Jack? She's a special one. Don't break her heart on me, okay?"

Despite her irritations, Charlotte didn't miss the mist in James's eyes, the way his voice wavered slightly between words.

"Yeah man, I'll uh, I'll do my best."

Awkward waves were passed between the three as James turned on his heel to slump back into his car, palming the back of his head as he went. When his steel Camry made a left out of the parking lot, Charlotte finally pushed a heavy breath from her lungs, sighing defeatedly, exhaustedly, as she perched her back against the driver's side door of her own car with a resounding *thud*.

"So that was…" Jack began, joining her with slow, tentative steps as he mimicked her position, crossing one leg over the other at the ankles.

"God, I'm so sorry about that."

Charlotte tipped her chin towards the sky, willing the clouds to open and take her somewhere far, far away.

"No, it's okay," Jack chuckled, shaking his head from side to side.

"We just...we got into this stupid fight and... I'm sorry. I didn't know he would be here."

Silence settled atop them like a soft sheet.

With his head cocked to the side, Jack finally asked, "He's your Friday nights, isn't he?"

"How'd you guess?" Charlotte replied, her voice small as she stared at her shoes.

"Just a hunch," he said with a shrug.

There was more silence then, crickets chirping their encouragement in the dark of night as she took another breath and closed her eyes to brace for his reaction.

"Listen, I know I invited you here and—"

"No, it's okay." Jack's voice was a soft chuckle, comforting more than anything. "I think it would be better if I went home. Plus, I wouldn't want to kill the anticipation of getting to see you tomorrow."

Her smile was shy as her shoulders relaxed against the frame of her car. The expression on her face screamed *I'm embarrassed* and *I'm sorry* and *God, I hope this doesn't scare you away.*

But as Jack pushed his palms against the back passenger door, he surprised her by swooping in to plant his lips against hers, his hands cradling her waist gently. A startled *Oh!* squeaked past her lips as *What am I supposed to do with my hands?* bounced around her brain. By the time she had made a decision, he was pulling away, his fingers curving along her skin, leaving a hot trail in their wake.

"I guess a little preview never hurt anyone."

She could only smile warily, the words caught behind her teeth as he scooted the distance to his own car.

After promising to call her tomorrow, Jack was driving off, too.

Her meal went mostly untouched, as she perched on her couch with a steaming cup of tea instead, her mind racing long after Friday night turned to Saturday morning.

June 2018

She was up before dawn, restless about her date and her fight with James and her *feelings* for James and her feelings for Jack and the whole mess inside her head, which had Charlotte peeling her tired eyes back while the sky was still grey and the birds were just waking up themselves.

It took hours of tossing and turning to finally admit defeat before she pulled herself out of bed and sulked in a bowl of cereal instead, deciding to save her shower for closer to date time. She chewed her fingernails in between pages of *Something Borrowed* before deciding that nine-thirty on a Saturday was late enough to call without waking him up.

He answered on the first ring, as if he'd been waiting.

Their *Hey's* were both soft, shaky even, and it took a round of *How long have you been up?* and *Being an adult kind of sucks sometimes* to get them to the root of the phone call.

"Charlie Kate...I'm so sorry," he began, the pang in his voice true. "I was...I'm an *ass*, okay? There's really nothing more to it. I shouldn't have said what I did. I shouldn't have shown up at your place last night. I've been doing everything so wrong lately. I just...I don't like fighting with you. I never have. I hate that what I said was so, *so* wrong, Charlie Kate, that I was the cause of your pain."

"You kind of hurt me, James."

"I know. It's just...I don't know, Charlie Kate, it's...still hard sometimes."

His voice trailed off, and he was quick to form new words before she could stop and ask.

"Your brother said something when Emma was born, that no man would ever be good enough for you, and you know how much I agree with that. I guess I just see Joey and Scotty and all of the guys who have caused your heart to break, and I don't want that to happen again. I hate seeing you hurt. It...it hurts me, too."

It was hard to hear him so vulnerable and open without seeing his face. In all that she was trying to process, in all of the ways he had hurt

147

and confused her in the past week, she still wanted to throw her arms around his neck and make sure he was okay, too.

"Yeah...I guess...I mean...thanks for apologizing. And, honestly, I wasn't planning on...seeing Jack last night. We got out of work late and it just sort of...happened."

She wasn't sure why she was apologizing or defending or whatever it was, but the words were tumbling out of her mouth, mocking her *moving forward* and *standing up for herself* by the letter.

"No, that's okay. I... you shouldn't have to apologize for wanting to hang out with your...with Jack."

His admission helped her to gain a bit of ground, smoothed the cracks in her confidence, as she let herself settle into getting *them* back.

"So. All ready for your big date tonight?"

"I'm kind of incredibly freak out nervous, actually."

"Oh, come on. He's obviously already head over heels for you. You should've seen the look he had in his eyes when he got out of the car."

"Yeah, well, maybe if I wasn't so distracted by the sleeping hobo in the parking lot, I would have."

Their chuckles were timid, but still present, which made her feel loads better about the situation.

"Hey, but seriously, call me if you need anything. *Anything*. If you guys have one too many and I have to haul both of your asses home, I'll do it."

"Thanks, Rango."

"Anytime, Smalls."

In retrospect, a Saturday afternoon date was almost worse than the nagging she would have to endure through skipping one Friday night with James.

Now, waking before nine, she had simply too much time to kill, which only translated into *simply too much time to overthink*.

The problem wasn't the thinking itself, but the way her thoughts were in an all-out war.

Her consciousness was a battle of *What do I wear?* and *How much eyeshadow is too much eyeshadow?* to *Why was James here?* and *What did he mean when he said, "it still hurts sometimes?"*

Chores that were thrown to the wayside throughout the week were useless, as *dusting the living room* became *staring at pictures on the mantle of Charlotte and James from when they were seven,* and *reorganizing the pile of tattered college notebooks* turned into *Jack, so kind and patient as a helper, but now he was turning into something more.*

Her head was stuffed, and her heart rate was increasing as if she was working out, which she almost never did. By the time she was able to decipher whether she wanted to vacuum or actually scrub down her shower for once, she threw the chores to hell and decided instead to just start getting ready. After a thorough shower, blow dry, and too much time spent on too little makeup to really make a difference, she had enough time to pace before the bell to her apartment was ringing.

For a first date where they were presumably going to *go have fun,* she hadn't expected the bouquet of flowers that he was peering over when she let him up.

His smile was directed towards his shoes as she filled the one vase she owned with water, and her fingers twisted together in a flutter of apprehension as she met him by the front door.

"So," he breathed, "you ready?"

"Yeah," she smiled, her eyes shining past the jitters. "Yeah, I think I am."

James Ramsey was the farthest thing from a runner, but with his legs positively restless and his head pressurized to the point of potential explosion, he just couldn't take it.

Vanessa even laughed when he grabbed his shoes and tossed a strangled, "I'm going for a run" over his shoulder on his way out the door, waiting for him to turn it into a joke. But here he stood, his feet pounding the pavement, his lungs barking from this sudden onslaught of motion that didn't stop as quickly as it did when he was playing a pickup game of basketball in the middle of a workday.

But the pain was good, welcomed even. It took his mind off the fact that somewhere across town, Charlotte Murphy was on a date, and that date was not with him, and his body was whining for him to make some sort of intrusion.

He could go to the boardwalk, he realized. Plenty of people ran along the pier, didn't they? It was always so annoying to have an ice cream cone in one hand and your lady in the other and almost get toppled over by some ignorant runners who thought the pier was for them and them alone.

But he could be that guy today. Yeah. He could be the guy who *accidentally* ran through their arms, haphazardly apologized, tripped when he realized who he was running into. Offer up an over-enthusiastic, "Oh my god! What are you guys doing here?"

Piss her off even more.

No. He couldn't go to the boardwalk to run.

The trails around his condo eventually veered him into the bike lanes that ran around the city, but seeing couples holding hands and eating at outdoor restaurants had the nausea rising, the bile and acid bubbling in his throat.

Closing his eyes would only have him running headfirst into an obstruction, and for one fleeting moment, he thought that diving into oncoming traffic might just be better than having to watch Charlotte Murphy fall in love with someone else.

So he headed back toward home, focusing on the humidity that trickled sweat down his back and the bite of his ankles with each pumping step, the rustle of leaves in the unusually blustery winds.

But he couldn't get the images out of his head.

A kiss on the cheek to end the perfect date.

Her inviting him inside.

Another man's hands on her cheeks, her hips, her bare skin that probably still held tattoos of his own fingerprints.

It was that fire that had his feet driving toward home, slapping concrete with a burn that he felt in his thighs, in his toes, in the fingers that grasped around Vanessa's waist as soon as he busted through the front door, his lips seeking her without so much as a word.

He was rough that night, his hands and his teeth and his tongue driven mad by the desire in his chest to push out any thoughts of what Charlotte was doing.

Would he drive her back to his place? Or to hers?

Vanessa's abdomen pushing insistently into his as his hands shoved the material of her sheer top over her head, his lips finding and claiming any square inch of skin they could, anything to distract himself.

Would they share a glass of wine in those dinky glasses that *he* had helped her pick out when they first moved in, the cheapest set they could find at Target so that they could celebrate the move *as soon as possible!*

His lips on her throat, letting the little noises she made drown out all of the commotion in his head.

Would his body be pressed against hers, their clothes still between them, as he lay her across the old, beat up couch? The one that he sometimes slept on if they'd had one too many to drink?

With clothes cast aside, every push of their bodies together was an attempt to distance himself from his thoughts. It was more heated now, his hands frantically clutching at her, wary somewhere in the back of his thoughts that she'd probably have bruises on her thighs from where he was grabbing, marks on her neck from where he'd buried his teeth. He couldn't afford to look her in the eye, not tonight.

Despite every effort to focus on the body beneath him, his mind took over, flashing back to *her*, to the way that *she* moved, the way that *she* reacted to his touch.

So he pushed harder, willing the sound of theirs bodies moving together to overcome it all.

But when his fingers moved over Vanessa, they rooted back to the ways that he knew would get Charlotte to writhe beneath him, not even twitching in the slightest when Vanessa's reactions weren't the same.

She lay in a heap on his chest, her arm draped limply over his waist, her breath coming in ragged pants over his skin that was still slick and sticky with sweat.

Her, "Oh my god, baby. I... I don't know what got into you, but

Jesus Christ," should have made his chest swell with pride, should've beamed likewise comments against her ears as he kissed her and held her and geared up for round two.

Instead, he kissed the crown of her forehead, pinched his eyes shut, and willed sleep to overtake him before he jumped out of his skin.

California weather wasn't much to complain about. It was the driving force behind Charlotte's desire to move out west in the first place. But in the middle of the summer, when the heat so typically made a habit of hitting triple digits, they couldn't have asked for a more perfect afternoon to be outside basking in the glow of the sun and the warmth of one another.

The flowing skirt she had selected earlier was light, swishing just above her knees while they walked along the boardwalk. The cool breeze made her curls tap her cheeks and fly behind her, but in a way that wasn't a nuisance, and only added to her innocence.

It was easy to be with Jack, to swap stories of growing up on the East Coast when she learned that he had been born and raised in Queens ("Don't worry, I'm a Mets fan, if anything. We can mutually hate the Yankees together").

He had plenty to dish about growing up in a Brownstone and taking the subway to school, and teased her mercilessly about the fact that her family only took the T *on special occasions.* They debated the merits of Disney World versus Disneyland as they traded stories about family vacations, and they let their fingers tangle together in the middle.

As conversation flowed freely between them, Charlotte marveled at the simplicity of the late afternoon, the way that Jack just made everything so *easy.* There was no pressure to fill voids in the conversation, no timidness in his light, gentle touches that were but whispers against her skin every once in a while.

His smile brought her comfort, squashed down any slight nervous tendencies before they could even peek over the edge.

He kicked her ass in darts, but she returned the favor in skee ball.

It wasn't until dinner, the golden hues of the setting sun screaming *cliché* in the best way, that she saw his smile fade for the first time into something sad.

It was her simple question of, "So if you're from New York, what brought you all the way out here?" that finally had light peeking through his cracks, his lips downturned for the first time since she'd really gotten to know him. His eyes met his plate of pasta, and she was acquainted with the top of his head for the first time.

"Touchy subject, apparently?" she squeaked, avoiding his eyes as she poked her own meal with a fork.

Jack's head shook twice from side to side, slowly, as if he was still trying to piece together his thoughts.

"Not so much touchy as...I just didn't think I'd be bringing this up on our first date."

He met her eyes then, his grin sheepish, his ears muffled in a shrug of his shoulder.

"Hey, you don't have to—"

"Nah," he interrupted with a brush of his fingers through the air. "Don't worry about it. It's okay. I want to tell you."

He took a deep breath, beginning only when she nodded and offered a smile that said, *Go ahead, I'm all ears.*

"Back in high school, I had a girlfriend. Molly. We were together from the middle of sophomore year on, and when she didn't hesitate from following me to college, I... man, I figured she was my soul mate."

She could see the ghosts that danced in his eyes, momentarily regretted even bringing up the innocent question before remembering that there was no way she could have known. Instead, she gave him her full attention, letting her heart hurt for the ways in which he had once been broken.

"Anyway, to make a long story short, we dated through college, and I proposed right after graduation. I had this really great job transition from being a writer's assistant to being on staff at a small show that filmed in New York City. Molly went to school for journalism, but she had been in the acting program all throughout high school, and I was able to bring her to set one day to kind of look around and see what the actor's life was all about. And then, about a month later, I caught her sneaking out of the dressing room of one of our lead actors."

He shrugged, took a deep breath, and gulped long sips of his water glass until nothing but clinking cubes of ice remained. Charlotte remained still, trying her best to process how someone could do something so cruel to this man who exuded nothing but kindness.

"And after that? I just couldn't take it, Charlotte. I had memories of her in every nook and cranny of that state. God, my place of employment was where it all went to hell. I had to get out of there. So, I called up one of my buddies from school who had decided to work in Hollywood over New York and stayed with him until I could find a job. I've been climbing my way up the ladder ever since. And now we're here."

At a loss for words, Charlotte let her lips part just slightly, the air from her lungs blowing away with the soft breeze that kissed their skin from the patio restaurant. In her silence, Jack took his time polishing off the glass of wine that he had abandoned while he spoke, his sips languid and slow. His eyes wandered meticulously over his dinner, hers, the tips of his fingers, before he slowly dragged his gaze back up to Charlotte's.

He smiled warmly and with more confidence this time, as, "You don't have to feel sorry for me," whispered past soft, upturned lips.

"Honestly, Charlotte. I'm okay. Yes, it's a painful part of my past. One of the most painful, if I let myself stew in it for too long. But I haven't, not for a long time. Because I like the life that I have here. I like the person that I've become in spite of everything I've been through. And, regardless of anyone who has broken my heart, I'm glad that tonight, I get to be here with you."

He reached across, gently pulling her fingers from their rigid posture on the tabletop, his embrace as warm as the eyes that took her breath away. In the same moment, the meaning of his words began to register.

"Me too," seemed like an appropriate enough response, one simple enough to acknowledge, and to break the tension so that it didn't linger over their shared dessert.

Jack held her fingers while their toes squished against the sand, the water ghosting her freshly painted toes. They'd moved on to trivial topics like their favorite bands, the Broadway cast of *Wicked* versus the touring cast, and whether or not the Baltimore Orioles should be considered a real baseball team. But as they walked together, their hips brushing and her head lingering more and more against his shoulder with every step, she decided to act on the nagging feeling that she should say more, should acknowledge his pain in a way that brought that smile back to his lips.

"Hey, so, I just...I wanted to let you know that I meant what I said earlier," she began, her quelled nerves beginning to bubble as heat and tension in her cheekbones. "I like that I get to be here with you, Jack. And, for what it's worth, that girl Molly lost a wonderful, wonderful man. I'm just glad that I get to be the one to have the pieces she left behind. Because, despite being broken, what you've put back together is a pretty amazing person. Consider it her loss."

She was smiling now, both at the prospect of what lay ahead for herself and this man whose fingers were squeezing hers gently, and in the pride she had for speaking her mind for once.

Though the sun had already faded beyond the horizon, leaving only twinkling beach lights to dance across the water's reflection, his smile still shined brightly back at her in the light of the moon as he turned to brush his palms across her cheeks. Her smile, warm and wanting, was reflected in his eyes when he ducked in to press his lips against hers.

Her first thought was that kissing him was nice.

His hands against her cheeks, his lips full and soft and moving slowly against hers, stirred up the butterflies in her belly. She grasped his forearms near the crook of his elbow as he held her, feeling the softness of hair beneath her fingers, the way his muscles tensed as he adjusted his grip to tickle his touch to her neck, to flutter his fingers up and through the waves of her hair.

But all the while, as he moved slowly and languidly, as the soft sounds of their kissing mirrored the way the waves crashed against the shore, there was a part of her that screamed *different*.

It was different than the way that James kissed her.

While Jack's hands were soft, his touch just skimming the skin of her neck, James's fingers were always confident, a confidence that was tender yet possessive, as if he alone had written the map for her body. Though Jack's lips were soft and gentle, James had a fervor about him whenever their lips would meet that was desperate, hungry, almost unquenchable, as if he would never, ever be filled of her no matter how long they spent with their bodies pressed together.

But when Jack was pulling back, resting his forehead against hers, she had to push those thoughts behind, had to remind herself to be in the *now* instead of living in her past.

"I'm glad, too," was warm on his breath as it touched her lips that were still plump from his kisses. He bent to kiss her one last time, one lingering peck before he wrapped an arm around her shoulder for the walk back to his car.

He was grinning from ear to ear, brushing his thumb against the back of her hand as he drove them home, stealing glances every chance he got. She had to giggle, both at the sheer joy that filled their little bubble, and at how much he looked like a little boy on Christmas.

But the bubble seemed to be leaking, at least, when he arrived at her apartment.

She didn't want their night to end, didn't want to go back into her same apartment with the same drab walls and the same monotony that drove her mad with indecision. But there were too many parts within her fighting to keep him out.

To not rush things. To do this right. To make sure he understood that she really did like him, really did want to make something work between them.

But also, to keep the island of solitude closed off, the one that contained only her and James, the one where her secrets were kept safe, and she knew how he would react, and she knew that the one constant in her life would be there waiting.

So instead of inviting him in, continuing their night, letting her brand-new bold self take a risk for once, she decided that the date itself was risk enough for one night.

He walked her to the door like any good gentleman should, held both of her hands between their bodies as he told her for the hundredth time that night how good of a time he had, the smile never leaving his face.

"I did too."

And she was telling the truth, under the shine in her eye and the still small voice that she was doing her best to squash down.

He tugged gently at her hands to close the gap between them, and she felt his smile as it widened against her lips after she let her eyes flutter closed against their kisses. His hands were itching at her cheeks, his forehead nuzzling against hers, when he was saying, "I'd better go," and she was saying, "Yeah, I guess," and they were kissing again with longer and longer pauses in between.

She told him to text her when he got home safely, and he promised that he would, and she crossed her arms over her chest as she leaned against the frame of her building and watched his car disappear around the corner and down the road.

Her body buzzed while she undressed and slipped into pajamas, buzzed as she rubbed her toothbrush against the purple of wine on her teeth, buzzed while she patted her face dry and dragged the headband from behind her ears.

She'd never done drugs before, but her body was positively on a high. She found her fingers tapping against her lips on more than one occasion as she poured herself a glass of water and tucked her legs to the side of her body as she crawled into bed.

Scrolling aimlessly through her phone in an attempt to settle down for the night, a buzzing in her palm was the paradox for her entire existence.

One New Message
From: Jack McKinney
Home safe and sound. Thanks again for the best night I've had in a while. I really enjoyed being with you, Charlotte. Sweet dreams.

One New Message

From: James Ramsey

You make it home safe and sound, Smalls? I don't have to string him up by his tighty whities, do I?

The message to Jack was easy. It was *I'm glad* and *had fun too, Jack,* and *I can't wait to see you again* and *Sleep well.*

But this uneasiness about sending a message to James, this mulling over her words and backspacing and rewriting brought her back years into her past, her bottom lip now void of its buzzing and instead privy to nervous teeth.

Eventually, she settled on *Safe and sound as they come. Please don't touch Jack's underwear. A sexual predator charge wouldn't bode too well for your record.*

James

Lol. You're right. How in the world would I be able to come and volunteer in your classroom anymore?

Charlotte

This conversation is getting weird, even for us, Ramsey.

James

You might be right. Hey, how'd it go? Did you two crazy kids have fun?

Charlotte

We did. We had a really nice time.

James

I'm glad. Well, I've gotta hit the hay. Big day tomorrow.

Charlotte

Big day? It's Sunday, Rango.

James
Exactly. Big day of sleeping in ahead of me.

Charlotte
Lol. Dork. Night, James.

James
Goodnight, kiddo.

Somehow, as she lay her head against the pillow, the puzzle pieces in her brain calmed down, settling the Jack parts and the James parts and the other parts to their respective corners in a way that had a smile content enough for now pulling her into a dreamless slumber.

August 2008

It wasn't a lie that the last summer before college absolutely flew by. But all the same, it wasn't so bad for Charlotte and James, who spent almost every waking moment together, whether on the baseball diamond, at the lake, or in each other's living rooms. Still, with college looming on the horizon, time was certainly fleeting. It wasn't the thrill of a new path that made the hands of the clock tick by so quickly, but the new feelings that made time slip through their grasp like putty. The thrill of sneaking stolen glances and touches only made the minutes evaporate quicker.

Although it was quite commonplace for the pair to sneak off for time alone, whether at the lake, a quick break between baseball games at one of his tournaments, or just time to breathe, it was a different sort of privacy that they sought now.

It was pinkies touching with hands resting between them on the bleachers as they waited in between games for his team to take the field. When they would return to the hotel after his games, and sleeping parents and siblings interrupted time together, they walked the hotel halls late at night where they would brush arms and bump hips and giggle quietly. Lunch breaks at work, where he would buy a milkshake from her at the register and ask for two straws with a wink before finding a secluded booth to wait in until she could clock out for fifteen minutes. Some days, his car was parked in the alley behind the kitchen, and she would meet him in the backseat instead.

It was off days at home when they would take long, aimless walks along trails that would find fingers linked together only once they were under the cover of the trees' shadows. Quiet nights in her basement or his bedroom, when the house was deserted, lips parting, hands finding skin under the cover of darkness, the shadows their friends, their accomplices.

There was never a conversation, nor words passed more than *Should we stop?* and the inevitable *No* that would immediately follow when touches would grow hot. So instead, they counted down the minutes left until they moved away, truly only across the city, with moments stolen in time.

He had always been a jokester, would do anything in his power to make her giggle or roll her eyes before swatting playfully at his chest. But now, he found his efforts were doubled; her cheeks were in constant, delicious pain from how often they were stretched, her eyes shining brightly as she watched him beam with pride. His efforts, too, were often otherwise occupied, not only wanting to see her laugh and smile, but now it was to cloud her vision, to get her to close her eyes and sigh, and react in a way that he had never quite explored before. Her body was the page, and his touch the manuscript, trying and trying again until he got each and every word right.

She had always been shy, but now, in the confines of his arms and his hands and his lips, she was suddenly more bold, wanting to prove that she was more, that she could speak her mind and come out of her shell, that it was *him* that made it all appear.

No one questioned it when, at two o'clock in the morning, they were curled against one another, her head on his chest, his arms flung loosely around her on the basement couch. It was commonplace at this point, almost expected. It wasn't a problem that she spent more nights at his house than in her own bed, or that Mrs. Murphy woke up early and often to James, bed-headed and squinty eyed as he searched in the Murphy's refrigerator for the orange juice.

The problem, always, was hiding the marks that they left behind, taking special care to find areas that could be hidden underneath clothing. But it eventually turned into a game, a secret, sneaky little challenge that had their eyes sly and ears tinted whenever a new place was discovered. When Linda questioned Charlotte as to why she wanted a one-piece bathing suit that season, she'd said it was a "new fashion trend." James, having never worn a t-shirt in the pool in his lifetime, was suddenly very wary of skin cancer.

Charlotte reveled in those moments when he would suggest a late-night walk, always waiting for him to find her hand first as they strode together under the stars. Sometimes he stood behind her, his arms wrapped firmly across her chest with her head tucked under his chin. All too often, she rolled her eyes at the couples in books and on TV who said that they *felt safe* and *found a home* in one another. But in those moments, she couldn't help but think of a puzzle, and how the pieces of him and the pieces of her just fit.

His favorite place to have her was with her head on his chest, her fingers wandering aimlessly across his body, and his arms snug around her. He saw himself in those moments as her protector, the one to keep her safe.

As the reality of their last night before college sunk in, less words were passed than usual. He held her tightly, but she held on more.

When move-in day finally rolled around, they were both exhausted from the previous night they'd spent, almost wordlessly, wrapped in one another. They caravanned from Newton, each taking the hour drive with their own parents because *You two are going to school together, give us a little bit of time with our babies*, obliging only because he could still discreetly text her from the back seat and she could very easily get away with telling her parents that her new roommate had a ton of questions.

They were lucky, requesting the same dorm building and getting placed only one floor apart. The Murphys and the Ramseys made quite the show of putting together their dorms before tears were shed and they were finally, at last, alone. Charlotte and James found themselves on James's bed, his brand-new comforter as odd and uncomfortable as the Insane Clown Posse posters that hung above his roommate's bed.

With the door cracked slightly ajar, the flood of people and furniture and chatter waving past the room was overwhelming, but it didn't supersede the tension that hung as their pinkies met on his bedspread, their shoulders bumping slightly. Her feet dangled freely in midair. His were planted firmly on the ground.

When their eyes finally met, he reached up to brush a stray curl behind her ears, her hair having grown wild in the mid-August humidity and the chaos of bounding up and down flights of stairs. His fingers lingered, curling around her ear, causing her eyes to flutter closed and her fingers to finally brush towards his thigh, effectively pulling them closer. His nose was brushing her temple, lips but a whisper from her skin, when four skinny boys were gamboling into the room, the ruckus sending Charlotte off the bed and onto her feet as

James's hands found his hair.

'Sup, dudes? were passed back and forth, and James felt the instant need to protect Charlotte as the eyes of the frat boy types eyed her with grins that made his stomach turn.

"Hey man, I'm James," he said, offering an outstretched hand to his roommate. "Nice to meet you."

Charlotte, with timidness in her eyes, stepped back, her shy smile saying *I'll see you later* as she edged towards the doorway. His frantic gazes between her and the newcomers led to quick strides of his long legs, his lanky arm catching her before she got the chance to leave.

"Hey, you don't have to go."

His voice was low and breathy, and she wished for a second that they hadn't been interrupted.

"No, it's fine. You should hang out with these guys. Talk about manly things. I'll catch up with you later."

His eyes dropped to where his fingers tangled loosely around her wrist, watching his own thumb trace soft circles on the inside.

"Are you sure?"

While her heart was screaming *No*, she took a breath, tugged her lips into a grin, and covered his hand with her own.

"Yes. Be a big boy. Go make some friends."

He grinned down at her, the look in his eyes and the parting of his lips wavering momentarily as if he were about to bend forward and kiss her. But he never did, settling instead for, "Okay. I'll text you in a little while about dinner," before she headed back towards the staircase.

In the chaos of freshman orientation, being randomly assigned groups and playing trivial ice breaker games, even being forced to eat dinner with their ice breaker classmates rather than choosing who to sit by, it was late into the evening "free hours" before they exchanged any texts, mainly consisting of things like ***Wow, our Student Mentor was on crack or something*** and ***If this is the kind of food we have to live off of for the next four years, I'm literally going to die.***

When a small crowd of girls gathered in her room later that night, the standard gossip of *Where did you go to high school?* and *What sports/clubs were you in?* and *What's your major?* quickly transformed into ranking the boys on campus and comparing notes. One of the girls—was her name Ginny?—pointed out the frame of Charlotte and James that sat on her bedside dresser, a photo taken two summers ago at the lake house of Charlotte and James in their standard pose: her on his back with her chin resting on his shoulder, their cheeks squished together, and Charlotte doing her best not to touch the sunburn on his chest.

"Well Charlotte already bagged the hottie from the third floor. Dear God, woman, would you *please* tell us how good he is in bed already?"

But after flushing red and watching several of the other girls go bug eyed, Ginny spoke again, her eyes narrowing as she took stock of the sweet and innocent little group they had gathered.

"Okay, apparently we're still too early in the night for *that* kind of chatter. Charlotte, girl, we'll talk later."

"Tell us how you guys met," chimed in another girl, and as blush now renewed with her smile, the tale of their friendship spun to the backgrounds of *Aww* and *So cute!* and *Oh my god, it's like a fairytale.*

She made the mistake of letting it slip that, "Well, we kind of spent the whole summer together, and now, I guess we're just seeing where things go," which came with a new barrage of questioning, the finality of the conversation dropping with the hammer of Ginny dragging her by the wrist and a curt, "What the hell are you still doing here, woman? Go get him!"

The encouragement from the rest of the room had her failing to bite back a smile. It didn't surprise her that Ginny, with no vocal boundaries, reached up to futz with her hair, tugged the zippered hoodie from her shoulders, and slathered sticky lip gloss to her shocked expression before telling her point blank, "If you're back before 2 A.M., I'll march you up there and undress you two myself."

She felt herself skipping down the hallway, a spring in her step as she bounded up the stairs. Her senses were overwhelmed, transitioning quickly from flowery scents and a distinct quietude on the girls' floor to loud noises, body odor and beer, and mass chaos just ten steps above. She avoided a flying soccer ball and a boy body surfing on a skateboard before sidestepping a pile of garbage to come upon James's room, a crowd similar to the one she'd just left gathered on chairs and beds and any open floor space. Her heart raced, teeth shining, when she saw him straddling his desk chair backwards, his mouth hung open in laughter, looking so casual and sexy all at the same time. As she lingered outside the door ready to knock against its frame, she backed up upon hearing her name come up in their locker room talk.

"So what about that chick you had in here earlier, Ramsey?"

"Who, Charlie Kate?"

"Yeah, the one you were about to bump uglies with when we walked in." His roommate snickered, and she could see him reach behind James to the frame that he had on *his* desk. It was that same pose, her on his back, from last summer. They were standing at Fenway Park underneath the glorious *Welcome to Yawkey Way: Gate A* banner that fluttered above them.

Suddenly, the frame was travelling from person to person, and she felt her face grow warm as she realized that she was being scrutinized by a bunch of guys she didn't even know. There was a *She ain't bad* and *I'd give her a solid 6* and one *Maybe if we were drunk* that had a lump forming in her throat before she heard James take the picture frame and settle it back to its place. He bit back, "Hey, knock it off guys, seriously," before his speech truly took off. He took a deep breath, his voice lower now.

"No, I mean, Charlie Kate's just...listen, we've been best friends, like, forever. She's...our families are like, super close and everything. We've known each other since kindergarten."

Her heart dropped to her stomach, that once wide smile now downturned in disbelief.

"Man, you can't tell me you've never hit that before. Kindergarten's a long time."

Just last night was ringing in her ears, while a wash of sensations, of his hands and his lips and that *look* in his eyes fought for her attention against the chatter of guys saying things like *How does she like it?* and *Was it good?* She wanted to run, but her shoes were heavy, like concrete was sucking her to the spot. She was only reassured when his voice, clearly growing more and more agitated rang, "Guys, seriously, cut it out." The familiar *thump* of his steps crossing the room and opening up his mini fridge, the crack of a Sprite can, took up the idle silence.

"So, you guys aren't together or anything? She's kind of cute."

"Yeah, I mean, no, I mean, she's...she's like my sister, you know?"

It cut her like a knife, the intake of breath sharp, loud enough, she feared, for him to hear in such close proximity. She caught the beginning of a new conversation starting before she summoned what strength she had left to dash down the hall.

"Good, because I heard that chick Lauren on the fourth floor has the hots for you and *man* does she have a *rack*..."

She was flicking tears away angrily. There was nothing to be upset about, right? They never *really* defined their relationship. Maybe it was just a way to finally get each other out of their systems before college. They could both do their own thing now with the weight finally gone.

So, why then, was her heart so stuffed up?

The vibrations of the door slamming behind her hadn't even subsided before it was ripped open again, and there was Ginny Edley, her arms crossed and her expression questioning. She'd barely gotten, "Little Miss Charlotte, I thought I *told* you" out before she saw blotchy tear-streaked cheeks, and her words changed automatically to, "Alright, whose dick do I have to cut off?"

Charlotte laughed through her tears, a noisy, junky sound breaking itself up in her throat as she tried to find the words. How was she supposed to unearth twelve long years of her life into something simple, when it was the complete opposite? As Ginny watched her mouth open and close a thousand times, grappling with what to say, she turned on her toes.

"I'm getting snacks and booze, and we're going to forget that he ever existed. I will *not* let your first night of college be remembered like this."

She shook her head in disbelief of the past ten minutes of her life as she watched Ginny disappear. While she changed into a pair of

166

sweats, reconsidering her decision to don one of many of James's shirts that she had stolen over the years, she was oblivious to the conversation occurring in the hallway.

James, having exhausted himself of guy talk, had bounded down the stairs, fully intending to crack open a soda and cuddle up with his best friend, the one who still had his heart going on a tear. The one whose touch his fingers itched for. The one who had his body screaming to just *hold onto.* Instead, as he raised his knuckles to rap on the door, he was stopped by the slender arm of a tall, skinny girl with brown chunks in her blonde hair. The scowl in her pursed lips had him on edge.

"Uh, hi," he started, his eyebrows quirking with questions as he shifted his weight. "Can I... get by?"

He watched as her eyes scanned him through tightly drawn slits, seeming to size him up in a menacing way that gave him the chills. When her eyes finally dragged their way back to his face, her lips quirked to the side before she spoke.

"You're James?"

It was phrased as a question, but the inflection said otherwise, and he nodded his head, matching her wary expression.

"In that case, you *can't* get by. We're having a girls' night. Bye."

He didn't catch much more than the glow of the television against the wall; Charlotte's bed was behind the door. Before Ginny disappeared, James put his hand up in protest.

"Well, hold up. I at least want to say good night. She's my…"

"Your what?"

He took it personally when, after a beat with no response, she said, "That's what I thought," and disappeared into the room, the door clicking closed behind her with a sinking finality.

He lingered by the door, his hand coming up to rub the back of his neck as he paced a few times before ultimately deciding to leave.

When Charlotte's phone buzzed and his name lit up the screen, Ginny was quick to take it, saying, "Oh no. If he's going to leave you in tears, he doesn't get the satisfaction of you reading his text messages. Now, spill. The quicker you get it all out, the better you'll feel, and the quicker we can get drunk and watch something trashy."

It was odd, how this girl had pushed her way in, was so concerned about her well-being after knowing each other for only an hour, but more so that Charlotte had a weird sense of trust. In not so many details, she clued Ginny in to how they'd spent their prom, the summer, the way that her feelings had been building since they were kids, how she never had the courage to mention anything. The conversation she had eavesdropped upon, and the words that were now plugging a hole in her heart.

All the while, her new friend listened without interjection, her eyes narrow and her expression unchangingly stoic as the story unfolded. When she finished, Ginny gave her a break, taking her own time to piece together the puzzle before responding. Charlotte's fingers itched to reach across to where her cell phone sat on the dresser behind Ginny, but she had the sneaking suspicion she'd get slapped.

"I guess you really have two options, Char. One: You march right up to his room and tell him how you feel and what you want. Or two: You leave it be, stay his best friend, but make the most of this college experience and move on. He seems like a good thing, but Charlotte, maybe there becomes a point when that good thing is just too much."

She was so used to James being her only voice of reason, the one person in her life who would tell her how it was and be honest and blunt, but this was refreshing. It was so black and white—take him or leave him—but the decision itself wasn't so simple.

She let Ginny talk her into one Mike's Hard, her new friend easily guzzling three, while they watched movie reruns and laughed about their respective orientation leaders. It wasn't until Ginny had stumbled out the door, something about *Mike from upstairs wanting to check out her ass*, that she peeled her cell phone away from the dresser.

One New Message
From: James Ramsey
Hey, Murph. I feel like I haven't seen you all day. I hope your first day went good. I miss you. Just wanted to say goodnight. Let me know if you need me to come check for monsters under your bed ;)

As her fingers hovered over the keys, Ginny's words resounded. *Tell him or move on.*
Her message travelled up one floor.

Well, if you've got nothing better to do, I think I heard a noise under the sheets that could use some investigation… :P

Her heart raced in anticipation, checking her phone and the hallway frantically until fatigue pulled her eyelids shut around 2 A.M.

His phone was lost under the hoodie he'd tossed off after being shunned from her room with his text message unreturned for over an hour. It turned out that Lauren from the fourth floor did *have the hots for him*, and had said so herself when she ventured down to his room around midnight.

Kissing her was weird and different, but she seemed to enjoy whatever it was that he was doing. When she had started to take his shirt off, though, he whispered something about taking it slow, opting to cuddle instead until she was falling asleep and he felt the inherent need to have her gone. For so long, there had only been one body to mold with his. Now, with this petite, itty bitty little thing all bony and strange wrapped around him, he began to feel itchy, like he was developing hives. He only checked his phone again once his door was locked shut and he was alone, chucking it to the floor in frustration when his messages came up empty.

Ryan, his roommate, woke him the next morning with a reminder of the mandatory orientation activities they had to attend, giving James a thumbs up and silent *Nice*, alluding to his previous night's engagements as he wiped the sleep groggily from his eyes.

His heart dropped to the floor when he cracked open his phone, a message from Charlotte terrorizing him from just fifteen minutes after he'd fallen asleep. On the edge of his own bedroom door, he realized that he still smelled like the Abercrombie perfume that Lauren had no doubt doused herself with before showing up at his door.

After tossing his clothes haphazardly near his hamper, he grabbed his shower caddy and headed to the communal bathroom, running his toothbrush twice for good measure before gargling a shot of mouthwash. While he was slopping body wash over his chest, he felt a rush of air as the light became brighter.

The shower curtain was open.

And stark naked, entering his shower stall, the one in the *men's* bathroom, was that girl from the hallway last night, the one who had stopped him from seeing Charlotte.

"Oh! Shit. Sorry. I didn't know this one was occupied," she said nonchalantly, not even bothering to cover herself, while James did his best to hide behind the half wall. She was on her way out when she turned quickly, her finger nearly colliding with his chest.

"*You.*"

His expression exasperated, hands still clenched awkwardly in front of his crotch, he mumbled, "Me?" over the roar of the water hitting his back.

"Yes, *you.* Is there anyone else in this stall?"

"No, and realistically, there should only be one of us here anyway."

"You need to sort out your priorities," she continued, ignoring his comment. "Figure it out before you end up hurting someone. Got it?"

Finally covering her chest with her crossed arms, he nodded furiously, having no idea what she meant, but wanting doubly for her to disappear.

He finished washing as quickly as he could when she exited his stall, throwing on a pair of khaki shorts and a Red Sox t-shirt before skipping stairs down to Charlotte's floor. She was gone when he got there, so with his head hung, he made his way to the dining hall, hoping to catch her before she finished her breakfast.

When Charlotte's roommate Holly invited her to breakfast, she hesitated for only a moment before pocketing her phone and keys and deciding that she didn't need to rely on James for everything. She could have other friends, after all. He certainly did. Holly picked up a few other girls in the lobby from her orientation group, and as they all chatted over fluffy waffles and burnt toast, the petite blonde sitting across from her said something that struck a chord.

It was the cute guy from the third floor, she said. *The tall one, with the shaggy hair. All the girls were talking about him.*

But she had decided to do something. She'd stayed past midnight. Her name was Lauren.

And she lived on the fourth floor.

The realization dawned on Charlotte just a moment before James's eyes found her from across the cafeteria, smile wide and fingers waving, until he took a seat next to her and was face to face with Lauren.

Lauren, who beamed immediately, the thought that he had joined *her*, and not the mousy education major on the other side of the square table. Lauren, who squeezed his fingers immediately, asking if he had *slept well without her*.

He wanted to chase after Charlotte when she immediately stood at Lauren's comment, the claim that she'd forgotten something in her room quick and rushed. His chest was tight, and not from the dainty fingers that were steadily creeping along his thigh. He watched the back of her head, those curls that he could pick out of any crowd, as they disappeared beyond the wall of windows that led out of the cafeteria. His hard stare followed her all the way out just in case she turned to change her mind.

It was a weird morning. A weird afternoon. Neither Charlotte nor Lauren were in his orientation group, so he had lucked out, concentrating on stupid get to know you games and scavenger hunts through unknown buildings rather than the pull of his heart, the slight ache in his temple after only a few hours in those buildings had already destroyed him.

He had been so close to saying something the night before. All it would've taken was that damn pesky friend of hers not kicking him out, and he would've held her in his arms all night long, told her that he wanted to spend college *together*, that the summer had finally kicked his feelings in the ass for good.

But then Lauren happened. And Charlotte was doing her best to both make new friends and avoid him. So, he was moving on too, right?

Rather than face either of the women who were currently racking his brain, he holed up in his own room, stuffing his face with the box of Cheez-Its that his mother had bought him the day before.

"That's it. You have *got* to stop moping."

Ginny was already in the mini fridge, a stolen soda can in hand, by the time Charlotte plucked her headphones from her ears and wound them around her iPod.

"Listen, Charlotte. There's a party at the guys' soccer house tonight. I'm going. You're going. We're going to raid your closet, find you something skimpy to wear, defrizz those curls, have a good time, and for*get* about James. Got it?"

Her eyes were trained on a loose thread in the carpet, her shoulders shrugged up towards her ears. But Ginny wasn't having any of it, and no sooner was Charlotte plugged into a playlist called *J&CK's Greatest Hits!* than she was being dragged up by a freshly manicured hand and down the hallway.

It was odd, seeing herself all dolled up like this. Not that she never did her makeup or curled her hair more attentively. But Ginny Edley must have had a magic wand in that makeup bag (more like makeup *suitcase*) of hers. After a good hour, Charlotte looked determinedly *hot*. Sexy, even.

Her curls, usually tight with a slight amount of frizz, her typical *straight out of the shower* look, were now large and loose, sleek and controlled after a few spritzes of product. She wasn't one for much more than a coat of foundation and a little eyeliner or mascara, but tonight, she was somehow pulling off the smoky eye *thing* that all of her friends had spent countless hours perfecting in high school. In lieu of one of her own less than stellar outfits, Ginny had loaned her a black mini skirt and shimmery silver tank top for the night. Though she was already pulling the edges of the skirt down, she had to admit that it made her legs look longer, her curves accentuated in all of the right places. With a bit of gloss on her lips, they were ready to go.

"See? There's no *way* guys don't throw themselves at you tonight," Ginny encouraged as she applied her own finishing touches. "James *who*?"

"Stop it," Charlotte chuckled. "This isn't about James.

We're...we'll always be friends. This is...this night is for *me*," she declared with a deep breath and a shy smile at herself in Ginny's full-length mirror.

"That's my girl."

Linking arms at the elbows—mostly to steady Charlotte as she walked in a pair of unfamiliar heels—they were out the door.

She and James hadn't spent too much time at parties in high school, though Newton South was notorious for throwing the occasional weekend banger. She didn't know what to expect, aside from what they'd glimpsed in cheesy 80's movies that had been watched in lieu of attending said parties, a bowl of popcorn often between James and herself. Entering the off-campus soccer house, she was greeted by a cloud of smoke, a deep booming bass, and several frat type boys with backwards hats and cutoff T-shirts.

Two of them surveyed the girls, looking them up and down intently, one even biting his lower lip as he—*growled?*—"*Damn*, lookin' fine tonight, ladies. Come on in," and offered them each a plastic red cup. In no time at all, Ginny located the keg, filled up Charlotte's and her own, and was halfway through her own beer and leading Charlotte to the basement.

It wasn't long before she was instinctively looking for James, checking her purse to make sure her phone and keys were still there, wondering if she should just book it out the front door before shit hit the fan. It was all very unnerving. People were already drunk, grinding against each other on the makeshift "dance floor" (a carpet in the middle of the cracked basement concrete). Others were sloppily kissing against walls, in the stairwell, in the bathroom. A circle of guys and girls alike passed around a joint. People sat on laps, touched in places that made her squirm for being in such a public arena. She felt bile rise in her throat, but not before Ginny's hands were dragging her to a new corner of the basement.

"Come on, Charlotte," she yelled, though her lips were touching Charlotte's ear. "Loosen up. Have some fun."

Ginny threw her arms up, the flask in her hand a clear indication that she was already tipsy as she gave her backside to a boy Charlotte had never seen before. Her eyes dropped to her own beer cup, fingered the rim several times, and looked up again with every intention of telling Ginny she was just going to head back, put on her pajamas, and throw in a movie. But as her head snapped up, her entire body ran hot.

Among the throngs of scantily clad college students dancing and grinding and moving about, she saw the tip of his Red Sox hat, turned backwards just like all the others. He had to bend down to accommodate the short frame in front of him, but his nose was undoubtedly brushing through the hair at the back of Lauren's head, his arms snaked around the front of her waist as they moved slowly to the beat of the music. The clothes that Lauren bore made Charlotte feel overdressed.

Suddenly, it was, "Screw this," a prolonged *chug* of her own drink—which gained her a few *Right on, girl!*'s from the people around her—and the hand of the first boy who offered.

She closed her eyes, her own fury driving the way she let her inhibitions fly as her body moved against the sweaty frame of a boy whose name she didn't even know. His hands were on her waist, playing with her hip bones and snaking up her sides. She rested hers on his shoulders, still tentative at first. But as she looked up to see Ginny giving her an encouraging smile and a slight wink, she switched gears, encircling his neck, tickling up and down his chest.

When his hands reached down to squeeze her ass, she almost recoiled, almost slapped him in the face. But then, she realized she didn't have to. There was no reason she couldn't be enjoying this, the attention of someone else.

Following Ginny's lead, she turned in his arms, gave him her backside, and moved to the beat of the music. She was scared at first, to throw her arms up in the air, to be so uninhibited like the other girls. But when she looked across the room, saw Lauren facing James and shimmying down his body like he was a pole, she clenched her eyes shut and gave in.

The foreign grip on her waist held tighter, pulled her closer, moved behind her and against her in a way that might have made her feel gross if she hadn't just chugged a beer. Her suitor was quick to offer her a refill on drinks, but with a head still clear enough, she pulled Ginny away to do it herself, returning to find his eyes glassy, half closed, but his arms waiting for her as one song flowed into the next.

It was easy to keep this façade, to keep her eyes clenched and focus the burn in her belly on loosening her muscles, freeing her body of tension, and being *somewhere else*. When Ginny offered her the flask, she only paused to pinch her lips at the burn in her throat as the liquid eased its way down, opening her even more.

She spent some time dancing with Ginny and a few other girls who had migrated their way, leaving the sweaty men to refill cups and stand back and watch. She was giggling, her head thrown back, shouting along to the songs that she knew and moving uninhibitedly when she didn't recognize the words. When the music paused between songs, those same arms returned, his nose tickling her ear when he mentioned, "I'm Mark, by the way." She shouted, "Charlotte!" followed by a giggle. Her voice was *so loud*! And she was looming on very drunk as the beat resumed, her hands unrestrained as the alcohol in her system made her suddenly bolder.

It was Charlotte that was pulling Mark's body to her now, her hands roaming along his chest, his hips, around to his ass to give a gentle squeeze. Suddenly, he was holding her tightly against him, his words thick and slurred in her ear as he whispered things like *You look so good in that skirt*, and *Keep moving like that, baby*. She didn't know how to take the compliment, the flush in her face a mixture of alcohol and immaturity. Instead, she focused herself on the movement of her body to the music, searching for Ginny in the crowd for a smile of reassurance. Only this time, when she opened her eyes, she was met with a stare that screamed rage. She thought for a moment that she could see literal flames in his eyes.

From where he stood, with Lauren still swaying drunkenly against his body, James had stopped moving to stare. But Charlotte's brow furrowed, the scowl she threw his way her own form of daggers as she purposefully gripped onto Mark tighter, stealing a move from Lauren as she twisted her way down the floor and back up. The yelp of encouragement from Mark, the way he pulled her against him when she was standing again and pushed their noses together, had James's body red and flaming. She cupped the back of Mark's head then, their lips coming together for sloppy, drunk movement that involved way too much of his tongue for it to even register as a kiss.

"Excuse me," James yelled, his grip hard on Charlotte's bicep as he yanked the pair apart. "I need to steal her for a minute."

In his state of inebriation, Mark only slugged back some of his own drink and stumbled off to find one of his buddies.

Charlotte's scowl remained, deepened, as James pulled her to an unoccupied corner of the basement.

"What the *hell*?" she shouted, this time raising her voice out of anger rather than necessity, her arms crossed against her shiny shirt, suddenly feeling the need to cover herself.

"What are you *doing*?" He pushed past her frustration completely, his arms thrown up as his face reddened. "Do you even *know* that guy?"

"Oh, *I'm* sorry, are you the friend police now? I can talk to whoever I want to, *James*."

His name was bitter on her tongue as her words spat above the music. His face softened a bit, his eyes flitting up, back and forth, before finding her again; the look she gave him stabbed through to his core.

"I didn't...listen, you don't even *know* that guy. I don't want him grabbing you like that."

"You don't get to tell me what to do." Her words were sharp, dictated, her pupils wide and focused as she jutted her finger into his chest. "I can dance with whoever I want to. I thought I left *David* at home."

He rolled his eyes, brushing off the implications she'd made about her brother as he snatched her finger in his fist, ignoring her gasp and the way her face scrunched.

"No, I don't, but when I see my *friend* making a *stupid* decision and rubbing up on some guy she barely knows, I *get* to step in. Did you even know that guy for longer than five minutes before you let him touch you like that?"

There was a pause, her words forming carefully as she quieted her tone to an eerie whisper.

"It certainly didn't stop *you*."

Finally, her voice broke. Whether from the alcohol or the emotions that she'd beaten down over the course of her first college weekend, she didn't care to think about.

She was usually never quick enough to get away from him; his legs were too long and most times he caught her by a simple stretch of the arm. But she had caught him off guard, rendered him stunned long enough for her to make it halfway up the stairs with crossed arms and tear stained cheeks before he was up and moving.

He was halfway to the stairs when an arm jerked him backward.

Suddenly, he was caught between *that girl from the shower?* and *I don't have time for this*, while he watched Charlotte wipe her eyes as she disappeared to the second floor. And then there was Lauren, with a refilled beer in each hand, snapping her gaze from James to Charlotte to Ginny and back again.

He had no time to respond to the mess he was in the middle of, jerking his body away purposelessly as a finger was thrust into his chest for the second time that night.

"Let her be. She doesn't need you chasing her right now."

"I—"

"No. You listen to me. That sweet girl up there doesn't deserve to have her heart broken on her first. Damn. Weekend. Of college. Leave her alone."

Ginny pushed past him then, clearly intent on following after Charlotte, but he wasn't about to have any of it.

"No. Listen. This is between me and her. I have to handle it."

His features softened, she noticed, pain and maybe regret past all that was bloodshot and wide.

He could tell that her thoughts were churning in the same way that her eyes turned to slits, surveying him closely as he pleaded with her to let him go. When he saw the slightest of nods, he was bounding up the stairs, taking three at a time.

He expected tears, expected to gather her up in his arms and not let her go until he talked, and she talked, and they were back to being *James and Charlie Kate* again. What he hadn't expected was a full-on screaming match on the front lawn. He was shocked as he shoved past the thick crowds upstairs, his eyes scanning for the curls that were loose tonight, the ones he had seen and, after being infuriated at the way that she was grinding against the douche in the basketball jersey, wanted to wind his fingers through and feel how soft they were.

It was the voices outside that pulled him towards the front door, fear clogging his throat as her words became clearer.

"...and if you wanted him so badly, you should've done something about it. But listen, bitch. I got to him first. You need to *back* the *hell* off, because I am *not* about to let you ruin—"

"*Lauren.*"

The word was sharp and cut deep. Charlotte had only heard that voice twice before. Once when he had confronted the boy who was bullying his baby sister. The other when he'd decked Joey De Luca at prom just months before.

"Hey." Lauren's voice was suddenly sweet again, but shaky, as she turned and approached him. Her hand was on his chest for no more than a moment before he pushed her away, cutting off her, "I was just—"

"You *don't* talk to her like that."

"Jimmy," she pleaded, her voice still wavering as she tried again to close a physical barrier. But he persisted, pushing her hand away again. "Listen, I was—"

"I don't want to hear it. You don't...I'm not even going to waste my time here. Stay away from *her*. Stay away from *me*."

When he turned towards Charlotte, with her eyes still puffy and red, his hand extended tentatively; his words were the ones to shake now.

"C'mon, Charlie Kate. Let me get you home."

He waited, terrified for a moment that she wouldn't accept his outstretched hand, that she would yell again or head back inside. But he let out a sigh of relief when her hand slipped into his.

Though the walk was only a mile off campus, in their state of drunkenness, it seemed like hours. She stopped to take off Ginny's heels after the first block, and when she stood again, he opted for his arm around her shoulders rather than just holding her hand.

The walk was silent, save for the crunch under his shoes, the occasional sniffle from her nose. It killed him a little more each time.

He wanted to offer her his shoes, his socks, pick her up and carry her the rest of the way when he heard her wince. But he wasn't sure how she'd respond. So instead, he took the time to stop, let her brush a stray stick or pebble from her soles, and continued on when she was ready.

He brought her to his room, knowing that his roommate—who had been the one to mention the party to him when Lauren was standing in the doorway—would more than likely be spending the night elsewhere.

After being surrounded for hours by a thumping bass, the dull light buzzed loudly overhead. He pulled one of his T-shirts and a pair of shorts from his drawer and handed them to her, leaving the room to wet a washcloth while she changed. When he returned, she was standing in the middle of his room, looking so small in his borrowed clothes that were swallowing her. Her eyes were still red and her nose scrunched as she stood there wringing her hands. She looked scared, almost, as if she didn't belong. He swallowed a lump in his throat, gestured for her to sit on the bed, and pulled her feet into his lap.

Wordlessly, he used the washcloth to dab at her feet, using gentle strokes to free her of the dirt. Then, his thumbs pushed and pressed, relieving the knots that had formed from their trek across town.

Her hiccups now mingled with the buzz of the lights, the small noises pounding in his ears, reminding him that they hadn't spoken a word since they'd yelled across the stuffy, smoke filled basement.

And then, her voice so small, laden with tears and thick with snot finally said, "James?"

He knew before she had to say another word by the pale green in her face. His trashcan was in her lap not seconds before she hurled. He rubbed her back, folded the washcloth backwards so that the clean side could cool the back of her neck, pulled the ponytail holder from her wrist, and wrapped up her curls.

When he was sure that she was spent, he took the can to the garbage chute, gathered a bottled water from his mini fridge, and instructed her with a simple, "Here, you need to drink," before watching her take small sips until it was at least half gone. After putting a new bag in the garbage can, he found her key, went down one flight of stairs, and grabbed her toothbrush.

It was a memory from being eight years old that reminded him of just how much she hated the taste of vomit. He had visited her all four days that she was out of school with the stomach flu in second grade and brought her a pack of gum—*Just in case you don't want to get up and go all the way to the bathroom.*

She was still nursing the bottle of water when he returned, but she let him help her to the men's bathroom on shaky feet, and he watched cautiously, ready to respond if she was going to puke again.

When they got back to his room, he pulled back the covers, praying to God that he'd gotten the smell of Lauren's perfume out of his bedding as he motioned for her to climb in.

"Are we...should we..."

It killed him, that look on her face. Her chin shaking, her eyes brimming with fresh tears, avoiding him in favor of the floor, the wall, the posters above his roommate's bed. He gathered her to his chest, tucked her head under his chin, and breathed for what seemed like the first time all weekend.

"Hey. We'll...we can do this in the morning, okay? Just...let's get some sleep."

He felt her nod against his chest, felt her fists clench just a little bit tighter at the cotton of the T-shirt he'd thrown on earlier that evening.

When her head was on his pillow, her eyes blinking slowly, he turned his back and shucked his clothes, finding a fresh shirt but opting to stay in his boxers. She curled into him as easily as he pulled her to his chest.

She woke in the morning with dry eyes and a headache that she could hear.

The clock on his desk blinked *7:54*, seeming to taunt and tease her as she groaned against his chest, burying her head into a place that had been so familiar, and yet so distant after the past seventy-two hours. When his arms tightened around her, she could feel the tears beginning to threaten again.

"Hey." His voice was thick and groggy. "What time is it?"

"Too early to function o'clock," she mumbled back, her words lost in the cotton of his shirt.

She felt his chest rumble beneath her as a laugh escaped him.

"Go back to sleep. We can go to brunch later."

As sleep began to pull her back under, she felt his nose nuzzle the top of her head, and she could've sworn his lips lingered as she slipped back into unconsciousness.

The room was brighter when she woke again. Her head was heavy, but the throbbing more distant as she sat up slowly. As she looked around his room, she spied a bottle of water, two aspirin, and a pack of gum on the desk next to his bed. She winced as she swallowed the pills, taking a final sip of water as the door opened to the smell of Dove for Men body wash and Suave shampoo. The very same way his pillow smelled.

He had on a fresh pair of jeans and a t-shirt, but his hair was still damp. He entered almost silently, slipped off his shower shoes, and put his shower caddy back on the floor as gingerly as possible, trying his best not to wake her. But when he looked over to the bed to see her sitting up, still swallowed in his clothes and blankets, he let a small smile invade his lips.

"Hey."

"Hey," she repeated, her own voice still scratchy.

Their movements were tentative, James slow to cross the room, Charlotte unaware if she should untuck herself from his sheets or stay put. Eventually, he perched himself on the edge of the bed, letting his legs swing off the side.

When their *So*'s tangled and the awkward laughter subsided, he finally met her eyes, apology written everywhere.

"What a way to start off our first weekend at college, huh?"

"Yeah," she chuckled, avoiding his gaze. "I guess I won freshman orientation bingo. Went to a party, wore a slutty outfit, got plastered, made out with a guy I didn't know, threw up in my best friend's bed."

He tried to hide the way his body responded when *made out with a guy I didn't know* rolled so effortlessly off her tongue. He recovered quickly, pushing banter over cringe.

"Hey, to be fair, you didn't actually *throw up* in my bed. You made it to the garbage can. You were very ladylike."

"Crap," she said without missing a beat. "How am I supposed to fill my bingo card now?"

"Free space? Hangover from hell?"

She smiled in response, her eyes shining for just a moment as she let herself hang onto *them* before they got to the root of it all.

"Listen," he started, his voice serious, though she could hear the fear behind it. "I... Charlie Kate, I'm so sorry about last night. I just...when I saw you with that guy…"

"You went into big brother mode," she finished for him, shrugging, pulling her arms inside of his long sleeves. "I get it, James. It's okay."

"That's the thing." He shook his head, backing up onto the bed so that his back was against the wall, so that her crossed legs were brushing against his outer thigh. "It wasn't okay. You...you're right. I *don't* get to tell you what to do. You're a big girl. You have your own life. I just…"

Why was it so hard for him to just say the words, to let her know how he felt? It was so simple, too. *I didn't want you to be dancing with him. The way he had his hands all over you infuriated me. You should've been with me.*

But instead, the words stuck in his throat like glue, nothing but strangled sounds making their way into the open.

"We're really bad at this, aren't we?" she laughed, picking at her nails.

He laughed then, too, relaxing finally as he let his shoulders fall.

"Yeah. We kind of are." But inside, his thoughts were screaming otherwise.

Just say it.

I went to your room the other night.

That really invasive chick wouldn't let me in.

I didn't even want Lauren to be with me.

I wanted you.

Your hair looked so pretty last night.

It still looks pretty now.

Waking up with you here has been the best part about college so
far.

Instead, he stumbled over, "I guess we never really got to talk about…" which tripped over her, "I'm sorry about your date."

The word *date* sunk to the bottom of his gut like a rock, the fury from last night, from hearing vile words attack Charlotte from Lauren's lips, causing his body temperature to rise.

"No. That's not even *worthy* of a sorry." He was quick to reset her direction, his head snapping sideways so that she could see it in his eyes. "That's…I can't even say it's done, Charlie Kate. It wasn't even started."

That's a start. Keep going. I was thinking of you the whole time I was with her...

He watched her shrug, saw her eyes fall into her lap, and wanted so much to just pull her into his arms and string words into sentences that would make her understand. But he was stuck, stranded in a weird limbo of *This is Charlie Kate Murphy, your best friend* and *This is Charlie Kate, the same girl whose eyes you get lost in and whose touch can make you crumble.* Stuck enough for her to keep going. Apparently, *she* was able to string words into sentences this morning.

"Hey, you can...you can date whoever you want, James. I mean, preferably not the girl who called me a *bitch* last night but…"

She found solace in the long sleeves of the shirt he'd given her the night before, the one that had their high school logo on the front. The one that said **RAMSEY** in bold letters across the back above the number *18*. The cuffs that trailed well past her fingertips gave her something to focus on instead of looking into his eyes. If she did, he would be able to read right through her, would be able to see that *You can date whoever you want* came with the subtext of *Please, please say you want it to be me* etched into her corneas.

She was no good at this idea of *speaking your mind*. It would be up to James to fill in the blanks. They'd perfected the practice of reading each other's minds so well over the years. This should be no different. Right?

She laughed as her words trailed off. He did not, just sat there in stunned silence trying to decide what to say, what to *do* next. So far, she'd done all of the talking while his brain turned to mush.

"Maybe college is where we find our person, you know?"

Her voice was so small, scared even, and he wasn't sure he'd heard her by the way she was still talking to his comforter. But when she picked her head up, her eyes begging him to *Just say yes so we can end this painfully awkward conversation*, he could only nod his head, let a strangled, "Yeah," escape in agreement.

Relief fell in a breath, and her eyes were finally something other than sad.

"But hey. If I have to stand up in your wedding five years down the road, I don't want it to be next to someone who tried to have me murdered during my first weekend of college."

He only chuckled because she did.

"So... breakfast?"

He jumped at her suggestion, waiting patiently outside her door while she changed into something other than his pajamas and her outfit from last night. After a little bit of teasing ("What, you *don't* go to breakfast in four-inch heels and a mini-skirt? Then I am doing this college thing *all* wrong!"), they found themselves at a circular table in the dining hall joined by several other hungover freshman, swapping war stories over carbs and tall glasses of water.

When Lauren walked in, he didn't even make a passing glance in her direction.

Ginny's keys and phone hit the table in front of an empty chair, and she told Charlotte over her shoulder not to leave as she went to get a tray. James leaned over then, whispering, "That girl is *something*."

Charlotte giggled.

"Who? Ginny? Yeah, I can't say I disagree."

"She jumped me in the shower yesterday morning."

"She did *not*."

"Oh. But she *did*."

Laughter and red faces dissipated upon Ginny's return as formal introductions were made.

"It'll be nice to stop referring to you as *that chick who jumped me in the shower,* let me tell you," James quipped, stealing a hash brown from Charlotte's plate.

"You're not the only one on that list," was her instant comeback. Although he shivered at the thought, hung his head low as he shook it slowly from side to side, James knew that she would get along with them just fine.

Charlotte declined his invitation to watch the Red Sox game on his floor in favor of returning Ginny's outfit and "promising to catch up with her," but she said she'd text him later. He tried his best not to let the disappointment be too evident in his expression as he stalked up the stairs, his plans of continuing their discussion, gathering the courage to tell her how he truly felt crumbling with her *No*.

She was barely through Ginny's doorway before Ginny was saying, "*Spill.* I wanna know *everything*." When Charlotte was done recounting all of the details, Ginny took a moment to process before responding.

"What a little tart. At least he had the common sense to get rid of her."

Charlotte was in the middle of a chuckle when Ginny continued.

"But seriously. You're going to let him go just like that? It sounds to me like that isn't what either of you actually want."

Charlotte hugged a pillow to her chest, flopping backwards onto Ginny's bed with a hearty groan.

"I don't know, Ginny. He's my best friend. He'd do all of that stuff for me *anyway*. We've taken care of each other before. That's all it was."

"Yes, but how many times did it end up with you *sleeping*

together?"

"*Sleep* being the operative word," she shot back. "We did not have sex."

"But you could have. And you wanted to. And he probably did too."

Ginny shrugged, crossing her room to grab a soda and offer one to Charlotte.

"You two suck at communication. But I guess I can only tell you so many times to just tell him and get it over with. That whole *lead a horse to water* bullshit and all. I can't make your decisions for you, Charlotte Murphy."

Ginny shrugged again and turned the volume up on the television when it was evident that Charlotte had nothing more to say on the subject.

When the game started, Charlotte returned to her own room, shut the door, and slipped James's shirt on over her clothes. Burying her nose in the collar, she let herself get lost in the thought of *wearing the name Ramsey on her back* for a moment in time. He texted her when Dustin Pedroia hit a three-run triple, and she smiled, sniffled, and texted him back.

She met up with him in the dining hall for dinner, merging their two groups of friends into one large table.

When classes started and new people joined their lunch and dinner rituals, it wasn't long before Ben took a liking to her. He loved the Sox and listened to a bunch of the same music that she did.

Not long after, James met Alexa.

She was an education major and had curly, blonde hair.

It wasn't quite the same, but they'd get there.

"Charlotte Murphy, are you hooking up with my writing staff? How very Hollywood of you."

Her coffee hadn't even cooled off yet, but already, Charlotte was getting the third degree.

"What are you talking about?" she asked, her face already red as she busied herself in her computer screen.

"I'm not blind, sweetie. I see the way you two sneak around on lunch breaks. Oh, and I saw you outside at The Sidewalk Cafe on Saturday night. Looking pretty cozy, I might add."

Charlotte's head snapped up, her eyes wide as though she'd been caught red handed. Before she was able to respond, the room flooded with people and commotion.

"Oh, good lord almighty, would you check out the way that man is trying to devour you with his eyes?"

"Ginny, oh my god, stop it!"

Ginny snickered as Charlotte backhanded her and did her best to retract into her own skin, making herself as small as possible at their end of the table. When Jack caught her eye and passed her a warm smile, she did her best not to split her cheeks.

"You're blushing. You really like him, don't you?"

She smiled at her lap, nervously brushing her wide curls behind her ears as she keyed up her Google Doc and added the day's date, making special note of the agenda that Dan had posted.

"What does James think about it?" Ginny whispered while Dan continued to tick off their goals for the day.

It was this question that gave Charlotte pause and caused her thoughts to come to a halt for the first time since the race had begun. They hadn't really spoken about her date, save for a few errant texts and the phone call Sunday morning. James's tone had been all apologies, and he seemed like he was happy for her, but at the same time, there was something foreign in the way his words formed together, something she couldn't quite put her finger on.

Pursing her lips, her fingers clacked furiously against the keyboard as she said, "He needs to be okay with it, whether or not he really is. He...Jack makes me happy. That should make James happy, too."

As she finished her words with a curt nod and smiled at Jack across the table, she tried her best to convince herself that they weren't said for her own benefit.

It was convenient, Charlotte realized, to be able to see Jack every day, whether it was being on set together for nine hours, or only catching the occasional glimpse and an hour lunch break together. But it was something that took away the ambiguity, the *When will I see you next?* She'd been with one too many pen-pals for her liking, and the fact that Jack made just as much effort as she did to seek her out on set or flash a smile her way or text or call her even though they'd just been together all day told her that this was so much different.

It was that feeling that had her asking him out for coffee after work.

She paid, insisting that it was only fair. They reclined in comfy lounge chairs, sharing smiles and swapping stories of where their love of writing came about. Jack told her about his first penned play back in fourth grade, how his teacher had encouraged the students in his class that year to branch out and had given opportunities for creativity rather than just stilted opinion essays. When his teacher had asked if he would be willing to submit his piece for a reader's theater performance, Jack recalled exactly how warm his chest was, the feeling of his muscles swelling to stretching capacity while he watched his words come to life with feeling and emotion, and how the audience laughed at his jokes and sympathized with his characters. It was that exact feeling that he wanted to replicate over and over again.

Charlotte then admitted to what spurred her reticence when it came to sharing her publications. David's name was mentioned when she recalled the incident on her first day of kindergarten. But it was when she recounted the details of reluctantly entering a writing contest in 6th grade, when she heard her name and her piece introduced in front of the whole school, only to be criticized and laughed at by every boy in the building, that her notebooks remained mostly hidden.

Another late night found Charlotte choosing to stick around the office to work on her book rather than going home and killing the workflow. Jack claimed to have script notes himself, and an hour later, they were enjoying pizza and vending machine sodas, swapping stories from college, where Charlotte learned of Jack's brief stint in his campus's improv group, a few drunken escapades, and his eventual "nice guy" schtick coming to fruition as he took on the role of RA for junior and senior year.

When he asked her to a more casual dinner on Thursday night, he laughed at her admittance to a brief gothic phase ("It seriously lasted a week, and then I was too scared to go back into Hot Topic anymore. And my dad took my black nail polish away. I'm pretty sure it's still decaying somewhere in the cabinet in my parent's bathroom"). She grinned with white, shiny teeth when he was blushing as he asked if she wanted to continue the night back at his apartment.

While they dabbled in the awkwardness of *being in Jack's apartment for the first time,* Charlotte's words traversed down the road of *first dorms* and *first apartments* and hot red cheeks as soon as she let it slip that she and James shared an apartment when they first moved to California.

Jack's throat bobbed as he gulped, and she tried to play it off like she didn't see the way his neck twitched before his hand snuck back to rub at the skin below his hairline.

"You guys used to live together?" he asked with a sip of wine.

"Uhm, yeah, yeah we did for a couple of years. In college, too, actually," she admitted, realizing that it was better to get it all on the table now than to have to revisit the subject later on.

She watched him, biting her lip and fidgeting with a loose thread at the hem of her shirt as the wheels in his eye turned, his words being woven carefully before he spoke.

"So, I guess...I should just ask this now, instead of letting it eat away at me. I mean, I know you said he's your best friend and all, Charlotte, but did you and James...did you guys ever date?"

It was the million-dollar question, really. Images danced in her head, of first kisses and the backseat of his car in the late summer nights, of waking up in his arms in her dorm, or their LA apartment, or the basement couch at his parent's place back in Newton. But as the thoughts played like a soundtrack to her life, so too did the wordlessness of it all, the countless times where words failed and were replaced by touches or silences or stumbling over a whole lot of nonsense before jokes piled up in a high wall of defense mechanisms, throwing them both off guard with a sigh of relief and an easy out once again.

She could feel Jack's eyes on her, realizing that she'd been lost inside her own head for a minute, and chose her words carefully.

"He, um...the short answer, Jack? No. No, we, uhm...we never *dated*."

The desperation in her eyes was palpable, the glassiness a plea for him to not press on, because she didn't have the time nor the answers to keep going. His sad smile and nod caused her shoulders to relax. He slipped an arm around her, pulling her against his body, and the tension slowly slipped from her pores.

When he suggested a movie and queued up something random on Netflix that she knew she wasn't going to pay attention to, he interrupted the vacancy of her thoughts with a question that struck her with nerves and hope all in the same moment.

"Hey, why don't we go on a double date with James and his girlfriend sometime?"

The way that his words were so soft, brushing the top of her head when he turned his nose towards her, had her body warm. Though she didn't want to move from where she was resting against his shoulder, she jerked her head up suddenly, her eyes wide and hopeful.

"Really?"

"Yeah, really," he replied, no trace of laughter or raised eyebrows or sarcasm in sight. Just Jack, calm, kind, cool Jack, who was making every effort he could to accept everything about her rather than shy away at the first sign of weakness.

Once plans were made to talk to James the next night and organize a date, her body seemed lighter, and she let herself relax into Jack just a little bit more.

It wasn't long into their movie and glass of wine that Jack's nervous hands were becoming more vocal, brushing and clenching hesitantly up and down her arms until she couldn't take it anymore and brought her lips to his.

She'd kissed her fair share of men over the years, but as Jack's hands covered her cheeks and wound in her hair and tentatively traced down her spine to the small of her back, she found herself comparing more so than letting herself enjoy the ride.

His hands, for one, were much smaller than James's lanky fingers. They covered less of her, had to do more to catch up, as they cradled her waist to draw her closer.

His lips were more tentative, but also softer.

This was something she had come to figure, though; his entire demeanor when it came to her was light and unsure and always with one foot still on dry land. She still didn't know what to make of it.

James was like that at first, but once he knew her lips and her face and her body, he wouldn't hesitate to do whatever he could to make her feel good, to push her over the edge, to let her know just what he meant to her.

So, in her quest to *move forward* and *break the cycle*, she did her best to take the initiative.

Her hands were on his chest, around his neck, in his hair. *Shorter hair. Stiffer hair. A darker brown than I'm used to—Knock it off!*

When his tongue so much as ghosted her lips, she opened beneath his, inviting him in like an open door.

Her hands tickled up and down his chest, lingering at the waistband of his jeans before skirting north again. Jack's lips turned up beneath hers, but he only continued to kiss her, to skim the surface.

James would've pushed his hips into me. He would've made some snarky comment about me being a tease. Would've pinned me back and would've been hovering over me with that wild look in his eyes by now—

Stop.

She couldn't put her finger on what possessed her to pull Jack forwards, to lay herself down across his couch and tug on his hands so that he followed. But when he was finally pushing the envelope, if only a little more with his lips on her throat and his tongue making her head fall back against the headrest, she let her head go dizzy and her eyes clenched shut and she willed herself to just enjoy this.

It wasn't until she was chest deep in water, when her hands were doing their best to clutch onto hair that wasn't quite long enough for her desires, when her knees were squeezing at his hips and his hands were finally skirting just beneath the hem of her shirt, that he was suddenly pulling back. His kisses were farther between, the space between them growing cold as he propped his body above hers on his elbows.

"Sorry," he breathed through closed eyes and a wide smile. "Got carried away."

She tried to brush off his apology, did her best to pull him back to her, but failed when he was tugging on her wrists and pulling her back into a seated position.

"Hey," she urged, her fingertips now desperate on his thighs as he sat upright on his haunches, her body buzzing with a sudden need to *do this* for reasons unidentified as she moved her lips closer. "Don't apologize."

She was kissing him again, and though his hands were cupping her face and he was kissing her back, it wasn't very long before he was pulling away again, curling his lips inside of a wide smile as he rested his forehead against hers.

"I just...Charlotte, I don't wanna mess this up."

It caught her off guard to say the least, the way he was so upfront for what she would call the first time since they had really started to get to know one another. He was staring down at where their hands were joined together in his lap. Suddenly, she felt incredibly embarrassed for trying to jump him.

"I really, *really* like you, Murphy. I don't want to make this seem like some kind of fling."

"No," she heard herself say, her lips curling into a smile as those doubts from earlier began to fade, to shift into the man on the couch before her. "No, I don't either."

"Okay. Good."

There was the Jack she had come to know, the one with the shy smile and the eyes that couldn't meet her. The one who was laughing nervously now, whose hands she could feel shaking.

So instead, she pushed back her own insecurities, pushed back his doubts, and kissed him, smiling against his lips, tugging on his hands again so that he knew it was okay to hold her hips and take it slow.

"I really like you too, just so we're clear," she murmured against his smile.

She felt the way that *Good* traced off his tongue and skirted past her lips, let him roam his hands along her back and up on her shoulders, let him nudge her gently so that her face was turning and she was barring her neck to him and his lips were doing soft, nibbling things to the skin below her ear.

She let him pull away, let him flash her this wide, toothy grin as his body hit the back of the couch with a resounding *thud*, his hands tangling through the hair that she hadn't already pulled out of place.

She let him hold her to his side, run his fingers up and down her arms, while the movie played on. When it was getting late and she was getting sleepy and he walked her to her car, she let him kiss her slow and long, his tongue smooth and teasing and eliciting little noises in the back of her throat that had her contemplating why he hadn't just invited her to stay the night.

But with Jack, things were different, and she could tell already.

He was serious about this. He wanted to take his time with her and do things the right way. It was a fleeting thought in her mind on the ride home, why he was this way. She also realized that, hopefully, they had the time to flesh it all out.

He had stuck by her so far, had endured an incredibly awkward encounter with her best friend, was willing to schedule their next date for Saturday instead of Friday, and still wanted her despite it all.

But still, as she wound down for the night and pulled on her pajamas and drifted off to sleep, her dreams fought between two different men, leaving her thrashing and restless.

194

"Oh my god. I am *done* with this weather."

It was May 18th, and despite the date on the calendar, Charlotte trudged through the doors to their on-campus apartment in heavy boots and a winter jacket. James, with feet propped up on the coffee table, chuckled over the top of his Saturday morning coffee. Finals were done for him, student teaching was finally finished for her, and on the brink of graduation, they were supposed to be packing up to move back home. However, as Charlotte had offered to head out to get more boxes, Sports Center had pulled James's butt to the couch and away from his promise to start taking the dishes out of the cabinets to organize them. He was afraid he'd be reprimanded, but he said a silent thank you to Mother Nature, as the snow had clearly distracted her.

"It *is* a little ridiculous," he retorted.

Throughout their childhood, he'd simply gotten used to the idea that Massachusetts weather was bipolar. Charlotte, on the other hand, was so vocal about the cold weather that he could parrot her words before they were even out of her mouth, which he did as she stung the air with, "It is *May*, James. The snow needs to *go*. I am *moving* to California."

Typically, she was too caught up in her rants, with her head thrown back and her fists clenched, to notice his little charade. But today, as she propped open the soggy boxes to dry, she noticed the way his face twisted while he mimicked her words, snickering at the end.

"Hey!"

"What?" He continued snickering, his hands held up in defense.

Her body language spoke for her, arms folded and eyebrows cocked.

"Oh, come on, Charlie Kate. It's *too* easy. You say the same thing every winter. And yet, here you sit, in the heartland of shitty snowstorms."

His smug grin only deflated her mood further, and with boots still on, she sunk into the futon, pulling the snow dusted beanie from hair that was speckled in moisture.

James joined her, changing his expression from heckling to reassuring as he tossed his arm around her shoulder and pulled her against his side.

"We're about to graduate college and move out into the real world, James. I'm twenty-two years old, and in four days, I'll be moving back into my parent's basement. What am I *doing* with my life?"

"Trying to figure it out like the rest of us?"

His eyes spoke calmly, reassuringly.

"I mean, I think I sent my resume out to at least a hundred different places, and that was just this week. Relax. You're on the doorstep to the rest of your life, Smalls. Why don't you just do it?"

Scrunching her eyebrows, she adjusted her position under his arm to see his eyes more clearly.

"Do what?"

"Move to California," he said seriously. "You've been threatening to leave since the first time you went to Disneyland, so it's obviously not just a fluke. You can get a teaching job anywhere. Why not there?"

Fear suddenly washed her face, her eyes bugging from their sockets as her lips scrunched smaller.

"I am *not* moving to California," she stated simply.

"Why?" He was pushing, but suddenly, he felt that she needed the challenge.

"I mean, I... James, my family is here, my home is here. God, *you're* here. My *life* is in Boston. I can't just...*move* across the country. I can't…"

The silence choked her words, and he could hear the hum of their heater kick in again.

"Yes. You *can*," he said, his tone low and reassuring, with a slight chuckle pulling at his lips. "The only thing stopping you is *you*, Charlie Kate."

They had gone from griping to serious life talk in the flick of a switch, and suddenly, it was all too overwhelming. Graduation. Getting a "real job." Being financially responsible for *everything*. Moving to California? Tears suddenly rushed to her eyes, pooling down her cheeks in fat streams.

He hadn't meant to upset her, but when her expression swapped out, *I'm pissed about the weather* for *Please help me, my life is falling apart*, he gathered her in his arms in an instant.

"Woah, hey, shh, it's okay."

Words weren't necessary to voice her fears; they were written all over her face in a language that only he understood.

Instead of throwing her fears in her face, he reached for the remote and turned on a Saturday movie marathon. He kept her clutched to his side as her tears eventually dissipated, her sobs stifled, and her cries turned into laughter at the drama on screen as visions of palm trees danced in her head.

California, the vacation she voted for each time her mom and dad asked the Murphy clan where they wanted to go next. She had fallen in love at a young age, not only with the warm weather and beach close by, but with the ambience, the sunny sky, and the fact that it never seemed to be sad and dreary in California. It wasn't a pipe dream, because as James had so clearly stated, she could take her degree and go anywhere. But no matter how many times she had walked up the beaches in La Jolla or skipped down San Francisco sidewalks, it was the fear of the unknown that had her rooted to her spot, stuck in familiarity and comfort.

Apartment 302 was eventually reduced to nothing but a truckload of boxes, one heading to her parent's and one heading to his. Being only an hour from home, it wasn't really a shock to be back in their childhood bedrooms, and days later, he made the familiar walk down Haynes Road under the shady trees in balmy, seventy-degree weather. The snow had melted almost entirely and children on front lawns were wearing shorts and t-shirts as they enjoyed the sneak peek of summertime. He had to chuckle. Massachusetts weather was indeed bipolar.

He'd long since foregone knocking or ringing the doorbell to the Murphy home, and as he slipped off his shoes next to the mat, he knew right where he would find her.

The basement had taken on many drastic transformations: first, a playroom, then a practice space for their fluke of a band, a rumpus room back in high school, and now a hodgepodge of storage and Will Murphy's workout equipment. But through the barbells, there was enough room to see the ancient box television, its picture quality somehow still hanging on. She was sitting cross-legged in the middle of the couch that had long since made its way down from the living room. The lights were off, leaving her in a grey overhang with just enough light cascading in from the well windows to make out her surroundings.

She turned her head, knowing without fail who was standing at the bottom of the stairs.

"Did you unpack yet?" he asked.

"Nope. Just been hanging out here for a little while. Figured I'd start when I really needed something from the bottom of a box."

"Good. Don't."

"Why not?"

"Because it would be *so* backwards to unpack all of your stuff when you're just going to have to pack it back up again."

He crossed his arms over his body, the crinkle in his eyebrow asking her why she wasn't yet privy to such obvious information.

"You wanna elaborate a little here? I'm not sure I follow."

"Pack your bags, Murph. We're heading West."

"What are you talking about?" she questioned, planting her feet on the floor as she turned to face him, finally giving him all of her attention.

"I got a job offer in LA, and I'm in desperate need of a roomie. So, I figured since you've done so much extensive research on the place, you might be able to give me a hand here? You've been putting up with me for the past two years anyway. I figured I might as well take someone with me who will make sure the dishes are done and that I don't live off of Ramen noodles."

It was truly one of his favorite sights in the world, right next to the Green Monster under stadium lights, when her eyes lit up and her smile widened like that.

"You're joking," she said, jumping from the couch, not a hint of irony in her voice.

"Absolutely not. The offer is on the table, just waiting for my approval."

"James." Her teeth reflected brightly in the dimness of the basement, and she waited for one more confirmation, a pinch to tell her it wasn't real, before she truly let her quickened heartbeat run free.

"So, what do you say? Roomies again?"

"Oh my *god*!"

She catapulted herself into his arms, letting him pick her up from the floor and whirl her around before coming physically back to earth. Mentally, she was on cloud nine.

As she clung to him, still squealing in his arms, he silently praised God for the still available positions that he had found when, just days prior, he was sitting cross-legged on his bedroom floor, surrounded by unpacked boxes, with one goal on his mind as he sent out his resume, one that had nothing to do with his own self-interests.

Of course, their parents weren't at all thrilled by the sudden change in direction, their two babies heading to the literal opposite side of the country. It made it much easier that they were doing things together, though. The tears were worse than the day they moved into college, but the entire family was there, packed into a rental van to help them make the journey west.

They stopped along the way in places like Chicago and Omaha, taking a detour to see the Grand Canyon, making a pit stop in Vegas even though Abby couldn't get into any of the casinos.

It wasn't until they were finally alone in their new apartment, surrounded by their childhood in cardboard boxes, that reality began to set in.

He would begin his big boy career the following week, working in a marketing department for a big corporation. She was scouting the area for schools in need of teachers with a few interviews set up so far: one in 5th grade and one in kindergarten.

Although Jerry and Will had helped assemble beds and Linda and Julie had washed the sheets and covered the mattresses before heading to the airport, they were huddled in the middle of their living room floor, surrounded by blankets and pillows and a set of cheap wine glasses that they had purchased at Target.

"We have to celebrate *now,* Rango!"

He just smiled and clinked their glasses together over *new beginnings with my oldest friend,* as they did their best to combat the fact that back home in Newton where their bodies still clung, it was already midnight, despite the mock of 9:00 PM from the clock on the wall.

Neither wanted to unpack just yet, so he settled for hooking up his XBox as a DVD player to their still cable-less television set and popped in the first movie he could unearth.

She scarcely paid any attention to *National Treasure* but was more aware of the way that James's breathing was low and slow, the way that he was perched so casually with his back against the foot of the couch and his legs crossed at the ankle in front of them. His arm was draped loosely around her, the way it so often was, as he polished off his wine and let the glass form a ring on the coffee table that his dad had let him take from the basement.

It hit her hard, snuggled up next to him, that they were truly alone. There would be no running—or even driving—off to Mom and Dad's if things got tough. That thought alone caused her body to go stiff, had her hands clasping more tightly to his thigh where they had been resting. He tended immediately to her reaction, tilting his gaze towards her.

"What's wrong?"

She had tears in her eyes when he tipped her chin up and forced her to look him in the eye.

"What if I don't know how to cook an egg?"

"What?" he replied, scrunching his eyebrows in severe confusion.

"What if I don't know how to cook an egg? And then the apartment burns down? What about taxes? James, I don't know the first thing about taxes! Or if the toilet breaks? I know we have a plunger, but do *you* know the first thing about plumbing, because *I* certainly don't—"

"Hey," he chuckled, putting distance between them as he turned to face her and took her shaking hands between his. "Breathe, slick."

She took a few shaky breaths, opening her eyes to find him too calm.

"You're not freaking out. Why aren't you freaking out?"

"Because, Smalls, we're going to be okay."

He shrugged. It was that simple.

He continued, told her things like, "We're here together" and, "Home is only a phone call away" and, "When in doubt, there's always Google." But it was the certainty in his tone when he shrugged and told her it would be okay, the confidence when he said, "And besides, I've got you, and you've got me. Frankly, that's about all I've ever needed," that did her in.

When she was in his lap with her lips pressed squarely to his, it didn't take long before his hands were at her waist, guiding her into a more comfortable position where she was straddling his hips and he could hold onto her more firmly.

He was on his back with her knees on either side when he finally asked against the hollow of her throat, "What are we doing?"

"Christening the apartment. Beating the time change. Does it really need a name?"

Her words were split with kisses and peeling his shirt over the top of his head, answered only with a swift *No* before he was moving her onto her back and reminding her that he was the only home she truly needed.

James was a bundle of nerves on Friday. It was the first time he would be seeing Charlotte since their fight, the first time seeing Charlotte since her date with Jack. It was too much time in his eyes, but that anticipation was made all the worse by the fire, the need that his body had to see her, as if she was the drug he'd been withdrawn from all those days long.

So he actually cleaned the condo for her arrival, wore something other than his after work sweats, showered and *shaved* before she was expected to arrive, all without the thought that this was *just Charlotte* because she *wasn't* Just Charlotte. When he answered the front door to her soft knocking, the tightness in his chest stole oxygen from his lungs.

It had nothing to do with her appearance—she was wearing a pair of jean shorts and a ratty T-shirt from college, her curls up in a high ponytail, any traces of the little makeup she typically wore already gone from her day at work. No. It was the fact that a piece of his heart, the missing, aching piece, was finally restored and standing in front of him. And the grin on his face, the way his smile was full, and his eyebrows were high, and a little chuckle was gathering in his throat, told him that he was home.

"You okay?" she chuckled. "You know I'm not Publisher's Clearing House, right?"

He took no notice in the way that her eyebrows were pinched, and one was cocked, and her eyes were wide with a smile tugging at her lips. Instead, he was trying to figure out where exactly the halo of light was coming from, since his porch was covered, and the door was facing eastward, away from the setting sun.

"I'm, uh, I'm just happy to see you."

He didn't even shrug, had no doubt for his emotion, and let her know it when he all but pulled her over the doorway and into his arms. He tucked her head firmly beneath his chin and to his chest, where he finally exhaled.

"I'm happy to see you, too," she whispered, letting her body sag against his, her arms tightening around his back as he breathed her in.

When they parted, he swept his arm across the entryway to beckon her inside, his grin subsiding to one that crawled up the side of his face instead of one that would blind her with its brightness.

He followed her to the living room, watching her take a pillow in her lap immediately as his own body flopped on the opposite end. He let out a contented sigh, his lips upturning once again, as she chuckled and shook her head.

"What's so funny over there?"

"Oh, nothing," she chuckled, shaking her head again. "You just, I don't know. I've always loved that goofy smile of yours, but I *can*not accept that it's just because I'm here."

"Well, deal with it," he said, chucking his own pillow at her with a smile. "I missed my friend. Especially after the past week we've had."

As her eyes asked *Are you sure?* and his immediately responded with *You'd better believe it*, she smiled a warm smile that softened her eyes and settled a blanket of calm over the room.

From there, it was cracked open beers and playing catch up and offhanded jokes until a deep yawn from Charlotte had James taunting her with, "You'd better not be flaking out on me, Smalls. It's only 7:30!" before Charlotte was squinting one eye and tossing back, "Hey, cut me some slack. I've had some late nights this week."

"Oh, are you guys doing night shoots or something?"

"No, uh…"

He knew what it was before the words could string into a sentence that would break him despite his stance in the whole situation. Still, they didn't sting any less when she stared into her lap and let them fly free.

"I've been hanging out with Jack a lot this week, actually. We got coffee and dinner a couple times. Honestly, it's really convenient that we work together."

She was laughing nervously, almost like she was trying to justify the fact that she'd seen him on three separate occasions in the six days since their first date. She peeled at the label on her beer then, offering James a sideways glance, a plea for him to fill the silence so that she didn't have to keep talking.

His *Oh* was soft, like a surprised breath, and he leaned back into the couch, trying to mask the fact that he was indeed sinking.

"So, you guys...you must be getting along pretty well then?"

"Mhm. I'd say so."

It didn't pass him by that she was still staring at her lap, still fidgeting with her beer bottle, but he didn't want to digest that, didn't want to ask and tear everything wide open. Not now. Not when he had just gotten her back.

In the next minutes of silence, the room was buzzing with the sounds of their thoughts on parallel roller coaster tracks, whizzing and dropping and trying to find a way out before the big loopdeeloop had them both jumping off in fear of being sick.

But like he always seemed to do, James jumped in and saved the day. Though his words were a whisper in the thick air, they weighed her down like a truck.

"Is he good to you, Charlie Kate? That's really all that matters."

She tried to stop her eyes from glossing over, tried to swallow down the tight ball in her throat that prevented her from returning more than a nod for a full minute.

Eventually, she managed to say, "Yeah, Rango. He's good to me."

A silent, slow wave formed between them, tickling the sands and brushing gently against their toes.

The rest of the night was warm and content, and although her head was in his lap as they watched the FX Friday night feature, he let his body revel in the fact that she was here, and she was happy. It was that realization that patched him up but made him bleed all in the same moment.

It wasn't *him* that was making her happy this time. It was *Jack,* and everything else that was happening in this *new* part of her life that he could only steal fleeting glimpses of. It hurt when it shouldn't, the happiness that he wasn't really a part of, made him ache when he glanced down to see her eyes fluttering closed and her head nodding as she fought to stay awake.

It took every fiber of his being to not let her fall asleep in his arms;

his body screamed at him as he nudged her with his knee and scratched his fingers across the crown of her head.

She couldn't sleep here tonight.

He couldn't, in good conscious, let her fall asleep in his lap, on his couch, when she was trying her hardest to get to know another man. Especially one that made her this happy.

He also couldn't, in good conscious, trust himself. Because the pain in his chest was screaming for him to scoop her up and take her to bed and hold her and kiss and do nothing but love her until they were all that existed.

So, he poked the bear, knowing it wouldn't be too bad since she was only on the edge of sleep and not fully engrossed just yet.

"Hey, sleepy head. C'mon, let's get you home."

She replied in muffled sounds and incoherent words that had him choking back a groan of frustration, peeling his eyes away as she twitched in her sleep. It was painful, because in some alternate universe where he actually spoke what was on his mind and had told her how he felt a long time ago, he would've been waking her up just to move her to the bed that they shared.

Instead, he got to watch in silence, with pocketed hands, as she slipped on her shoes and rubbed the sleep from her eyes, getting ready to return to an apartment where she slept alone, where someday soon, she might be sharing the couch and the bed with someone who wasn't him.

But suddenly, she was wide awake.

"Oh! Before I forget: Jack wants to double date with you and Vanessa soon."

"He does?"

"Yeah. It was his idea actually. He said we could do something fun, like go mini golfing or something. Do you, uh...do you think you guys would be interested?"

He had no choice in the matter, because the way her big green eyes were asking, he literally couldn't say no.

"Absolutely. Just so long as he realizes that I *can* and *will* kick his ass in front of his new girlfriend and he's just going to have to deal with it."

The word *girlfriend* tasted weird and bitter on his tongue, but it helped a little that she jumped back at the mention of the word, too, following with a hurried, "Oh, he's, uh, we haven't really…" before he jumped in and saved her with an, "I'm kidding," and a jab on the shoulder.

"Now, go home and sleep. You're delirious, Smalls. You owe me a full movie with no naps next time."

She smiled sleepily at him as she leaned against the open door jam and rested her eyes.

"You've got it, Rango."

"Hey, text me when you get home so I know you didn't roll off into a ditch, okay?"

She nodded and folded her tired body into him warmly for a goodbye hug, and he couldn't tell whether the feeling in his chest was his heart expanding or breaking.

Charlotte spent her drive home tossing her thoughts around anxiously just to keep herself awake. James's demeanor was different tonight, different than all of those other times she had talked with him about a boyfriend. He used to get defensive, would brush it off in a tone that still scoffed annoyance.

But tonight, he was soft, warm, the look in his eyes hauntingly sad, like he wanted to say so much more than he had.

Then again, the few words he'd expressed on the subject carried so much more weight than a monologue.

I'm just happy to see you.

I missed my friend.

Is he good to you?

God was her heart heavy.

It only made matters worse that, when she pulled into her driveway, she had a text from James and a missed call from Jack.

James's text was one she could have copied and pasted from any of the past twelve years.

You make it home okay, kiddo? Don't make me drive across town to tuck you in.

It was usually easy to respond, to find humor and wit and make him eat his words while they carried on a pointless text conversation for the next hour and a half. But she found herself as wordless as they'd been all night, choosing **Home safe and sound** instead of jokes this time.

She waited until she was inside and in pajamas before she called Jack, settling into her pillow as the call rang on the other end. The background noise when he answered reminded her of a crowded bar or restaurant, and her suspicions were confirmed when he answered with, "Hey, give me a sec, I need to step outside," and then, moments later, "Sorry about that, it was too loud in there."

"That's okay," she chuckled. "You out painting the town red without me, McKinney?"

"Not even close," he laughed back. She could imagine him standing on the sidewalk, his body leaned up against the building as he hunched over and stuffed his free hand inside his pocket. "A friend of mine invited a few guys out to dinner. They're all on about round number seven, while yours truly has been trying to find the appropriate moment to sneak away for the past forty-five minutes now."

"Oh really? And why's that?"

"Don't get me wrong, dinner was nice. The *getting drunk* part is something I tried to leave in college though. Plus, I was spending too much time thinking about you instead of enjoying my night out."

This newfound confidence that was peeking through the cracks of Jack McKinney made her veins tingly, her face flush.

"Well, I certainly don't want to hold you back from having fun," came out as a whisper, her vocal cords suddenly tied.

"I'd be having more fun if you were here."

It took her until he spoke again to realize that he couldn't see her blushing and smiling, that when you were talking over the phone, you had to use words in order to communicate.

"Hey, did you have fun with James tonight?"

"Oh, yeah, we watched some shitty movie and had a few beers. It was nice to catch up. He said he'd love to do a double date next Friday, if we're free."

"I'm glad you had fun. And interesting. Are we a *we* now?"

She could hear the laughter in his voice, could picture his eyebrows pinching, and wondered if his confidence was brought on by the mask of telephone lines, too.

"I mean, I could very well go by myself and third wheel—"

"You know I'm teasing you."

She giggled and brushed him off.

"I guess that's a conversation we might have to have tomorrow night, huh, Murphy?"

"Can't wait."

She made him promise that he would text her that he was home safely from his *night of drunken escapades* as they said their goodbyes, and her heart beat in a wild cadence as she plugged her phone in and tried to wind down for the night.

But as she checked her notifications one more time, realizing she'd been texted while she was on the phone with Jack, her emotions blended once again.

Good. I don't know what I'd do without you, Charlie Kate. Sleep tight. Don't let the bed bugs bite.

July 2018

Charlotte's knee bounced wildly in the front passenger seat of Jack's car. She chewed her fingernails, her nerves bringing a flush to her face in the otherwise mild summer day. When a warm hand rested on her thigh, she twitched her gaze sideways, where Jack was doing his best to keep his eyes on the road.

"You okay there, Miss Jitters?" His words were smooth and cool, laced with a chuckle.

She rolled her eyes, letting out a loud breath as she groaned.

"I don't know why I'm so nervous. I shouldn't be nervous, right?"

"Considering he and I have already met and made it through a seemingly awkward conversation without killing each other or spontaneously combusting? No, you shouldn't be nervous."

He gave her hand a gentle squeeze, puffed out a breath of laughter, and turned his attention back to the road.

"What are you so nervous about?"

"I don't know," she mused, peering out the window. "I guess...It's just, I *need* you guys to get along. You can't *not* get along, because that would just...it would ruin everything. I need my best friend and my boyfriend to get along, or the world might honestly implode."

It was new, this word *boyfriend*. She felt like she was back in high school, throwing it around loosely so that people would know she was taken. But now, in adulthood, it was less about *celebrating one-week anniversaries* and *being Facebook official,* but so much more about knowing that this man wanted to be with her, and only her.

He had told her so the previous Saturday night, over an impromptu picnic hike that had taken them through Runyon Canyon Park, where he'd confessed that it hadn't been this way since Molly, that he had been so scared to have these feelings again, but he knew that he was ready and willing to try, if she was.

And boy was she willing, as emphasized by her words and her smile and the move of her lips softly against his.

Now, as her voice trailed and her thoughts wound together like a knotted ball of string, she let out another strong breath of air, her eyes pleading in his direction.

"It's okay. I get it." His voice was calm as he put the car in park and turned to face her. "This is important to you. I will do my absolute best job to not hate your best friend."

She wrapped her fingers around his outstretched hand and squeezed, offering him a relieved tight-lipped smile, and a "Thank you."

Charlotte and Jack walked hand in hand, their arms swinging between their bodies as Charlotte chewed nervously on the fingernails of her free hand. They approached the ticket window of the miniature golf course where several groups and couples were making their purchases and walking away with clubs and balls in hand. When Charlotte spotted James's tall figure sticking out of a crowd of other milling patrons, her body tensed, her face running warm.

But he smiled when he saw her. It wasn't quite his goofy grin, but a genuine, warm smile, his lips closed and full with his head nodding in her direction.

She did her best to quell the churning in her gut, the way it always seemed to kick up a notch when she saw his fingers knotted with Vanessa's.

It was always strange to see him in new clothing that she hadn't helped him pick out at the store, but the blue and white plaid suited him. It also, she noticed, disgustingly matched the navy top and white shorts that Vanessa donned. Her fingernails were brushing her lips again when Jack squeezed their hands, his whisper low and reassuring in her ear.

"Next time, remind me to text you before we go out so that we can coordinate our outfits."

She snickered, her nose turning to brush his shoulder as she let her free hand fall to her side.

"Stop it," she whispered breathily.

"No, I'm serious. I feel out of place. Are we the inferior couple now?"

That word *couple* had her stomach churning with a new feeling altogether.

"Not at all," she replied. "But, just so we're all on the same page, that is one-hundred percent Vanessa. James hates plaid."

It wasn't the admission that James's girlfriend could be controlling whenever they went out in public that struck her, but the fact that *James hates plaid* rolled so easily off her tongue, that stopped her for a moment before she was yanked forward again.

When they were close enough, Charlotte dropped Jack's hand and greeted James with a hug and *Good to see you* before moving on to Vanessa.

She then watched in stunted anxiety as Jack did the same, winding his arm around Vanessa to greet her with a hug before exchanging a handshake with James. Realization dawned on her that, at any second, these men could fist fight over her, and for a fleeting moment, she wanted to crawl into a hole and hide.

But then they were all smiles, and the gentlemen were being gentlemen as they paid for clubs, and James pocketed the scorecard as they found the wall of multicolored balls to choose from.

"Oh! They have teal," Charlotte exclaimed.

Without missing a beat, James pulled a quarter from his pocket, eyed Charlotte competitively, and flipped it into the air.

"Tails, Rango," she said victoriously. "Fork it over."

She smiled smugly as James rolled his eyes and plopped the teal ball into her hand, his head turned back towards the sky as he groaned. He chose the navy-blue ball before selecting his club.

While Charlotte followed James out to the first hole on the course, Jack and Vanessa gathered their balls and clubs. As Jack pulled the forest green ball from the PVC holder, he spoke, his gaze still trained on the technicolor array of spheres.

"Do they always do that?"

Vanessa, also transfixed as she chose hot pink, rolled her gaze up to meet Jack in a way that said *You've got a lot to learn, pal.*

"Only if there's a teal ball. Otherwise, he gets navy blue and she gets purple."

She shrugged, offering an ironic chuckle, and headed out the door.

Jack shook the squalid feeling and followed to join the group.

Despite the awkward moment, mini golf turned into an evening of laughs and friendly competition. They agreed on guys versus girls, losers to buy ice cream, which paired Charlotte with Vanessa in a tight night of conversation that was lots of hushed whispers and giggles in the direction of the men.

This, of course, gave Jack and James a lot of forced time together at the ostracizing of the ladies.

As James watched the two best women in his life conspiring at the start of hole five, he realized that this was important to Charlotte, that he get along with Jack. It brought him back to his first weeks with Vanessa, to the nerves that overfilled him when he had introduced her to Charlotte. He wanted them to get along, to click, to be best friends and take each other shopping and kick him out of the room so that they could have sleepovers. Granted, it clearly hadn't transpired in exactly that way, but they were more than civil, and the least he could do was return the favor.

So he sucked in a breath, sucked up his pride, and nudged Jack with his shoulder.

"Hey, what do you say we try to throw them off their game here?" he said with a faux suggestive look in his eyes. "Can't have the ladies knocking us down."

"Yeah, that could be fun," Jack said back, as the two men began to conspire.

He didn't realize that his plan would backfire, as he saw Jack sidle up behind Charlotte with his hands on her hips as he pretended to help with her stance. It got under his skin, the way that her face blushed, the way she giggled and backed into him playfully.

He wouldn't admit either way if that had any impact on the sudden kiss that he pulled Vanessa into, the one that surprised her, had her gasping as he blinked down with a hazy smile.

It went along like this, the little game of *touch tag* that they were unconsciously playing. Whenever one of them would so much as scoot closer to their significant other, the other would do the same, in a one-upping cycle.

Jack would lean in to whisper something to Charlotte, and James would immediately snake his arm around Vanessa.

James high-fived Vanessa after a hole in one, clasped their hands together, pulled her in for a quick peck, and suddenly Charlotte's hands were running over Jack's chest in a light scratching motion.

After the ladies came out victorious and they made their way for ice cream, it was James who placed the orders, wincing slightly when he realized that he only had to turn to ask Jack what kind of ice cream he wanted, because he had already placed orders for himself, Vanessa, and Charlotte.

But it was all taken in stride, a few backhanded comments from Jack to the tune of, "Man, do I have a lot of catching up to do," and "Vanessa, do you feel like we're at a disadvantage to the crib mates here? Maybe we should team up," that put everyone at ease. Everyone except James.

Later, they settled into reclining chairs at the movie theater. He didn't give a damn about the movie he'd just paid twenty-two-fifty for, as his wide eyes peered over the top of Vanessa's head, burning holes into the image that was Charlotte and Jack. They looked cozy. Jack leaned down to whisper something into her ear. She giggled, angling her head towards his body. His arm draped comfortably around her shoulder like it belonged as he continued to smile, to speak softly to only her. She pushed up the armrest to move their bodies closer, to tangle their feet at the end of the recliner.

James felt the air rush quickly out of his nostrils, bounce off of Vanessa's hair and back to his own face. Angrily, he jerked his body so that it was facing forward, determined to lock his gaze with the movie screen for the next hour and a half instead of torturing himself with the giggling and the soft touching that was going on four feet to his right.

He knew it was a comedy only from the laughter that shook in his ears like he was underwater, from the way that Vanessa's body occasionally jerked against his shoulder. His focus, though, homed in on the breathy noises, the slight snort that he knew so well, though it was muffled into the arms of another.

His own grip around the shoulders of his girlfriend tightened as he whispered something nonsensical and pressed his lips to her ear.

This was where he belonged. In the arms of the woman who was snuggling into his body, who laced their fingers together and laughed about some superficial joke on screen that he couldn't give two shits less about. He scooted lower into his chair, effectively killing his line of sight short of anything that wasn't Vanessa's bright blonde hair.

His ears rang every time Charlotte's muffled words or laughter floated above, seeking him out like a siren trying to pull him under. But it was in those moments that he held Vanessa tighter, squeezed her hands, pressed his lips almost too roughly into her temple, anything to distract himself from the noises in his head.

And then the thought hit him that, for the first time in a long time, he was *sharing* his Friday night. The one day of the week throughout his life that was the most routine, was sacred between them, had two other bodies intervening.

That thought only deepened his uncalled-for anger and put him in an even funkier mood. He blamed it on the ice cream and popcorn when both Vanessa and Charlotte had matching frowns of concern once they stepped into the light of the vacant theater lobby.

"We'd better get you home, then," Vanessa insisted, feeling his forehead with the back of her hand.

But as Jack's hand clasped firmly in his for a handshake, it was, "Thanks man. Charlotte was super nervous about this whole *boyfriend-best-friend* thing, but I had a really great time with you and Vanessa tonight. We should definitely do this again soon," that had him suddenly guilt ridden.

They said their goodbyes, and it pained him like a fire in his chest to see her fingers laced with Jack's, to watch some other man pull their bodies closer at the center, to see their faces turned in and smiling in some shared secret that he wasn't privy to.

It didn't take much to convince Vanessa that he just needed to go to bed, despite her comment that he *Didn't seem so sick during the movie,* and that look in her eye that told him she wanted more of him tonight.

But he remained huffy, pissed off as he flopped backwards onto the bed and kicked off his shoes. He rubbed his temples, choosing to shuck off the button down that Vanessa had forced him to wear and sleep in an undershirt and boxers.

He didn't get much sleep. The whir of their bedroom fan was like nails on a chalkboard and Vanessa's faint snore was a freight train screaming in his ear. Even the light traffic outside had him fed up. He punched his pillow as he tried to bury his head beneath it, but to no avail.

Eventually he found himself in the guest room, with no fan and no windows that faced the street and no second body to remind him that if he continued to let himself have these feelings, it was going to cost him.

Charlotte's lips tattooed *Thank you's* across Jack's face as she sat in his lap, letting his hands span her back and cup her body closer to his. The half empty bottle of wine was long forgotten in favor of breathy laughter and hands on cheeks and shoulders.

When she was all but attacking him, short pecks darting across his cheeks and his lips and his nose, he was pushing her back far enough to see her, cradling her face in his hands while he traced small circles into her skin with his thumbs.

"I had such a good time tonight," she breathed, her smile wide as she traced her nose along his. "God, I can't believe I was even nervous. You...you amaze me, Jack McKinney."

He tipped his head back, pressing his smile into hers for a soft, slow kiss that was nothing but gentle admiration.

When she adjusted her position to tuck her bottom into his lap and lay her legs across the couch and fit her head into his shoulder, he wrapped his arms around her tightly and kissed her temple.

Annoyance buzzed around James like a swarm of mosquitos in the summer heat.

It was something Jack had said on their double date, some off handed comment that was meant as a joke and, in all honesty, was probably something he'd said to lighten the mood, to recognize and acknowledge the relationship that James and Charlotte had.

But all it did was swim around in James's head, mixing with Vanessa's comment the day after that: "You and Charlotte sure do have your quirks."

She was referring to the coin flip and the golf ball, but now, as the words on his office computer all blurred together, it morphed into so much more.

It wasn't intentional, but the differences started floating like contrasting images, one black and one white, with his grey as their only commonality.

Vanessa always slept on the right side of the bed.

But Charlotte insisted on sleeping on the left side of the bed. She had often made a point in the past to shove him over with her cold feet against his thighs. She slept on the left side and couldn't fall asleep otherwise. But she had this little quirk, in that her cell phone was plugged in on the right side of her bed, and her nighttime ritual required her to turn over and face away from her phone, almost as if in recognition of her body shutting down for the night. But every time, no more than two minutes later, she was rolling onto the left side again.

It wasn't anything Charlotte had ever mentioned to him, but rather, something he'd come to expect after years of noticing that she only turned in her sleep once. Then again, he had also come to notice it from years of staying awake long after she'd fallen asleep to watch the way her chest puffed slowly up and down.

Vanessa only shaved two or three times a week. It was an offhand comment that he remembered, something about her hair not growing fast enough to *waste ten minutes every day.*

Charlotte complained constantly about shaving. He mocked her, of

216

course, with comments about sharp legs and how she needed to keep warm for the winter somehow. She showered every day in the summers, he noticed when they hit puberty. But he also took notice when they lived together, that sometimes it was twice a day if they were going to the beach. He joked often that she should be the one paying for the water bill.

When they were teenagers, he noticed band aids at the backs of her ankles on the regular, but even into adulthood, they remained. It was a constant that he depended on, one that connected them to her childhood, and reminded him that everyone was flawed.

Vanessa's father was a tall, skinny man who liked his golf and his LA Kings. He insisted that James call him Ben.

But he knew how Will Murphy liked his eggs in the morning, what kind of beer was his winter beer and what kind was his summer beer, and understood that he only cried on three separate occasions: funerals, weddings, and any time he watched *Field of Dreams*. And still, all these years later, he respected Will Murphy enough to call him *Sir*.

Vanessa's taste in music was thanks in large part to her father, and when she was behind the wheel, she wouldn't hesitate to belt out Queen at the top of her lungs.

Charlotte was very adamant that her collection of alternative music was, "the only real music," insisting that "pop music was tacky" and "country music was just an excuse to get drunk and talk about your ex-wife." He could match every playlist in her iTunes library with its corresponding mood or situation. Still though, in the right moments, she would sing Taylor Swift with the best of them, those guilty pleasure tracks hidden in covert playlists on her iPod that he snuck peeks at just to confirm.

But the best part was when they were alone, either on a long car ride, or locked away in her bedroom or his basement with the music flowing, when she would actually try to sing. Because Charlotte truly could carry a tune. She had a soft, pretty voice, that she let very few people hear. So when they were 40 miles into a trip to the lake, or it was late at night and they were settled against her bed frame with textbooks piling across her comforter, that sweet little tune would paint his eardrums with colors brighter than he had ever imagined.

Some of the songs were from pop radio, some were show tunes, and some were just annoying little diddies that she'd picked up along the way that she knew would dig under his skin. But most of the songs had lyrics that he could only hope meant something deeper to her, artists that she'd found while listening to her older sister's collection or had heard in the background of a stray YouTube video that caught her attention. Whether it was "Poison and Wine" by The Civil Wars, "So Long, Goodbye" by 10 Years, or "Hello My Old Heart" by The Oh Hellos, each new set of lyrics opened a part of her heart that was hidden from even him. Of course, every time he would catch her singing, actually focusing on the pitch and the small bit of vibrato in her throat, she would turn red and over exaggerate the tunes and start singing in ridiculous accents to throw him off and make him laugh.

He teased her once about listening relentlessly to a Kelly Clarkson song, "So much for not listening to any pop artists," waggling behind his eyebrows before she retorted, in all serious business, "It's not on any of her albums, so it doesn't count. I had to rip it off YouTube," before she popped her headphones back in and continued on her way.

It took him one night to learn the simple chord progression to "Don't," the words hammered into his brain after the fortieth listen-through, those lyrics piercing his every nerve as he tried to decide if they were haunting her, too.

Charlotte's favorite weekday was Thursday, because it was, "like Friday Eve!"

Charlotte, at twenty-eight years old, still stuck her tongue out to the side whenever she was deep in concentration.

Charlotte could not brush her teeth without her lips foaming up like a rabid bunny. The more he teased her about it, the more she tried not to, and the foamier she became.

She hated Christmas music with a burning passion, refused to decorate for the holiday until after December first, but would watch the movie *Elf* any day of the year.

She did a little dance, this wiggle and bounce of her head back and forth, whenever she was in a happy mood. Most of the time it was whenever she had food.

When Charlotte laughed a true, uninhibited laugh, she always covered her teeth with her hands. She'd only told him this once, when they were eight, but it was because she "didn't want anyone to see down her throat," and the habit had just stuck.

Every time Charlotte got a new book, whether it was from the library or Barnes and Noble, she judged it first not by its cover, but by flicking the pages in front of her nose and inhaling.

If they were eating any meal that came with fries, she would pick at the entrée, claiming she was full, but always proceeded to finish the entire order of fries, and whatever was left of his plate.

She had exactly four scars on her body. One in the crevice of her thumb, where the wheel of a wagon burned her when she let her hand trail out the side when she was three years old. The second was a pretty stamp of childhood summers in Newton, coming in the form of a darker shade on her right kneecap where she'd skinned herself learning to ride a bike. The third, a faint white line on the back of her knee, was from her first time shaving, the time that her mom told her she could have a razor when she was thirteen but she was getting impatient and didn't know what she was doing and used her father's face blade to rip a chunk of her skin off.

The last was so faint that you'd have to hear the story to know it was a scar. It was just behind her left wrist, a small dot that you could only see if it caught the light in the right way. They'd been doing homework, or at least pretending to, during the 2007 World Series. When JD Drew blasted the grand slam, James's pencil-clenched hand slammed right into her wrist. It took them ten minutes after the celebration to realize that blood was still trickling down her arm.

Vanessa had scars too, but he didn't really have any goddamn emotional attachment to any of them.

He found himself doodling aimlessly on a pad that was reserved for taking notes before he realized that he hadn't really done much work in the past forty-five minutes. Instead of putting together a package for his latest client, organizing price points and mock-up designs, he was creating a list of all the things in his life that he knew about Charlotte, things that Jack was slowly but surely beginning to cross off his own Boggle list.

It was a list that he held sacred, and after hearing the word *boyfriend* and watching them be so goddamn *happy* together, he decided he earned one day of being a petulant child, of sulking and stomping his feet and sucking his thumb and hiding in his bedroom with his blanket.

That night, Vanessa stared for a minute before ultimately rolling her eyes and throwing a, "Let me know when you're done PMSing" over her shoulder before disappearing for the night.

It had been so long since Charlotte had ventured into the world of healthy relationships that she was beginning to question if and when her new reality was going to pop.

Every day with Jack was a new adventure, a new door opened to a world that she never thought possible. She had been scared at first to move quickly, wanting to take her time and test the waters and make sure that this was right. But she had been careful for too long, and the more time she spent with Jack, the more she found herself diving in headfirst.

He was patient and kind, understanding that it took a lot for her to open up. And yet with each day that she knew him, she wanted to open the floodgates and tell him everything, let him into the nooks and crannies that formed Charlotte Murphy.

It was an awkward struggle, navigating the intricate parts of her without mentioning James, but the thing about Jack was that he *got it*, and he did so without putting up a fight or stomping his foot like a baby. He asked questions, wanting to piece together Charlotte from the ground up regardless of how much of the foundation was built around James Ramsey.

Eventually, she found herself growing more confident.

When Jack said, "You don't have to protect me from James, Charlotte. He isn't going to scare me away," she took the end of that thread and let his truth expose her nerves a little more each time they talked.

That was what usually did her in when it came to boyfriends: James would be too much for them to handle, and would conversely be the very thing that picked up the pieces when men left her in shambles. But Jack was taking every reality she'd ever known and turning it on its head by diving right in with her.

It wasn't only the ways that she was letting him in, but the way that she saw his heart healing from the pain he'd shared with her. He was slow to heal, too, after the heartbreak that Molly had put him through, but he was letting go, and letting her in, and she was learning so much about this man, hoping it would never end.

She was catching onto his little quirks, like the way that he had to keep his music volume on an even or round number ("5 counts, too!"), that he hated having the windows down in his car, and that he always left his dishes in the sink to soak overnight.

Jack needed something to fidget with constantly, and his go-to was pens. If he was nervous, he would click them. Anxiety played on in capping and uncapping. Frustrations were drawn out in swift taps against tabletops.

He laughed at almost everything, but she knew he found something truly comical if he snorted. The first time he did, she had busted out laughing herself. But from then on, she came to find it endearing.

He avoided cracks in the sidewalk, which she started doing too, because it made him blush. When she was kissing him, the skin on his chest would redden first before the rest of his body warmed to her touch. His body was a hotbox when they cuddled, but his feet were always, always cold. He could recite *Good Will Hunting* from beginning to end and pick up anywhere in the middle.

He was comforting, warm, kind, and affectionate.

When they were together, Charlotte truly lost sight of the rest of the world, of her worries and her anxieties and the things she kept bottled up inside.

With Jack, she was beginning to see why she had to struggle and suffer and endure so many dead ends. He was the light at the end of her tunnel, the end of a road that had been broken for so long, she hadn't known it needed mending until he came through with his warm eyes and kind smile and gentle hands to show her exactly what it felt like to be loved.

And in those moments where life was so simple, where their hands were twined together and the smile on his face as he gazed down at her put the sun in the sky to shame, she began to wonder if she was falling in love with Jack McKinney.

It wasn't just Jack that had her summer bursting at the seams; the way that she dedicated herself to penning her book gave her a newfound confidence.

Although she couldn't put her finger on just what it was, the summer had Charlotte filled with a new surge of focus and determination, a work ethic that had her buckling down to finish her book and put something that she created into the hands of others. The prospects were thrilling as she let herself imagine seeing her book on shelves and in classrooms, her words known across the country, twinkling in the minds of children whose smiles mirrored those of her own kindergarten students.

Her nights became encapsulated by the clacking sounds of her keyboard, bubbling caffeine from empty soda cans, and dark circles under her eyes. But it was all worth it to see her characters springing to life, her plots driven and focused, the conclusion in her sights like a finish line.

And Jack was there through it all. He was supportive as a boyfriend on nights where she needed to be left alone, or those where she needed a break to catch her breath. But he was also a supportive professional; he helped guide her through the process that he had dipped his foot into a time or two, helping her edit and craft her words to be ready for publication.

All the while, amidst midnight snack runs and nights spent curled together on her couch with his lips soft and his hands wandering and his smile making her feel warm and fuzzy, James was there too. He lingered in the shadows just when that good feeling was almost finally settled.

It was as if he had a sixth sense of all things Charlotte that kicked in to find her when she least expected it. Growing up, it had been nice.

He was always there, out of the blue, right when she was ready to break. But now, as she was finally feeling confident and comfortable and on her way to a new sense of security, he was popping up again.

Things like a mid-afternoon text, when her fingers were cramping from typing, or her head was pounding after being run the gambit by Ginny, where his *Hey, Smalls. Just thinking about you. Hope you're taking care of yourself* had her eyes pricking and her heart longing for a night on his couch or in his arms.

Or an unexpected visit, when she hit a wall of writer's block, and suddenly her buzzer rang despite the fact that he had a key. He always came with food and a smile, but now it was also with the strange habit of leaving after only an hour or so, unlike the nights where he would crash on her couch or stay until dawn was sneaking up on them. It was those nights when she felt empty as soon as he left, barely skimming the surface before he was out the door again. It left her mind in a constant state of wondering why: why had he stopped using his key? Why was he letting her get to sleep at a reasonable hour instead of keeping her up until dawn with a smile brightening his tired eyes? Why was he suddenly changing the habits she'd come to rely on?

James was so respectful of her time with Jack that it almost made her angry. They had always held Friday nights sacred, and yet he was constantly double checking: "Are you sure Jack is okay with us hanging out? Just let me know if we have to cancel a Friday. It's okay," made her so frustrated that she almost wanted to scream at him.

But then again, maybe there were things in his life that she suddenly didn't know. Maybe Vanessa's schedule had changed, and he didn't want to let on. Or maybe he was just that perfect of a man, to respect her boundaries and make sure that she was always happy. Maybe this was growing up?

Jack was beginning to catch on to her frustrations, as they spent an entire Saturday afternoon making final edits to her book and going over professional editors and publishing companies from a list of connections that he had from college.

"So, I guess the three best choices I can give you are going to be with my buddies in New York, Chicago, or the one guy out here.

Obviously, New York is going to be at the center of big publishers, but...hey, Charlotte? You home tonight?"

She was staring at a shadow on his wall, watching the way that the dim candlelight made the picture frames on his mantle dance. What had begun as a night of writing and wine had suddenly brought her mind wandering back to James's comments just the other night, when he had showed up out of the blue for a quick mid-week catch up:

"I've gotta say, I'm really proud of you, Charlie Kate Murphy. I don't remember the last time I saw you so dedicated to something. You're going to blow the world away one day soon."

And with that memory, poor Jack had been taken out to sea.

"Sorry, baby, I'm just..."

He watched her eyes wander to another place and time, and decided to table the discussion, along with his wine glass, in favor of pulling her against his chest and kissing the top of her head.

"What can I do to help?"

She sighed, her body pushing him back gently into the pillows as she absently traced the lines in his palm.

"It's James."

She could feel him tense beneath her and regretted her words for only a moment before remembering that James and Jack were separate, that Jack understood, and was only reassured further when he relaxed a bit and said, "Tell me about it."

So she tried, really tried, to string together thoughts like *He's just been weird lately* and *I feel like he isn't telling me something* and *We tell each other everything, you know?* without sounding like she was more emotionally involved in another relationship. But Jack was patient and kind and offered the best advice that he could.

"Have you talked to him about it?"

"No. I don't know, I'm not sure how to bring it up, really. But maybe I'm just overthinking things, right? People change. I just...I guess we've always changed together, or at least, when we were changing, we were always there to help each other through it. It almost feels like something major is going on and I'm not there to…"

As she let a sigh cap her thoughts, she snuggled her way into Jack's chest, propping her chin to squint up and gauge his reaction.

It was his turn to stare out into his apartment, searching for the right words to say.

"You know, Charlotte? Maybe this is good, though. Maybe, in order for you to grow individually, you two have to learn who you are without each other."

It was this thought that truly took her by surprise.

She wanted to be offended, wanted to pull back in shock and shout things like *How dare you!* and *Are you out of your mind?*

But that feeling never came. Instead, it was the shock of retaliation, the pain that he might actually be right, that scared her the most. As she grappled with that fear, tried to form her next thought, he was already detouring her next move.

"But hey, you two have an entire long weekend coming up to sort it all out. Why don't you talk to him? I hate to see you so upset, and I can't do much else to help you fix it."

He was right. Emma's third birthday was the following weekend, and Charlotte, James, and Vanessa would all be boarding a plane on Friday morning to head to Newton for a long weekend of highly anticipated family fun. While she had initially expected a long and exhaustive conversation with Jack on the subject of *going home to meet the families*, he was entirely understanding: they'd only been dating for a couple of months; of course he understood that she was still apprehensive about taking him home for a weekend. It made perfect sense. They wanted to do things the right way.

But still, she felt nervous about leaving him, nervous that he would be on edge about her every move while she was away. And of course, she would miss him like crazy. But what she felt for Jack was real, and real scary at that. She didn't want to bring him home and have her family pick him apart when they were still so fresh into getting to know one another. And what's more, James's family was part of her family. It was a battle she wasn't yet prepared for, especially after the disaster that had happened when Vanessa first accompanied them to

225

Newton.

So she agreed, reluctantly, that she would have plenty of time to sort things out with James once they were home, pushing aside the fact that family weekends were *family weekends* where both sets of parents demanded the undivided attention of their *traitorous children* and they were exhausted and running on fumes by hour twelve at the latest. Not to mention there would be almost no way to get him alone with Vanessa tagging along. But she wasn't in the mood for spending her time with Jack focusing on James.

She changed the subject, asking him to go over his list of friends in the business one more time, the pros and cons of all three options, before his stomach was rumbling. Then, they were both sharing laughter and a take-out menu and saying *to hell with work!* in favor of a trashy Netflix movie and cuddling that found Charlotte doing her best to bury her way as far inside of Jack as she possibly could.

August 2015

It was odd, being home in Massachusetts for a week in the summer when they both had "big kid jobs" out on the west coast. But sitting on the couch in her parent's basement, riding the waves of the cushions as James shimmied back and forth in an effort to control what the characters in his video game were doing, it was as if nothing had changed.

He was a man now, but the length of his bangs—that were in need of a good cut if he was going to vie for the promotion at work—and the way he concentrated so intensely on steering the sports car on screen, said otherwise.

"God *damn*it!" he exclaimed, whipping the controller down with both hands but keeping his grip. After the incident when they were twelve—the controller hitting the concrete floor, the shock of the impact running from the cord to the Nintendo 64 to fry the console, and David nearly beheading them both—he had since learned his lesson.

Charlotte chuckled, looking up from the notebook in her lap to raise an eyebrow in his direction.

"You know, maybe if you stopped driving the way that you do on the Mass Pike, you'd be able to stay on the road without crashing into so many poles."

"And maybe if you were as good of a couch-seat driver as you are a car-napper while I'm driving, I'd be able to concentrate."

He reached across her body to where an opened bag of Doritos lay and popped a few into his mouth. Charlotte pretended not to notice when his fingers brushed against her thigh on the way over. James did his best to hide the blush that crept up his cheeks as he chewed.

She watched for a minute in contented silence as he dragged his Corvette through stop lights and ran over pedestrians in an effort to finish the race that he had already lost three times. It wasn't until an exclamatory voice from upstairs yelled, "You guys!" that they both stopped paying attention. Taking a moment to share wide toothed grins, they raced one another up the stairs.

The clinical cleanliness of the Mass Gen hallways prickled James's nose, causing him to scrunch and wipe at it with the back of his hand as he tried to keep up with Charlotte's quick pace. His goofy grin was all thanks to how excitedly Charlotte bopped down the hallway at just short of an actual run.

"I can't believe that my big brother is a daddy!" she exclaimed for about the sixteenth time since he'd pulled out of her parent's driveway. "I mean, just yesterday, he was bribing me with a trip to Cabot's to not tell my parents that he had a girl in his bedroom, and now…"

It was the first time since they'd arrived at the hospital that she was actually pausing, slowing down to take a breath. He had to backtrack a step, but when he did, he was overwhelmed by the color in her cheeks, the spark in her smile. They said all new mothers had a glow about them, but nothing prepared him for *Auntie Charlotte's* radiance.

His grin was lopsided, all pulled up to one side of his face, just like it had been when they were kids. After a moment of staring and drinking in the excitement that bloomed from her eyes, he whispered, "You ready?"

Her smile quirked as she slipped her hand into his palm. It was unexpected, but a warm welcome. He thought for a moment that her hand seemed to have a home here.

He wasn't prepared for the quietude in the room. He had expected buzzing energy and excitement, or at least some sort of bustle. When Abby was born, his mom's hospital room had been overflowing with people: nurses, orderlies, both sets of grandparents, and his brother Kyle. It was mass chaos.

But this stillness was so much less, which made it so much more.

Charlotte's older brother David sat cuddled in the bed with his tired but glowing bride Marie, a pink bundle nestled between them in Marie's arms. She was fast asleep, and against James's own instincts, his breath caught in his throat.

Charlotte's parents, first time grandma and grandpa, were out in the waiting room already having had their turn; they took the time to make frantic phone calls and brag to anyone passing by that their first grandchild was here. It was just the five of them.

He felt his arm pull, noticing that Charlotte was creeping slowly across the hospital room with their hands still clutched together. Her steps were timid, almost as if she were afraid the floor would break out from under her if she wasn't careful enough.

Her, "Hi," was quiet but pitchy, drawn out for at least a full four counts. His hand was cold when hers left to cover her mouth, to hide her smile, to show her awe for the new little human in the room. Although she had her back to him now, James knew that there were tears in her eyes.

He watched as big brother embraced little sister, a relationship whose ups and downs he had been privy to while growing up. In the end, though, David had truly been there for both of them more often than not. When Charlotte and David pulled away, and Charlotte bent to hug Marie, James offered a handshake that turned into a hug.

"Congratulations, daddio," he muttered into David's ear. The two men exchanged proud smiles before they turned to see Charlotte wiping the last of the hand sanitizer into her palms, taking a seat as Marie lay the baby gingerly across her awaiting arms.

It was quite a sight to see. James turned, pretending he had an itch as he wiped at a stray tear before allowing himself to truly marvel at this woman, his best friend, holding her newborn niece. His mind wandered for only a second to her future, to the babies she would have, and his own role in the hospital room, the different versions of stickers playing at *New Dad* or *Just Visiting*.

"Oh my goodness, you guys, she is *precious*," Charlotte whispered through smiling teeth.

She cooed at the baby, running a finger along the girl's plump cheeks, the smile on her face only growing wider.

"What's her name?"

"Emma. Emma Katherine Murphy."

Charlotte beamed at her brother, at his wife, before her attention was focused on the baby again.

"Emma Katherine Murphy. Well, little miss Emma. Welcome to the world. I'm your Auntie Charlotte. *Boy* am I going to spoil you rotten."

A soft chuckle filled the room as the baby shifted in Charlotte's arms, yawned widely, and blinked her eyes several times before ultimately falling back asleep. Charlotte's excited laughter made her cheeks glow, as James looked on in awe of his own.

"Well, not just *aunt*, hopefully," David said with a shrug, stepping between Charlotte and James as he lay a hand on each of their shoulders. "We were hoping that you two would be Emma's godparents."

Charlotte's expression went from confused to elated almost instantly, her smile stretching wider than her cheeks would allow as tears fell from her eyes again. James's close-lipped smile was beaming, his eyes shining now too as he nodded his head, far inferior to Charlotte's, "Of *course* we will be!" that shook with tears.

After smiles and hugs were passed around, James made his way to the chair that Charlotte sat in, crouching closer to get a look at his new *goddaughter*. The word itself suddenly turned this whole event into something more profound. He would have been *Uncle James* anyway, but now, he was so much more.

He teared up a bit himself, taking in her plump pink cheeks and the tuft of brown hair peeking out from underneath her pink beanie cap. After a quick hand wash, Charlotte transferred the baby into his waiting arms, and his breath was gone again, the tiny weight of seven pounds and six ounces both light and heavy. He rocked her gently, but mainly he just smiled, trying to keep his tears inside this time.

"Soak it up now while you can," David said. "This will be you two in no time at all."

Charlotte pulled her attention from the baby long enough to snort in her brother's direction.

"Oh, come on, David. Don't even say that."

"What? It's true," David replied without hesitation. "You're next in line. And with any luck, maybe it'll be the two of you *together*. Lord knows I haven't liked any of the other guys you've brought home."

David shrugged, futzing with the tag of his hospital bracelet, keeping his eyes trained somewhere other than the godparents of his newborn baby girl.

"That's because I haven't *brought* any other boys home," she quipped, her eyes trained on the tiny bundle in James's arms in an attempt to hide her embarrassment.

"Exactly," David replied, wiggling his eyebrows in their direction.

In the silence that followed, James handed the baby back to Marie and pulled two cigars from his pocket, offering one to David while the women rolled their eyes, and the men headed down a flight of stairs and out the door before lighting up.

"So, how are you feelin', Daddy?"

"Honestly?" David replied, blowing out a puff of smoke. "I'm the happiest man in the world, Jimmy. Hands down. These girls are the greatest thing to ever happen to me."

They exchanged a warm smile and took a drag on their cigars.

"Are you sure you want to trust us as her godparents?"

James was a bit nervous as he asked the question, his words tailed with a chuckle. David laughed it off with a clap on James's back.

"Of course we are, man. My baby sister, and the little brother I never had. There's not a doubt in my mind that you two would take care of our little girl if anything ever happened to Marie and me."

"Thanks, man. That really means a lot."

"And I meant what I said earlier, too."

At this, James turned, his cigar now half spent and dangling between his thumb and pointer finger. He cocked an eyebrow, encouraging David to continue.

"You're the only guy I've ever trusted around my little sister. You mean the world to her, James. And I know the same is true for you. Don't take what you guys have for granted."

James shied away, tapping his forefinger against the back of his cigar to watch the stray bits of ash drift around in the air before him.

"Come on. She isn't dating any of those college doorknobs anymore, and neither are you. You're both free. Make your move, man."

With one final clap on the shoulder, David snuffed out his cigar, popped a mint in his mouth, offered one to James, and turned to head back inside. James remained on the sidewalk, toeing the ground with the tip of his sneaker before following after David.

When he re-entered the room, there was something different about the atmosphere, like the air had shifted. He could've attributed it to the setting sun, the quietude, or the new baby smell. But in the halo of light surrounding Charlotte as she held that baby, standing and swaying softly while she quietly cooed and made faces at the little girl whose eyes were now wide open, his world was turning on its axis.

Charlotte glanced up, feeling his eyes on her and smiled, wiping the stunned expression in his eyes into one of joy and hope. He closed the distance in the room between them, sidling up next to her to stare down at the bundle in her arms. With the fingers of one hand gripped in a tiny baby fist, he let the other trail down Charlotte's spine, coming to rest at the small of her back. His skin tingled when he felt her lean into his touch. He was warm in all the right ways.

"Hey, can we get a picture of you three together?"

David pulled out his cell phone, snapping a few photos of baby and godparents before giving them a few more minutes to *aww* at baby Emma.

Goodbyes were reluctant but joyful. Charlotte and James had taken the entire week off knowing that they would want to see that the new baby made it home safely and to get in a few extra cuddles before returning back across the country. The backs of their hands brushed together as they walked back to James's car, smiles wide each time they caught one another staring.

"Oh my *god,* I just can't believe how precious she is!" Charlotte exclaimed once they were back on the highway, the sun now low beyond the horizon.

James had run through the drive-thru at Friendly's and was sipping on his shake as he chuckled, murmuring, "She is cute," around his straw.

"God, where did the time go?"

"What do you mean?" He passed her a questioning sideways glance.

"I mean, my big brother has a *baby*, James. Not to mention my sister's wedding two months ago. Everyone is just...moving onward and upward in their lives. It's exciting, but kind of scary when you think about it."

"Hey," he started, placing his shake in the cupholder and slipping his hand around hers. She shuddered at the shock of cool in his fingertips but gripped onto him tightly. "We've still got our entire lives ahead of us. And just think: we get to use that little baby for all the cute stuff and then send her home to her parents for all the whining."

She laughed, which lessened the pressure in his chest, and she squeezed back a thank you, not letting go of his hand until her phone buzzed in her pocket.

"Who is it?"

"*Aww.*"

James glanced away from traffic, noticing the way her smile was stretching wide again and her eyes were sparkling.

"David just sent me the pictures of us and Emma. Oh my god, look how cute we are!"

As he pulled to a stop at a red light, James smiled, clutching her phone in his hand to see the image better. With their heads bent together around the little pink bundle, he couldn't stop the swelling in his chest, the smile that curled up the side of his face.

It wasn't until she muttered, "I can't wait to have this one day," that he had to refocus on the road, had to stop his mind from wandering back to the conversation with David and the feeling of her hand fitting so warmly and so perfectly in his.

Her parents were planning on getting things ready at David and Marie's house that night, choosing to stay overnight in Boston in their guest room rather than coming home. With the house to just the two of them, the agenda was full of movies and snacks, but he said he had to run home first. He was short of breath when he slipped his shoes off at the front door, sweating by the time he found her up in her bedroom already in pajamas.

This Charlotte, the one wearing the oversized Red Sox T-shirt and fuzzy pajama pants and mismatched socks, took his breath away. He was across her room with her cheeks cradled in his palms before she could open her mouth to ask him which movie he wanted to start with.

She was surprised at first, a little, "*Oh!*" caught in her throat, swallowed by his kiss that was powerful, decisive, the declaration in his lips claiming her. His lips moved over hers with an assertive hunger that caught them both off guard when he was pulling away suddenly, his nose touching hers. His eyes were wide, telling a story of his want as his thumbs traced small circles high on her cheek bones.

It was written in his eyes, the desire and the need. But what was etched into hers was a desperation that seemed to call to him from somewhere distant, piercing him deep within his soul.

It was Charlotte who started the kissing this time, the fervor evident in the fingers that dug into his hair and pulled him closer, the way her body was already humming so close to his as she pulled him backwards, falling into place, into a rhythm that fit together like a harmonious symphony.

Staring at the ceiling of Charlotte's bedroom afterwards, his eyes were wide, afraid that if he so much as blinked that he would miss something important. He held her to his body like glue, pasting every inch of his sticky skin to every warm part of her, his strong arms wrapped around her shoulders in a way that made it hard for her to breathe in the best possible way.

When she did, it wasn't what he expected, her laughter coming in hot puffs of breath against his bare chest causing him to flinch.

"What?" he whispered, frantic and nervous. Nothing about this was funny. Nothing about the burning in his heart was funny. But yet here she was, laughing against him.

"I can't believe we let ourselves get that carried away."

Despite her words, she was nuzzling closer to him, wrapping her arms more tightly around his back.

"What, what do you mean?" He stumbled on his words, anxiety kicking itself into high gear as he wondered what about that was *carried away.*

"I must have let the new baby fumes go to my head," she replied, still tapered with remnants of laughter.

At her explication, his cheeks grew hot, his arms stiff around her. "I... uh..."

It was happening all over again, the words clinging to his throat, the ideas, so clear in his mind when he'd walked into her bedroom: *I love you,* and *It's always been you,* and *Can we finally make this right?* now curling around his tongue like a vice that refused to let them all escape.

It was all lost, swallowed by her giggles and *carried away* and *this is all just alive inside our heads.*

Maybe that was where it was meant to stay.

Defeatedly, he settled for, "Yeah, you...must be right," sounding a lot better in response than, *Yes, but also, I think I'm in love with you.*

Harder still was the way her body was contradicting each and every thing she said, tightening around him though her words loosened him, hiding her nose in the crook of his neck and pressing her lips there though he was already drifting backwards down the path of *Keeping this all in my head.*

She muttered, "You're going to stay tonight, right?" despite his every want and need to just *leave this place* before it broke him again.

Of course he said yes.

The same way he always had and wondered then if he always *would.*

What he failed to realize, as his own head swam wildly, doing his best not to overanalyze, was the churn of emotions going on in *her* head, too.

The hesitance in her voice, the slight shake, the tremble of her lips, went completely unseen, pushed back in favor of his own overthinking. Because when she'd laughed, it had been to cover her nerves. When she blamed their actions on heightened emotions, it had been a defense mechanism, a hook and line that she hoped he would sink onto, that he would catch her lies and tell her that she was wrong, that he didn't come over and grab her by the cheeks and kiss her breathless because *David's wife had a baby,* but because he was finally realizing what had been there between them, and was finally going to let the lid fly off the top and spew the potential they had building.

It was all of that and more that had them stuck inside their heads as they held one another through the night.

In the morning, it was slower, less frantic, but so much more needy. His lips mapped her skin, covering her neck to her collarbone and worshipping every bare inch of her before finding a home on her lips. When she moved beneath him, she clung to his body in a way that molded her fingerprints to his hips, that left handprints on his back and neck as if branding her claim. It reminded him of desperation.

In a way, he wondered if this would be their goodbye from any chance that was left. When the thought crossed his mind, he made it that much more, cataloguing every touch and kiss and feel of her fingers on his skin and in his hair, every sigh and moan and muttering of his name hot on her lips, locking it away for safe keeping.

The remainder of the weekend was filled with babies and parents and more food than he could think to handle, but he was grateful for the distraction, for the fact that she was as caught up in the frantic bustle as he was.

He did his best to put a physical distance between them, making sure that when she was helping the moms in the kitchen that he was outside with their fathers, a mask of *quality time* the perfect cover for *This is too painful to keep doing to myself.*

But when he saw her from across the living room, or through the window, with that little pink bundle in her arms, her smile wide and her eyes bright, the tightness in his chest was overwhelming.

The plane ride back to California was quiet, long moments of processing and introspection happening over the course of those six hours.

When her head hit his shoulder, her slowed breaths warm against his neck, he grit his teeth, crossed his arms, forced his eyes shut, and focused on their one last moment together before the bubble popped.

But as she slept quietly against him, he let his mind wander to what it was that was stopping him from just *going for it*. David's words echoed in his mind, how *they were next* and *Make your move, man.*

Neither was tied down anymore. David had that right.

His college girlfriends had been flukes, wasted time that did little to diminish the feelings he had for Charlotte that were too often left unsaid.

The feeling of her head on his shoulder was a warm weight tingling beneath her curls. Suddenly, he was incredibly eager for the plane to land.

It wasn't a surprise that he carried both bags, paid for the parking garage, held the door for her as she climbed into his car. But the hand at the small of her back as they walked through the terminal, the arm around her shoulder when the crowds in LAX thickened, the fingers that he linked across the dash as they drove home, all spoke of hope on the horizon; the way he held on just a little bit tighter than normal was the desperation inside of him to not let her go this time.

But when they were home, she was calling Ginny and making plans to go to the bar. His heart busted open when the door closed on the heels of, "Maybe David's right, James. Maybe I should put myself back out there, you know?"

Each drunk text from her that night was another stab to his gut, his ears ringing with each notification.

James
Hey buddfy i friggggen luv u
Some guy gav me his phone nuber!1!

When she arrived home at dawn with McDonald's breakfast and *Scotty, Scotty, Scotty* was all she could talk about, he took it as his sign to turn it all off again, to shut it down, bury his feelings six feet underground, and keep them there for good.

August 2018

For the first time since Christmas, they were going *home*.

Emma's birthday was Friday with a Saturday party to follow, and there was absolutely no way that Auntie K and Uncle JJ would miss it. With luggage packed for the long weekend, Charlotte, James, and Vanessa waited in line to board Southwest Flight #373 for Boston, Massachusetts.

As they stood toward the front of Boarding Group B, James pulled a penny from his pocket, cocked his eyebrow at Charlotte, and flipped it in the air.

She was always tails, and he was always heads.

Uncovering the piece of dulled copper, he dropped his head in exaggeration. She would have the window seat on the way there.

While Vanessa was certainly used to the little charade that often accompanied these airport visits, it didn't mean she had to like it. And while she understood that she had essentially plopped herself into the folds of a bond already cemented with traditions, she didn't have to like that either.

Maybe, just this once, *she* wanted the window seat.

But it didn't matter. She was going home early this trip, unable to get out of work on Sunday evening. She could have an entire row to herself, if she really wanted to.

The three gravitated immediately towards the middle of the plane as Charlotte and James always did, so that they had a perfect view of the wing. James lofted each of the three carryon bags into the overhead bin and let Charlotte scurry towards the window seat before following in after her.

"Are you sure you don't want the aisle, babe? Your legs are going to be cramped."

It was a useless argument, but without fail, Vanessa attempted each and every time they boarded a plane. But his gangly body was always perched in the middle seat, smack dab between Charlotte and Vanessa.

"Nah, I'm good. But I appreciate the offer."

He gave her a quick peck on the cheek, found his seat, and turned immediately to Charlotte as she produced two magazines, two bags of gummies, and her earbuds. The bag of worms and the *Sports Illustrated* went to James, and the bears and *People* stayed in her lap. Vanessa fastened her neck pillow snugly atop her shoulders, inserted her earplugs, and pulled her sleeping mask over her eyes as James and Charlotte split each end of a pair of headphones. Vanessa was out before they had made it through the first song.

Despite the frequent back and forth between coasts since they had moved, the time change and the six-hour flight still took its toll on their bodies. Huddled around two long tables that were pushed together in the Murphy's backyard, Charlotte, James, and Vanessa found themselves the victims of cruel teasing when James had announced that they wouldn't be joining the adults at the local bar for a night cap.

"You're really painting the town beige tonight, son," Jerry chortled, clapping him on the shoulder.

"Lay off, will ya Dad?" he chuckled back. "We jumped from ten AM to dinner time, and Vanessa went straight from work to the airport. We're here all weekend. I'll see you plenty."

"Isn't your generation supposed to live a little?" Will Murphy chimed in as everyone began pressing up from the tables and heading into the Murphy home.

"I'll live after I've gotten a good night's sleep."

James tossed the words over his shoulder as he claimed "his" spot on the Murphy's living room sofa. Charlotte joined him, waving goodbye to their parents as they gathered purses and shoes and filed into vehicles to head downtown. Vanessa stood at the end of the couch, picking awkwardly at the cuff of her sweater when James turned on the TV.

"Come take a load off, babe. We finally have some peace and quiet."

He extended his arm, encouraging her to join them while he flipped through the channels for something to settle on. He only turned when Vanessa failed to join them, his eyebrows crunched together as he took in her slouched body and the way her fingers were meshing and pulling apart in the middle.

"Everything okay?"

"Yeah, I'm just really tired."

"Come sit. You'll feel much better."

She shook her head slightly. He clearly wasn't getting it.

"Actually, I was thinking we could head to the hotel for the night. I have a feeling that if I fall asleep here, you aren't moving me off the couch."

The disappointment pulled at James's lips immediately, although he hadn't meant for it to show. He glanced up at Vanessa, then sideways to Charlotte, chewing on the inside of his lip like his mother had just told him to come wash up for supper while the rest of his friends all got to stay outside.

"I guess we'll see you in the morning," he said to Charlotte, patting his thighs and pushing up off the couch not moments after he'd just gotten comfortable. He noticed the matching disappointment in Charlotte's eyes, but it was mostly masked by how tired she was, despite the fact that it was still late afternoon on her body's clock.

Vanessa took the keys to their rental and left to start the car while James lingered a bit longer to say goodbye.

"Can you remind me again why, after all these years, you two still shell out the cash for a hotel instead of spending the weekend with your parents?" she asked as he began to tie his tennis shoes.

"I don't know. Just easier on them, I guess. They don't have to entertain us for the *entire* weekend. Plus, we get our own space." He shrugged knowing that, although she wasn't about to believe a word of what he was saying, she also didn't have the time to call him out on it right now either.

Charlotte's eyes seemed to say *Whatever you say* as they rolled around in one complete circle.

"See you in the morning?"

"Bright and early, Ramsey! We don't get these Massachusetts mornings very often. Gotta make 'em count."

They passed warm smiles as goodbyes, and he reluctantly walked out her door and drove Vanessa and himself twenty minutes down the road to the Boston Marriot instead of walking a block and a half to his childhood home.

After kissing Vanessa goodnight, she passed out at the drop of her head to the pillow. James flipped aimlessly through TV stations, grumbling that the Sox game was already over as he found no solace in any of the other Friday night cable lineups.

If they were staying at his parent's, he'd have access to their Dish, their movie collection, and his old XBox.

But they weren't.

And as he clicked off the TV, sliding his tennis shoes on with his pajama bottoms to pace the familiar halls of the hotel, he sighed, knowing that it was his own fault.

He didn't *want* Vanessa staying at his parent's house. In his childhood bedroom. Showering in his *Finding Nemo* themed bathroom that his parents refused to remodel. It was stupid, he knew that. But after two years of dating, he thought he would've gotten over the insecurities by now and let her in all the way. Of course, now more than ever, he was starting to see why he was keeping those walls up. Not minutes later, he was hovering over a different name is his contact favorites.

"Is this a booty call?" Charlotte asked as she picked up on the first ring.

"From the lobby of my hotel? I think I'd get a few suspicious eyes from concierge if I asked what you were wearing right now."

"Well, luckily for you, I'm wearing the same thing I was when you left." Though she tried her best to stay in sultry character in an attempt to get a rise out of him, she couldn't help the laughter that tailed her words. At least he was joining in.

"Couldn't sleep?"

"Nope. You?" he replied, propping his feet up on an ottoman.

"I thought I was exhausted, but I can't shut my eyes. It's only 7:30 at home."

"Time changes are a *bitch*," he muttered, running his hand over his face and into his hair.

"Hey, do you remember when we first moved out to California? And it took us like a week and a half to defeat jet lag?"

He could hear her body shift, and pictured her legs folding crisscross underneath her body as she prepared to reminisce.

"And we did all that dumb shit to try to stay awake?" His words were already laced with silky laughter, the memories pouring over him like a wave.

"The seven-hour Monopoly game was my personal favorite."

"Oh, bull*shit*, Murphy! You cried *twice* and flipped the board on me at two in the morning."

"That's because it was two in the morning!" Her laughter filled his ears, and he pictured the way that her teeth were probably showing, and her curls were probably bouncing as the laughter coursed through her body. He had the sudden urge to be back on the couch and sitting next to her.

"What about the cooking extravaganza?"

"I think you mean *disaster*."

It was so easy to travel down memory lane when their entire past was intertwined. The conversation slipped seamlessly from their first weeks on the west coast to summers spent in hotels at baseball tournaments. She poked fun at him for his momentary goth phase ("You were Hot Topic's primary source of income for a good two weeks there, Rango") while he retorted with, "Do we *need* to revisit the time that you dragged me into Abercrombie, spent ninety-five dollars on a pair of jeans with holes in them, and then made me stash them in *my* closet so your mom wouldn't find out?"

He could place the blame on a product of environment, being back in their hometown spiraling old habits and comfortability, but he knew that was all a lie. No matter where they ended up, they were always the same James and Charlotte.

The buzz against his ear stilted his laughter. When he pulled his phone away, he saw a text from Vanessa.

Where are you? peeked just above the open call screen that read

Charlie Kate
2:47:32

The clock read after one AM, but he felt like he'd only been sitting in the lobby for ten minutes.

"Hey, I think I'm going to head to bed."

"Aww, wimp. I was just getting to the good part!"

But he could hear the exhaustion in her voice even as she protested.

"Get some sleep, Ace. We've got a big day ahead of us tomorrow."

"Ugh. You're right. You'd think we lived across the country or something with the itineraries that our parents whip up when we come into town," she giggled. "See you bright and early for breakfast?"

"Eight AM on the dot."

"Goodnight, James."

"Sleep tight, Charlie Kate."

He let her end the call, watching the blink fade to his home screen, to a photo of himself and Vanessa on the beach from several weeks prior, both of them squinting into the basking California sun.

"Hey baby, where'd you go?" Her voice was riddled with sleep and grit when he came back to the room, the hall light breaking up the pitch blackness that she slept in.

"I couldn't sleep, so I headed to the lobby to watch TV. I didn't want to wake you," he whispered as he climbed into bed and pulled her back against his front. Her arms folded over his as she nuzzled her cheek into the crook of his elbow, and he buried his lips in her hair before he closed his eyes.

Morning came too quickly, but Vanessa's body clock was used to the odd hours and had figured out how to ignore her body's protests by this point. She was up and showered before James was able to hit the snooze on his own alarm. She sat gently on the edge of the bed, wiping the mop of hair from his forehead.

He barely moved when he slept; it was a mystery that he always woke up with bed head resembling Animal the Muppet. She watched his parted lips close and open again to let a strangled sigh escape, while his limbs twisted out from behind her soft touch to stretch wildly before he rolled over, his back to her.

"Five more minutes," was mumbled into the pillow that he violently shoved his cheeks into, and she rolled her eyes before yanking the blanket from his body.

"Baby, you barely have enough time to shower as it is. Come on. You know how your parents hate it when we're late."

"I'm their precious baby boy. There's no *way* they start passing out cinnamon rolls before I get there," he said with a smirk, flopping onto his back to face Vanessa.

Her eyes pleaded with him to be serious, and she cocked her head to the side when he reached his long arm to grab her hand, dragging her closer to where he had propped himself against the headboard.

"James—"

"Hey, they'll be fine if we're a few minutes late. Promise." He was trying to meet her halfway, one of his large hands grabbing her by the waist as his lips sought hers. But she was pushing away with more force, quickly up and buried in his suitcase to toss an outfit of his across the bed. Her movements were frantic and frazzled, and no sooner was he shaking his head at her attitude than was he ducking under warm water for a quick shower.

"You okay?" he offered as he wiped the toothpaste dribble from his chin.

"Yeah, just...don't want to be late."

She was tapping her foot, appearing almost nervous as he laced up his shoes. He cocked his head, urging her to press on, and she rolled her eyes and picked up her purse and keys.

When, "I just don't want your parents to be mad at us, James. Now, can we get going please?" finally hit the air, realization crashed down on him with a bang.

"Hey," he started with a chuckle, grabbing her forearm lightly. "They're not going to be mad. Seriously. They've known you for like, a year and a half now. They *like* you. They're not going to jump down your throat if we're five minutes late."

Despite his chill attitude, James didn't see the tension thinning around Vanessa's eyes. He took the back roads and passed a few speed limit signs in order to make it home by 8:01 AM.

He did his fair share of checking in throughout the morning as the Ramsey and Murphy clan piled around the large island in Linda's kitchen for a big breakfast buffet. He watched the way that his parents and siblings and the Murphys interacted with Vanessa, in a generally accepting manner, as they had since she had started coming around two Christmases ago. But there was a wariness in her eyes, in the way she was chewing on the inside of her lip, and the way her words were so carefully chosen and her laughter was stilted, almost forced, that had him going between worrying and rolling his eyes about the whole thing. If she wasn't comfortable by now, would she ever be?

Rather than let himself get hung up on the details, James busied himself, sharing a mid-morning beer with his father and the men of the house while the women rushed around getting last minute odds and ends finalized for Emma's party.

Although she now lived on the opposite coast, Charlotte would always consider her parent's house in Newton *home*. Staring at the photos on the mantle, all representative of her growing goddaughter, her fingers paused on the framed image of an hours old little peanut, clutched in the arms of her Auntie K and Uncle JJ. Her smile emanated as the memory of that day flashed quickly, disappearing into the sparkles that filled the air.

"God, I can't believe this was already *three years ago*," she marveled, turning to face her sister.

"I know. They grow up so fast," Kelly replied as she continued tying pink balloons to the chairs in the dining room seated around a table that would soon be toppling over with an avalanche of gifts for the guest of honor.

"Just think: pretty soon, she'll be calling you at three in the morning and asking you to pick her up from some party that she snuck out to when she's too afraid to tell Mom and Dad that she's not actually sleeping over at her girlfriend's house like she promised she would be."

"Oh, stop it! I don't even want to think about that yet."

As Kelly's giggle drifted into the background, Charlotte, with eyes wide, set the frame carefully back onto the oak shelf, preserving the thought of Emma as a precious baby into her mind.

"So, how's the job been treating you?"

For the first time in a long, long time, Charlotte's response to that question wasn't an eye roll or a mimed gag, but a genuine smile.

"I'm really, really loving it."

"Squirt, I'm so happy for you. It's good to see at least one part of your life looking up."

She nodded, adjusting the lavender tablecloth so that it hung evenly, purposely evading the suggestive nature of her sister's words. She wasn't going to go there. Not this weekend. She was here for quality family time, not for another rousing episode of Blunt Lectures with Big Sis.

So instead, she let her sister ask questions about her book, purposely avoiding the subject of Jack. It didn't feel right, all of a sudden, to have him in this sacred space, the one that held photos of James on the mantle and his mother's cookie recipe baking in her mother's oven.

"The goal is to at least have all of the writing done and out of the way by the time school starts in August. That way, I don't have to worry about juggling two things at once. I've already got plenty to manage with working for Ginny and trying to get everything in order for this book as it is."

"Hey, try wrangling stray dogs and cats for eight straight hours; *then* you can start complaining," Kelly chortled as she straightened bows and adjusted streamers.

"I don't need to wrangle dogs and cats; I've got enough on my plate with *this* little munchkin!"

The octave in her voice positively raised as she bent down to pick up and twirl the petite, Rapunzel-dress clad three-year-old, whose giggles sang a sweet song as Charlotte spun her in the air. She set Emma back to a steady place on the ground, still clutching the little girl's tiny fingers in her own palm.

"I'm the birfday princess, Auntie K!" The purple wand in her free hand waved mightily in the air.

"You sure are, Emmy Bear. Are you all ready for your princess party?"

"I wanna go in the bouncy castle!" she replied with a nod.

As per tradition in the Murphy household, no birthday party was complete without a moon bounce. And, as per the theme of the party, a Rapunzel-style castle was being installed on the Murphy's front lawn.

"Aww, sweetheart, we can't go in the bouncy castle yet. They have to blow it up first. We'll go in later." Seeing the signature pout and knitting of brows begin on her niece's face, Charlotte jumped in quickly. "You wanna help me finish putting up these balloons?"

"Yes!"

Charlotte followed her niece around the table, toddling after the three-year-old and doing more correcting of Emma's work than anything else.

"Well, hey, I hope you don't mind adding a little more to your plate soon," Kelly interjected. For the first time that she could ever recall, Charlotte sensed an unfamiliar hesitance in her sister's voice. When she turned to face her, a wide grin spread across Kelly's cheeks.

Kelly's palm was resting on her lower belly, and Charlotte didn't so much as blink as the balloon in her hand hit the ceiling when she ran to embrace her big sister.

"Oh my God, you're not!"

"We are."

"I should've known something was up when you and Bill bought a house in the suburbs. You hate the suburbs."

It wasn't often that Charlotte had these moments with her big sister, where they were all giggles and teasing and just genuinely happy for one another. Of course, naturally, it popped, as Kelly went on about, "And in no time, it'll be you, squirt," and joy suddenly started to fizzle around the edges.

"I know you're always slow to bring guys home, but have you been dating anyone lately?"

Immediately she thought of Jack. Kind, sensitive, amazing Jack, who was waiting back at home for her. Jack, who understood that she didn't bring men home lightly. Jack, who was being patient with her.

Jack, whom she hadn't so much as texted since they landed.

So instead of broaching the subject, she opted instead for *No* and *not really* and *Like I said, with the book and everything, it's just been busy. Maybe when all of this has calmed down a bit I will.*

The bubbles in her gut were making her queasy, but she couldn't put her finger on their source, whether she was feeling guilty about lying, guilty for neglecting her boyfriend for the past day and a half, or just generally fearful about the subject as a whole.

Because all of a sudden, with the word *Future* screaming at her from the living room of her parent's home, she wasn't entirely sure what she wanted.

"Well, put yourself out there, kid. You never know when you're going to stumble across Mr. Right."

She shrugged, wanting immensely to just be out of the conversation. "I guess I'll know him when I see him."

"There's my favorite birthday girl!"

His voice perked the ears of three different people for three separate reasons. By a stroke of luck, Emma's feet pattering across the floor as she threw her tiny body into her godfather's large frame was enough to distract Charlotte and her sister from the deep maroon that had stained her ears.

"Uncle JJ!"

No sooner was Emma shish-kabobbed around James with her arms around his neck, her head resting on his shoulder, her little legs barely clicking together as they wound around his waist.

"Uncle JJ, I'm *free* now!"

"You're *three?* Well, you know what that means, don't you?"

Her baby blues lit up in wonder, inches away from the man who held the secrets.

"You get three big, wet, birthday kisses from the birthday monster!"

He began blowing raspberries on her cheeks, elevating her to spray her tummy. Charlotte wanted to laugh along, but any semblance of a response to the scene playing out before her caught in her throat. She fidgeted with the silver chain around her neck, only stirring from where her thoughts had trapped her by Kelly, whose voice was low enough for only her to hear.

"Seems like you've got a pretty decent guy right across the room."

Kelly didn't need to angle her eyebrows, didn't need to point subtly at James with the pair of scissors that she had been using to skewer curly q's at the end of the balloon ribbons. Charlotte understood her sister's intent quite clearly. But Kelly did it all anyway, squeezing Charlotte once around the shoulder for good measure as she made her way out of the room. The color deepened in Charlotte's cheeks as she grasped for the wine cooler that was awaiting her on the table.

Once Emma's laughter died down and Charlotte's body temperature dissipated a touch, she approached James, hugging him as well as she could with a child balanced on his hip and a large present box on the other.

"Thanks for coming over early to help set up," she murmured into his ear, lips brushing almost as closely as her words did.

"Aww, you didn't really think I'd miss Princess Emma's Princess Party, did you?" His voice still had that touch of childlike wonder, making sure that Emma could hear the enthusiasm. Charlotte's giggles mirrored that of the three-year-old on his hip. Glancing around his shoulder and into the kitchen, she furrowed her eyebrows.

"Where's Vanessa?"

"Oh, she found someone out front that she knew. It must be one of your brother's friends that's helping with the bouncy house or something. I guess they went to college together. Small world, huh?"

He shrugged. She nodded.

"Uncle JJ, let's go to the bouncy castle!"

"The bouncy castle? Aww, kiddo, I'd *love* to go in the bouncy castle. But you'll have to convince your Auntie K to come with us, too."

He waggled his eyebrows at a heels-and-sundress clad Charlotte, whose eyeballs had positively popped out of her skull upon hearing his words. Exactly the reaction he'd been hoping for.

"Oh, no, no, no. You two go have *so much fun—*"

"Puh-*leeeeeease*, Auntie K?"

Emma's eyelashes batted expertly, her lips pursing into a puppy dog pout as she lay her head on James's shoulder.

"Yeah, *pleeeeease,* Auntie K?"

James mimicked the facial expression of the three-year-old, the two looking like twins as they tried to persuade Charlotte to join them.

While Charlotte could typically resist James and Emma pretty easily on their own, it was hard to combat the eyes that batted so willingly at her. She was cornered with no choice but to submit, if for five minutes of the day.

"Now, how could I say no to *those* faces?"

"Yay!"

Jumping from her perch on James's hip, Emma grabbed a hand from each adult and all but dragged them to the yard where guests had already begun to cover the grass. As they arrived at the opening of the un-jumped-upon inflatable, Emma's plastic Rapunzel shoes and James's Dockers found a new home in the grass.

His large hands engulfed the waist of the three-year-old as he lofted her through the mesh doors, following right behind her through the small opening. Pausing on all fours, he observed Charlotte's dainty frame, dressed in tight cotton and bathed in sunlight. She was giggling at what was obviously a comedic scene: he was six-foot-three; he didn't belong in a bouncy castle.

Extending his lanky arm out the opening, he chuckled.

"Oh, don't think you're getting yourself out of this one, Smalls."

"Hey now! I agreed to come out *to* the bouncy castle. Never in that agreement did I say I would enter. I am *not* dressed for a bouncy castle. I am specifically dressed for refilling the cheese and cracker plates when *you* inevitably clear them."

"Well, that's your own fault."

Without another word, his hands were clutching her hips and effectively yanking her inside. The force of his actions knocked him onto his back, banging heads with a flustered Charlotte. As the immediate pain subsided, his body was suddenly hyper aware of their position, that she was straddling him in her cute little sundress with her hips covering his, her small hands clutching at his chest for stability, her curls brushing his cheeks with their foreheads still whispering against one another.

Her body tensed immediately at the heat that now positively overwhelmed her. She had felt his body, hard and strong and comforting against hers hundreds of times. But as the conversation with her sister trickled into her mind, the electricity that used to pulse under her fingertips all those years ago was suddenly present once again. In their close proximity, she could feel his breath passing over her lips in shallow waves.

She wasn't sure when the, "Ow," escaped her throat, but as Emma responded to it with innocent childlike wonder, Charlotte was grateful to be pulled from the intensity of the moment, from his strong hands that were still clasped tightly around her hips, his thumbs absently stroking up and down over her dress.

"Auntie K, did you get a booboo?"

She gulped, shaking her head once, twice, before turning her attention back to her niece. She pursed her lips into a pout. It was meant to be overplayed for the likeness of the little girl, but instead, all her gesture did was form beads of sweat on James's forehead.

Although he knew that she was only trying to be silly on Emma's behalf, the nature at which she was still perched upon him, her knees hugging him from either side, her lips *pouting*, her fingers trembling on his chest, was suddenly making it difficult for him to breathe.

"Yeah, your clumsy Uncle JJ gave me a booboo. It hurts really bad."

"I'll kiss it and make it better."

With the tulle of her dress bobbing up and down, Emma bounced towards them, completely unphased by the heavy tension that had suddenly settled into her kingdom, and planted a sloppy kiss atop Charlotte's head.

"Uncle JJ, kiss it and make it better, too. Say you're sorry."

Gazes that were momentarily drawn towards the child were suddenly forced together again, the intensity behind his turning a deep forest green. Charlotte dragged her bottom lip between her teeth, suppressing a groan.

"Kiss it and make it better, Uncle JJ!"

For a three-year-old, she already had the attitude of a teenager, making demands with her hands perched on her hip. The plastic wand she held in her right hand was almost threatening, as if she would wave it upon him and turn him into a frog if he didn't comply.

He had to move, to shift his body's focus from the position that they had gotten themselves into. Sitting up didn't help, didn't help at all, because when he did, she was sitting in his lap with her knees still astride his hips. Her hands didn't lose their place on his chest, but rather loosened their grip and drifted to his shoulders, her fingers leaving a deadly trail as they found their new home. He was absolutely on fire despite the shade that the moon bounce provided.

Her eyes were locked on his, and he did his best to keep his own gaze from wandering to her lips again. The persistent tapping foot to his right encouraged him from the trance that her sun kissed skin had him under. Her hair must have become tousled in their grand entry, and as he lifted a tentative hand to brush it back from her forehead, his fingers lit a trail across her skin. He held her gaze for only a second more, his eyes whispering the words he wanted to say, the promises he wished he could make her, as he gently cupped her cheek and met her forehead halfway. His lips sealed a healing kiss to the spot where they had collided only moments ago.

She had been kissed by him before, several times, in fact. But in this moment, her entire world froze, his lips hot and cold at the same time, his prior gaze haunting everything in her life that she knew to be true. More quickly than not, he was pulling back, a tinge of regret snaked behind the green that was fading back to its original color.

His voice, strangely gravelly, broke her from the daze that had encapsulated her.

"Hey, I got a booboo, too. Don't I get a kiss to make it feel better?" he breathed, his gaze still holding tightly to the woman in his lap. His words were meant for the three-year-old, but Charlotte was all he truly saw.

"Daddy says boys are tough," she shrugged, and planted her hands on her hips as if to put an end cap on the conversation.

All of a sudden, the moment was gone, lost to the awkward laughter that shook through Charlotte's body and reverberated into his. He was sad but grateful as she slunk from his lap, an almost defeated look in her eye when she was pressed solely into the vinyl of the moon bounce. Finally, he turned his attention towards Emma, the puppy dog pout making a return.

"So, no kisses for Uncle JJ?"

"Oh, Emma. *I* know who will give Uncle JJ as many kisses as he wants."

James shook the chill from his body, bringing himself back to a reality where Charlotte wasn't his, and instead his expression contorted, noticing the scheming pair of ladies who were beginning to encircle him. The girls faced one another, shared a knowing glance and nod, and screamed in unison, "The tickle monster!"

No sooner was he ducking for cover than was he under a dogpile assault of tiny bodies and fingers and a mass of giggles. Eventually they made their way upright, and general bouncing commenced, the tension momentarily forgotten.

Across the yard, condensation from Vanessa's beer bottle dripped slowly over her fingertips as her eyes burned holes through the mesh walls of the moon bounce, the glass clenched so tightly in her grasp that she was surprised it hadn't popped.

August 2018

"Vanessa?"

The voice, belonging to her college friend Ben, pulled her back to the conversation that had been interrupted by the questionable actions that had just transpired in the moon bounce across the yard.

"Sorry," she fumbled, pulling herself away from moon bounces and laps and forehead kisses, and doing her best to pretend that she hadn't just witnessed every last thing.

Despite being grounded back to the present, her eyes were still fixed on the three people bouncing and giggling across the yard. It was similar to a train wreck: she wanted to look away, to focus on herself, but she just *couldn't*.

"Charlotte and James." Ben's Bud Light was pointed in the direction of her boyfriend. Now outside the shelter of the castle, James and Charlotte were swinging Emma by the arms between them.

"That's David's little sister and her best friend; they're Emma's godparents. They've been like glue since they were, like, five years old. Might as well just get married already. They already act like it."

Her stare hadn't wavered from the trio, but Ben's words stung her ears and fueled the scowl that was contorting on her lips. She hadn't even thought to mention the name of the "boyfriend" she had told Ben that she was here to accompany. To him, or any casual passerby in attendance at this party, Charlotte and James were the couple that had yet to be. She didn't even belong in the picture.

Distraught, with no other response as her veins ran numb, all she could think to mutter was, "Yeah, might as well," before she excused herself to the cooler for another beer.

Vanessa stood at the back corner of the throng that gathered to sing "Happy Birthday" to the precious three-year-old, whose presence shouldn't have been having this dampening effect on her day. She tried not to focus on the fact that Emma had an arm around James and the other around Charlotte, that her little legs were being cradled by James's bicep, that the two adults in the picture began a frosting war with the little girl as soon as the candles were plucked from the cake's

254

surface and that every other onlooker giggled in response.

Instead, she did her best to focus on the way that the child's face lit up through it all. The child, who was their reason for being there. That little girl's happiness was what Vanessa chose to focus on, even as her beau's eyes found hers for the first time all afternoon, and a sheepish smile was all that he could muster.

James set Emma down as she began to devour her large slice of pink frosted cake, grabbed a napkin, and maneuvered his way to Vanessa's side as he wiped the frosting from his nose and cheek, the product of not one, but two culprits: one three years old and carefree, the other too close to home, a threat she thought they had long since avoided.

"Hey, where have you been? I feel like I haven't seen you since we got here. How's your friend?"

"Good, he's good. How's Charlotte?" She didn't mean to let snark drip from her words, but at the same time, she didn't regret letting her emotions show for once.

"Charlie Kate? She's fine. Why?" He continued to wipe at the remaining bits of frosting, completely unphased by her line of questioning. She didn't know whether to be angry, shocked, or defeated.

Eventually, she settled on the latter.

"No reason." Her eyes dropped a beat after the words left her mouth, focusing on the label that she had been peeling off her beer bottle. Suddenly, his large hands were atop her shoulders, his head sneaking into her bubble.

"Hey, everything okay?"

"Yeah, I'm fine."

"Good." He smiled, giving her a quick peck on the forehead. "I'm gonna go grab a beer. Do you need another?"

"No, I'm alright."

As he sauntered back towards the house where the line of coolers awaited, a thought crossed her mind: she wasn't *losing* him.

She had already lost him.

"James?"

He caught her words and stopped in his tracks. His body remained poised in the direction of travel, but he turned his head attentively, his grin almost bringing tears to her eyes.

"Yeah?"

"I love you."

His lips pulled up, but the way that his eyes were turned down only assured her worries.

"I love you, too."

Vanessa watched as he became sidetracked on the way to the beer cooler because a Rapunzel dress was wrapping around his legs for the umpteenth time that day. James lifted Emma into the air and carried her back to the makeshift throne that had been set up in front of the pile of unopened presents, where Charlotte was already waiting. The two crouched near Emma, watching with identical grins as she tore at bows and scattered colorful paper all over the patio. Vanessa was an onlooker, an observer on the outside looking into a group of people that she never belonged to in the first place.

After the party concluded and they stayed to help clean up ("Why *wouldn't* we?" he had asked her with more than a hint of defensiveness to his tone), they made the trek back to the hotel. A warm sunset seeped through the windshield that forced James into his aviators. With hands clasped in her lap, she stared out the passenger side window, admiring the way the light created soft shadows on the suburban sidewalks.

"You've been awfully quiet today." His voice pulled her from her thoughts, silky and rich like a spoonful of honey. "Did you enjoy the party?"

"It was nice. I'm just tired." She'd used the excuse hundreds of times when it actually matched her situation. Oftentimes they found themselves at home and in bed much earlier than he'd have liked due to her state of sheer exhaustion after back to back shifts. Sometimes, she just needed a moment to herself. But tonight was different. Tonight, her words dripped with a falsity that she hadn't adopted until recently.

She just didn't want to do this tonight.

"Well how about when we get back to the hotel, I'll order us a nice bottle of wine, and we—"

"I think I'm just going to go to bed."

Her typical candor failed as she noticed that the time on the dash read 7:42. She could go to bed early, but not eight o'clock early. James's body shifted, tensing as his knuckles gripped the steering wheel a bit more firmly.

"Vanessa, is everything okay?" There was an edge to his voice that sparked parts alarm and concern. Her sole job in that moment was to reassure him and put them back to a place where she could push her thoughts away for just a little while longer.

"Yes, James, everything is fine. I'm just really burnt out. I had a long week, we were on a plane for six hours yesterday, and we've kind of been *go-go-going* since then. I just want a few minutes to relax, that's all."

He was used to this burnt out Vanessa. Maybe not with quite as much attitude, but he resonated with her all the same. He gave up his inquisition, shifting his gaze sideways so that his sympathetic smile was noticed, and grasped both her hands in his right one, rubbing his thumb over the back.

As Vanessa cuddled into their less than pristine hotel bed later, James's words trickled to her from the bathroom almost as effortlessly as the toothpaste dribbled down his chin.

"Hey, I forgot to tell you: Charlie Kate and I were thinking about taking Emma to the zoo and maybe coming home Monday instead of tomorrow night, if that's okay with you. Sort of a birthday present from her godparents, you know, since we don't get to see her that often."

His casual tone, as he wiped his chin and padded barefoot towards the bed, registered as one he might use when he asked her if she minded pizza instead of Chinese takeout. She sat up from her lounged position, bracing herself for the fight that she was trying her hardest to put off. But if she was going to fight, she'd do her damndest to make her voice heard. Eyes rimmed more with sadness and exhaustion, she took a deep breath before plunging straight into the deep end.

"What if it's not?"

She watched the features in his expression flinch quickly from confused to angered to *maybe I didn't hear that correctly.* So she spoke again.

"What if it's not okay with me?"

This time he heard her loud and clear, and his eyes told everything that followed on his lips.

"I mean, I'm not exactly sure why it wouldn't be—"

"You, Charlotte, Emma. Going to the zoo together?"

"Yeah. That's exactly why I'm—she's our goddaughter." His hands were prone in front of him, posed in frustrated questioning that knit his eyebrows, clearly not understanding where all of this was coming from.

"Yes, James. But Charlotte is not your wife, nor your girlfriend for that matter. Your *girlfriend* is flying home early and thought that she'd see you at home on Sunday night."

The confusion turned straight to frustration, anger even, as she noticed the lobes of his ears turning a deep shade of crimson.

"I'm not even sure what you're getting at here—"

"I saw you two today, James. *Everyone at the party* saw you two."

This time, his eyes, his cheeks, his neck flushed with a sense of knowing. She wouldn't label it embarrassment or guilt, but she could tell by his reaction that he knew exactly what she was referring to.

"Did anybody outside of the family even know that I was there with you? That *I'm* your girlfriend? The woman that you share a home with. The woman that you're supposed to love?"

"Vanessa, where is all of this coming from?"

That was his answer. Not, *Of course I love you,* or *I'm so sorry, of course people know that we're together,* or *You're right, I fucked up royally today.* He was defending himself. Trying to get her to shed light on every insecure part, every fault of her own. But she was done with it.

"What do you want from me, James? From this? What do you want from *us*? Because the way I see it, you can get everything you've ever wanted from Charlotte."

"Vanessa—"

"No. I'm not done. I... what are we *doing*, James?"

The way her voice broke, the pleading in her tone, knocked him back on his feet. He was stunned, watching the skin on her face pull downward, and her eyes fill with water as her shoulders slumped and pulled her body into an unending hole.

It was a shock to his system, her existential question, her *What are we doing?* that finally had everything crashing down around him, that finally had a defeated, "I don't know," whispering past his lips as he sank to the bed and put his head in his hands. Everything he had been trying so hard to cover up was thrown immediately into sight.

Their fight went well into the morning, topics thrashing back and forth, ranging between everything from Charlotte, to where James's intentions lay, to *We've never stayed at your parents' house, James. Am I embarrassing to you?*

Voices raised, screeching past the point of raw throats, until a neighbor knocked on their door at two in the morning and politely asked them to *Knock it off, for fuck's sake!*

But it was the hushed tones, the whispers, that he realized were even more painful. When her words were bitten and almost silent, piercing every part of him that had ever loved her like a knife. Each tear that dropped from her eyes stung worse than the next, but he was in no place to reach across, to wipe them away and comfort her, because those hands that were itching to reach out were the very same ones that had hurt her in the first place.

It was her, "I'm done, James. I'm tired. I'm tired of all of this," with a defeated wave of her arms that did him in and broke the dam of his own tears. He watched her through his own haze as she crawled into the king-sized bed without changing out of her dress and let her eyes close under the weight of gravity.

He didn't dare try to comfort her, didn't try to crawl into that bed, but he was torn between staying and leaving. On the one hand, she didn't want him there in the slightest. But on the other hand, walking out that door would be the nail in the coffin to something they clearly weren't finished discussing.

Eventually, under the pressure of his own exhaustion, he collapsed in the stiff corner armchair, his neck crooked at an awkward angle that he decided he deserved every bit of.

When he awoke to the bathroom door opening and closing only a few hours later, an eerie silence enveloped the air. Vanessa's hair was damp, her eyes patted in powder that was no doubt to hide her dark circle tattoos.

His sad eyes did their best to communicate the sorrow, the indecision, because he knew that spoken words were not just yet an option.

They packed their suitcases in silence, brushing past each other carefully as not to touch, which created for stiff backs and sharp intakes of air.

Holding her hand as they walked into The Paramount for Sunday brunch with his family was tense, but they did their best to keep up appearances for the sake of everyone else. It wasn't until they were in the car, following the invitation to head back to his parent's for Sunday hangout, that she spoke directly to him for the first time since three AM.

"I think I'm going to head back now. Instead of going to your parents'. I'll get some rest before my shift. Clear my head a little."

The pause between them was pregnant and thick as he debated his response. He knew that a swift *Okay* would be the final twist of the knife, but begging her to stay would be too much, inconsiderate almost.

He settled instead for a soft, "Can I drive you to the airport?" that was all but whispered past his lips, his shoulders hunching in defeat when she whispered back *Okay*.

When James walked through the front door of his parent's house, there was something different about the way that he carried himself. Charlotte had ventured inside from where the rest of their clan was relaxing on the patio to refresh her drink when she heard the front door peek open and seal closed, the ghost of her friend so quiet as he all but tiptoed into the house. His demeanor frightened her in more ways than one.

"I don't like that look on your face, James Ramsey."

She had gotten so good at reading him over the years that it was uncomfortable when she couldn't place an expression. His eyes were tired but wide; his lips set in a straight line, but full, like they were loaded with words he wanted to scream. Lines of worry stretched across his forehead, but frustration was also etched deep into the creases.

At first, she was worried that he was going to confront her on what had happened the day before. The tension from the moon bounce had lingered in her body all through the night after he had left, dawdling the entire time she had been on the phone with Jack on a call that she tried to convince herself wasn't entirely made out of guilt. But when James finally spoke, she began to realize that there was so much more to it than her own selfish worries.

"Vanessa's gone," he said right away, learning so long ago that there was no point in trying to hide things or beat around the bush when it came to Charlotte. "We had a fight last night. A pretty bad one. A *really* bad one. I just dropped her off at the airport."

He sat on his parent's living room couch with elbows balanced on his knees so that he could rest his forehead in his hands before he let out a groan, expelling a large gust of air through his lungs as he did so.

Charlotte was quick to his side, concern washing over her in waves that began with biting her lip and ended with a soft hand on his shoulder.

"Talk to me, Rango. What do you need me to do?"

It was another sigh as he picked his head from the cradle of his large hand, a long stare around the room and up towards the ceiling, and a defeated shrug before he finally spoke.

"I don't know. I don't want to see anyone though. Not my parents. Not your family. God, Charlie Kate, I just want to like, bury myself ten feet underground and scream."

She pondered, but not for long, before she grabbed his hand and hauled him from the couch, stumbling slightly.

"C'mon. I know exactly where we can run away to."

His gaze questioned her still as she merged onto the highway, one eyebrow cocked over her bright eyes and mischievous grin.

When he refused to sing along to the radio despite the fact that she had immediately put on his favorite station, she knew it was worse than she had imagined.

Flicking through her phone as she kept one eye on the road, the shrill telltale voice of Kristin Chenoweth pierced his ears long enough for him to pass the smallest hint of a smile.

She began with "Popular" from the *Wicked* soundtrack. They had the over exaggerated voices and character faces down to a routine science by now. By the end of the song, with Charlotte passing him many glances and silly expressions to the tune, he was finally beginning to soften up.

By the time "What Is This Feeling?" came on shuffle, James was taking on his role of Elphaba, and the entire car was booming with noise and laughter and *loathing!*

"Always know how to make me feel better, don't you, Smalls?"

She laughed, a light and airy sound that made his ears ring and run hot. For that moment in time, it was only them, and she was twelve years old with the brand-new CD he had bought her at the t-shirt stand during intermission. He'd made fun of her, because *that one chick's voice sounds like nails on a chalkboard, Charlie Kate! Do we really have to listen to it again?* But no sooner was he complaining than he was giving in, because hearing her laugh and giggle and become the characters on the CD was just something that his body had learned to crave.

They made their way through the album before switching to a Top

40's station, continuing with the obnoxious dancing and singing while the stares from other cars on the highway went completely ignored.

Once she took the exit toward North Mill Pond, a wave of relief flooded his nerves. For the first time since his body had tensed the night before, he was breathing fresh air.

The lake house was a property that his parents and hers had invested in together the second summer that they knew each other. When both families agreed that they all needed somewhere just a little bit farther than Crystal Lake, somewhere that felt like a "real vacation" but still wasn't too far from home, the decision was made. Whenever they weren't on the baseball field, they were up at the lake, using and abusing every water toy imaginable. The summer he was finally able to drive the jet ski was one for the books for sure.

But as Charlotte turned down the gravel road under a canopy of trees that beckoned them forward to safety, as they crossed the threshold from city and suburbs into their own shielded world, a cinema of memories played out in his mind.

The entire first summer at the lake house was less swimming and more wading ankle deep while Charlotte stood with her toes barely nudging the water.

He held her hand to lead her in, swearing up and down that it wasn't as cold and full of *slimy fish that could touch her!* as she claimed.

She did more playing with Abby in the years to come, because Abby's swim floats stayed in shallow water. While running off to play with David and Kyle on the skis was fun for a while, he would inevitably end up rolling his eyes while he sat on the sand and helped Charlotte and his baby sister make sandcastles and puddle around the shorelines.

When they were old enough to swim out to the diving raft, he spent an entire summer pleading with her to follow him out to the platform, to jump into the water with him. On their last night of the year, she was cutting off the circulation in his arms as they swam out to the middle of the water, but she made the sunset jump with him and finally broke her hesitance with water. That same hesitance was only brought back the first time he flipped her off the back of the jet skis when they were twelve.

Needless to say, as soon as he helped her back on and she shoved him over the edge, that fear took off like she did when she left him wading in her wake.

As they got older and curfews were extended, it was the time that they spent wandering the shore at night, sitting on the beach and having late night talks, that he came to cherish. The water, the boats, the fun times were guaranteed. But time spent with her was coveted.

Time that waned during those summers when he would invite his girlfriend or she would invite her boyfriend, but they somehow always made up for it.

Now, as the sun was already moving toward the west, toward *home* now, it seemed that they had so, so much to *make up* for.

It wasn't until they were seated at the edge of their dock, socks and shoes abandoned behind them while their toes skimmed the surface, that the words dripped from him like a faucet.

He told her everything, feeling her body tense beside him at the realization that *her* name was so primarily involved in this major crack in all that was *James and Vanessa*. But he focused more on Vanessa's insecurities than his own thoughts, his own faults, how Vanessa was always timid and scared and untrusting, but never once admitting to the fact that his own actions could have—and definitely did—contribute.

She sat and listened, letting him pour it all out; she stayed calm in his silences, knowing that he was thinking and processing and that he would pick back up eventually. He liked to pace, so eventually she was following him down the beach, watching him chuck smooth, flat rocks at the water's surface as he continued to speak, more processing out loud than needing a response.

He said things like, "I mean, she knew you were part of the deal when this all started. Why is it bothering her now?" and, "She wants so badly to impress my family, but I think she gets so caught up in being perfect that she spends the entire time being uptight and overtired." But he caught himself, folded inside for more thought, and then started over again.

264

It was forty-five minutes, an hour, the sun beginning to set behind them when his parched lips finally expelled a sigh, and with a shake of his head, he started towards the house. Wordlessly, she followed.

The house was vacant, musty with a layer of dust that had settled since the last use weeks prior. With the setting sun poking through the pulled curtains, a hazy gray settled over the faded hardwood, creating eerie lines and small shadows to accompany them.

"I feel like a rebel," she giggled, her voice just barely above a whisper. "I'm not allowed in the *boys' room*."

"Oh, come on," he chuckled, standing back so that she could duck under his arm and cross into forbidden territory. "Don't tell me you never once stepped foot in here."

"I didn't!" she insisted, crossing her arms with both her eyes and her smile wide. "The rules of the lake house were unflinchingly rigid, James Ramsey: No girls in the boys' room, and no boys in the girls' room, or you'd spend the summer cleaning the boat instead of riding it."

"Then I have some serious deck swabbing to make up for."

"James!"

She swatted at his chest as his smile grew wider. He shook his head then and settled on the edge of the queen bed, watching as she tentatively took up residence at his side, her feet swinging in the open air in contrast to his that could reach the floor.

The creak and steady hum of the old fan spinning above them provided a filler for the otherwise still air, accompanied only by the buzz of their thoughts.

"So, how many other rules did you break that I don't know about?" she teased, keeping her gaze on their feet.

"Oh, well," he chuckled. "You remember that one time the jet ski *mysteriously* got totaled? Definitely took it to the beached area. Definitely let the gravel eat the bottom of it. Definitely went a mile and a half out of my way to make sure it didn't look like it was my fault."

"Oh my god! *You're* the reason we all got banned from driving for the summer?"

He nodded, trying and failing to suppress a laugh through his closed lips.

"James! We had to clean out under the porch all summer because of your dumb ass?"

"Yup. Afraid so. But you're one to talk, little miss perfect. You can't tell me *you* were all rules and regs when we'd come up here."

It went that way for a while, with memories being traded and laughter melting the bags of tension that he'd brought in on his back. It wasn't until memory lane morphed into *Ghosts of Significant Others at the Lake House Past* that she felt her cheeks growing hot and he felt himself suddenly swinging his feet a little more towards the center.

"Do you remember that one summer?" Her voice was shy as she stared at the tanned skin of her thighs and bit her lip.

The summer before college, where the thrill of sneaking around only added to the chase, and they spent more time hiding in the woods for stolen kisses and ducking out for midnight drives to empty fields and parking lots than they actually did on the lake. It was the longest time they had spent together; though without title, the significance was evident.

He sidled into her softly, his smile wide and boyish under the cover of his falling bangs. "Come on, of course I remember that summer."

Their red cheeks matched, and as they realized that they were each holding back grins, the tension loosened a little, bodies seeping a bit lower into the mattress.

"We were kind of wild, weren't we?" he chuckled, his eyes rolling up towards the ceiling as he let his mind drift away.

"We had *no* idea what we were doing." She laughed, partially from nerves, but mostly from the chill of those memories now.

"Hey, I give us credit," he defended, turning now to face her slightly. "For being newbies, we eventually got the hang of things."

"Yeah, I guess you're right," she agreed, the nod of her head slow as her ears began to burn.

"That, uh...you definitely knew what you were doing that one night.... you know, after that Sox game, when we drove out to that parking lot?"

His bottom lip was tucked between his teeth as he awaited her reply, his eyes shy again until he saw recognition in a sheepish form in hers.

"Yeah, that was...that was a good night."

A smile crept up her crimson cheeks, and he buried his stare in his lap as he nodded in agreement, the memories making his body tingle.

"Yeah, yeah, it was," he nodded, suddenly eighteen again, his body abuzz with nerves. "We had to be pretty creative."

"Yeah, we definitely didn't have very many options."

"Oh really, miss *put your hand in my gym shorts pocket while my mom was in the kitchen*?"

Echoes of the past whispered into the air.

"Charlotte Katherine my mother is in the next room."

"Mmm, I like when you call me that. Say it again."

Her giggles and his sighs combined to form an almost private symphony.

"Do you want me to stop?"

"I don't know how to answer that question."

"Hey, I don't seem to remember much complaining from your end," she jabbed to break the silence.

"Oh, trust me, I *complained* in my room when you, uh, left before the job was done."

Their laughter then was soft, like the tail end of a long breath that came from parted upturned lips and pink cheeks.

"We never really got each other out of our systems, did we?" she asked more to her knees than to him as her smile pointed downward.

"Hmm? What was...?"

"Oh, it was something stupid Ginny said. Forever ago. She said that you and I should just...you know...get it out of our systems. I guess we never really did."

She shrugged, tucking her chin atop her shoulder as her eyes ticked from his hands to his eyes and back again.

James chuckled, a puff of breath that was low and warmed the air between them. Her eyebrows rose at his perception of humor, and he turned his eyes to the ceiling before finding her gaze, his words steady

267

and strong as he said, "I don't think I could ever get you out of my system, Charlotte Murphy."

Their eyes clicked in the middle then, the intensity in wide stares matching in a fire that only climbed higher when he nudged his hand across the mattress to meet hers in the middle. When her breath was noisy, a little moan caught in the back of her throat, it was all over.

They met with a force, her cheeks in his palms under a pressure that was almost painful, but it urged her forward that much more.

Their kiss was a mess of lips and teeth and tongue, wet sounds competing over the top of the breaths and grunts and groans that bounced from wall to ceiling. Hands were flying in a fury to cover both ground and time lost, as he pulled at her shirt and pulled her into his lap and lost his pants to the furious work of her hands.

A fury that only stopped when he was hovering above her, nothing but cotton underwear separating their pulsing, sweating bodies that were peppered with marks where kisses and fingernails had already lay their claim.

With his nose brushing the tip of hers, breaths so close that they were sharing oxygen, his hands finally slowed their pace, took stock in smoothing the hair behind her ears, doing his best to read the intentions in eyes that had blown up in size and turned shades darker than her typical golden green.

He was asking in stuttered brokenness, things like *Charlie Kate,* and *Are you…?* and little squeaks when her hips jumped up to meet his. His nose was like a paintbrush against her cheek as he tried to maintain his bearings, tried to anchor himself to her before he literally floated away with the torch of desire that his body carried for Charlotte Murphy.

When his name was squeaking off her lips, that *James* so full of want and need, he was suddenly eighteen again, and her hair was frizzier, and her eyes had more fear in them. She was on his childhood bed, the sheets probably overdue for a wash, his hands still bruised with every lesson he had taught Joey De Luca, with every reason he had to love her.

In that moment, there was no Vanessa, no Jack. It was James and it was Charlotte, and he would do everything in his damned power to make the sun revolve around her.

It occurred to him then that his whole world was in his hands, his future lying at the fingertips that wound up in her curls and trailed along her jaw and down her abdomen. This dawning stopped him in his tracks, slowed his frantic moves to dull idle strokes, despite the look in her eye and the way she was biting her lip and doing her best to shift herself beneath him, to urge him forward and fast. Instead of speeding along, he kissed her slowly, tenderly, praying that the words stuffed up in his head would somehow be conveyed through his touch.

He couldn't mess it up this time. He had to do right by her.

So, his lips were tender, and his hands found all of the places that he knew she liked, letting their bodies communicate, responding to her in the ways that he hadn't lost all those years ago. She wasn't a habit though, because she wasn't something he could ever break himself from knowing.

His hands shook, fingertips burning as they traced familiar paths, remembering the different ways in which she would respond when he kissed her neck or nuzzled his way down her body. By the way she was bucking against his fingertips and doing her very best to make their kisses more heated and frantic, he was being blown back to that summer, to all of the times before when having her come undone was as simple as untying a shoelace. But he didn't want to unravel her like he was trying to prove a point.

No. Not when the point he was trying to prove was how much love every fiber of his being held for only her.

He was kissing down her neck, his tongue skirting the skin and tasting the salt, sucking at the base of her throat so slowly that it made her squirm. The way her fingers were growing tighter in his hair, the way that she was panting and letting loose those soft sounds, told him that he was doing it right.

So he continued onward, letting his lips be the pen that wrote a manuscript of his love along her body, across her skin, down her abdomen, her symphony of sounds the accompaniment to his never ending saga.

Her legs twitched beneath him, her toes curling against the mattress as her feet dragged along the backs of his knees, making his core run hot and his face redden.

He never expected her to drag him back up, for those fingers in his hair to be firm and insistent at his cheeks, for the fervor in her kisses to steal his breath away. But he complied all the same, wrapping his arms around her back to hold her as tightly to him as humanly possible while he breathed every intention into her lungs.

Her touch was hot but fleeting, her fingers trailing the length of his spine, the broad expanse of his shoulders, the curve of his ass, massaging his temple. She was everywhere, and in that moment, if he were to die being consumed by her, he wouldn't mind in the slightest.

When she wrapped her legs around him, hooked her ankles at the small of his back, buried her nose into the crook of his shoulder and kissed the skin there tenderly, he had to stifle a groan.

He pulled away then, but just enough to stare down into her eyes, to brush away the curls that were skirting past and impeding his field of vision. With her eyes so hazy, her nose skirting back and forth across his as she tried her best to lock their lips together again in the center, he tried his best to use real words this time, to just *fucking tell her* before things got out of control.

I love you.

I want you.

I need you to know that it's always been you.

But when her cell phone rang, the shrill tone cut through the air like a knife, severed any intention that was still on his lips, and her body tensed immediately under his touch.

He tensed too, but so differently, as his arms tightened around her to hold her in place. He couldn't let this go, couldn't let her go, not when she was finally here. Not when they were finally so close.

His voice was almost pleading when he brought his lips to her ears and whispered, "Let it ring," but then she was listening to the tone, and saying, "It's David, I have to take it," and wrapping the comforter around her body like a vice.

Letting his feet swing over the edge of the bed, he expelled a sigh and rested his elbows on his knees, running his fingers back and forth across his scalp. When he looked over, her eyes were wide, but he couldn't tell if the shock came from the news on the other line or what they'd just been interrupted from finishing.

It wasn't until she said, "Kelly's in the hospital," that he stopped thinking about himself and whipped his clothes on faster than he had on their first night.

The entire car ride was silent, save for her brief explanation of *Heat exhaustion* and *Making sure everything is alright with the baby.* He kept the music off, doing his best not to lose himself in the battle of thoughts that were her and Kelly and feelings and what exactly he was supposed to do right now.

He dropped her off at the front and watched her run through the automatic doors before finding a parking space. As he threw the car in park, he rested his head on the steering wheel and let a groan fill the otherwise silent cabin.

It wasn't hard to find their circus crowd of a family that filled the waiting room. Emma was kneeling on the floor in front of a table with a box of crayons and a coloring book. She was still wearing the plastic Rapunzel crown she'd donned at the party the day before. The rest of their family, parents, siblings, significant others, crowded around nervously. The absence of Charlotte had him assuming that she was in Kelly's room, which was confirmed when her mother told him so.

It was some time before she came back out, dried tear tracks staining the cheeks he'd been cradling not long ago. He stood then, wiping his hands on his thighs and cocking his head down the hall. She nodded and followed him wordlessly. They turned three corners before he spoke.

"How's Kelly?"

"She's fine. Stable. They're going to keep her for a few more hours to make sure she's hydrated and that the baby's okay."

"Good. That's good." He nodded, rubbed his hands together, and tried to think of the appropriate way to say *I didn't want us to stop, Charlie Kate* when she had just left her sister's hospital room.

It was her next words that stopped him cold, a twitch shocking him back to earth when she said, "I think you should go after Vanessa."

"Uhm, sorry, what?" He grappled, his eyes wide and searching. James watched her take a deep breath, her eyes closing to compose herself.

"I think you should go back, James. You need to talk to Vanessa. You need to...to figure things out. I'm going to stay here one more day and make sure Kelly's okay. You should go home. You probably still have time to change your flight."

He looked lost then, more lost than he'd appeared when he entered his parent's living room mere hours ago, his world seemingly shattered. But in all reality, it wasn't *then*, after his cataclysmic fight with Vanessa, that his whole being was beginning to crumble. It was now, with her pushing him away, that he felt the ground beneath him give way.

Pleading did nothing but force her to shake her head more rapidly from side to side, to cause the lump in her throat to well even larger in size. He couldn't be the one that brought her pain. Not now. Not after everything he'd put her through. So with tears of his own causing his water line to redden, he nodded curtly, folded his lips into a tight line, and made his way back into the waiting room with his fists balled at his sides.

Goodbyes were brief, abrupt, but everyone understood. He passed along well wishes to Kelly through her parents and turned to leave. When he caught Charlotte's gaze head on, the tension in her expression that was more from an effort of trying not to lose it than anything else, he couldn't stay any longer. He couldn't watch her break, couldn't be the source of her crumbling any longer. So, for the first time in his life, he left her behind.

May 2016

"Woah, there, Murphy. Starting early tonight or what?"

James chuckled, watching Charlotte chug down a good quarter of a Sam Adams before she even closed their refrigerator.

"James. Don't *ever* become a teacher. You'll *die*."

"Oh, come on, you don't mean that," he chuckled, stealing a bottle from the six pack.

"No. I don't. I love my job. But summer hungry kindergarteners are literally out for blood this week. I'm lucky I made it out alive."

"Alright, lay it on me. Storytime. What was it today?"

"Pee. Literal pee. Everywhere. Three kids, James. *Three*. It was like ping-pong piss. One peed their pants, so they all started."

"And this is why *you* went into the field of education and *I* chose to sit behind a desk all day."

"Exactly. And that's not even the half of it."

"Oh?"

He cocked his eyebrow, waiting for her to go on, but received a pathetic, *help me please* look that he immediately pitied.

"You know what this means, right?" he asked as he reached into the refrigerator, yanking the six-pack of beer from its spot on the bottom shelf and plopping it in the middle of the coffee table.

That got her smiling.

She praddled on, telling him another of her affectionately dubbed "Kindergarten Horror Stories" as they knocked back a few beers apiece, her stress from the week slipping out as the alcohol slipped in.

"She did *not!*"

"I swear to god, James. Scout's honor. She walked up to me and said, 'Excuse me, Miss Murphy? I'm sorry, but I think I just sharted.' How? *How* do you react to that?"

With his eyes pinched in laughter, he slapped an open palm to his forehead.

"How *did* you react to that?"

"I don't even remember. It was an out of body experience. I'm pretty sure I sent her to the bathroom with the aide. God, if I'd wanted

273

to deal with bodily fluids all day, I would have just become a nurse."

The buzzer to their apartment stalled James's laughter, and at the sound of Scotty's voice, he was simultaneously pushing the button to let him up and pulling the Pizza Hut menu off the refrigerator.

Charlotte sidled to the door with her third beer half gone and let Scotty in, all five-foot-eleven of his wide, stocky frame. He was a California surfer boy through and through, with the tan, the blonde pushed-back hair, and the muscles to back up a childhood spent on the beach.

"Hey baby, how are you?" He pulled her against his chest after she'd closed the door, her small body so comically enveloped by his broad torso. "I see you survived."

"Ugh. Barely," she mumbled to his pecs.

"So, do you wanna vent about it?"

"Actually, I think I just need to chill out. James already got an earful and I think the only thing my mouth wants to do for the next three hours is this," she replied, pressing the cool bottle to her lips again.

Scotty's eyes twisted downward, pulling his mouth along with them before his gaze wandered to the clock.

"Oh. Well, do you want to hang out for a little while before the game then?"

"Sure. We're just getting ready to order a pizza if you want to hang with us," she said, joining James on the couch.

Scotty followed, leaning his chin on crossed arms on the back of the couch to bow closer to her ear as he muttered, "I was kind of thinking just *us*, you know? I haven't really seen you all week."

But as the familiar NESN theme bounded from the speakers, he knew it was a lost cause, and he dropped his forehead to rest on his folded arms for just a moment.

When Charlotte turned with eyebrows furrowed to face him, he propped his chin up on his arms and raised his eyebrows in equal parts annoyance, pleading, and defeat. He cocked his head towards the door, and for the next ten minutes, James could hear muffled voices raising and lowering to different pitches and grunts in the hallway before the door was opening again.

Scotty was saying, "Call me after the game?" but his tone was admittedly annoyed.

"You know you're always more than welcome to join us, Scotty," James said, facing the sullen man before the crack of the bat pulled his focus back to the television.

"I appreciate the offer, man, but you know baseball's not my thing. I'll talk to you later babe, alright?"

"Alright. I'll call you after the game."

James watched Charlotte give Scotty a stilted peck on the lips before skipping back to the couch, joining James's chorus of, "What the fuck, Buchholz?" as he threw his hands up in frustration.

Scotty was out the door reluctantly, lingering just a moment longer, patting the doorframe first before officially heading out with a "Kay."

Charlotte found the spot on their couch that had essentially molded to her butt since they had moved in, taking a swig of her beer as Xander Bogaerts turned a double play to end the first inning.

"What was his problem tonight?" James asked once the commercial break hit.

She shrugged at first, hoping he would drop the subject and just enjoy the game, but his less than satisfied grunt had her spouting ambiguous words.

"I don't know."

"Come on, Charlie Kate. You guys are obviously fighting about something. Talk to me."

"I think he's mad that I kick him out every time the game comes on."

"Hey, look, I've told him time and time again that he's more than welcome to—"

"That's not it, James." She chewed the inside of her lip, grateful for the return of the game to bide her time. After a one-two-three bottom half, he seemed to pounce right back to the subject.

"So what is it then, Smalls? C'mon, I know you're holding out on me."

"He's upset that it's *you*, okay?"

For once, James was stunned into speechlessness. He stared at her, mouth agape, for several moments before settling into the couch and running a hand through his hair.

"He knew I had a rough day, and he wanted to be there for me. But the game's on, and he knows that this is our thing, and that watching baseball with you would help to fix my shitty day long before he got to swoop in to save me. He had a lot of...not so nice things to say about the amount of time I spend with you. I think he feels threatened by you or something."

"Threatened by me? Do you hear the words that are coming out of your mouth?"

"Yes, I do," she retorted, her lips furling into an annoyed grin. "How does that not make sense to you? We live together, for Christ's sake, James. I'd certainly understand if he did feel that way."

"If you wanted him to *swoop in to save the day*, you'd have skipped the game. Admit that to yourself."

He rolled his eyes before stalking to the refrigerator to pour himself a glass of water in favor of polishing off their beer entirely.

"Am I doing the right thing, James?" she asked as he returned to the couch, gnawing on her fingernails.

"What do you mean? Staying in and watching baseball? That's your call, Charlie Kate. If you want to be with your boyfriend, you have every right to—"

"I meant in general."

Suddenly, she was quiet, her eyes doeish and wide, her body now incredibly small in her corner of the couch. He'd been so surface level that it took until that moment for him to realize that she was questioning so much more. He nodded his head, urging her to continue.

"I just mean...Scotty's all wrong for me, isn't he?"

For the first time, he broke their sacred rules of "Only talking about the game during the game," and hit the pause button, setting the remote carefully on the coffee table before turning his body to face her fully.

"I... I can't tell you who to date, Smalls. Does he make you happy?"

"I don't know," she confessed, flopping backwards. "I guess...it makes me happy to be in a relationship. But that's not the same thing, is it?"

"Not quite, kiddo." He offered her an apologetic smile and reached for her hand as she rolled her eyes to fend off unwanted emotions.

"It just sucks, Rango."

"What sucks?"

"Just that...I don't know. I found someone who wants to be with me, but I don't think I want to be with him. I want to be with the idea of someone wanting me. If I end it, I won't have that anymore, you know? And then it's back to square one."

He pulled her into his arms then, his heart hurting for his best friend.

"Hey. You have to do what's best for you. If you love him, and you see a future with him, then by all means, you should probably chase after him. Maybe sacrifice a Sox game or a Friday night every once in a while. If you don't, well then, you kind of have a choice to make."

She sniffled and wiped her fingers across her nose, pulling away enough to stare into her lap.

"But, at the same time, you have to know that...Charlie Kate, Scotty shouldn't be your end all be all, okay? Think of him as a steppingstone. Be grateful for what you got out of this relationship, but then move on with the knowledge that there is someone out there who is going to love every part of you, and you every part of him. Don't settle for something just because it fills a hole in you for a little while."

She had tears in her eyes as she peered up into his, her smile sheepish, but grateful all the same, as she whispered, "Thanks, Rango."

"Always," he said. But as, "You know my bias stands that no man will ever be good enough for you," glided off his tongue, tucking her under his chin for one more hug, he couldn't find the courage to meet her eyes.

He waited up for her that night, after she left to confront Scotty, until almost four in the morning. Her red rimmed eyes led her through the front door, and her nose was a deep cherry color when it hit his chest and continued sniffling. The sun came up before sleep overtook her wholly, but he remained awake, relishing the feel of her hair so soft against his neck, the way her left leg had curled across both of his, the two soft fists curled one against his chest and the other at his stomach. She was fast asleep by the time he finally succumbed himself.

When she woke, she found him with his feet up on the coffee table, his laptop propped on his thighs, his eyes fixed on the screen in concentration.

Hearing her feet pad up behind him, he snapped the lid closed and faced her with a wide grin.

"Hey," he offered, his tone loud and cheerful.

"Well someone cleverly avoided the hangover bug this morning," she retorted, squinting at the light coming in through the kitchen window.

"Get dressed." He avoided her retort, tossing his laptop to the couch, passing by her on the way to his own bedroom. "Something Red Sox related would be appropriate!"

She raised an eyebrow to no one in particular, as the door to his bedroom had already closed. Shrugging, she picked out a pair of jean shorts, a t-shirt, and her favorite Nomar Garciaparra jersey, brushed her teeth, and found him in similar attire waiting in the living room.

"Alright, what's going on?" Her smile was more apprehensive than the proud, smug look that had overtaken his cheeks.

"You busy today?"

"No, I am not," she replied warily.

"Good. The Sox are still in Seattle today and tomorrow, and we, my friend, will be sitting behind their dugout for both games. We should probably get going. We've got a flight to catch."

She wanted to cry, wanted to squeal and jump into his arms and call up Julie Ramsey to tell her just how much money her baby boy had dropped on her moment of panic. Instead, she settled for quirked eyebrows, a grin that hinged on the brink of tears, and her head buried in his chest while he enveloped her in a big bear hug. Her breathy

Thank you was squished between the buttons of his jersey.

Conversation on the drive to the airport was split between heated baseball debate and a joyful but nervous contented silence. When they reached the aisle of the plane and he produced a quarter, his seat on the airplane really didn't matter in his mind. It was his fate, in retrospect, that spun in the air, tossing and turning the options in the pressurized cabin with the flip of heads or tails. When the end result was a smile on her face, he took that as a good sign.

She refused to let him pay for his own snacks since he was refusing to let her drop a dime on the tickets or the hotel, so he just thanked her and polished off his bag of sour worms as their plane headed north.

Shared earbuds and trivial conversation helped to melt away all of her worries, to push back the reasons for the tears she'd been up all night expelling. James kept her laughing, and she spent more time than she cared to admit peeking over to admire the way his face glowed against the dim cabin lights.

After dropping off their luggage, they headed straight for Safeco Field, spent too much time against the mesh during batting practice, and enjoyed a 4-2 Red Sox win under the guise of a few beers and plenty of French fries. It was hard to say when she had last laughed this hard or cast her cares to the side without effort, but James was so good about bringing that out in her.

Rather than exploring Seattle's nightlife, they retreated to the hotel under James's exhausted eyes and the fact that, in the end, they'd had a grueling twenty-four hours. There were two beds, but as they changed into pajamas and settled down from the buzz of their whirlwind of a day, Charlotte found herself drawn to her best friend, finding no reason to be ten feet apart in separate beds when they were more than likely going to stay up watching late night television and laughing for at least another hour.

Her head nodded against his shoulder while Jimmy Kimmel put them to sleep. Unbeknownst to Charlotte, James was wide awake; his own words, the echoes of David's not so long before, had his thoughts in a vice.

And with any luck, maybe it'll be the two of you together.

You mean the world to her, James. And I know the same is true for you. Don't take what you guys have for granted.

So, when she awoke to his arms around her the next morning, his breaths slow and steady across the top of her head, she snuggled in a little closer, let the comfort of home surround her before disturbing their cocoon.

It had always been fun to explore new places with his best friend, but walking around Seattle now was so much different. As new ideas began to form, as words unsaid for far too long took shape, so did the boldness of his hands, the need to hold her close against the chilly Seattle temperatures.

She was the one person on the planet who knew his whole soul, and she seemed to be holding it welcomingly between their palms.

Despite the Sox loss that afternoon, they both shared beaming smiles on the way to the airport, shy peeks across the cabin followed by awkward giggles that spouted endless conversation.

This, this was his home.

She nodded off quickly into the plane ride, and he took the time to settle into his thoughts, to solidify everything that he wanted to say, that had been building in his heart since the first day he'd met her, all finally coming together.

They retreated to their own bedrooms to unpack, the knot in his chest and the tightness in his throat competing as the words in his head formed and backtracked and rewrote themselves into sonnets upon sonnets that he feared would never be enough.

But when he found her in the bathroom after changing into a pair of simple grey sweats and a white undershirt himself, clasping his palms nervously against the gathered sweat, his entire body was uncomfortably warm, like the edge between drunkenness and being uncontrollable.

She was bent over the sink, her lips poised in an "O" as she applied a coat of mascara to her lashes. It wasn't until she offered a *Hey, what's up?* over her shoulder that he noticed the outfit she was wearing, the shiny black top and high waisted shorts, the way her curls were looser, and the air smelled like her perfume.

"Uhh, nothin'," he started, quirking an eyebrow. "You going somewhere?"

She gave herself a once over in the mirror, smacking her freshly glossed lips as she replied, "Yeah. Ginny texted and invited me to girls' night. I'd let you tag along but you have too much chest hair."

Her face scrunched in jest as she scratched her fingers lightly over his chest, passing by him to edge her way out the bathroom door. But his pulse quickened under her touch, captured the wind in his chest, and before she was able to squeeze her way out the door, he grabbed her fingers in his hand and pulled her towards his him.

She was caught off guard, and a tiny squeak caught in her throat as her eyes passed quickly up and down his body, from his eyes to their hands and back again.

"Are you...uh...you sure you have to go out? I was thinking we could...I don't know, hang out or something."

He was licking his lips, a nervous habit of his, as his eyes widened, wandering as quickly as hers, trying to find purpose behind her still dumbfounded expression. All too quickly, she was blinking several times, shaking out the nerves and cocking an eyebrow at him.

"Yeah. I mean, Ginny and I haven't seen each other in a few weeks. And besides, I just spent like an entire weekend with you. We can hang out when I get home, okay?"

She said all of this while pulling her fingers from his grasp and disappearing into her closet where she pulled out a pair of heels that rarely saw the light of day.

But she was determined, her bag packed with extra makeup and hair irons as she grabbed her purse and said something along the lines of *I'll see you when I get home.* No sooner was the door clicking behind her than his hands were tangling through his hair, a frustrated groan biting in his lungs.

He sent her a few texts throughout the night, one to make sure she got to Ginny's safely, one to ask how her night was going, and one to double check that they had a ride home. She stopped replying after his

281

third query, and eventually the exhaustion of his own thoughts wore him down and dragged his eyelids closed.

Hours later, he was awakened by her key scratching at the lock, her giggles resounding off the hallway walls. He popped up, cursing himself for sleeping so long as he pulled the door open and caught Charlotte against his chest as she fell through the door laughing.

"*Oh* my god, *James* Ramsey!" she giggled, her grasp hot on his t-shirt.

"Oh my god, Charlie Kate Murphy," he chuckled back, doing his best to hold her upright as her purse tumbled to the floor and her keys followed shortly after. "You, my friend, are drunk."

"I know. I'm drunk," she agreed, her giggles continuing as he helped her the short distance to the living room.

Sitting next to one another on the couch, her body slumped into his, her head landing with a *thump* on his shoulder. She breathed out an *Ow,* giggled again, and sighed comfortably as he wrapped his tense grasp around her shoulder.

"So, Murphy, did you ladies have fun?"

"So much fun," she nodded, her eyes closed, her smile warm and dreamy.

"Good. I'm glad."

She continued nodding intermittently against his shoulder, and his eyes painted her slowly as he pictured himself taking her to bed, wrapping his body around her until the sun rose, and accompanying her morning hangover with a conversation that would probably bust their world wide open.

But as he swept her matted curls from her shoulder and reveled in the way that she was breathing contentedly against him, the perfect ways in which she fit him wholly, he noticed the brown and purple bruise at the base of her throat, and his body was suddenly stiff and hot. The air was stuffy, and his head was certainly swimming much more than hers was as he imagined just whom she had been with all night.

"I think you'd better drink some water and get to bed," came out mechanically and forced, and he couldn't decide if it was more painful

282

to help her into her own bed and walk away, or to just keep himself away from her altogether.

He slept restlessly, knowing that it was entirely uncharacteristic of him to just put a garbage can in her room and leave her be for the night, but he knew she'd be alright. And maybe that was the harsh reality that he didn't want to face: maybe she *didn't* need him there all the time. Maybe they didn't need to be so codependent after all.

So he woke with the morning sun and did his best to shower the scowl off of his face, to force his soliloquies down the drain. He made breakfast when he heard her stirring but left it ready on the table with the plan to be out the door before she was anywhere near his space. Of course, she caught him as he slipped into his shoes, her voice groggy as she padded sock-less into the living room in an oversized t-shirt and a pair of old boxers.

"Hey. Where are you going?"

He froze like he'd been caught stealing, his eyes wide and his fingers frozen on the laces of his Nike's, his unresounding *Uhhh...* earning him beckoning fingers and *Come eat with me before you go.*

It was the very opposite of what he wanted to be doing, pushing pancakes past his lips that tasted like rubber and scarred his throat on the way down, because her hair was up in a knot on top of her head, and his eyes were glued to the spot on her neck where the purple hues still taunted him.

"Sorry I kind of passed out on you last night. I hope you didn't stay up too late."

"No. It was fine."

"So, did you do anything fun?"

Thought about you the whole time?

"Not really. Watched TV. Read a little bit. Went to bed early. It was a long weekend."

"Yeah, that's true."

He hated when the air between them would settle into an awkward smog, and as the silence ticked by, and the bruised skin on her neck mocked him from beneath her high ponytail and he just couldn't take it, he pushed himself away from the table. He mumbled something about heading to the beach for a run before making himself scarce for the rest of the day.

As she watched James disappear out their front door that closed with a resounding *slam*, Charlotte chewed the inside of her lip, staring at his empty seat before busying herself with cleaning the table, unpacking her bags from the weekend, and icing the burn on her neck that a tipsy Ginny had given her with a curling iron.

She thought about the night that had quickly turned into Ginny's couch, a long heart to heart, too much tequila, and lots of tears after the words, "God, Ginny, I think I'm still in love with James" slipped from thought into existence.

Charlotte Murphy had never craved a weekend respite as much as she did after what she had affectionately dubbed "The Week from Hell."

She spent most of Monday in Boston by her sister's bedside, fluffing pillows and bringing her water and eventually earning her a *Jesus, Charlotte, you were never this annoying when you were actually trying to be,* only to have her break down at Kelly's bedside.

"I'm supposed to be comforting *you*," she had whined, sniffling back the tears that her big sister immediately brought an end to.

"Exactly," Kelly snorted back. "So what gives?"

"Nothing. I think...it's just been a long weekend. And you scared the shit out of me."

Which was partially true. But with her sister still bedridden and being pumped full of Gatorade, Charlotte was not in the business to unload all of her personal drama upon her. So instead, she brought it all as a carry-on for the plane ride back to Los Angeles.

When he picked her up from LAX on Monday night, Jack knew immediately that there was something wrong, something off.

She couldn't so much as relax in his embrace before he was whispering *Talk to me* and *Something happened* came on the tail end of a sob which eventually opened the floodgates.

She wanted him to yell and scream and throw things and ask her why, but instead he listened as she all but begged him, told him how much she cared about him, how much she wanted to fix this and make it work, how it had been a mistake, and how it wouldn't happen again.

It made it that much worse that he was being patient with her, that his reaction was so quiet and steady, that only a couple tears made their way down his cheek when he cradled her face and said, "Charlotte, I'm so sorry, but I can't keep doing this to myself," before he kissed her on the forehead and walked out her front door.

She even tried texting to make sure she got home okay, finding his **Yeah** to be the final nail in the coffin. It was hell on earth, trying to compose all of her emotions in a few quick hours before she would be back in an office space where his presence was certainly about to be overwhelming. Her heart hadn't hurt this much in a long time, she realized, as tears dampened her pillow. She had ruined a genuinely good thing, and she only had herself to blame.

She didn't sleep much before going into work, looking about as hellish as he did from across the room where she did her best to catch his eye and he did his best to avoid every attempt.

She made it until Thursday, nursing glasses of wine and a silent cell phone, before Jack approached her at the end of lunch. The expression in his eyes was so cold, almost dead, that she wanted to start crying all over again, wanted to drop to her knees and beg at his feet. She had put it there, and there was no hope in putting the light back.

"I wanted to make sure you got that list of publishers before the summer is over," was all he offered her before handing a crisp sheet of paper across the table, his fingers clutching the far end, though she could still feel her body tingling as she muttered a high *Thanks*. Before she could utter his name, his was already out the door.

The weekend left her seething, all of her emotions directed at James.

She was blaming him, planning it all out in her head, how she would yell and accuse and threaten and make sure he wallowed for the rest of eternity, because Jack was a *good thing* and he had *ruined it*.

But in the dark of night, under a blanket of moonlight and wine, that night came flooding back.

He was no more to blame than she was.

Teacher in-services were beginning soon, a brand-new school year with new students and new challenges looming on the horizon. It would be good, she decided. A good distraction from the personal hell that she had been dragged through over the course of her summer vacation. Something she would have to keep to herself when the fresh five-year-old faces asked her, "What did you do this summer, Miss Murphy?" and she had to reply with, "Lost everything I've ever cared about."

The writing staff had a cake for her on her last day, which hadn't really happened in the past. Hugs from people she barely knew, a few *We're really going to miss the extra set of hands* before she was shutting down her things for the last time that summer.

She sought Jack's eyes as she lingered at the door, but all she saw was the back of his head as he turned away.

It wasn't so much a surprise as something she'd been awaiting, almost dreading, when her door creaked open and pressed softly closed like it would any other Friday; it was so silent that she watched the shadows of the door dance along her walls to confirm that he was truly there.

James looked about as run down as she felt, his shoulders drooped, his eyes hollow, either from lack of sleep or pure exhaustion or both.

What caught her, though, was the spark of hope that existed in his eyes, the way his lips were upturned, only slightly, creeping along the side of his face. It was all in stark contrast to the way that his hands were shoved roughly into his pockets, the way that his body screamed to be on edge.

She unfurled her legs from beneath her to place her socked feet on the carpet and watched him take tentative steps until he was on the edge of her living room.

"So... Vanessa's gone."

She peered at him from below, her eyes asking him to continue, because there was no way she was going to be able to make words come out of her mouth coherently just yet.

"I think we got a lot of it out back home, but when I got to my place on Sunday night, she wasn't there. She came back Monday after work to pick up a few things and...I... I get it, Charlie Kate. I completely understand everything she threw at me."

He moved to her armchair as he settled his chin atop his clasped hands.

"I wasn't always...there. She knew it, and I did, too, but I never wanted to admit to it, you know? Who wants to tell the woman they're supposed to be with that his heart belongs in large part to someone else?"

He shrugged, that hint of a smile wistful as he gazed off into nowhere, lost in the past, back to the memories of Seattle's aftermath, and the day he'd met Vanessa.

He had been in the hospital three times that week to speak with the Chief of Surgery about rebranding, always waiting at the nurse's station, always during her shift. On the first day, he noticed her smile. On the second day, she'd made fun of his misbuttoned shirt, and his heart thumped in his chest just a little harder. On the third day, he wore an extra spot of cologne and shaved the stubble from his jaw that had collected in the three days since Seattle and feelings and hickies and his heart being torn from his chest and salsa danced on top of.

There was something new on the nurses' station desk today. A whiteboard. Right now, it was blank, and something bypassed the butterflies churning in his stomach as he exchanged a silly yet nervous quip that somehow ended in a game of tic-tac-toe while he waited for the Chief of Surgery to show up and go over the final details of their deal.

As he placed his "O" in the top right-hand corner, he was surprised when she asked, "So, what's the wager?"

"Huh?" he asked, hands poised with the marker midair.

"You know. What do I get when I win?"

"Wow, Nurse Harding. You sure are cocky, aren't you?"

"Not cocky. Confident," she corrected him, adding a second "X" to the board. "So, when I win, you have to tell me what your name is, since we've gone three days now, and my nametag gives mine away."

"Well, in that case, when I win, Nurse Harding," he started, masking the shake in his voice by tapping his fingers along the edge of the counter, "you have to give me your phone number."

It was bolder than he had been as of late, when his typical dates were night long endeavors that were heavily assisted by a flow of alcohol, which also conveniently got him out of taking the girl home after, under the pretense of I don't want to take advantage of you; I'll give you a call tomorrow. *Which he never did. Because while she was coming home with Scotty, he was still hopeful that one day, she would wake up and realize what she had waiting for her.*

So today, under the haze of this new smile and big blue eyes, and the utter heartache that he had been trying to repair over the past week with online dating apps and loud music and alcohol, he needed something to plug the hole, to make it stop hurting for a little while.

She called him out on their first date, after she had won the game of tic-tac-toe, wiped the board clean, written Vanessa *and a string of digits on the now blank slate before rushing off to a page.*

"You don't usually do this sort of thing, do you, James?"

Because now, she knew his name, too.

He blushed, ducking his eyes in the same manner that he had when he'd given her his ultimatum not hours prior.

"No. No I don't." He told his chicken parm, rather than her directly, because he still couldn't believe the balls that he'd grown all of a sudden. The same fight that had him finally dragging his stare up, to meet her gorgeous blue eyes under the lowlights of the Italian restaurant that he'd chosen. "But there was just something about you that pulled me up."

He shrugged down at his plate, knowing that the "thing that pulled him up" was the constant ache in his heart that he figured her smile could maybe bandage for a while, could ease the pain just a little.

When it was months into their relationship, and she was finally asking about Charlotte and about why they still lived together when he had more than enough money to live on his own, and maybe their relationship could move to the next level if he had his own place, he was having that conversation, helping Charlotte find a new apartment, wiping her tears as they both realized that this was the first time they would truly be without one another.

He kept telling himself that this was good, that he was moving on, that buying the condo and making three keys so that Vanessa and Charlotte could each have one was being mature and growing up. But in the back of his mind, he knew that he was still using her as a defense, was hoping that if he played house long enough that he could convince them all that he was okay. That this façade was indeed reality.

It was hard, especially when Charlotte was helping him pack the

boxes and reminiscing over every single item they stowed away and
hugging him so tightly that his lungs were on fire. When she fell asleep
on his floor that first night, Vanessa was scowling, but he couldn't even
see it past the way that Charlotte's curls spanned the deep green of the
old comforter of his that he draped across her body. He had to
convince Vanessa that having a slumber party in the living room was
way more fun for their first night, that she could have the couch, of
course.

But as they continued to grow together, and he continued to play
along with each and every step in the relationship that Vanessa wanted
to take, reality began to manifest itself into a hard shell of over two
years that buried every falsity that he wanted hidden.

It wasn't that his feelings for Charlotte were gone, no. It was more
that he had convinced himself that Vanessa was hiding them well
enough, that they were playing pretend long enough, that he actually
believed it himself.

"I don't know why I thought I could convince myself otherwise," he
said, shaking his head and laughing in more of a puff of air from his
nostrils than actual sound. "It's always been you, Charlie Kate. God,
it's always been you."

She stiffened then, still so freshly wounded that she wasn't sure
her body could handle another blow.

But he looked so goddamn *sure.* There wasn't any other way to
describe it. He wasn't being cocky or confident or righteous. No. He
was stating facts, his eyes more crystal than she'd ever seen them
before, the clarity making her stomach tighten.

His smile, that goofy smile that she'd known since he was a boy,
was rimmed with the smallest tear as he searched her face, gauged her
reaction, and fell with every passing second that she didn't jump into
his arms. She was paralyzed, with fear and regret and so many things
that she simply couldn't move, couldn't begin to process what was
happening.

She couldn't bare the sight of him, of his eyes looking so sure and
so hopeful, of his lips falling down at the corners. So she sought solace

in her lap, where she picked at the skin around her fingernails and did her best to right herself and her thoughts before the dizziness toppled her over.

His feet toed at her carpet, she noticed out of the corner of her eyes. As she blinked her gaze slowly up his body, she could see all the telltale signs of his nerves: his knee bouncing erratically, his eyes wandering to the side, his hand rubbing errantly at the back of his neck.

She had to put him out of his misery, had to say *something*.

"James...I..."

The words were stuck, a traffic jam of too many different highways trying to barrel up her esophagus that tangled into the sob she was trying to repress.

"I don't know what to say."

It was the most honest answer she had. He was out here telling her everything that she'd ever wanted to hear, everything she had been internally begging him to say.

But it was all wrong now.

She watched him swallow down a sizable lump, watched him cock his head toward the ceiling as he blinked rapidly.

"James. You left Vanessa, what? An hour ago? You can't honestly tell me that you're ready to...I don't even know what you think you're ready for."

"This," he stated decisively, his lips in a firm line as he stood and spread his arms out wide. "I'm ready for *this* Charlie Kate. I'm finally...it took me way too goddamn long, but we're here now."

"*You're* here now."

It was like watching him absorb a punch, the way that blow had him dropping his arms to clench at his stomach, the way his head dropped, and his eyes closed in pain.

"W-what?"

"You're here now, James. *You* are. I've...I was *here* a long time ago." She chuckled then, in irony, as she stood and crossed her arms, the bitterness, the resentment beginning to take control of her words. "I've been *here* from the beginning. Throughout all of our ups and downs, I was *here*. For all of the girls that I had to watch you date, through every broken heart, James, I was *here*. I was waiting, leaving a piece of myself with you every single time. But I was finally putting those pieces back together, letting *Jack* help me put those pieces back together, and somehow, you figured out a way to shatter it all again."

He looked wounded, every word piercing through his skin.

"I broke my back trying bend myself for you, James. To make sure that every little thing I ever did included you and made you happy."

"And you don't think I was doing the same thing? God, Charlie Kate, look at where we are! Do you think California was for *me?* My entire *life* is on the other side of the goddamn country, but here I am, because it made *you* happy."

"I was finally at peace, James. I had finally decided to *let you go,* and now...God, I should've just expected this, honestly."

"Expected what?" he asked, his voice full of gravel and grit.

"Expected you to finally want this just when I was getting my feet back on the ground."

He was crossing the room in two large strides now, his hands reaching for hers in a grip that said he wasn't letting go, that he would hold on for dear life if he had to.

"I've always wanted this," he pleaded. "I've always wanted you, Smalls. You've gotta believe that. How could you not know?"

He pressed his forehead into hers, their noses touching at the tip so that his words were more like shared breaths.

"Why didn't you say something then?"

He sniffled in their silence and licked his lips.

"Because I was scared—"

"Don't you think I was scared, too?" She pushed away from him then, needing to move, to shake the feeling of her crawling, buzzing skin away. "Scared of losing the only thing in my life that ever felt right? It terrified me, James. Every time something would start between us, I would be up at night sick with the thought of you turning me down or walking away. I couldn't stand the thought of not having you somewhere in my life."

"But you *do*," he promised, trying to reach for her again, his words curling up at the ends. "You've got me. Charlie Kate, I'm right here."

"No, that's the thing. I don't." She stopped then, shaking her head with a pained smile on her face as she closed her eyes to compose herself. "I have this...this idea of you that I've built into a box, James. I've done everything in my life, calculated every move I've made, so that you could somehow fit. I'm starting to think that I've been forcing a square peg into a round hole for too long."

"You can't say that," he demanded. "You cannot honestly stand here and say that we don't work."

"Not all the time, we don't!"

"People aren't meant to be perfect!"

"Maybe that's our problem," she finally breathed. "Maybe we've been trying to perfect one another for too long."

The sound of heavy breathing was alone in the tense atmosphere of her apartment, but the buzzing inside of their heads was real. The chase of thoughts and new revelations doing their best to morph into a new semblance of reality, one that would usher the stilted conversations forward.

"I don't need you to be perfect, Charlie Kate. I just...I need you to be *you*. To be the you that I've always known."

His words were so small, but beseeching.

"See, that's the thing," she continued, her eyes clenched shut with the falsity that if she couldn't see him, the pain in his eyes wouldn't hurt her so badly. "The *me* that you know? That person is broken, James. She's broken, and she's hurting, and she...I have to figure out a way to put her back together. On my own."

"What are you saying?" He reached for her again, his grip tight around her wrists. But she refused to meet his eyes, focused instead on their hands and the way that his made hers seem to disappear.

"James...I think I... I need to figure out who I am without you."

He was finally frozen, his eyes wide with only the expression of fear as he let a whispered *What do you mean?* fill the space between them.

"I mean...James, you're all I've ever known. All I've ever really let myself know. I...it might be...good for us if we..."

And then he was kissing her, hard and fast, his hands enveloping her face as he held onto her cheeks like she was his life anchor. In the midst of his lips and his hands and the way that his nose was digging into her skin, he was whimpering like she had wounded him so deeply that he could barely breathe, each sound pinging in the air like a final plea, each final peck of her lips dotted with *Please, please, please.*

"We can't…" she started, only to be cut off by his lips again, "keep doing this."

He rested his forehead against hers, a slow stream of moisture dripping from his eyes and painting her cheeks. The way she clung to his forearms, shook her head against him like she was trying to crawl inside, contradicted her every word.

"We need space, James."

A hitched sob, his breathing high and whiny.

"It'll be good for us, I promise."

Her own promise breathy and high, her fingernails digging into his skin.

"I don't wanna do this."

His words tapered, his lips pressing into her cheek as he pulled her closer.

"I know."

She let him, pulled herself into his body, wishing he would just swallow her whole. The bone shattering grip of his strong arms around her was sure to leave marks that she would trace like tattoos in the days to come.

"Are you sure?"

The way that his voice sounded so young, like the little boy who used to hold her hand on the playground and make up stories with her in the treehouse and protect her from every evil that the world had to offer, almost had her backtracking, apologizing for every word and dragging him to the nearest surface where he could hold her so tightly, he might just put every broken piece of her back together.

But she was nodding, the motion of her head causing his t-shirt to rise up and down. He breathed out hard and fast, his lungs puffing under her face, his breath hot on her head as he squeezed her tightly one more time before pulling away.

When she looked up through her own red-rimmed eyes, she almost broke down again, almost let his deep set dark eyes and tear stained cheeks and runny nose destroy her. It was the look of such utter defeat in his eyes, in the cold, hard green that was void of any and all emotion besides brokenness, that had her biting her lip, had a squeal skipping past her lungs as she squeezed his hands before breaking all contact.

He breathed deeply, stuffing his hands into his pockets as he exhaled.

She studied his feet as she followed him to the door. His black and white Converse, the pair that she'd helped him find, the last size twelves in the store, mocked her from a place of *all you've ever known.*

She could be strong, she kept telling herself, though his hair was mussed out of place on the left side and she was itching to reach up and fix it. She could be strong, she pleaded, as he wiped the back of his hand across fresh tears, dismissing them with a pointless flick of the wrist as new ones slid down his cheeks immediately anyway. She could be strong, she gasped, when he was actually opening the door, ready to leave.

But it was his, "Goodbye, Charlotte," the hitch in his throat on the name he never called her, that had her crumpling to the floor.

Life without James Ramsey was decidedly empty.

It wasn't as though her life had no purpose and time ceased to exist and the floor had opened up below her and swallowed her into a fiery abyss.

Quite contrarily, the world seemed to move on as if nothing monumental had occurred, as if her world hadn't just shattered into unsalvageable pieces in a matter of minutes. In the minuteness of her life, there were moments of absurdity that had her urging to stop what she was doing and jump onto a table and bounce as highly as her feet would carry her while screaming, "Doesn't anyone care? Can't you see what's happening? He's gone, and we're done, and nothing makes sense anymore!"

But then, she would realize that no one in a Los Angeles Starbucks at 2:37 PM in the middle of a Tuesday *did* care, that to any passerby, she was just any other woman seemingly having a mental breakdown by her red-rimmed eyes and the way her hair appeared unshampooed and the rate at which she was guzzling down espresso. For downtown LA, she might even be considered normal.

Life continued to progress at its regular, almost dragging pace. She longed for emails to start showing up from her principal, to get back into her classroom and focus on decorating and organizing and pulling out her lesson plans for the new year instead of how much of her apartment reminded her of *him*.

But her classroom screamed *James* too. As she painted on a façade of happiness, or some sort of contentment at least, trudging in with a fresh roll of tape and Sticky Clips to put a dent into her classroom preparations, she was swept away by a tidal wave of *him*. She was instantly taken back to her first weekend in this classroom that he spent helping her unpack boxes and arranging and rearranging tiny desks and chairs again until she was satisfied.

That first year, he'd pulled her against his shoulder on that very same floor, with empty take-out bags at their feet, his lips pressed into her sweat-dampened hair as he said, "You're going to be the best teacher, Charlie Kate Murphy. These will be the kids that take over the world someday."

Suddenly, putting her bulletin boards up wasn't remotely important anymore. Not as important as it was to sit against the filing cabinet and will herself not to press the *CALL* button next to his name.

She was grateful for the way that Ginny sincerely tried to console her, but it was no use, and she was almost embarrassed by the way that she dumped herself onto her friend's couch to do nothing but blubber and sob for close to three hours before she fell into an exhausted sleep. When she tried to apologize in the morning, after awakening to a blanket draped across her body and a pillow under her cheek, Ginny cut her off immediately, gave her a cup of coffee, and pulled her into a hug. Any trace of snarky comments or high eyebrows or *I told you so's* were gone in favor of utter sympathy.

The realization dawned on her, as she put in the news of her unexpected resignation with her principal, and said her final goodbyes, that every waking memory she had of this place was all consumed by him.

It was a hard decision to move back to Massachusetts, but ultimately, it was the first step. She needed support, and the people she had out in California just didn't get it. It was the first of her big decisions that she made without him, which only made the band-aid more sticky and painful to rip off.

She thought about calling him, stopping by, just to let him know. She couldn't just disappear without a trace, after all. One of their parents would let him know, anyway. It would be better coming from her, in the end.

It took three days, several drafted emails that sounded way too business-like, and a bottle of wine to finally send the text.

I'm moving back to Boston next week. I need to do this. For me.

She had erased all of the *This isn't about you's* and *I'm so sorry's* and the stray *Please don't follow me, you'll only make this harder.*

The little bubbles in their iMessage chat popped up almost

immediately, but she wiped away all thoughts that he'd been sitting around for three weeks and doing nothing but waiting to hear from her, assuming that he'd just had his phone in his hand.

I understand. Good luck out there.

It was another two days before she stopped wondering if he had struggled, too, with *Please don't go's* and *I'm coming with you's*.

David and Daddy came out to help her pack, her apartment reduced to boxes after long hugs and *I'm so sorry's* and an impromptu trip for frozen yogurt. It only took one truck to pack away every belonging, and she chuckled at the irony that when she thought she was leaving her entire life behind, it all actually fit into one, mid-sized U-Haul.

The first day of the drive back, switching off turns in her Elantra with David, was mostly silent, save for their iPods. That was until a song would come on that held too many memories and she was sniffling behind the wheel and David was shutting off the music entirely.

She tucked herself into bed at the hotel in Albuquerque, leaving a worried pair of Murphy men behind.

David finally broke the silence over drive-thru Cokes on Highway 44.

"I'm sorry that all of this is happening, squirt."

It was the *squirt* that did her in, that had her head sinking as her tear-laced words said, "I can't anymore. I love him so much, David, but all we do is hurt each other in circles."

"Then maybe you're doing the right thing," was where he left it, his hand clenched firmly around her shaking ones.

Being home was odd. Her childhood bedroom was still *hers*, though the pieces of Charlotte were long gone, now packed into a storage container. She spent her days doing her best to avoid the stares and wait on baited breath for one of the Ramseys to walk through the front door, or appear in her kitchen and scold her, or pass along a disapproving look like the time that she and James had come in after curfew for the first time.

What surprised her even more was the phone call that she received to her parent's landline, because they still had one and refused to get rid of it. Julie Ramsey was inviting her over, and when she hesitated, Julie's voice hitched almost in realization, and asked if she could meet Charlotte in her own home instead.

Charlotte was blown away by the tears, by the tightness of the hug from the woman who she had started to call *Mommy Number Two* when she was in middle school.

"Just know that we are always here for you. I know you two are both hurting so much right now, but it will get easier. Don't ever hesitate to call. You're still family. You always will be."

Though Julie's words were meant to be comforting, she left Charlotte with even more congestion in her heart.

Eventually, she realized that at twenty-eight years old, she couldn't just live at her parent's house forever, helping Mom with the dishes and folding Dad's socks when the dryer was done. It was Kelly who offered a room, since things would be getting hectic once the baby was born, and she and Bill could use the extra hands anyway. Just until she was back on her feet. So her things were hauled to her sister's new home with the four bedrooms, one of which was turning slowly but surely into a nursery for her nephew. The remaining two rooms were up for grabs.

Though she didn't want to go ahead and *make this place home*, she allowed for a few trinkets up on the walls: photos of all of her kindergarten classes, plenty of Emma, a ball from her first game at Fenway.

The photos of James remained in the box that she eventually tucked into the closet.

Moving into Kelly and Bill's was a lot easier considering the relationship she had with her big sister. No one forced her to talk, and they could be focused on the baby instead of Charlotte's pathetic drama.

Most importantly, it was a place that James had never touched, where his memories were nonexistent. She could turn the corners in this brand new house where he'd never been and not be afraid to find him sitting on the stairs or perched on the bed that Kelly had set up for her. He wouldn't be in the kitchen, rummaging through the fridge for a snack, or lounging on the couch whenever she wanted to relax.

But he *was* everywhere.

She couldn't turn on NESN without thousands of memories with him at Fenway assaulting her. The image of a little boy, at seven years old, trying to impress her by doing Nomar's entire pre-at-bat ritual in front of the television before she was calling him out for skipping the arm-band adjustment and laughing at the way that his eyes bugged and his jaw hit the floor when she was doing it all perfectly, was suddenly playing out in front of her like a projection.

In monotonous tasks like stopping at Wegman's to pick up a few things for dinner, he was buzzing around the aisles with his feet up on the edge of the shopping cart, staring into her eyes as she perched on the back, her head thrown in laughter just seconds before they were thrown out.

He was down every side street, leaning against buildings, in front of store fronts, seated on benches where the ghosts of their past still existed. He spanned the entire Charles River, no path left untouched by the tire treads of their bikes or the soles of their shoes.

He was in the North End, perched on the curb outside Ernesto's when all she wanted was a quick slice of pizza. Not seventeen-year-old James with his arm around her shoulders. Not mid-Thursday afternoon tears hitting the pavement of Salem Street.

His face replaced the photos on every bottle of Sam Adams, reminding her of nights on couches and summers on his back porch and their twenty-first birthdays, when she waited the four days between hers and his to drink, because really, what was the difference between October 18th and October 22nd anyway, aside from getting to celebrate with him?

It was easy at first to resist the temptation to see what he was up to on social media. James only had Facebook, and even then, he hadn't really posted since 2016. But then, there was the knowledge that women liked to tag men in posts and photos on Facebook, and the suspicion haunted her around every corner. Would new photos show up on his page? Did she want to see who would be cozied up next to him?

Even when she was doing her best to make the most of being in the same state as her family and doing the big Murphy Sunday Brunch thing, he was there in too many places. On the front porch swing, tanned and shirtless in the pool, out on the back lawn playing catch with the boys while she did her best not to stare because then he might catch on, might know what was going on in her head.

He was there in Emma's smile, despite the lack of blood relation, in her giggle and in her mannerisms. The little girl trounced her way across the freshly cut grass and asked a simple, "Why are you cryin', Auntie K?" and she did her best to force a smile as she said, "No reason, baby girl. My heart just hurts."

After Emma bent down to place a sweet kiss over Charlotte's heart, she stood up, embraced her in a tight squeeze, and had to take a walk. But there he was again, all over Haynes Road, riding bikes and playing hopscotch or walking home from school with his hands flying wildly as he told stories upon stories. He was in the dark with his hands in her hands, tugging her around the corner before his lips were all over her, or leading her to the park where the cover of trees sheltered them away from the rest of the world.

In the moments of silence where James's ghost seemed to take pity and give her a brief respite, she found herself wondering if this is how Jack felt whenever he was in New York, surrounded by all of the love that had hurt him.

And a whole new form of guilt entirely overtook her.
Jack.

The one man who was about to pull her through the ice and bring her into a new *Charlotte* altogether, and she had let him go, let him slip through the cracks and underneath the water.

Yet here she was crying over the other man who had shattered it all.

Seeing Jack's name in the credits of Ginny's television show as it premiered that fall made her feel pride and sadness all in one fell swoop.

She called Ginny that evening, beaming and glowing for her longtime friend, congratulating her on the success, and wishing her well as they caught up on the surface level.

Ginny was good, still as tough as nails and refusing to take anyone's bullshit. But success had tamed her, brought her to a higher degree of focus that Charlotte hoped would keep her on track.

It was when Ginny mentioned Jack, subtly inserting her two cents that he had survived, but it had taken him awhile, that she truly wanted to cry.

But that evening, after she hung up and readied herself for bed and lay awake with her thoughts, she travelled back to something Jack had said on their first date, after spilling all he had to tell about Molly.

I like the life that I have here. I like the person that I've become in spite of everything I've been through.

It was then that she finally snapped; the need to stop feeling sorry for herself and do what she came home to do, to live for herself and simply *be* without him was suddenly overwhelming.

Although it was far too late in the year to apply for any teaching jobs, she found a local daycare and a spot in the three-year-old room. It was a big change from kindergarten, but the toddlers never failed to put a smile on her face for the part-time hours that she spent wiping boogers and reading books to kids who fought over rights to sit on her lap. It made her feel good, to be doing something with her time other than moping around.

It also gave her time to pick up the loose end of the book she'd once been so diligently putting together for the better part of the summer.

Her life became about routine: Wake up in the morning and make a list of everything you're thankful for while you lather, rinse, and repeat. Go to work. Eat lunch with someone new. If you can't find someone new, go out and find a place to eat that you haven't been to before. Head straight from work to the library. Do not stop to pass go or collect two-hundred dollars, but by all means, stop to smell the roses every once in a while. Work on your book until you've hit a wall.

302

Then, check out one from the shelves, for inspiration or just for fun. Go home and spend time with your family. Laugh, cry, be silent sometimes. When it's late at night, and you're on the edge of sleep, it's okay if he creeps up every so often.

Her life had purpose, and it was a purpose that she was initiating. So, while she was working part-time and living in her sister's guest bedroom, she decided to take stock of what she *did* have control over, and make the most of it.

Writing a book was definitely hard work. She tried her best not to think about Jack, and how simple it had been when she was stuck to phone him up and have him walk her through whatever was blocking her path. But now, she was forced to deal with the challenges head on, to pick apart her plot and piece it back together all by herself. She saw it as a metaphor for her own life, and chuckled at a dimly lit computer screen one night at two in the morning as she willed her characters to shift before she realized that sometimes, people need to just be stuck for awhile.

There were also nights, when it was clear that Kelly and Bill didn't really mean *We don't mind if you sit and hang out with us* and she holed up in her bedroom. Those nights were when she wanted so badly to text James and see how he was doing, if he was hanging out in his bedroom at his parents' and wanted to sneak down to Cabot's for a late night order of chili cheese fries and a cookie jar sundae.

Nights when she wondered what he was doing out in California. If he was okay. If he was missing her.

The text on her birthday surprised her, sent her into a tailspin to search for meaning in his uber simplistic ***Happy Birthday, Smalls. Hope you're doing alright out there.***

She returned the favor four days later, hoping that they'd keep talking but conversely praying for the opposite.

Watching the Red Sox win the World Series without him was an occasion that she felt empty celebrating, despite the beers being passed around her parent's living room and the endless loop of "Dirty Water" playing through bluetooth speakers. It almost didn't feel right.

Christmas was especially hard. The weeks leading up to it had her on pins and needles as she thought about him coming home, and would he want to see her, and would he avoid her or be kind out of sheer civility. But then it was Christmas Eve, at the Ramsey's this year, and Julie mentioned in passing that he had decided to stay in LA instead. Something about work getting hectic in the holiday season.

It was all a lie, she knew, but as she stirred her eggnog and did her best not to notice the extra set of Jingle Jammies under the tree for him, it was hard not to wonder if he was back with Vanessa or with someone new. Those thoughts were what kept her from sending him a picture message of the pajamas, from razzing him and wishing him well. When he called his mom to wish everyone a happy holiday, she was suddenly super interested in cleaning up the dinner dishes.

When she rang in the New Year with David and Marie and a sleeping Emma all tucked in on the couch, she vowed to spend it bettering herself.

On January second, she started the search for an editor.

Baby Carson was born on January 27th, and she immediately fell in love with all eight pounds and four ounces of him. It was super sweet to watch Emma hold her new cousin, and even funnier when he started to cry and she was handing him right back with a look on her face that shouted pure disgust. It was practice for being a big sister, David announced later that night, because Marie was due in July.

It was a practice in patience for Charlotte, living with a newborn. Kelly and Bill truly had it made, with two extra hands and an extra body for midnight wake-up calls when they needed it. There were nights when she would shove her head under a pillow or plug in headphones to drown out the noise. There were also peaceful nights, with a sleeping baby in one arm and the last revisions of her book propped on the table beside her that had a certain contentedness soothing her warmly.

At the start of February, in torrents of snow and bitter cold Massachusetts temperatures, she was longing to do something productive. Google was a big help in the process of finding an editor. Her fingers itched for the sheet of paper that was somewhere at the bottom of her purse, the one Jack had given her as his parting gift. Something about that felt wrong, though. She had to do this on her own.

Query letter after query letter and rejection after rejection made her head spin with equal parts doubt and contempt and frustration. She turned to the experts in the field when she truly hit a dead end on her story, and the kids at her daycare provided not only a confidence boosting attentiveness, but also suggestions and criticisms for her book. Being back at the drawing board this time was refreshing, as she tweaked and polished and took as many suggestions from the kids as she could, save for the student from the 5-year-old room that said, "Miss Charlotte, I think Emma's superpower should be that she can shoot mashed potatoes out of her hands!"

But publishing a book was still hard, she quickly began to realize. It was the editing process during late nights and being shot down by publisher after publisher that had her driving her head into a wall. Then one night, while she walked the halls with a fussy baby, her eyes landed on a photo of her kindergartners, her cheesy posters bright and bubbling in the background, one big and bold declaring *I can't do it YET!*

Another four-AM feeding had come to the rescue.

Pre-spring in Massachusetts, where snow was melting away from its first round and dull greens were poking through in front lawns, when the weather was warm enough to maybe only wear a light jacket for the two week tease that she knew from experience would be gone too soon and replaced by a truckload of winter round two, had her biting at the bit, bound and determined to not be cooped up in her sister's house.

So she took Baby Carson on walks in the afternoons and admired the scenery that she knew would only last for a few days longer before making its official debut later in May. She wrote in the park instead of in the library, which was beginning to grow stuffy anyway. She took respite from her prized children's book, from fictional Emma's tales, to start on a few new ideas that she'd developed over the past months of heartache and self-discovery. These, she decided, might spin their way into fiction novels themselves.

It was during a Wednesday afternoon diaper change, when Carson was cooing and giggling, and he had peed on her sock a little bit, and she had baby powder on her left cheek, that the phone call came.

Suddenly, she was one step closer to being a real author.

But as she scheduled her first meeting with the editors and her agent (agent?!), there was a certain hollowness, a pang in her chest that screamed for *him*, that pleaded for her to *put aside your differences* and *just call him for God's sake! He's going to be over the moon.*

Instead, she choked down her pride, swallowed the insistence, and called her parents, told her brother, and shared a celebratory bottle of wine with Kelly and Bill after Carson was down for the night.

It was a first, of sorts. Her first "big moment" to which he wasn't her first phone call, or any phone call, at that. The guilt was seeping, threatening to flood her the more she sat on it. But then she realized that she was surrounded by people who loved her, people who were happy for her. More importantly, in the quiet of the night, under the guise of a bit of wine and the buzz of happiness, she told herself it was okay to be sad, that it was okay to cry about it, that it was okay to *feel*.

In the morning, she awoke content, and more ready than ever to start this new chapter.

After lengthy calls with her agent about next steps and edit letters, Charlotte's pace of work became a fury of focus. Revisions from the publisher were a gold mine in her hand, and she ate up every single one as she polished and perfected her story. It took three revisions back and forth before everyone was confident enough for submission, and by that time, the summer sun was peeking over the horizon.

She found herself on her parents' back porch one Sunday evening as the sky danced before her in purples and pinks, deep in thought about this process as a whole.

There were times when she was reading over her edit letter, or having just hung up with her agent, where she wanted to throw a fit and curl up into a ball and cry. She was angry and upset that things still needed to be changed, that the perfection in her head just wasn't "good enough." It was all of those reasons in the past that kept her from wanting to put her writing in the hands of actual people in the first place, her fear of criticism and of failure and of all the in between that would shed light on her insecurities.

But this new Charlotte, the one who moved back home to start again, wasn't about wallowing, and she gulped down more than a grain of salt as she bettered herself, stood up for herself when she felt the need to fight for an idea, and took matters into her own hands. This baby was all hers, she realized, and she had done it on her own. Despite the help from Jack and encouragement from James, when it came down to the nitty gritty of it all, she had done this by herself, and *for* herself. For the first time, without anyone to back her up, she felt immensely proud.

Summer was a flurry of activity that included applying for teaching jobs in the Boston area and surrounding suburbs, going to Red Sox games with her dad and brother, and catching up with old friends from high school who hadn't ever ventured outside of Newton. There were a few weeks of apartment hunting before the U-Haul was packed and her things were moved out of storage. She started to make Quincy, Massachusetts home in her cozy little apartment while she prepared for a new adventure teaching second grade and continuing to write in her free time.

It was nice, to be independent but to still be within a short drive from her family, from people she could count on. Still, it made for time to grow, time to continue to find out who she was and what she was capable of without a sizable crutch.

She joined a book club at the library, took a yoga class, quit a yoga class, took a jazzercise class instead. It was odd but refreshing to form new friendships this late in the game, and the few social activities she allowed herself gave her time to breathe, to have fun, and remember to just *be*.

Dating was still out of the question, but she did allow a few girls from the gym to take her out for drinks on a few separate occasions.

While she was waiting for the bartender to finish refilling her drink, a ghost from the past was booming in her ear to the tune of, "Charlotte Murphy! It's been quite awhile, hasn't it?"

It had been some ten or so years since she'd last seen Joey De Luca, and the last time, his face had been a little banged up, at that. But now, those bruises were replaced by lines of age, less boyhood baby fat, and a few gray hairs around his temples.

"It certainly has," she said with a chuckle and a raise of the eyebrow. "How have you been?"

"Oh, busy, that's for sure," he chuckled, waving down a bartender as he placed his order. "Having two little guys under four keeps us on our toes."

It was then, as she played in the condensation of her own drink, that she noticed the wedding band around his finger and the pretty brunette he waved at who had settled herself into a table behind them.

"So what about you? You and Ramsey still together? Last I'd heard, you two had flown the coop and ditched us for greener pastures."

He wasn't the first person to bring up James since she'd come home, but for some reason, this one seemed to sting just a little bit more. She thought of bruised knuckles and almost confessions and feeling at home for the first time in her life, lost in her own world before Joey was waving a hand in front of her and saying, "Woah there, Murphy. I think I lost you there for a second."

"Sorry," she flushed, staring down at her drink. "I guess you did."

"Well, hey. I've gotta get going. But say hi to James for me, will you? It was good to see you, Charlotte."

"Yeah, you too."

During the week of Emma's fourth birthday, amidst the party preparations and special birthday outings, a shipment of mock-up books was delivered to her new address with a fresh wave of *beginnings*. The book was all bare bones, very bland and picture-less, awaiting approval before the illustration process began. Her fingertips tingled with anticipation and hope as they danced across crisp white pages and stiff binding, her words now tangible in subtle bumps that registered like mountaintops beneath her touch. She had done this. This, this was hers.

So, too, were the words that she had spent so much time debating, rewriting, backspacing. The ones on the very first page.

To Mom and Dad for giving me the tools,
To Emmy Bear for giving me the inspiration,
and to my Number One Fan, for believing in me always.

She brought the box and her overnight bag to Mom and Dad's for the party weekend extravaganza, excited to share the news with those she held close. But pulling up the drive, she was startled with silent tears and a sudden loss for words.

His hair was shorter, less of a styled mane now and more stiff and composed. His skin was certainly tan, as if he'd spent more time in the California sun this summer than normal. The lines on his face were somehow more defined; whether from the time it took for a year to pass, the new and unfamiliar facial hair, or from damage done, she couldn't quite decipher.

But he was there, all the same, throwing a baseball across the front yard with her big brother while their goddaughter did her best to swing a bat with all her might. Charlotte could hear Emma yelling, "I'm Mookie Betts!" as she fouled a ball off behind her.

When she shut her car door, her duffel bag slung over her shoulder and the box of books suddenly light as a feather in her arms, he finally turned to face her.

His expression was shocked, sad and glad, remorse and hope and *I never thought this moment would come* all rolled into one. As her feet began to move of their own accord, she saw the tears in his eyes, too.

David said something along the lines of, "Hey, Emmy, let's head inside for a bit, okay?" but Charlotte paid David no mind as she was suddenly left face to face with *him* on the sidewalk in front of her parent's home, their feet seeming to trace prints left behind from years ago as they stood a cement block apart. The emotion in their eyes swirled in patterns that screamed with too much and not enough all at once.

When he finally managed a strangled, "Hey," it was like breathing fresh air for the first time in a long time.

"Hey yourself."

He offered to help carry her things in the house, but she refused, on the basis that this box was the only thing keeping her sane and stable. She was grateful for the bustle of the day, that as soon as she put her things down in her bedroom, activity and itineraries seemed to take over. He was there, constantly glancing over to her, keeping her in his proximity, but she was right there, too. Their every intention spoke volumes, in glances over lunch and the way he sought her out in every crowd, in every room, following one another just to ensure that they still existed.

She found it a little strange when he was pulling out his guitar after dinner, when all twelve of them were crowded on the back porch. It was something she hadn't seen or heard since maybe high school, a pipe dream they'd had as kids. Still, his fingers flowed and melodies sung to the tune of slightly off-key lyrics, folk songs and popular songs from the radio. It was kitschy, she realized, straight out of a Hallmark movie. But even as he missed notes and fumbled around for purchase on the strings, every single part of her was warm.

The rest of the night was lost in the bustle of cleaning and preparing for the party in the morning, and by the time every surface of the Murphy household was vacuumed and spotless, he was gone. But she knew exactly where to find him.

If her instincts hadn't been so keen and developed over the years, the light guitar melodies would've given him away.

His bedroom had long since been turned into a guest room, with his shelves and knick knacks replaced by a fresh coat of paint, standard furniture, and hotel-esq paintings and decor. Even the bedspread was new, a forest green that somehow encapsulated his eyes perfectly. He was lying with his eyes closed and his back propped up against the headboard, his feet crossed at the ankles, the guitar in his hands seeming to play of its own accord.

As the doorframe held her sinking body up, she began to recognize the tune to "Far Away" by Nickelback filling the room, filling her ears, filling every part of her. It was a wonder she didn't drop the book that she was now wrinkling beneath her tight grip.

The sniffling gave her away, but the way that his eyes and smile were opening slowly told her that he knew she was there all the while.

"Why are you sittin' all by yourself?" she asked, her words a whisper in the air, echoes of the past and a kickstart to the future.

His smile choked back threatening tears as he tried instead for humor.

"So…am I rusty?"

"If it wasn't for these damn tears in my eyes right now, I'd be giving you so much shit for playing Nickelback," she managed through laughter and a teary smile and the backs of her hands swiping furiously at the strays that remained.

"Hey now, don't rip on Nickelback. We both know that they don't deserve the hate they get."

"You're right. They don't."

She was in the room now, but in limbo, trying to decide whether she wanted to sit on the bed or continue to awkwardly sway between the bed and the dresser. When he sat up and adjusted his body so that he was now cross-legged, she felt comfortable enough to perch herself on the edge of the bed, the charge in the four feet of space still overwhelming enough to heat her entire body.

"So, Ramsey, when did you decide to pick up your dream of becoming the next Jimi Hendrix again?"

"Oh, this?" he scoffed, twisting the guitar over in his hands. "I've just had a lot of time on my hands lately. Figured I'd use it wisely."

His shrug said all that he needed to say, said more than that even, as she glanced down to the white binding in her hands.

"So, what did you bring me?"

"Oh, this?"

Her cheeks were suddenly red, that immediacy of *needing to be good for him* creeping back in as though it had never left. But it dissipated slowly, and then ran out altogether, as she tentatively crossed the distance, handing him the book.

"I finished it."

His smile was warm and proud. His eyes beamed behind the shadows that had grown into a semi-permanence over the past several months.

It was ages before he opened it, because he was reading it with his fingertips, tracing the lines in the cover, going over the curves of her name in simple Times New Roman block on the front. He looked up when he was ready, earning her approval with a steady nod before he opened up and dove in. He paused only once, after reading the dedication page, that choked up smile creeping back before he became lost in her fictional world.

He had tears in his eyes, doing his best to avoid letting them fall onto the crisp new pages, as he closed the book carefully and clutched it to his chest.

"I'm so proud of you," he whispered over the top of the white binding. "I'd say I can't believe it, but that would be a lie. It's been there along. I'm just...I'm so glad you got to find it for yourself, Charlie Kate."

It took a moment, of eyes meeting and disappearing, of smiles strained to fight back tears, before they were letting go and bodies were colliding into a fierce hug that left them both holding on and gasping for a breath that could only be provided by their embrace. For the first time since she had moved back to Boston, Charlotte finally felt *home*.

It was minutes, hours, days, before either wanted to let go, but eventually, Charlotte was hiccupping and James was chuckling a gurgled sound against her shoulder where he had buried his face, and they were pulling apart in a way that said *I don't want to let go but I need to see you to remember that you're real.*

"God, we're pathetic," she chuckled as she wiped her eyes and watched him do the same.

"Maybe a little bit," he agreed.

She scooted her body so that they were sitting together, side by side, not quite touching, but close enough for their shoulders to whisper against one another. It was no time at all before he was kicking her softly with his toes.

"I've missed you so much, Charlie Kate."

"I've missed you, too."

They played a skeletal version of catching up, skirting around any and all issues that immediately dealt with *how have you been getting along without me?* He was still working at the same company, still playing pick-up basketball twice a week with some of his coworkers. He'd taken up running, apparently, which explained the tan. She didn't ask why.

She told him about her new apartment and the writing she was doing, and about her new job teaching second grade.

"Oh, and by the way, Joey De Luca says hi."

"De *Luca*? When did you see *him*?"

"A couple of weeks ago, actually. He's married with two kids."

"Absolutely not. Now you're just pulling my leg."

"Would I make this up?"

"Absolutely, you would."

It led to another in a round of many pauses for awkward laughter, but as their giggles subsided, James was noticeably tense.

"God, that seems like a lifetime ago."

"What does? Your days as an extra in Rocky Four?"

"No, dork. Just...high school. Joey De Luca."

She smiled, scratching idly at the comforter.

"Yeah, no, you're right. I get that."

The silence was comfortable, but still charged, still buzzing as he took in all the air in the room with his next breath.

"You know, I was going to ask you to prom that night."

It caught her off guard, the sudden change in direction.

"What night?"

"You know. That night that you came over and said that Joey had asked you. I had this whole schtick prepared, too. And then, of course, I went and blew it all to hell."

He was meshing his fingers together and apart while he focused on the far wall, doing his best to keep his body from imploding.

"Really? Well, if the *schtick* was to make a complete and total ass of yourself, you did a spectacular job," she chided, doing her best to take away some of the tension. Just because she was growing up and *being on her own* didn't mean she couldn't still try to protect him.

"Thank you, truly," he chuckled, tailing off into silence once again.

"So," she picked up, "do I get to see this schtick, then? I mean, way to lead a girl on and then leave her hanging."

She sidled into him, the skin where their shoulders touched igniting. But all in the same, he gulped down the lump in his throat that nerves had built upon, and reached once more for his guitar.

"You said you'd always wanted someone to write you a song, so," he began, focusing all of his attention on adjusting and readjusting his lavender, button-filled strap. "Now, keep in mind, I wrote this in high school, so no comments from the peanut gallery, please."

She felt the tightness in her own throat constricting her every breath from the moment she realized what he was about to do. Age be damned, she hung on every word that came out of his raspy throat, absorbed every melody that his fingers strummed. Because this right here was the boy she had fallen in love with, the man who she knew deep down inside, in every nook and cranny and dark hidden cave. He reached her to the depths of her soul, and had been doing so all this time.

She finally began to breathe again when his fingers let the last note trail away. His eyes, so fixed on the six strings for the past two minutes of her life, slowly found her again. In that moment, everything he hadn't sung, the words that followed from high school and beyond, the feelings that he had fought and battled and shoved to the wayside for all of those years, were crystal clear in his eyes.

"Now, I can't very well ask you to prom, but I hear there's a Dunkin' Donuts that stays open until midnight down on Boylston. What do you say?"

His eyes were shy but hopeful as he waited with bated breath.

"You know what, Ramsey? I'd say it looks like we've got a lot of catching up to do."

Hello Reader!

Thank you so much for going on Charlie Kate and James's journey with me! I hope that you loved their story as much as I loved bringing them to life on these pages (or on this e-reader device. Technology is cool, right?). If you enjoyed this book, please feel free to share your love on Amazon or Goodreads!

If you enjoyed hearing from Ginny, a sneak peek of the rest of her story, *Five Mississippi*, is coming up next! You can find both Kindle and paperback versions on Amazon starting August 18th, 2020!

.

Catch a sneak peek of Ginny's story in Five Mississippi!

Ginny Edley has always prided herself on living an organized life. Structure. Order. ***Control***. After growing up in an environment with a complete lack of stability, and having any semblance of hope slip right through her fingers, she has made it her mission in life to only ever rely on herself.

Until Jack McKinney comes in and threatens to ruin everything that she has spent her life building.

Working on the same television show as staff writers, Ginny and Jack get to know each other quite well. When secrets from Jack's past are unearthed, Ginny makes it her mission to distract him, and "Mission: Make Jack Happy" becomes her summer project. But Jack's past heartache leaves Ginny questioning her own happiness, and as his friendship begins to poke at old wounds of her own, Ginny is caught between letting her past define her and allowing someone else into her life in a way that might let those old wounds begin to heal instead of scarring over.

As her relationship with Jack grows, planting new roots in parts of her heart that she had thought were otherwise dead, Ginny finds herself struggling with just how lonely life can be when the only person in your corner is *you.*

1

"No, we already established Rachel's point of view during this first season: she doesn't think she's going *anywhere*. She has told Todd repeatedly that they're going to make their relationship work, regardless of his estranged daughter showing up on his front porch. We can't just cut her loose without so much as an explanation. And frankly, dismissing her character from the show is only going to cost us. We keep her on because her drama gives the script conflict when necessary. That's my two cents, and I'm sticking by that opinion."

Mark Frese, one of the staff writers on my primetime show *Unexpected Grace*, was talking out of his ass.

"We're not cutting her loose without an explanation," I explained, doing my best not to patronize him even though I really, really wanted to. "We're phasing her out. We set Rachel and Todd's relationship up for failure since day one for a reason. Keeping her on any longer than absolutely necessary is only going to flake out the character, and that isn't fair to anyone."

"Come on, Ginny," Mark continued to argue idly. "She's a prominent source of drama—"

"*Was* a prominent source of drama. In season one. When we were using her to set up *Todd's* character arc to give him an unfulfilled life. And we have done that. Several times, actually. Several times with*out* the help of Rachel's character."

Leaning back in my chair, I crossed my arms over my chest. He wasn't going to win this argument, and I had enough ammunition to keep me going all day. But poor Mark just didn't learn, and it was entirely evident by the size of his head and the steam coming out of his ears.

"Listen," I continued, "keeping Rachel on as a character will bleed every other storyline dry. We've built up enough backstory now that we can focus solely on the drama between Todd and *Riley*. *Their* past. *Their* daughter that she kept from him. Which, might I remind you, is the entire heart and soul of our show anyway. I don't see Rachel as a valuable tool in any of this moving forward. And while I understand that every character needs to have multiple points of conflict, Rachel does *not* need to be one for Todd. He has his job and his nagging parents, on *top* of being a good father and struggling with Gracie suddenly entering his life—not to mention the fact that we're bringing

Riley in this season. We are *not* going to turn this show into some nighttime, love triangle bullshit. There are plenty of those on Netflix if that's what the audience wants."

With his little fish lips pursed inside his mouth, Mark glanced around the table where three other staff writers and our show runner had been watching our ping-pong match intently. Heidi shrunk back into her chair away from the conflict, and while Jenna was eating up our argument like she was at a buffet, Jack had his chin tucked into his chest and an annoyed scowl on his face. Without any support from the rest of the staff—who were either avoiding his grueling stare or shrugging, *Give it up, pal; Edley always wins and you know it*—he rolled his eyes and huffed, sinking into his chair as he finally surrendered. Tucking my straight blonde hair behind my ears, I tilted my head modestly. Momma always said that the slight upturn of my nose was God-given as a pair to my confidence. With the decision finally made to phase out the character of Rachel, the rest of our writers' meeting could finally move on.

Unexpected Grace had been my baby for a while now. I had worked at Lemon Sauce Productions as a writer on many shows, but *Grace* was my heart and soul. Seeing it come to life on the set of our thirteen-episode first season was like a dream come true. It was also the first show that had been officially picked up with my name on as a staff writer, which gave it a special place in my heart. That, along with my gritty and tenacious nature, made me uber protective of the characters and the storylines. While I knew that the show was not solely *mine*, I fought like hell for the storylines I believed in.

When the meeting wrapped, the rest of our staff shuffled out to their respective offices to work on their own scripts. Dan, our showrunner, stopped to pull Mark and me aside. He cocked his head towards the conference room, his flour white, mad scientist crazy hair swaying like wheat in a field. I took my seat across from Mark, with Dan at the head of the table, and pulled my MacBook out of my bag. I logged in as Dan situated his thick square frames on his face and made sense of the disorganized stack of papers he'd just collected.

"Listen, I appreciate the conversation that the two of you brought to the table," he began, clasping his hands over his tumbling stack of papers. "We got to see all sides of that argument. Mark, while I agree that you brought up several good points about keeping Rachel on for the drama," he tilted his head, extending one finger to Mark before shifting it in my direction, "I have *got* to go with Ginny on this one. Your points were *good*. But I don't think any of us envisioned this script as a relationship drama—in *that* sense. The drama that we're really trying to paint is about Todd's relationships with his daughter, with his parents, with his past, and with himself. If, and when, we think about bringing in a romantic relationship for him down the road, we want it to be something stable that can make Todd better. Don't we?"

I nodded in agreement, lifting one brow in Mark's direction as I wore a sly smile, doing my best not to be too cocky. He rolled his eyes, more at me than Dan, and blew a strand of his black hair out of his eyes. Mark hated being wrong, but he hated admitting that I was *right* even more.

"Good." Dan clapped his hands together forcefully and drew our attention from the little silent brother-sister-esq spat we'd been having. "Here comes the fun part."

Rubbing his hands together, I realized quickly that Dan had his two best writers in the room with quite possibly the trickiest piece of B-plot that we'd seen to date. Instantly, I felt my body tense, knowing exactly what was coming.

"I want the two of you to work on this together. We have a two- to three-episode window to write Rachel out in a realistic fashion. Don't just chop her out and make her seem like useless plot filler. Put your heads together and get 'er done."

Our eye-rolls were synchronized, but Dan was so caught up in pushing his glasses back up the bridge of his nose that he didn't even recognize our mutual disdain. The problem with Mark and me working together was that we were both hot headed, stubborn as they came, and had an inherent desire for control. Putting us in the room together to work on a project that Mark had clearly lost all creative rights on when my idea had been chosen was a recipe for disaster, especially with his impending attitude of doom. But Dan was already halfway out the door, and there was no use protesting.

Not when I'd worked this hard to make a name for myself, one that was branded on the credits of three of our thirteen episodes—the most of any staff writer for season one.

Not when we were already renewed for a second season.

Not when the story arcs I had typed and ready to bring to the table when it came time to *really* plan out season two were so intricate and deep and rich with direction that I could almost taste my own brilliance as the words had flown beneath my fingers.

I had to buck up and work with Mark, no matter how grueling the process would be. At least, underneath the layers of being an asshole, he was almost as equally brilliant at his job as I was.

Almost.

"Alright. Where do you want to start?" I asked, keying up a new Google Doc that I shared with both Mark and Dan before creating a header.

"I don't care," he huffed. "It's your idea."

Rolling my eyes, I glared at him over the top of my open computer and his closed one. Apparently, I was working with a fifth grader. His hair had fallen in his face again, but the annoyance in his green eyes was evident.

"Listen. I know that we tend to disagree on...most things. But we're working together on this one. So why don't we both just swallow our pride and figure this out? Come on. I'm sure you have as many good ideas for how to phase a girl out as you do to string them along. I've seen you do both with enough sorry women as it is."

I lifted one brow, smiling as I tried to lighten the mood.

"Yeah, fuck you too," he huffed, but the lift of his lips told me that he was at least going to suck it up for the sake of the script. Scooting my laptop to the middle of the table, I turned my screen to face Mark as I began to type.

"So here's what I'm thinking..."

It only took us a few hours to knock out three different B-plots that would successfully write Rachel off the show in a dignified manner. The goal was to keep her on for half the season and write the character off in an arc that would play out around the mid-season finale—Dan really did care for us like a family after all. We had two three-episode arcs and one two-episode arc that we were equally proud of. All three options did the job without affecting the rest of the plot too drastically, and could stand alone as their own source of comfort for the characters of both Rachel and Todd. After lunch, we brought them to Dan and decided on the winner.

"The stage direction on this is brilliant," Dan noted as we started fitting the sides into the scripts that we were already outlining.

"That's all Edley," Mark stated, nodding his head in my direction.

I don't blush often, but I bit my lip, trying to put at least a small damper on my timidity.

"Thanks. I just have a...a very specific vision in my head for the way that they're looking at each other while all of this is happening. I mean, Rachel *is* Todd's first 'successful relationship' after Riley. He'll mourn the loss."

"Absolutely. Absolutely." Dan nodded, continuing to cut and paste our text. "Listen, Mark, you can head on out and work on whatever it is that you need to get done. Ginny, come around here for a second."

I nodded at Mark's half-wave and half-grin as he headed out, glad that we'd gotten to be on the same page in a short amount of time. As I rounded Dan's desk with my arms folder over my chest, I watched him affix the last of our words to their new script home, reading possibly my favorite lines that I'd typed all afternoon that wouldn't *really* see the screen, because they weren't actually dialogue. They were stage direction for the characters.

> ***TODD*** *gazes at **RACHEL** longingly. This longing is a mixed bag, because at this point, he is longing for so much. Longing for a love that now has no place in his life. Longing for his daughter to finally accept him. Longing for the pieces of his life to finally make sense for the first time in what feels like forever. And we watch it all play out on his face as **RACHEL** quietly clicks the front door closed.*

"I mean. Ginny Edley. What can I say?" Dan smiled, rubbing his palms together as he leaned back in his chair.

I shrugged, smiling smugly.

"I want you to direct this."

The way that he delivered that line, the way he'd been so matter-of-fact, made my heart leap into my throat. My rapidly lifting smile betrayed the modest, calm-cool-collect that I'd been wearing for most of my life to maintain my own sense of control, throwing me a little off kilter inside. Directing had been the dream, but I knew from the very beginning that I had to fight my way into making that my reality. I poured my entire being into my scripts, planting the little mind movies for my characters with as much detail as I possibly could so that when the script was handed over to a director, there was absolutely no doubt as to what the actors' intent should be. Of course, I valued each actor's craft, and trusted them wholly with my words. There had been several times already when I'd seen something I had planned change as soon as it came time to film, and there were several times when my direction was maybe a little bit wrong. But when a director or an actor called to me on set and asked me to clarify my intent because they *just wanted to get it perfectly right*, I felt my heart swelling with pride.

"Definitely the last part of this episode, at least," Dan clarified. "The 'official break up scene' as you might call it. But this is yours come season two. It's one of your scripts anyway, so I guess you'll just be all over that week's credits," he chuckled. I joined him, a little jittery; I definitely wouldn't need my afternoon coffee now. "Take a look over it and when the time comes, we'll sit down and really hash this baby out."

"Thank you," was really all that I could muster. "Thank you so much for the opportunity."

I clasped my hands together, biting the bottom of my wide smile as I willed the totally out-of-character squealing that I wanted to let rip, stay inside of me.

I let myself out of Dan's office, giving in to a little skip-jump as I closed the door to my own office. It wasn't much, the office on our studio lot. We each had our own small workspace that we used more often now that we were filming. I had a standard oak office desk, a chair that I'd purchased myself from Staples because the ones offered to us were honestly kind of shitty, and a file cabinet in the back corner. There was a bookshelf along the side wall that was littered with textbooks from college and old script binders, and two arm chairs across from my desk in case I had visitors. Which I rarely did. I didn't really prefer people in my space. And that was a direct reflection on the phone call that I struggled to make with my good news.

My best friend Charlotte was in no mindset to take a phone call with *my* good news; she was still trying to piece back the shambles of her own life that had recently deteriorated. There was no frame of mind that would ever have me picking up the phone to dial my Daddy's number. It was one I'd long since forgotten anyway. So even though it wasn't Wednesday, I scrolled through the very short list of favorites in my phone and dialed Gram.

"Alright, who died?"

"No one," I chuckled, the sound of my grandmother's voice instantly soothing me, bringing my buzz to a delightful high. Once she knew my news, it would truly be real. "I just have something exciting to tell you."

"Oh? What's his name?"

"It's not a *guy*, Hazel, you old bat."

"A grandmother can dream, can't she? So, what's the news, darlin'?"

"I get to direct an episode."

I sounded so much like a little girl in that moment, like I was in fifth grade and my crush had given me a Valentine with a cheesy message on it. After having lived through a deprived childhood, these moments where I reverted back to acting an age I had never experienced were few and far between. I didn't let that escape me as I listened to Gram cursing in excitement on the other end of the line.

"This calls for a celebration!"

The telltale sound of bottles clinking in the background made me laugh.

"Let me guess: gin?"

"You know me too well, baby. What other way would there be to salute my Ginny?"

"I don't know," I smiled, "but I'm sure there are healthier options."

"Probably are, but this one gives me a buzz."

I could hear the wink all the way from Boston as Gram poured gin into her tea.

After hanging up with Gram, who had spent the entire short phone call telling me how wonderful I am, I decided to send Charlotte a quick text anyway. There was no harm in warning her that our phone call on Monday would contain a little bit of excitement. As I sat at the bar alone that night surveying my potential clientele, she texted back *omg! Can't wait!*

There were plenty of guys I could convince to take me home tonight. But I let the tequila sunrise warm my veins as I did my homework first. Tall-blondie at the bar was a little too socially distant and kept checking his phone despite the fact that he had two different girls hanging near, which meant he'd be all sorts of cocky in the sack—and not in the way I was looking for. Short-and-stocky-red-head had it a little *too* bad for the girl beside him that—obvious to everyone else in the bar besides him—wasn't interested. I was looking for a little one-night fun, not to be someone's shoulder to cry on. There was an entire group of surfers who reminded me of the frat boys from college. No matter who I chose, he would no doubt talk a big game and finish in less than two minutes, only to ask for a full recap of his performance. But I was a storyteller, not a paraphraser. All five of them were out.

When I met the eyes of a single guy with soft, light brown hair and piercing blue eyes at the other end of the bar, I knew I'd found my target. I cocked my brow in invitation for him to join me. That was all part of the game: I made them think that they were in control, putting even more of the power right into my hands.

Elliot was twenty-eight. Had lived in LA for about six months now. Didn't really have many friends outside of work, and was contemplating taking himself back home to Portland from where he'd been promoted. His family was back there anyway. He didn't entirely fit in here. But maybe, he promised as he slid me another drink on his tab, he would have one more weekend of meaningless fun before he decided for sure.

Bingo.

Meaningless fun was my middle name.

I didn't bother telling him about getting named director on the episode when he asked what I was doing at the bar all alone. *Celebrating* was the extent of the answer, and by the spark in his eye and the lack of any follow-up questions, I knew that he was just here to play the game too.

I let him make me feel good atop his sheets from Portland, in his not-really-all-the-way-unpacked apartment. I let him writhe beneath my fingers in a way that I knew most men would, let him beg a little before he turned me over onto my back and gave us both what we truly wanted. And then, I gave him what he *truly* wanted out of this entire charade when I stood up after we'd both caught our breath and started putting myself back together. I knew he was watching me, with my back turned as I got dressed and collected myself, a Cheshire grin facing the stack of boxes at the end of his dresser.

"This was fun," he said as I looked back over my shoulder at Elliot from Portland, with his sheets draped casually over his waist and his hands laced behind his head as he leaned against the wall without a headboard.

"Good luck in Portland," I offered, smiling slyly at him without ever turning fully around.

I'd forget his name by the morning. And that was all part of the game.

acknowledgements

I started writing *Too Much of a Good Thing* as a screenplay back in 2011. It came off of a monologue that I wrote about *not always getting what you wanted in the end.* I thought that monologue was so profound, some *big power piece* when I finally got over a crush and thought, *I don't need him! I don't need men! Screw the patriarchy!* First of all, it wasn't actually that good. Big surprise.

Funnily enough, that monologue never made it into the novel, nor did the notion that I had for Charlotte (I still can't call her Charlie Kate) to end up with*out* James, for him to pick Vanessa and wind up engaged at the end of the book while Charlotte went on to become some prolific author, to prove that *She didn't need no man!* Ha. Ha ha. Funny, Allie.

When I picked it up again years later, I was in the middle of several online publications (FanFiction, okay? It was FanFiction) and had the "creative genius" running through my veins again. Charlotte and James kind of picked up my silly little screenplay and turned it on its head, basically telling me how they wanted their story to end up. And trust me, I fought with both of their stubborn hearts along the way.

While turning it into a novel, I ended up cutting entire chapters (there was a whole thing about them watching the *Lost* finale together and getting into an argument over who Kate truly belonged with, mainly because I wanted the world to know my opinions on the subject. Team Sawyer, by the way) and rerouting several plot elements that just didn't make sense.

The more that I wrote, the more I realized that what I was teaching to my 5th grade students about editing their own essays was still true to me as a novice novel writer, so I got to use my own book as a teaching tool. I brought in a hard copy to show my kids that I was literally tossing twenty-seven pages into the recycling bin. One girl cried (one girl aside from *me* cried, I should clarify).

I wouldn't have gotten through this without the support from several people.

Dad, I'm sorry this is a love story (but please stop rolling your eyes). Mom, no there isn't anything inherently "naughty," but maybe skip the end of the chapter about prom. And the lake house part. Probably skip those.

Mary, who was the first person to finish, to give me the best criticisms, and to FaceTime me at odd hours of the night to design book covers and be the best book worm I know.

Angie and Lisa, who insist that they'll read it "when the movie comes out." And Chuck, who still thinks he should've been the "male model on the cover."

To Lilly, who hates this genre to a T, but still read it cover to cover in about a day and designed an amazing cover at the price of tickets to a couple of Red Sox games. To Lizzy and Jenny for spending your coveted teacher summer time indulging me. Lizzy especially, for picking out all seventy-billion "James's" to correct. The James's and I are forever in your debt.

To Shannon and Coley, who gushed and beta'd and distracted me with about a billion other story ideas (for FanFiction, okay? For FanFiction) but pumped my ego full of praises anyway and made (still make) me believe that I am good at this.

And to my Number One Fan, for believing in my always.

It's scary to give my babies to the world. Be kind to them.

about the author

Allie Giancarlo is an elementary school teacher first and an author once all of her papers are graded (sometimes even when they're not...shhh...). She enjoys traveling, spending time by the lake or the bonfire with her family, and live-Tweeting every Red Sox game from March thru November.

Follow Me on Social Media!

 @alliewrites_

@allie_g18

Made in the USA
Middletown, DE
02 May 2021